FURY
of
SEDUCTION

FURY
of
SEDUCTION

COREENE CALLAHAN

Montlake
Romance

Text copyright © 2012 Coreene Callahan

Published by Montlake Romance
P.O. Box 400818
Las Vegas, NV 89140

ISBN-13: 9781612182964
ISBN-10: 1612182968

To Mom and Dad:
As always, thank you for being You.

Chapter One

Sleep always eluded Mac. Night, day...it didn't matter. A solid eight hours of REM never made it onto his schedule. He'd tried everything: swapping his firm mattress for a softer one, kitting the thing out with silk sheets and the best pillows money could buy. Stretching out in his La-Z-Boy recliner. Hard-core sex before bedtime. Nothing helped. No matter what he did, the most he ever got was three hours in a row.

Which explained a lot.

Like why he stood by himself in the gymnasium he shared with the other Nightfury dragon warriors instead of tucked in his bed getting the recommended number of Zs. Seven stories belowground, their lair, Black Diamond, boasted the best of everything: state-of-the-art workout equipment, a basketball court, and a room full of tools used to sharpen dragon claws. The fact he was alone said it all. None of his brothers-in-arms suffered from insomnia. All were no doubt deep in la-la land, laid out under feather down, getting hot and heavy with an imaginary dream girl. Which...

Made Mac the sole patient in the sleep deprivation department of chez Nightfury.

Damned annoying. And even more of a problem today.

Combating a boatload of pissed off, Mac rolled his shoulders to work out the kinks. He couldn't afford to screw up. Or let his new family down. Not again. The other warriors were counting on him. Trusted that he'd learn to master the magic he commanded as a Dragonkind male to become a solid member of the Nightfury pack. Did it matter that he'd only just learned he was half dragon? That the magic encoded in his DNA had jump-started the *change*—allowing him to shift from human to dragon form and back again—just over a month ago?

Not even a little.

Time didn't wait for anyone or give a shit about ability. And neither did Mac.

To fight alongside his brothers, he must prove he belonged with them. So, yeah. He needed to pull it together...right now.

Too bad the plan was goat-fucked six ways to Sunday.

His dragon half was AWOL, getting in his face, fucking up his flow, denying his will to control it. Cajoling didn't work. Neither did babying the bastard. And threatening it? Shit, he'd gotten zapped with nasty-ass energy shards the handful of times he'd tried that approach. So what did that leave him?

Begging.

Mac blew out a long breath. Just the thought gave him a raging case of *no can do*—the obstinate SOB belonged to him, after all, not the other way around—but desperate times called for desperate measures. If he continued to screw the pooch, he wouldn't get what he wanted. Hell...

make that *craved*. He needed the Nightfuries' acceptance. Without it, he wouldn't get his warrior status rubber-stamped in the war against the Razorbacks, a rogue faction of Dragonkind whose endgame included the extermination of the human race.

He glared at the weight machine nearest him. Steel rattled, picking up the vibe he threw off, and shifted against the rivets that kept it bolted to the floor. As the calamity got going, clanking out a rhythm, industrial-grade fluorescents flared above his head, crackling through the quiet. A second before the lightbulbs exploded, Mac shut the energy overload down, more disgusted with himself than ever.

KOing gym equipment wouldn't get him anything but more attention. The kind he didn't need from the crew still asleep upstairs. He snorted. Now there was an understatement. Bastian, his new commander, would deep-fry his ass if he wrecked anything else this week. Especially since he was still on the hook for putting his fist through a wall.

Raising his arms, Mac cupped the back of his head and pressed down, pushing his chin toward his chest. Taut muscles pulled, and pain screamed up his spine. As agony slammed into his skull, he frowned at the real estate between his bare feet. The Velcro of the exercise mats lined up, connecting the whole, not even a millimeter off as each clung to its counterpart. Any other day, he would've appreciated the precision. Enjoyed the tidy corners and neat edges. Today, the sight just made him sick.

So together. So on the same page. So perfect in every way.

Unlike him. He was a total frickin' catastrophe. The only guy in Black Diamond who didn't have his shit together.

Mac's headache morphed into a full-blown throb, pounding between his temples. The whole thing was a total mind-fuck. The failure. Each defeat. The fact his magic defied him. And as fear and uncertainty came calling, he shook his head. It shouldn't be this difficult. He'd always excelled at everything—school, sports, the military, and martial arts. Nothing had ever pushed him to the edge of what he could endure…until now.

Why was he having so much trouble? Was it the water angle? Most dragons hated water and spent their lives avoiding it. Not Mac. True to his water dragon roots, he preferred to be in the ocean. The deeper the better, but any body of water would do. Give him a lake, river, or Olympic-size swimming pool, and he was good to go. The difference between him and the other Nightfuries, though, didn't explain why his magic refused to obey him.

He frowned, turning the questions over in his mind, searching for answers. None came. No clever explanation. No aha moment. Just another big doughnut hole in an information string full of them.

Inhaling deep, Mac filled his lungs to capacity, getting back in the game. *Surrender* wasn't a word he ever used, and as he held the breath, relishing the burn, he prayed the last time was the charm. He needed to connect with his dragon side like he needed legs to stand on. Letting the air go, he drew another lungful and released it.

Draw. Hold. Release.

Mac repeated the sequence over and over, using the breathing technique he'd learned in the navy. After a while, his heartbeat slowed. His body calmed. As the chaos in his mind receded, a sinking sensation grabbed hold and pulled him deep. A snick echoed as something unlocked inside him, releasing a flood of energy. The Meridian. Mother of God. He'd found it, tapped into the electrostatic current that fed Dragonkind.

And, oh man, it was beautiful.

Power personified, magic rushed through his veins, making his muscles contract and his heart thump, lighting him up from the inside out.

"Come on, beautiful," he whispered, nursing the fragile connection. "Stay with me."

His words swirled through the quiet, echoing in the gym, reminding him he was alone. Good thing too. He didn't want anyone witnessing the train wreck if he failed again. Call it pride. Call it ego. Call it a severe allergy to ridicule. Whatever. It didn't matter, just as long as he caught hold of the magic and mastered the cloaking spell. The ability wasn't optional. If he couldn't cloak himself—go dark and invisible against the night sky—he couldn't fight alongside his brothers. And if he couldn't contribute as a warrior, he wasn't worth the space he occupied.

Deep in the zone, Mac closed his eyes. As he shifted mental focus, he drifted toward the energy stream, afraid to lose the thin thread if he moved too fast. On the brink, he reached out with his mind, eager to touch and taste it while—

"You still at it?"

The rich brogue startled him, and Mac flinched. His dragon recoiled, turning away, causing the magic to whiplash. With a curse, Mac struggled to hold on, clinging to the fragile connection as he coaxed it to stay with him. The magical tether fractured, then faded, leaving him standing empty-handed in the darkness. Opening his eyes, Mac glanced toward the main entrance and snarled at the newcomer.

One shoulder propped against the doorframe, Forge raised a brow. "Not going well?"

"Son of a bitch," Mac gritted between clenched teeth. His hands curled into fists, ready to open a can of whup-ass on Forge for interrupting. "What does it look like?"

"It looks tae me like you need a break." Crossing his arms over his chest, Forge leveled a no-nonsense look in his direction. "And some sleep. When did you last eat?"

Good question. Mac didn't know the answer. Didn't much care, either. "Motherfuck. You screwed me up. I was seconds away from—"

"Touching the Meridian?"

"Yes, goddamn it."

"You're not ready for that, Mac."

He threw his new friend a load of fuck you.

"I'm not saying it tae fuck you up," Forge said, sounding so sincere Mac wanted to rip his head off. "You're rushing things...pushing your magic tae dangerous levels. 'Tisn't safe, lad. You went through the change just over a month ago. No way you should be trying to conjure a cloaking spell. You've a shitload to learn before we get to that. Need to be a helluva lot stronger too...which is why you should be eating and sleeping between training ops."

The "we" in the sentence pissed Mac off, even though it shouldn't. Every Dragonkind male was assigned a mentor after going through the *change*—a full-fledged warrior to teach him the ropes and get him through dragon combat training. Forge was his, and, honestly, Mac was thankful for the lethal SOB most of the time. But after screwing with his flow a moment ago, the male was officially on his shit list. "Go away. I need to get a handle on this before the others get up for the night."

"Everyone's already awake and in the kitchen."

Mac gritted his teeth. He was out of time, and with the evening meal on the table, out of luck too. In another hour, the Nightfuries would ramp up for a night filled with their favorite activity...hunting and killing Razorbacks. Where would that leave him? Climbing the walls as he got left behind. Again.

"B send you to get me?" Mac asked, trying to stem the flow of disappointment.

"Bastian wants the entire pack together," Forge said, pushing away from the doorjamb. "Something about a shared meal."

Stretching out his shoulders, Mac nodded. Probably not a bad idea. The Nightfury pack had suffered a shake-up in recent days as everyone adjusted to the fact he and Forge were now in the fold. Accepting new members into a tight military unit was never easy. Mac knew it from experience. His time in the human world—first as part of SEAL Team Six and then as a detective for the Seattle Police Department—had taught him a few things. First among them? Trust was imperative to solidify a group. 'Cause, yeah: if you didn't trust a guy, no way you wanted him protecting your six in a firefight.

The fact Bastian not only understood the principle but was taking steps to rectify the problem wasn't a surprise. The Nightfury commander was tight in the head, solid in the heart, and wicked smart with a shitload of vicious up front and center. The pack's cohesion and the health of each member was priority one for him. Especially considering the volatile mix of personalities and short tempers that called Black Diamond home.

"So…" Mac raised a brow. "We gonna have a love-in or something?"

"I wouldnae go that far." Forge flashed straight white teeth, the grin devilish. "Frosty's still pissed at me."

"With good reason," Mac murmured, fighting a smile. Rikar (aka Frosty and the Nightfury first-in-command) wanted his pound of flesh, and Forge topped his list of *I'm-gonna-rip-your-head-off*. Thank Jesus. Mac had enough to worry about at the moment. Getting his face rearranged by Rikar for leaving the guy's mate unprotected during a showdown with the rogues was something he didn't need. "Ange'll bring him around."

"Shite, I hope not." A twinkling in his eyes, Forge grimaced, feigning alarm. "I'm looking forward tae the fight."

Mac shook his head, enjoying his new friend's cocky attitude. He shared it most of the time. Too bad the strain of the day had sucked the swagger right out of him.

Returning his gaze to the gym mats, Mac said, "Go eat, man. I'll be up in a bit."

"Mac—"

"Give me another hour. I've almost got it."

Movement flashed in his periphery, and Mac cursed under his breath. Fucking Forge. The male had no intention of leaving him alone. Planned to drag him out of the underground lair by his balls and haul him topside for the meal. Mac knew it like he was standing there, bare feet planted, heart pumping, and fists clenched. He could smell Forge's concern as the soft thud of footfalls echoed across the gym, ping-ponging off cinder block walls, coming closer by the second.

His head down, Mac tracked the sound, his peripheral vision sharp. Black combat boots came into view. Forge stopped at the edge of the exercise mats. Mac tensed, waiting for the male to cross into his airspace and get in his face. Fuck him, but he hoped Forge made that mistake. He needed a fight. Yearned for a ball-busting, knuckle-grinding brawl. Maybe then he'd feel whole again. Less like a failure and more like himself.

Mentor or not, it didn't matter. A target was a target. And if Forge decided to accommodate him and slap a bull's-eye in the center of his forehead, all the better.

Chapter Two

The only thing Tania Solares hated more than ugly shoes was being late. The first problem, after all, a girl could fix. Improve. Improvise. Whatever. The second, however, meant she was screwed. Which, come to think of it, pretty much summed up her day. And as far as mistakes went? Not her favorite in the perpetual string of crap that had been thrown her way over the last few weeks.

Forget about running on empty into emotional and mental overload. She was in quicksand territory, waist-deep and sinking fast. No life preserver to grab onto or rescue crew in sight.

Blowing out a long breath, Tania raked the hair out of her eyes and downshifted into the S curve. Her '64 Mini Cooper purred and swung around the bend, catapulting her into the next turn. Oh yeah, she loved this stretch of highway. It was fun to drive. Made her feel powerful, like a Formula One driver racing for the finish line.

Not today, though. The usual feel-good vibe was 100 percent absent, leaving her feeling empty inside. Nothing but one big ache as she thought of her sister...the entire reason behind the solitary road trip. Tania did it twice a month, opening up her baby's performance engine around curves and down straightaways on the drive from Seattle to Gig Harbor.

Which was just plain awful.

She really needed to make the trip more often. Should visit her younger sister every weekend, not twice a month. Thank God J.J. understood the demands of a busy career. Always wanted to hear about her job and the cool projects she worked on.

A landscape designer at a prestigious firm, Tania had plenty of stories to tell: project management, design problems and solutions, clients with more cash than brains sometimes. The subject didn't matter. J.J. soaked up every tidbit. But that didn't make it right. The demands of her job shouldn't come first. Not when her sister needed her. She was all J.J. had—her sister's only lifeline to the outside world, so…no, the long stretches between visits weren't okay.

But God help her. She couldn't keep up. Couldn't swallow her fear or push back the feeling she wasn't doing anything right. No matter how many pep talks Tania gave herself—or how many lists she made—something always fell through the cracks. Too many balls in the air. Too many demands on her time. Too many opportunities to screw up.

And joy of joys? Today qualified as a big, big, *big* one.

She was late. So very late. Now her sister would be waiting…wondering…worrying she wasn't coming.

Her throat went tight. Classic. Another ball dropped, more guilt to throw on the ever-growing pile. Another thing to apologize for…'cause, yup: it was her fault. She should never have picked up the phone on her way out the door. That had been her first mistake. And the second? Being too nice, getting suckered into answering a bunch of survey questions about her shopping habits. Tania grumbled and, shifting gears on a winding incline, shook her head.

Curse her gung ho "Sure, I'll help...no problem" nature. She really needed to learn to say no. And mean it.

And while she was at it, *refusing* to take no for an answer might be a useful skill to master. The perfect example? The flipping Seattle Police Department. They kept blowing her off. No matter how many times she went to the precinct—being a superpest was fast becoming her specialty—and asked them to *do something*, no one ever listened. And the detectives in charge of the case?

Total jerks.

Tania swallowed past the lump in her throat. Ah, nuts, not again. She needed to keep it together. Crying wouldn't solve anything. Lord knew the waterworks hadn't done anything but mess her up all week, but...

She blinked, berating herself as her vision went blurry, tears defying her, pushing to the surface while she tried to hold them back. Tania wiped beneath her eyes. Well, snap...so much for her mascara. Not that she cared about the way she looked at the moment. A case of raccoon eyes, after all, was the least of her worries.

Myst was still missing.

Gone, kidnapped, dead, Tania didn't know. Her best friend could be in the hands of a serial killer or worse—although, come to think of it...a psycho killer was the absolute worst she could, or wanted, to imagine—and what were those bonehead cops doing?

Nothing. Not a damned thing.

Certainly not returning her calls. Big surprise there. She figured they'd call her back just to get rid of her...

particularly since she overloaded their in-boxes with messages every day. But neither Keen nor MacCord had responded. Worse than that, though? Tania suspected the detectives had gone missing too. And she should know. She'd been forced into stalker mode, trying to get a line on them.

So far, though, she'd come up with exactly nothing. A big fat zero on the information front. Which pushed all the wrong buttons on her internal PlayStation and Tania into a pile of trouble. Case in point? Her decision to team up with a reporter, a man-eater with no moral fiber and too much ambition. Now she was the star interviewee in an ongoing exposé about police incompetence in the cover-up of missing Seattle women.

She cringed, her hand tightening around the gearshift. Not her proudest moment. But with Myst's life at stake, getting down and dirty to light a fire under the cops' butts seemed like the best option.

Spotting her turnoff ahead, Tania swiped at another tear and braked, slowing down to wheel her Mini into the driveway. The short lane dumped her into a huge parking lot. Maneuvering like a pro in the tight space, she turned into the first aisle and scanned the row of vehicles, searching for a spot. Saturdays were always busy at the Washington State Correction Center for Women, a popular time for family and friends to visit those locked behind bars and barbed wire. Her sight line even with back bumpers and all-terrain tires, she trolled for a minute, looking for—

Red taillights flashed up ahead.

An early bird. Thank God. She didn't have time to muck around. Not with an hour left of visiting time. By now, J.J. would be climbing the walls. Which, yeah, was a pretty good analogy considering the size of the double-occupancy prison cells.

Awful in every way. But if you did the crime, you did the time.

Her sister was no exception.

The five years her sister had been incarcerated, though, hadn't made visiting J.J. any easier. Tania missed her little sister more with each passing day. The absence left a hole in the center of her life, the place where family lived, and ever since losing their mom to cancer, she—

Tania shook her head. Nope. No way she was going there. The loss was still too painful, the memories more than she could bear on a good day. And today didn't qualify as one of those.

Braking to a stop in the middle of the lane, Tania flipped on her turn signal and waited for the early bird to pull out. The Chevy's V-8 rumbled, cracking through the quiet as the driver drove away. Tania put her foot down and zipped into the empty space, enjoying the maneuverability of her Mini. Red with white racing stripes, her girl was a classic. A throwback to a simpler time and place, one without active park assist, GPS chips, and built-in cell phones.

Fine by her. She didn't need all the bells and whistles, just a performance engine and a whole lot of open road.

Shifting her baby into park, Tania cranked the emergency brake and reached for the oversize handbag sitting on the passenger seat. After tossing her keys inside, she plopped it in her lap and, with quick hands, found a hair elastic in one of the side pockets. Raking her thick strands back in a hurry, she ran through her usual checklist. Ponytail? Check. Wallet with ID and keys? Double check. No personal items and...

Oops. Her iPad had to go. No sense bringing it inside and giving Officer Griggs (aka the weasel) any more ammunition. The oily prison guard always worked Saturdays—oh joy, lucky her—and never missed an opportunity to go through her stuff with a fine-tooth comb.

And getting frisked by the weasel? Oh so not on her list of things to do...ever.

With a grimace, she tucked her favorite gadget into the workbag sitting on the floor in the backseat, between the stack of dog-eared architectural/landscape plans and client files. All right. Good to go. No contraband. Nothing too personal in her purse. She was ready to face Griggs and his barrage of crude innuendos.

Taking a fortifying breath, Tania popped the door open and slid out. Treetops swayed against the darkening sky, skeletal limbs rising above the SUV parked in front of her. As she watched the shadowed redwoods dance in the autumn breeze, she palmed the top of the car door and, with a flick, slammed the—

"Ouch!" she yelped as the sharp door edge clipped her. Pain streaked up her thigh. Tania dropped her purse. Holding the side of her knee, she hopped around on one foot. "Oh shit...oh shit, shit, shit."

Man, that stung. She gave the sore spot another rub. "Frickin'-frack, that's gonna leave a mark."

Gritting her teeth, she snagged her handbag off the wet pavement. Time to go. Her sister was waiting, but as she hurried across the parking lot, dread welled in the pit of her stomach. Visiting J.J. always hit her the same way... like a sucker punch. She loved her sister but didn't like coming here. Hated seeing the toll prison took on her sibling. Hated the steel doors, barbed wire fences, and stark, businesslike hallways. But most of all, Tania hated knowing there was nothing she could do to help.

No matter how hard she tried, she couldn't make it better.

Heavy heart weighing on her, Tania jogged up the front steps, her focus now on the entrance. Flanked on one side by a monstrous green wall, the glass doors weren't much to look at, and yet every time she saw them she wondered the same thing. How could the entryway to a prison look so ordinary? So run-of-the-mill? So office building pleasant? The effect—or camouflage...whatever—seemed a sort of sacrilege. As though the perfectly manicured flower beds with their red chrysanthemums and sculpted shrubbery belied the true nature of the place. Hid the ugliness that went on beyond the tailored front entrance day in and day out.

Mounting the last step, Tania walked across the landing and swung one door wide. The hinges hissed behind her, the sound soft and familiar as she crossed the small entryway and into the hallway beyond. The fast clip of her boot heels echoed along the empty corridor, joining the harsh buzz of fluorescent lights overhead.

Silence prevailed, no murmur of voices or clang of reinforced steel bars. Odd, really. She usually arrived with the late afternoon rush—amid the chatter of an excited crowd as each person waited to be allowed in to visit loved ones. But now? The absence of sound struck her as eerie. And for some reason...dangerous. A kind of calm before the storm reserved for horror movies...you know, the moment right before the psycho jumped out and massacred somebody.

Rubbing her upper arms to chase away the chill, Tania kept herself moving. Her wet soles squeaked against the floor tiles, cranking her tighter as she turned the corner into the—

"Ah, Ms. Solares. There you are."

The voice slithered from the far side of the room. Tania went rigid. White-knuckling her purse strap, she scanned the glass booth in front of the door to the visitor area. Nothing. No Griggs. The weasel wasn't in his usual spot. She looked to her left. Ah, crap. He was unleashed, out roaming the waiting area instead of caged behind the command center. But even worse than that bit of bad news? The second guard that usually worked the evening shift wasn't with him.

Terrific. No go-between, which meant no buffer to keep him in line.

Raising a brow, he tossed the magazine he held onto a scarred side table. Leather steel-toes creaking, he stepped around a double row of chairs in the middle of the room. As he walked toward her, Tania made a beeline for the front counter.

"You're late, Solares. What gives?"

She shrugged. "Car trouble."

"Really," he said, tone edged with sarcasm. He didn't believe her. Tania didn't blame him. She never told him the truth. About anything. The weasel was a chronic snoop: calling her at home, contacting her boss under the guise of completing prison records, digging into her background until he unearthed the fact her good-for-nothing father had walked out on her mother, abandoning Tania a week before her second birthday. Which, of course, he used to belittle her every chance he got, poking at the open wound the way a sadist taunted a cornered animal with a sharp stick. "I could help with that if you'd—"

"Nothing my mechanic couldn't handle," she said, her tone so sweet it made her teeth ache.

"So disappointing." He hooked his thumbs on his leather utility belt, drawing attention to the gun holstered at his hip. "Why not be nice to me, Solares? Give your sister a few perks on the inside?"

Tania's stomach rolled. The greasy jerk.

Ignoring his creep factor, she stopped at the high counter. The overhead lights reflected in the glass that rose from counter to ceiling. She kept her eyes forward but her peripheral vision sharp as Griggs came alongside her. If he so much as touched her, she'd—

The weasel flicked at the end of her ponytail with his fingertip.

She shifted sideways, hating his proximity, and planted herself in front of the rectangular opening in the glass partition. Her chin level, she met his gaze head-on, then glanced toward the wall-mounted camera at the rear of the booth. "Smile, you're on camera."

His gaze followed her sight line. Tania swallowed the urge to crow in triumph. She'd outflanked him. Standing where she was, the security camera was all seeing. One wrong move, and the warden would have a bird's-eye view.

"Smart girl," he murmured loud enough for her to hear. Her stomach churned as he brushed by her. Anger perfuming the air around him, he opened the door into the command booth and stepped inside. His back to the camera, he leered at her. "Let's see how well you do on the way out. I'm off at seven, *sweetheart*, and got nothing to do but wait."

Until visiting hours were over.

He didn't say the words. He didn't need to. Tania knew what he meant. The bastard was escalating, moving past veiled threats to outright intimidation. Though what Griggs thought he could do in a parking lot monitored by security equipment, she didn't know. Follow her maybe? Figure out where she'd booked her hotel room for the night? Well, she wished him luck with that one. She drove like a speed demon, better than most race car drivers. He'd never catch her once she hit the blacktop stretching between the prison and Gig Harbor. She and her Mini would be long gone before the jerk clued in and put his 4x4 in drive.

Thank God for high-powered performance engines. Oh how she loved her wicked smart mechanic.

Clearing her throat, Tania put the kibosh on her amusement. Laughing at him would only make Griggs meaner, and cranking him up another notch? Not a good idea.

Wasn't power grand?

And here—inside the prison walls—Griggs possessed the ultimate leverage, every bit of authority. But no matter how many times he insinuated that her sister's chances at parole would increase one hundredfold if Tania decided to be "nice" to him, she refused to play that game. J.J. would kill her, for one thing. And for another? She didn't sleep around—or trade sexual favors.

Ever.

Now all she needed to do was get through the security check. Without kicking Griggs in the balls with her fancy new boots. If she didn't, J.J. would suffer the consequences. No way Tania would allow that to happen. Or give in and let the scum-sucking weasel win.

Chapter Three

Nightfall couldn't come fast enough. Ivar wanted out of 28 Walton Street and the confining spaces inside the Razorback lair. And away from the thoughts banging around inside his head. He needed the rush and chill of winter against his scales. Yearned to shift into dragon form, stretch his wings, and soar above the cityscape. To hunt the female down before he lost his mind.

He was dangerously close to the edge already. Way off base with no hope of pulling back to the saner side of safe anytime soon.

Sitting on the edge of his bed, Ivar hung his head. He cupped the back of his neck and pressed down. Discomfort nagged at him. He pulled harder, stretching tense muscles, distracting himself with physical pain as an ache of another sort expanded inside his chest. Like a surgeon with rib spreaders, the sorrow cracked him wide open, engulfing his chest cavity, devouring what little remained of his heart. He closed his eyes, combating the mind-fuck of unimaginable loss.

Or at least, it had been...until three weeks ago. Until his warriors had returned and delivered the terrible news.

Lothair—his best friend and XO—was gone. Dead. Murdered by his enemies.

Now he choked on the grief. And didn't know how to handle the pain. He'd never been one for sentiment or brotherly love. Emotional excess belonged to other males— weaker ones with attachment issues—not him. Never him. Death, after all, happened more often than not. Was as inevitable as the rise and setting of the sun in the war he fought against the Nightfuries and the Dragonkind males that supported his enemies' cause.

But losing Lothair...

Fuck him, that hurt. More than he'd thought possible.

Planting his elbows on his knees, Ivar raised his head and stared at the wall opposite him. With all the lights off, the row of plasma TVs should've faded into the darkness, leaving the flat screens indistinguishable from the wall. But he saw everything in high-definition. Even from behind the dark lenses of his Oakleys, his night vision was pinpoint sharp, throwing each detail into stark relief: the textured surface of sea grass wallpaper, the fine grain in the bamboo floorboards, the crystal glass and empty bottle of Jim Beam sitting on the marble-topped bar.

Sucking back the JB hadn't helped. Hadn't put a dent in the pain or given him the oblivion he craved. Nothing ever did. Clarity was his cross to bear—always sticking with him, laying out the best course of action like playing cards in a poker game. Logical. Straightforward. Precise. His mind never failed to see all the angles, which meant he needed to get off his ass. Go hunting. Set the wheels of plan A in motion and avenge his friend.

Too bad daylight was screwing with his flow.

His brows drawn, Ivar pinched the bridge of his nose and took off his wraparounds. Fingering the twin arms, he twirled the sunglasses between the spread of his thighs. The pair were his favorites, something he always wore in human form, but things changed. He was done with the bullshit. Done lying to himself. Done apologizing for the flaw in his chromosomal DNA…for the bright pink eyes he'd been born with and ridiculed for all his life.

"Weak," his sire had said. A color worn by newborn babies and little girls, not warriors.

Well, fuck that. Eye color was the least of who he was… or what he'd become, a powerful male in command of the Razorback nation. Throw in his scientific expertise and…shit. What the hell was he doing living in the past and hiding behind dark lenses? His pansy-ass pink irises meant next to nothing in the scheme of things. Lothair hadn't given a rat's ass about his genetic shortcoming, so why the hell should he?

Pushing to his feet, Ivar dropped the Oakleys. The pair landed with a clatter on the hardwood. His eyes narrowed on the black frames, he lifted his foot and crushed them beneath his boot heel, enjoying the snap-crackle'n-pop as he ground them into the floor and—

"Hey, boss man." The German accent drifted through the closed door behind him. "Need a word."

With a mental click, Ivar flipped the dead bolt with his mind and swung the door wide. Well-oiled hinges sighed as light from the corridor spilled over the threshold, illuminating the darkness. Squinting against the glare, Ivar tilted his head, inviting Denzeil into his domain. "What did you find?"

A determined glint in his eyes, Denzeil crossed the threshold, long legs eating up the space between them. He stopped on the other side of the bed, a pale manila folder in his hand. "The female isn't home."

"Where is she?"

"I got nothing on her car. It's an older model…no GPS to track."

"But?" Ivar said, waiting for the punch line. Denzeil wasn't stupid. He wouldn't show up—put himself on Ivar's radar or in the line of fire—unless he had intel to share.

D smiled, but his dark gaze remained flat. No echo of humor. No spark of pleasure. And rightly so. Lothair's murder had hit all the Razorbacks hard. No one would be laughing for a while. And if his warrior felt so inclined? Ivar would work the male out so hard it would take him weeks to recover from the beat down. "Her credit card was used at a hotel in Gig Harbor."

Ivar's brows collided. "Where the fuck is that?"

"A couple of hours south…near Tacoma, off I-95."

"We leave at sunset. Inform the others."

"Ten four." With a nod, Denzeil tossed the folder onto the king-size bed. As the file's contents spilled onto the duvet, the male said, "One more thing, boss."

Ivar tipped his chin, asking without words.

"Rodin called from Prague an hour ago. He's looking for—"

"Fuck." Just what he didn't need…Rodin, leader of the Archguard, snooping around.

Lothair's sire was a pain in the ass. More so in recent days. But money talked, so Ivar couldn't afford to walk. Not yet. Not until he received another infusion of cash. The breeding program and his supervirus experiments were barely off the ground. Add in the fact the new lair needed additional work to take the construction from half-done to complete, and having a wealthy patron with deep pockets was priority number one.

Funding. Soldiers. Intel about the political climate within Dragonkind ranks. You name it, Rodin provided it.

Too bad the male couldn't keep his yap shut. The aristocratic know-it-all liked to be kept in the loop, which was annoying as hell, but having an influential member of the Archguard—head of one of the dynastic families that ruled Dragonkind—under his thumb furthered the Razorback cause. So, yeah…keeping Rodin happy ranked as important.

Powerful friends, after all, made excellent allies.

Which meant lying his ass off to keep Rodin in the dark awhile longer. Oh, he would tell him of Lothair's death… eventually. But not before Ivar made the male responsible for his friend's death pay first. The murdering SOB belonged to him, not Rodin's death squad.

So, step one…keep it quiet and off Rodin's radar.

Step two? Find Tania Solares.

Lothair had hunted her before his death. Was Solares the last high-energy female he needed to round out phase one of the breeding program? No clue. But after checking out her picture, Ivar suspected it would be a whole helluva lot of fun finding out, so…

Call it killing two birds with one stone.

By capturing her, he would honor his friend—finish what Lothair started—all while playing mind games with the enemy. Another missing female for the Nightfuries to chase. Add that gem to the fact Denzeil had discovered Solares was BFFs with the Nightfury commander's mate and…you guessed it. Instant torture to a pack of males more interested in protecting humans than their own kind. The double whammy would distract Bastian, drive him and his band of bastards insane as they tried to find her.

All the better for him.

The frenzy would be entertaining to watch. From a distance, of course. He'd be too busy breaking in his new captive: playing cat to her mouse, tossing her in a cage, toying with her until she screamed for mercy, all in the name of payback. And once he had his fill? He'd put her on the end of a hook. Dangle her as bait for the Nightfuries, then close the trap around them when they came to her rescue.

Annihilation inevitable.

Ivar's mouth curved. Time to stop living in the past indeed. He smelled Kentucky Fried Nightfury in his future. So, yeah…

Rodin, and his pissant Archguard problems, would have to wait.

Chapter Four

Good news traveled fast, bad news even faster. Fortunately for J.J., her news hadn't traveled anywhere at all. Just the way she liked it—everything buttoned up, information on the down-low. The last thing she needed was for word to leak out. At least not until she was ready to share, and that wouldn't be anytime soon.

Not if she wanted to stay under the radar.

And she did. With all her heart.

Strategize for the coming battle first. Celebrate the victory later.

The plan was a good one. But only if she could pull it off in a place full of nosey parkers and prison yard bullies. Drawing the attention of the hard-core element inside the cellblock wasn't advisable. Not if she wanted to stay healthy. So she needed to move fast, and getting her sister on board was a definite must. Secrets, like raw meat, didn't keep inside a prison for very long.

Taking a calming breath, J.J. played it cool, her attitude all about ordinary as she waited outside the last checkpoint.

Steels bars in front of her, a series of locked doors behind her, she stood in limbo as the guard checked the logbook. With a nod in her direction, he unhooked a clipboard from the wall, slid a pen from beneath the metal clip at the top, and wrote her name on the list.

Different day. Identical story.

Check in. Check out. Same old, same old as the guards followed each security measure to a T. Head counts at lights-out every night. Regular cell sweeps designed to crack down on the contraband problem on the inside. Three squares a day. Nothing but routine day after day, month after month.

Right now, though, J.J. didn't mind the watch-and-wait from inside the cage. Wasn't annoyed by the double check or the time it took. Today was visiting day, and for the first time ever, she had something other than doom and gloom to share with her sister.

J.J.'s mouth curved. *Good news.* Secret, incredible, fantastic news. An ache bloomed in the center of her chest. The sensation was unfamiliar...long forgotten. And no wonder. After four and a half years inside, she'd forgotten what hope felt like.

"Jamison Jordan." The raspy voice, flavored with a down-home hint of Georgia, came from the other side of the bars. "You gonna be a problem today?"

Startled from her thoughts, J.J. blinked and glanced up. Dark brown eyes met hers. Round face decorated by dark skin, the guard gave her a stern look. Anyone worth their salt would've taken the warning seriously. Not her. J.J. smiled instead. Sometimes a hard shell protected a soft center or, in Officer Rally's case, a big heart.

"Nah, not today, Reggie," she said, her tone edged by the amusement he always brought out in her. "I'm in a good mood."

Dark eyes twinkling, he snorted. Keys jangled, bumping against his utility belt as he approached the steel door. "Good to know, missy. Let's keep it that way, shall we?"

"Don't I always?"

"Ha! Trouble wrapped up in a small package, that's what you are," he murmured, teasing her.

God love him. Reggie was a real gem, the only guard who'd ever truly given a damn about her. Like the father figure she'd never had, he encouraged her every step of the way. Pushed to her to work harder, think faster…be better. And thanks to him, she *was* better. Smarter too. Without him, she never would've finished her college degree. J.J. shook her head, marveling at the irony. Go figure. She'd gone to prison to get an education.

Totally off-the-wall crazy.

Reggie unclipped the key ring from his belt. The collection jingled in his hand as he unlocked the door and swung it wide, inviting her to step through. Brushing by him, she came out clean on the other side, one right turn and sixty-three paces from her entrance into the visitor center. She knew because she always counted out the steps. Call it habit. Call it boredom with a slaphappy helping of the mundane. But those sixty-three strides mattered. Each one brought her closer to Tania when she visited.

And on those Saturdays, her sister became the center of her universe.

The urge to get a move on poked at her. J.J. ignored her itchy feet and waited, following protocol as the steel door clanged shut behind her and Reggie locked up. Seconds away from being unleashed, J.J. leaned forward, chancing a quick peek around the blind corner and down the double-wide corridor.

Yup. Nothing but ordinary in a sea of normal.

The two guards flanking the solitary door—backs facing the wall of frosted glass, arms crossed, and expressions set—weren't paying attention. Not to her. Not to Reggie, either. Excellent. Just the chance she needed. She was dying for an update.

Reclipping his keys, Reggie stopped alongside her.

"How's Helen?" she asked, keeping her voice low.

"Better," he whispered back. No one, least of all Reggie, wanted their friendship broadcast. The father–daughter thing wouldn't go over well. Trouble started that way. Inmates would squawk. Accusations of favoritism would fly—even though it wasn't true. If anything, Reggie pushed her harder, expected more from her than anyone else. "Doctor says she'll make a full recovery."

J.J. smiled her relief. Thank God for excellent doctors. The last thing Reggie needed was to bury his beloved wife. "Good news."

"Almost as good as yours."

J.J. froze. Her gaze snapped back to his as she ping-ponged, her happiness for him turning an ugly corner into fear for herself. Struggling to breathe, she swallowed the sudden swell of panic. "Who else knows?"

"Just the warden," he said, his tone soft with understanding. "Don't go getting all twisted up about it. I'm not telling, and the warden's got better things to do than piss on your parade."

"Hey, Rally," one of the guards in the adjacent corridor called. "What's the holdup? She coming or what?"

Playing the game, Reggie gripped her arm, curling his big hand around her biceps, and walked her around the corner. Giving her a stern look, he gave her a gentle push, urging her along the corridor. "Get moving now...visiting time's almost over."

With a nod, J.J. did as she was told. As she walked the length of the hallway, her shoes didn't make a peep on the newly waxed floor. No surprise there. She hardly ever made a sound. Silence was her thing...the weapon of choice in a place where flamboyance and mouthing off got you all the wrong attention.

All the more reason to keep her secret undercover.

Inmates were like vultures: constantly circling, waiting for the right time to strike. And when they found a weakness? A shakedown almost always followed, so...yeah, fading into the background—helping people forget you existed—was always the best survival strategy.

A prison guard pulled the door to the visiting center open for her. Murmuring her thanks, J.J. slipped over the threshold into organized chaos. She stood unmoving a moment, scanning the crowd, listening to female voices mixed with deeper male ones. The symphonic hum collected against the high ceiling before rebounding, bouncing off white cinder-block walls stenciled with NO SMOKING and NO PROFANITY warnings. Heavy-duty furniture dotted the landscape: table legs bolted to the concrete floor, uncomfortable seats welded to steel frames, nothing but utilitarian, old, and ugly.

Funny thing, though. No one ever complained about the lack of comfort. No one cared. All that mattered was the contact, the sit-chat-and-catch-up as inmates reunited with families, lovers, and friends. J.J. watched the animation a moment—absorbing the comfort of smiling faces, fluttering hand gestures, and bright eyes—then scanned the tables, looking for her sister in the crowd.

She spotted Tania near the back of the room. Her mouth curved, happiness lighting her up from the inside out. It never failed. Loyal to a fault, her sister always showed up, and J.J. was so grateful she fought a flood of tears every time she saw her sitting there. Waiting patiently. Facing the reality of her situation without flinching. So much love and acceptance in her eyes it made J.J. wonder what she'd done to deserve it.

Nothing, she knew. In fact, quite the opposite.

She'd shot and killed a man with a stolen .22 caliber.

Did it matter that she'd had little choice? That his threats to kill her hadn't been idle, but imminent? No. Not even a little. To protect herself and Tania, she'd lured her abusive boyfriend into a trap, provoked him into attacking, then pumped him full of lead. So, no, she didn't deserve her sister's understanding or the biweekly visits. But the manslaughter charge along with a fifteen-year sentence were worth the loss of her freedom. Thanks to her, Tania was still alive, and so was she.

As she approached, Tania smiled in greeting but didn't get up. It was safer that way. J.J. needed a hug so badly she could taste it—and her sister wanted to give her one—but physical contact wasn't allowed. The one time they'd broken that all-important rule and embraced, the guards had gone one hundred shades of badass on her, revoking her privileges for a month.

"Hey, Baby J." Planting her forearms on the pitted tabletop, Tania leaned toward her. "How goes the war?"

"Better than yours, I think," J.J. said, getting a load of the anger in her sister's eyes as she slid onto the bench seat opposite her. Yikes. That didn't bode well. Whenever Tania got upset, tornado-like chaos followed, taking out everything in its path.

Tania grimaced. "My pissed off is showing, isn't it?"

"Thundercloud times ten." Rubbing the inside of her wrist, J.J. traced the corner of the letter she'd tucked beneath the material of her long-sleeved shirt. She breathed out in relief. It was still there. Still folded end over end, safe and sound, right where she needed it to be. "What's the matter? Griggs get in your face again?"

"The little weasel made me take off my boots," she said, her tone a shade shy of murderous. "Again!"

"Jag-off."

"No kidding. What does he think I'm smuggling in them...a switchblade? It's not like he doesn't put me through a metal detector or anything."

"Probably just has a thing for your toes."

Tania huffed. "Foot fetish scuzball. One swift kick—"

"And good aim."

"—that's all I need."

"Forget the riding boots, then," J.J. said, grinning like an idiot. She couldn't help it. Tania always made her laugh. "Invest in some solid steel-toes. Better crunch factor."

They both laughed, enjoying the fantasy. The guard patrolling their side of the room glanced their way. Nothing unusual about that. Tania always got a lot of attention. Men loved to look at her. And with her sable hair pulled off her face and burgundy-flecked eyes full of laughter? Tania's gorgeous factor doubled.

Not that her sister knew it. Heck, she didn't know she was pretty at all.

Sure, Tania dressed to kill—always wore the latest and greatest—but that was just a defense mechanism. More about their upbringing, about never having enough and going hungry every day. But most of all? Her sister never wanted to hear anyone call her poor white trash ever again. J.J. could relate, although not on the same level. After their mom's death, Tania had shielded her: giving J.J. her share to eat, working two jobs to keep a roof over their heads and shoes on her feet.

At eighteen, Tania had been smarter—and more responsible—than most people twice her age.

Swallowing past the lump in her throat, J.J. shrugged off the pain. The past was the past. She couldn't change it or her mistakes. But here…right now? Today held the promise of tomorrow and maybe…just maybe…the second chance she needed to make things right.

"So…" One eye on the guard, J.J. waited until he pivoted and strode in the other direction. When he reached the midpoint in the room, she slipped the folded letter from her shirtsleeve. Trapping the paper between her palm and the table, she met Tania's gaze. "I've got some news, but you have to promise me something."

"What?"

"No freaking out." Stacking her forearms in front of her, she leaned in and whispered, "And keep your voice down. No one else can know, okay?"

"Cross my heart."

Exhaling long and smooth, she pushed the folded white square toward her sister. Her fingers trembled as she relinquished her secret and drew away, leaving the letter for her sister to grab. Tania plucked the paper off the tabletop and, after a quick check on the guard's location, unfolded the paper.

"Oh my God, J.J." True to her word, Tania kept her voice down, but when she looked up tears filled her eyes. "This is from the parole board."

"I know," she said, blinking to combat the rise of her own tears. Goddamn it. *Don't cry…do not cry.* But even as she fought the growing tide, hope swelled inside her, making her chest so tight she struggled to breathe. Hanging on by a fingernail, she beat back the surging tide of emotion. "The hearing's in a month. Tania, if all goes well, I could be—"

"Released." Her gaze locked on the letter, Tania rasped, "Out on parole. Thank God…oh thank you, God."

J.J. nodded, feeling as shell-shocked as her sister looked. The ache started up again. Raising her hand, she rubbed the spot over her heart, struggling to stay calm, willing Tania to do the same. But, man, the possibility of parole was unexpected, so mind-boggling that even now, a whole two days after receiving the news, J.J. couldn't believe it. Couldn't accept that a mistake hadn't been made…that the contents of the letter weren't meant for someone else.

Someone better. More deserving. Less guilty and regret-filled.

The paper trembled, crinkling as her sister's hands shook. Ah, crap. Not good. If Tania lost it, she would too, and a blubber-fest in front of witnesses was the last thing she needed. Especially surrounded by inmates who wouldn't hesitate to make her life hell—maybe even try to muck up her chance of parole by setting her up with the guards—if they knew about the letter.

Jealousy, after all, was an awful thing, and "accidents" happened all the time. Drugs got planted and people beaten up—or worse...stabbed—for a lot less than receiving a chance at freedom.

So, yeah. Tania needed to keep it together. Otherwise J.J. would be in for a world of hurt when she got back to her cell.

Chapter Five

Mac grunted as he unwrapped the uppercut beneath Forge's chin. The male's head snapped back. Pain throbbed up his arm. His muscle screamed, burning with fatigue. He growled in pleasure. Oh man...hitting his mentor was *so* the shit. The real frickin' deal, exactly what he needed to kill the frustration. A ball-breaking fight without an ounce of regret.

No worries. No need to hold back or pull his punches. No one would die here today.

End up bruised, bloodied, and headed to the in-house clinic in the underground lair? Fucking A. But Mac didn't give a damn. Forge handled himself beautifully: fists raised, purple gaze shimmering, giving as good as he got. And, oh baby, the backlash—each punishing blow the guy landed—felt like heaven, so damned good Mac didn't know what to do first...hit Forge or thank God.

He settled for both and nailed the male again. Bone cracked against bone. Forge cursed and stumbled sideways. Showing no mercy, Mac unleashed another body shot, hammering the guy's rib cage. An unforgiving crack echoed, ricocheting off the gymnasium's high ceiling. Each curse and groan played like a heavenly sound track—a lullaby that soothed Mac's pride—as the fight moved from brutal and intense to halfhearted.

Mac circled left. Forge limped right, struggling to stay on his feet. About time too. Built like a tank, the guy could take a lot of punishment, but it was getting ridiculous now. With his anger fading, Mac didn't want to fight anymore. Too bad he couldn't stop. Pride wouldn't let him. The sting of failure was still too fresh. He needed to win at something, instead of failing at everything. So, yeah…no way was he backing down until Forge cried uncle.

Which posed a major problem.

Pride, it seemed, wasn't a one-way street. Proof positive lay in the fact he and his mentor were doing the two-step down the middle of it, 'cause…yeah, Forge didn't want to lose, either. But worse than that? The male hadn't yet realized he couldn't win. Not against Mac in human form. Sure, Forge might be lethal in dragon form, but with fists and feet, Mac reigned supreme. A martial arts expert, he'd been trained in hand-to-hand combat and taught to inflict maximum damage. Which meant sooner or later he'd be forced to back off or hurt his buddy.

His brows drawn tight, Mac took a step back, giving his friend some breathing room. Wiping a trickle of blood from beneath his nose, he asked, "Had enough yet?"

"Bloody hell," Forge rasped and, pressing his elbow to his side, hugged his rib cage. With a groan, he bowed his head, hit one knee, then crumpled into a heap on the floor. "What the hell was that?"

"Kung fu."

"Bugger me...where did you learn it?" Giving up all pretense, Forge turned belly-up. Splayed out in the middle of the basketball court, he stared up at the ceiling. "Bruce fucking Lee?"

"Got interested while I was on an op with my SEAL unit," he said, the adrenaline rush fading. Agony took its place. Mac winced, feeling each blow Forge had landed. Exhaling hard, he collapsed next to his friend on the hardwood. "Been studying it ever since."

Forge swiped at the cut above his eye. His fingers came away covered in blood. With a grunt, he wiped a red smear on his T-shirt. "You're going tae teach me...every last move. And tae shoot too."

"You like guns?" Mac flexed his fingers. Pain screamed up his forearm as he checked for busted knuckles.

"Never held one, but I want tae learn."

"Done."

It was the least he could do, considering he'd just beaten the snot out of the guy. And as perverse as it sounded, he was looking forward to another round. Teaching Forge the basics would give him the opportunity to smack him around some more. 'Cause, man, now that he'd burned off the excess energy, his muscles unlocked, unfurling into relaxation.

Pure heaven.

Now all he needed was a swim. Too bad Black Diamond didn't have a pool. At least not yet.

Daimler—the Nightfuries' go-to guy—had something in the works with some hoity-toity landscape firm. Mac couldn't wait to get his hands on the plans. The sooner, the better, but he was exercising patience...and trying not to think about the company Daimler hired. But it was hard.

Especially since he knew who worked there. Tania Solares, sex kitten extraordinaire and best friend to Bastian's mate. So, yeah, he understood the connection and why she'd been given the contract, but…shit. No wonder he had trouble sleeping. He couldn't stop thinking about it. Or her. *She* polluted every thought that ran through his head.

Which didn't work for him at all.

He'd only met her once—barely talked to her—but from the moment he'd seen Tania across the SPD squad room…

Bam! Reason ceased to exist while desire took control.

With a sigh, Mac rolled to his feet. Time for a distraction. The last thing he needed was another go-around with the woman who invaded his dreams.

Stretching out his bruised shoulder, Mac glanced at Forge. "You coming?"

"Do I have tae?"

"Ah, poor baby."

"Go fuck yerself."

Effective if a little less than poetic. "Come on, man. You want Daimler down here kicking our asses because we ruined the meal?"

Like all the males in the lair, the thought of upsetting Daimler put Forge in gear. The Numbai was awesome to the next power. No way anyone wanted to piss him off. Whoever did might end up neglected. As Forge pushed to his feet, he grumbled, "You know I'll get you back. Just wait until dragon combat training tonight."

Mac put his middle finger to good use and flipped his friend the bird. "Pansy."

"Fledgling." Purple eyes glimmering, Forge smiled around his split lip. "You know you're gonna—"

"What the hell are you two yahoos doing?" The deep voice rumbled across the gym, drifting beneath the buzz of industrial-grade fluorescents.

"Shite…company." Forge threw him a warning look.

True enough. Had he listened, they'd already be upstairs, making Daimler happy with their unbruised, unbloodied presence.

"Playing pin the tail on the donkey," Mac said, sarcasm out in full force as he turned toward the gym entrance.

Shitkickers planted between the doorjambs, Rikar's pale gaze moved from him to Forge, then back again. "Which one of you is the ass?"

"Him," he and Forge said at the same time, pointing at each other.

Rikar's lips twitched. "Who won?"

"Me."

"Unfair advantage." Wincing, Forge rubbed the side of his knee. "Fucking guy knows kung fu."

His XO's amusement widened into a grin. "Handy."

"Only if you're not on the receiving end," Forge muttered.

Mac shook his head but felt his heart expand. His chest went tight around a flood of gratefulness. Frickin' guys. He knew what they were doing. With each word, they shored him up, making it clear that, despite everything, they valued him. Trusted him. Knew that sooner or later, he'd get in the game and master the magic—become one with his dragon half, so to speak—and become a full-fledged member of the Nightfury pack.

All he needed to do was believe.

Mac stifled a snort. Right. *Believe.* Simple, yet oh so complicated. Faith had never been his forte. He was a doer, not a believer. And sitting on his duff praying everything worked out day in, day out? He hated every second of it.

Conjuring a T-shirt to go with his faded Levi's, Mac strode across the gym. No sense avoiding the inevitable. He could argue with Forge—tell the guy to screw off and leave him alone—but not his XO. Rikar wouldn't give him a free pass.

Nor should he.

The guy had saved his life, finding him before his dragon DNA kicked in and the *change* took hold. Not that Mac recalled much of it. Most of what occurred that day was nothing but a big blank. But he remembered Rikar with total clarity. Could still hear the male's voice inside his head. Feel him as he connected through mind-speak, talked him through the pain, keeping his energy levels stable through seven hours of pure hell.

And that connection? A huge deal in Dragonkind circles.

The shared experience formed an unbreakable bond…a father–son vibe that spanned decades and demographics, shoved differences aside and tied males together. So, yeah, his respect for Rikar ran more than marrow-deep. He wanted to make the guy proud. To prove to himself and the others that Rikar's faith in him wasn't misguided.

"Everybody waiting?" Mac asked as he came even with the doorframe.

"Yeah. Daimler's having six fits. The food's getting cold." Pale eyes roaming, Rikar scanned his face, the concern in his gaze palpable.

Mac ignored it, refusing to acknowledge his own worry or that his XO shared it. Talking about that kind of crap never helped. Doing something about it was the only way through.

After a second, Rikar bowed out, respecting his silence, and glanced at the bruise on his cheekbone. "Feel better now?"

"Immeasurably." Mac flexed his fist, enjoying the residual pain as the nicks pulled at his skin. "I should kick his ass every day."

"You won't get any argument from me."

"Clever, lads," Forge said, an eye roll in his voice. "And tae think, you wankers are now my brothers-in-arms."

Amusement sparkled in Rikar's ice-blue eyes. Mac grinned back. Thank God for Forge and his wicked sense of humor. Okay, so the Scottish lingo took some getting used to, but it was worth it. No one lightened the mood better than his mentor. Or would allow himself to get kung fu'ed for a good cause.

He hadn't felt this relaxed in days.

Mac slapped the Scot's shoulder to show his appreciation. When Forge nodded, Mac left the party of three and stepped into the corridor, where quiet took on a new meaning. Under the buzz of the heavy-duty industrial lights, the silence hadn't been so complete. But outside it? Noise curled inward, playing keep-away, staying contained. Even the polished concrete floor was in on the game, absorbing each of his footfalls, eating the sound as he strode up a slight incline toward the elevators. The strip of halogens embedded in the floor acted like twin runways, throwing V-like splashes of illumination up the stone walls to touch twelve-foot ceilings.

Old came to mind.

Honed from solid granite, the underground lair reeked of history. A century's worth? A millennium's? As far as Mac knew, the Nightfuries didn't have a clue. No one talked about it…or cared. Safety mattered more than passing months unfolding into years. As long as the lair stayed secure—off both human and Razorback radar—no one gave a rat's ass about the hows and whys of Black Diamond.

Walking beneath the foyer's vaulted ceiling, Mac stopped in front of the elevators. He reached toward the control panel. A second before his finger made contact, he stopped, hand hovering an inch away, curiosity poking at him. His brow collided as he stared at the up button.

Baby steps.

Forge had been talking about the "little things" all week. About the sequence of learning. About respecting the magic enough not to rush it. Mac blew out a breath. Maybe it was time he pulled his head out of his ass and started to listen. To accept his mentor's coaching instead of fighting to do it his own way.

Seemed like a good plan. No time like the present to take a baby step and give it another shot.

Dropping his hand, Mac closed his eyes and retreated inward, looking for the thread of magic he'd lost in the gym. Energy sparked. He sank into the heat, fanning the ember into flame. As the ball of energy grew deep inside him, he nurtured it, held the power close a moment, then tossed his request out like a pair of dice. His heart thumped as magic rolled, whispering like static, filling the air around him. Machinery hummed, grinding into motion, obeying his command. His mouth curved. The elevator pinged a second before the stainless steel doors slid open in front of him.

Tears burned the back of his throat. Finally. Holy fuck...*finally*. He felt it. Wasn't fighting to hang on or grasping for control. He was connected to his dragon, no longer less than half, but whole. Combating the sear of emotion, Mac inhaled smooth and exhaled long. With a respect born of time, he repeated the breathing technique, exorcising the stress as the fractured pieces inside him clicked together.

A heavy hand landed on the back of his neck.

Mac glanced over his shoulder. Giving his nape a gentle squeeze, Rikar nodded. The show of approval hit Mac chest level. Mother of God. That felt good. The surge of magic in his veins. The pride he saw in Rikar's eyes. The hope both gave him.

Stopping alongside him, Forge nudged him with his shoulder. As Mac rocked sideways, bumping into Rikar, he met the male's gaze. He tipped his chin, thanking him without words for his patience over the past month.

"No sweat," Forge murmured, stepping past him and into the elevator. "Now enough of the bullshite. I'm famished."

Mac's stomach growled. Not a good sign. As a fledgling male, he needed to refuel often. Daimler wouldn't be happy with him for pulling a disappearing act all day. The Numbai worried about the Nightfury crew, working hard to keep them in good eats and give each what was needed to thrive. But he'd shifted focus this past month, babying Mac...overjoyed by the prospect of putting him into the calorie overload his body required to endure the ongoing changes and the new abilities that each shift brought.

Good thing too. Mac didn't know what he would do without the guy…and his monster triple-decker chocolate cake.

His mouth watering, he stepped into the elevator behind his comrades. The smooth ascent took less than a minute. Without making a sound, the doors slid open, dumping him into the aboveground lair. Hanging a right, Mac entered the double-wide corridor and beat feet, heading for the kitchen.

Antique doors marched like soldiers, trim, orderly, equally spaced on either side of the hallway. Paintings hung between them above the wainscoting, brightening the white walls with splashes of vivid color. Done by guys with names like Monet, Renoir, and van Gogh, the space was more gallery than hallway. A beautiful way to get from point A to B in the lair, the place would make curators and art connoisseurs the world over jealous.

Not that Mac knew anything about art, but…

Wow. The juxtaposition was appealing. Soothing, even. He'd never seen nineteenth-century landscapes play nice with modern, geometric pieces and charcoal etchings. The balance and flow was a big departure from the graphic art posters plastered on the walls inside the *Sarah-Jane*, his forty-seven-foot yacht and home for the last five years.

But not anymore.

He was 100 percent out of the human world. No more homicide squad at SPD or catching bad guys without a shitload of scales, claws, fangs, and the wherewithal to use them. And as surprising as it seemed, he was A-okay with the switch-up. Especially since it came complete with a crew who thought and acted just like him. The ultimate accessory to his lifestyle makeover, though? Daimler. Hands down. The Numbai took culinary wizardry to a whole new level.

His stomach rumbled again. Mac picked up the pace. The smell of roast beef and fresh bread pulled him toward the kitchen, slingshotting him over the threshold into—

He stopped short. Ah, hell. Not again.

Mac shook his head, struggling not to laugh. It never failed. He always walked in when Bastian was in Don Juan mode. Kind of embarrassing. Not that B cared. He was a little preoccupied. Standing at the far end of the kitchen island with his arms wrapped around Myst, Bastian hugged her from behind, hands traveling as she tried to slice a loaf of bread. *Tried* being the operative word. It wasn't going well, the uneven pieces, some thick, some thin, telling the tale.

"Would you quit that?" she said, exasperation combining with laughter. With a sudden twist, Myst bumped her mate's chest with the back of her shoulders, searching for separation. The nudge made Bastian bolder. While she squirmed, he got busy nuzzling the side of her neck. "God, you're a pain in the—oh, hey Mac."

Meeting her gaze, Mac tipped his chin in greeting.

Bastian's head came up. Green eyes lit him up like twin spotlights, then narrowed, taking inventory, cataloging his injuries, making assumptions. Not surprising. B didn't miss much, but…shit. Mac could've done without the visual pat down. It made him feel fifteen again, caught behind the bleachers with a cheerleader's legs wrapped around his waist. On the one hand, a great memory. On the other, not so much after the principal got hold of him. But like it or not, the Nightfury commander had that effect on him.

He hoped that changed when he got to know B better. Maybe it would. Maybe it wouldn't. Either way, Mac went on high alert as his commander raised a questioning brow. Resisting the urge to hide his beat-up hands behind his back, he walked between the bank of wall cabinets and the island, moving toward censure instead of away. He'd always been like that...a take-it-in-the-teeth kind of guy.

Slowing his roll, he stopped beside the pair. As he leaned his hip against the island's marble lip, he reached out and snagged a piece of bread off the bamboo cutting board. And oh man, it was still warm. Thick, fluffy, right-out-of-the-oven delicious. Shoving half of it into his mouth, he swallowed the load of umm-umm-good and met B's gaze. His commander didn't say a word, just waited.

Mac sighed. No time like the present. "So...had a little mishap in the gym."

"Really," B said, tone loaded with *yeah, right*. Mac didn't blame him. Not after KOing a wall last week. "Anything broken besides your face?"

"Just my fist." Cocky as ever, Forge slung his arm around Mac's neck and held his hand up for inspection. Dimmed down, the halogens above their heads highlighted the damage, throwing contoured shadows across his beat-to-shit knuckles.

"You gonna show him your cracked ribs too?" Icy air rushing in his wake, Rikar pulled up beside them.

Mac stifled a shiver, combating the sudden deep freeze. It was always like that. Everywhere the guy went, the temperature dropped into single digits. Par for the course for a frost dragon. Though how Angela—his best friend, partner in the SPD's homicide division, and now Rikar's mate—handled the cold without turning into an icicle, he didn't know. Magic, probably. Hard-core, never-say-die love? Without a doubt.

His expression in neutral, Rikar reached around him to grab his own slice of heaven. After taking a bite, he umm-yeahed around the mouthful and said, "Forge'll be walking with a limp for a while."

"One word." Releasing his hold on Mac, Forge spun and ass-planted himself on the countertop opposite them. Shitkickers dangling against white cabinet facades, he said, "Kung fu."

"That's two words, buddy."

"Who asked you, Frosty?"

As Rikar threw his favorite words—*fuck* and *off*—into the ring, Mac laughed.

Bastian grinned and, after giving Myst a gentle squeeze, let her out from between him and the island. No dummy, she escaped Mr. Grabby-Hands, scooped up the cutting board—bread knife and all—and hightailed it into the dining room. B watched her go, then glanced from him to Forge and back again. "You boys work it out?"

Rotating his sore shoulder, Mac nodded. "All good."

"Better be," B murmured, turning toward the dining room. "Let's eat before Daimler goes postal."

Sounded like a plan. Especially if it meant getting another slice of homemade bread.

Moving in sync, Mac followed his commander, passing beneath the heavy timber-beamed archway into Café Nightfury. As he cleared the threshold, he glanced at the glass French doors leading out onto the patio. Imbued with magic, each pane rippled like black water, lapping at the window edges, cutting off the garden views…blocking out the orange glow of the setting sun.

A shame, really. He loved watching the sun sink beyond the horizon. But that wasn't an option anymore. Not unless he wanted to go blind and get fried…in that order.

Dragonkind didn't tolerate sunlight. Their eyes were too light sensitive, hence the need for enchanted glass on all the windows. The stuff served an important purpose, shifting from light to dark, protecting them from the harmful UV rays during the day, lightening at night to allow moonlight into the aboveground lair. But where sunlight stopped, candlelight took over; the golden glow bounced off the collection of covered dishes on the long table and antique sideboard. Like expensive jewelry, cut crystal sparkled alongside fine china and expensive silverware.

Mecca for a hungry male.

And he wasn't alone. Wick and Venom had already made the trip. Per usual, the two sat side by side, Venom's arm slung over the back of Wick's chair. Wick growled a greeting. Mac nodded, making eye contact, getting plugged by the male's golden gaze in return. Venom he ignored, doing the usual as he pretended the guy didn't exist. It was either that or load a matched pair of Sigs and shoot the obstinate jack-off.

Ruby-red eyes trained on him, Venom followed his progress along the opposite side of the table. "About frigging time, fledgling."

"Stow it, dickhead," he said, resigned to the grind. Venom always came at him hard, like a sidewinder with fangs bared and poison rising. No trust. No faith. Just in-your-face aggression. Mac understood it to a certain extent. He was new and unproven, still unstable in a lot of ways and a potential minefield to the warriors Venom considered his to protect—the possessive SOB. "I'm here, so fuck off."

Venom shifted in his chair. Wick grabbed his forearm, keeping him seated as B yelled, "Yo, Sloan...unplug, man. Time to eat."

"In a sec," Sloan said, sounding distracted.

Uh-oh. Not good. He knew that tone. And whenever Sloan—resident computer genius, hacker of impenetrable databases—used it, shit usually hit the fan. Mac changed course and headed for the living room. Chair legs scraped against the wooden floor as the wonder twins pushed away from the table. As he bypassed the massive double-sided fireplace separating the two rooms, Bastian rolled in on his six.

Sitting on the back of the couch, shitkickers planted on the seat cushion, MacBook on his thighs, Sloan looked up as the entire crew filed into the room. Shaved head displaying his mocha-colored skin, he pegged Mac with dark eyes and an intense look. "We got a problem."

"We?" Mac skirted the ass end of the sofa. He wanted a sneak peek at what was playing on the computer screen. "Or me?"

"Both."

Rikar's eyes narrowed. "Put it on-screen."

Fingers flying, Sloan remote accessed the lair's cyber network. A second later the wall of plasma TVs flipped on. A few more keystrokes and...eureka. The six o'clock news started playing, pain-in-the-ass reporter Clarissa Newton front and center on-screen, talking about police corruption. And joy of joys, Mac's sudden disappearance from the Seattle scene.

"Jesus help me," Mac muttered.

"The little witch," his partner said at the same time. Hazel eyes glued to the screen, Angela slipped beneath

Rikar's arm, snuggled into his side, and scowled at the reporter. "Never could stand her."

Per usual, Angela was bang on. *Witch* summed it up nicely. The powder-puff reporter had been a problem for them while working cases with the SPD. And now? Here she was again, poking her nose where it didn't belong, smearing his good name, accusing him of a cover-up.

Him, for fuck's sake. The straightest, least corrupt cop on the entire frickin' force.

Flexing his hands, Mac unclenched his teeth and forced tense muscles to relax. No sense getting bent out of shape about a reputation that didn't matter anymore. So what. Big deal. Screw the humans and their idiot assumptions. Still, a mess was a mess, and this one needed to be cleaned up before the reporter got too close to the truth. He glanced at Bastian. "We need to find Newton—"

Glass shattered, splintering against the floor with a crash.

"Oh no." One hand covering her mouth, a broken water pitcher at her feet, Myst stared at the TV.

Mac's attention snapped back to the screen. His heart went jackrabbit. Caught fast by the image, he froze, hands and feet going numb, breath locked in his throat.

Mother of God. *Her.* His dream girl decked out by high definition, giving an interview to the cream-puff reporter.

"Tania," he growled, sounding more animal than human.

And no wonder. His dragon half stood at attention, instincts rising as need dragged him toward her. The closer he got to the screen, the more powerful the longing became.

Mine.

The word—possessive, territorial, and…mind-torquing terrible—echoed inside his head. Desperation turned the screw, twisting him tight, and as yearning took hold, he struggled to stay even. To hold on to the self-imposed exile he'd clung to all his life and the emotional distance that insulated him from the inevitable pain of betrayal. But not anymore. The sight of her made detachment impossible.

"Bastian," Myst whispered, fear in her violet eyes, face gone pale. "If we're watching this, so are the Razorbacks. If Ivar gets a hold of her, he'll…oh God, he'll…you have to find her first."

A quick about-face. Two long strides and Bastian reached his mate. Wrapping his arms around her, he pulled her close and held her tight. "I will. Don't worry, *bellmia*. I'll find her." Nestling his cheek against the top of Myst's head, B nailed Sloan with shimmering green eyes. "How much time?"

"Sun sets in an hour."

The time frame cranked Mac into overdrive. Tearing his gaze from Tania's face, he growled, "I'm going with you."

Rikar cursed.

B shook his head. "Mac—"

"No one touches her but me." He drilled his commander with a glare, daring Bastian to contradict him. Let him try. The male might be big, but he wouldn't get far. "Any of you go near her…I'll rip your heads off."

No contest. He didn't give a damn about protocol or the chain of command. The how and why of his reaction to Tania didn't matter. She belonged to him. He would protect her at all costs. End of story.

As the prisoners left single file, Tania waved at her sister. Dark as a raven's wing, J.J.'s long hair shimmered as she tipped her chin, returning her good-bye. Love mixed with envy. She loved her sibling, no question. But honestly, she'd always coveted her sister's pin-straight do. And wonder of wonders? J.J. still dreamed of one day having her wavy J. Lo–like locks.

Strange, wasn't it? To want what you didn't have.

Today, though, Tania didn't want to change a thing. She felt grateful for the first time in, well…she didn't know how long. Forever maybe? It seemed like a stretch—like an exaggeration without end—but it wasn't. Not after all she and J.J. had suffered together. And now, in the fading light of the closing day, bright and shining hope came calling. Finally something good had come home to roost. Knocked on their collective doors…whatever. The analogy didn't matter.

The letter in her back pocket, however? That mattered a heck of a lot. Meant everything and more as she watched her sister disappear from view. To return to her cell, nothing but a number printed neatly on the top of a prison file folder.

Well, not anymore. Parole. God help her…*parole*!

She rechecked the back pocket of her jeans. The piece of paper was still there. Snug. Secure. Safe from nosey parkers and away from prying eyes. Just how her sister wanted it. Too bad, really. Had it been her, she would've wanted to keep the letter with her…to read it over and over, early in the morning, late at night, between meals and trips to the prison yard, until the shock wore off and the contents began to feel real. Like a serious possibility instead of a homespun dream.

But it wasn't her neck on the line. And if her sister thought smuggling the paper out of the prison would keep her safe, Tania refused to argue. Squabbling, after all, took time, which was something she didn't have. Not right now.

Spinning toward the door, Tania hightailed it out of the visitor center. She needed to get to her cell phone and make a call ASAP. Before she sank any deeper into trouble. Before bad became worse. Before that stupid interview on KING channel 5 news went live and she screwed up J.J. for good.

Worry streamed through her, hitching her heartbeat into a gallop. Feet moving rapid-fire, Tania crossed the threshold into the waiting room. Without an abrupt "excuse me," she breezed by a woman with a bad perm and, ignoring the dirty look thrown her way, skidded up to the guard booth. An exchange took place, the plastic claim tag she held in return for the officer's scowl and her oversize handbag. She swung her purse off its perch. The monstrosity knocked against her thigh, throwing her off balance for a second. As she shuffled sideways and turned toward the exit, she blew out a long breath. Downsizing in the handbag department sounded like a good idea, and after this? She would go smaller. Become more practical on the fashion front and less, well…ridiculous for lack of a better word.

Slinging the Versace over her shoulder, she beat feet and, retracing her steps, headed for the front door. She needed to make the call outside. Prison walls had ears, so no question. The farther away she got from the guards and their snoop-o-meters, the better.

Boot heels ringing in the corridor, she unzipped her bag and dug for her iPhone. Stalling the reporter was mission critical. Vital for more reasons than one. Not the first of which involved keeping the SPD happy. Pissing off a bunch of cops, after all, wasn't the best idea.

Tania shook her head. What the hell had she been thinking? Well, all right. Dumb question. She knew the *what* along with the *why*. Myst was still out there, alone, probably scared, and in need of help. The kind only the SPD could provide, but somehow it had all gone sideways, not to mention upside down and backward. The brilliant plan to save her best friend had backfired on her sister. J.J. couldn't afford the police attention. Not after killing the younger brother of one of SPD's finest.

Which meant...

Yup, you guessed it.

Big brother cop would show up at the parole hearing if he got wind of it. A first-rate asshole, the guy didn't care that his brother had been a bad guy—a drug-dealing, abusive jerk with nothing better to do than hurt her sister. Nor did he give a damn that J.J. was a good person who'd gotten caught up in a bad situation and made a big mistake. Blood ran thicker than water, and the bonehead would muck up J.J's chances just for the fun of it.

Going round two with the inside of her bag, Tania frowned. Where the heck was it? She could have sworn she'd pocketed her cell phone before leaving—

"Ah, jeez," she said, slowing from speed walk to stop. Rooted to the floor in the middle of the corridor, Tania tipped her head back and closed her eyes. The name-calling came next. "I'm an idiot. A total freaking schizo."

She'd plugged in her iPhone for a quick recharge while she'd used the landline, then forgotten it. On the kitchen counter. Again. It happened at least once a week. But unlike those times, she didn't have the luxury of turning around and driving back to her apartment. And a two-hour drive to collect her cell phone? Just plain stupid on the strategy front.

With a sigh, Tania flipped her bag shut and made for the exit. As her feet picked up the pace, she rethought her plan. A forgotten iPhone wasn't the end of the world. She might not have her contact list at her fingertips just this second, but her iPad sat in her car, waiting to be used. God, she hoped she'd synced the thing lately. Otherwise she wouldn't have the reporter's phone number or contact information.

Cold metal chilled her palm as Tania pushed through the prison's front door. Thunder boomed overhead. Her brows collided. Weird. Another storm, one more violent than the one that had rolled through on her drive up to Gig Harbor. She glanced skyward, squinting when lightning forked, stroking the underbelly of angry clouds. The first raindrop splattered the concrete steps in front of her. Not wasting a second, she jogged past the perfect flower beds and down the stairs.

Halfway across the parking lot, a truck engine roared to life, the deep rumble joining another round of thunder. Flashing bright white, high-beam headlights lit up the pavement in front of her. A prickle of warning ghosted along her spine. Tania ignored it and, head down, angled her body against the autumn wind gusts.

She needed to grab her iPad and get over to the hotel, into her room, and on the phone. The sooner she reached Gig Harbor and nailed down the reporter, the safer her sister would be.

Chapter Six

A curse echoed down the stairwell behind him. Mac didn't slow down. Or bother to look back, either. He hauled ass, arms and legs pumping, combat boots hammering the stair treads as he descended into the bowels of Black Diamond. The landing zone. He needed to reach the LZ first...wanted to be in dragon form and airborne before Rikar got hold of him.

Or tried to ground him for the night.

Reaching the landing between flights, he grabbed the steel railing and pulled into the turn. Taut muscle stretched. Pain screamed up his arm and across his chest as the soles of his boots slid against the floor, slingshotting him onto the next set of stairs. Another flight down. More ground-eating strides. Each of his footfalls echoed, joining the slam-bang of shitkickers worn by the warriors chasing him down the stairwell.

The second he cleared the last corner, Mac went airborne, leaping over the last section of treads. Wind whistled in his ears. He landed at the bottom with a bone-jarring thud, feet sliding on the polished concrete of the next landing.

Two flights behind and playing catch-up, Rikar dropped another f-bomb. Mac ignored him. His XO could go to hell, along with the unhappy collection of kick-ass hot on his heels.

Screw 'em all.

To hell with protocol. To hell with his fledgling status and the fact he couldn't cloak himself yet. Tania was out there somewhere: alone, vulnerable, easy prey for Ivar and the Razorbacks. No way would he sit on his hands inside the lair and do nothing. Not while the other Nightfuries went out and hunted for her. Not when he could find her faster.

"Jesus H. Christ."

Loaded with pissed off, the growl sliced through the cool air. Bastian. Terrific. Just what he didn't need: the Nightfury commander in on the chase, watching him break rank and disregard a direct order. Mac gritted his teeth. No doubt about it. The second B got hold of him he was in for a serious ass kicking. The trick, though…the ace up his sleeve? Don't get caught. Get good and ghost—out of the lair and airborne—before the other warriors laid hands on him.

Rikar hollered at him. "Mac…hold up a second!"

His XO's voice reverberated in the enclosed space, ping-ponging off stone walls and polished concrete. Mac glanced over his shoulder. Shit. Not good. Rikar was closing in fast, leading the other warriors roaring down the stairs behind him like an organized hurricane, glacial eyes glowing, expression set, his I'm-gonna-fuck-you-up attitude locked in place.

Jesus. He probably should back down. Talk Rikar into letting him go instead of pulling a flash-and-fly. Mac upped his pace instead. He couldn't chance it. If anyone else touched Tania—another member of his pack, a Razorback—he would...

Lose it. Go totally freaking AWOL.

Which was so messed up.

Being territorial and possessive wasn't his usual MO. He didn't do commitment, never mind the hassles that came with it. But he couldn't deny the pull that drew him into Tania's sphere, telling him she was his responsibility. That he needed to keep her safe. And along with the mind-fuck of obsession came the sensation. Like a blip on a radar screen, her bioenergy lit him up, plugging him in until he felt the throb of her heartbeat in his veins. And as it pounded on him like a drum, Mac tossed his normally nonchalant attitude and abandoned his principles.

Sayonara, scruples. Hello, insanity.

Heartbeat raging against the wall of his chest, Mac shook his head, trying to clear it. He took the next flight three stairs at a time. His teeth slammed together as he launched himself off the next landing. Down...down... down. His shitkickers bang-bang-banging. Maybe if he jarred himself badly enough, knocked some brain cells together, he'd understand.

His reaction—the pressing need to shield Tania—didn't make any sense. Only bonded males reacted to a woman this way. How did he know? Dragon combat training. It wasn't just about physical prowess and aptitude. Forge expected him to hit the books too. And he had...hard, wanting to learn everything he could about Dragonkind and his magic. So, yeah, he knew exactly how a male acted—and reacted—when energy-fuse took hold. Shit, he lived with two prime examples inside Black Diamond every damned day.

His commander and his XO epitomized the bonded male crap: protective, loving, considerate to the point of Pukesville. Now, it seemed, he'd landed in the same muck hole. Nothing else explained his desperation. Or the fact he could *feel* her.

Except…

Mac frowned. How was that even possible?

Energy-fuse didn't just happen. The emotional pairing was difficult to achieve. So rare the knowledge of it had been lost over time, until Bastian rediscovered the bond with his chosen female. Now Rikar and Angela enjoyed the energy mating too. Fantastic in so many ways. Not the least of which was the fact Mac got to keep Ange in his life—his sister by choice if not blood. But his partner's luck with her man didn't explain Mac's reaction to Tania. Energy-fuse required a couple of things. One…acceptance from a male's notoriously fickle dragon half. And two? Contact. A male needed to get close to a female; so close skin met skin and passion exploded as he tapped into the Meridian through her, feeding from the electrostatic current that kept his kind healthy.

Excellent in theory. The problem? He'd never touched Tania. Had never been close enough to kiss her, never mind make love to her.

More's the pity.

'Cause, wow…he thought about it. A lot. And his dreams? Oh baby. Nothing PG about them. Hot, sweaty, so beautifully satisfying the images of him entwined with Tania seemed real, like memories instead of fantasies. God, sometimes he swore he could taste her; he actually relived the softness of her skin, the decadence of her scent as she moaned his name and begged him for more.

Desire licked through him.

As need curled into must-have, Mac cranked the door to the underground lair open. Reinforced steel slammed into the wall, then rebounded. Avoiding the backlash, Mac roared over the threshold, leaving the other Nightfuries in his wake. The boys didn't waste a second, heavy footfalls slamming out a rhythm, spilling through the doorway as Mac sprinted down the double-wide corridor.

Round lights embedded in the concrete floor led the way, throwing light up the chiseled stone walls. He blew by the entrance to Sloan's computer lab. Empty. Thank God. The last thing he needed was for the guy to jump out and ambush him. But the computer genius was tricky like that. Sloan loved shortcuts, using them to reach the underground lair and the com center the male slept in most days. The medical clinic came up on his right. Mac glanced through the sliding glass door, getting a flash of stainless steel cabinetry and state-of-the-art hospital equipment. No one milling around in there, either.

Home free. He was almost there, one more stretch of corridor to navigate before he reached the magical portal that led out to the LZ. Just in time too. His spidey senses were tingling. The sun was setting. In less than a minute, night would descend, blanketing Seattle in a cocoon of darkness. And the instant it did? He'd shift into dragon form and leave the lair, fly south toward Tania and hope like hell he reached her in time.

Before she landed on the Razorbacks' radar and Ivar came out to play.

Standing in the anteroom of his laboratory, Ivar stared through the two-way mirror at the dying humans. He took another sip of his Jimmy Beam. Ice rattled, playing clink-and-bump with the rim of his glass. He shook his head. Goddamn good-for-nothing humans. The insects always did the unexpected. And surprises? Oh so not his thing.

He liked measurable results. Pie graphs and chartable outcomes were more his speed. Not the fistful of fuck-all he had right now.

Disgusted with himself, Ivar sighed. His attitude needed a readjustment. A serious one. Otherwise the failures would get to him. Make him give up instead of pressing on to discover the right biological weapon (aka Project Supervirus).

Frowning, Ivar swirled the whiskey in his glass. The low light reflected off the ice cubes, sending a prism of color arching against cut crystal. The rainbow chilled him out, and as his tension eased, he reevaluated, clinging to reason. Science wasn't perfect. Experimentation and the results of any controlled study zigzagged, never traveling in a straight line. And really? After years spent studying, he ought to be accustomed to the twists and turns by now.

"Patience," he murmured to himself. He tipped his glass again, swallowing more of the color-me-happy JB. "Adapt and adjust. Do it better next time."

His motto. Somehow, though, his go-to pep talk pissed him off today. Fucking humans. Bane of his existence. Why couldn't they just die predictably? But oh no…no amount of scientific testing or viral load adjustment evened the playing field. No matter what he threw at his test subjects, they surprised him: fighting off his bioengineered superbugs, their immune systems reacting in strange ways.

Defiant. The assholes were a biological nightmare. How the hell was he supposed to work with that?

He needed the precise kill ratio, the right combination of time and contamination before setting a group of sick humans loose in the world to infect the entire race. Mass genocide without the mess of violence. The perfect way to free Dragonkind from the ecological disasters headed their way as the planet died a slow, agonizing death. As the human race pumped more and more poison into the air, contaminating the ground soil and water tables that sustained all life.

Simple. Pure. Effective. That's the plan he needed.

Too bad the perfect viral cocktail kept eluding him.

Ivar cursed under his breath and downed the rest of his drink. Look at them in there...dying way too fast. Damned annoying. He really couldn't stand much more of the humans' stupidity. Christ, another hurricane had rolled up the coast last night, KOing half the Eastern Seaboard while tornados ravaged the Midwest. And the insects thought that was normal? A coincidence? Just another series of monster storms without a cause and effect?

Well, he had news for the idiots.

They were the cause—the whole nasty lot of them—and the continued damage to the planet, the effect. It had to stop. All of it before the point of no return and recovery became impossible.

With a growl, Ivar glared through the glass. Six human males lay on the other side, barely breathing, puss-filled blisters oozing poison, polluting the hermetically sealed chamber where he'd imprisoned them. Bloody handprints marred the limestone floor where one had pulled himself out from behind the kitchen island. Now he lay still as death, but Ivar knew he wasn't. He could see the rise and fall of his chest, mucus and blood splattered on the tile in front of his face.

Ivar almost felt sorry for the human. Almost, but not quite.

Pain and suffering were necessary parts of the process. He needed to see, measure, and catalog the symptoms and half-life of his superbugs. How else was he to know how his babies would react and spread in the wilds of human society? But just like the first virus, this one—officially named Baby Number 2—was a bust. It killed too quickly. Wouldn't thrive in a human host long enough to spread to others and wreak maximum damage.

Turning away from the window, Ivar crossed the antechamber. The bank of wall monitors gleamed in the low light. He issued a mental command. Color exploded across the screens as the computer came online and gears whirled into motion. The sound made him hum. God, he L-O-V-E-D the lab in his new lair: state of the art, effective, and deadly…his favorite combination in the world.

Ivar set his empty glass on the black countertop. Fingers flying, he typed his password into the prompt box on the touch screen. No sense screwing around. Time to gas the insects, put them out their misery, and start a new batch. Although cleaning up the apartment and tossing in another group of humans would have to wait.

Night was coming.

The prickling awareness slid across the nape of his neck. Ten, maybe fifteen minutes before the sun set, releasing him and his warriors from lockdown. Ivar couldn't wait.

Revenge and his enemy awaited. Denzeil had it all figured out. Thank fuck. He didn't have time to chase the female around Seattle and set the trap at the same time, so—

"Hey, boss man."

Ah, speak of the devil.

Ivar smiled and tapped on the blinking green button in the middle of the touch screen. The closed-circuit ventilation system went to work, hissing as it dispensed the deadly gas into the chamber for the humans to breathe. "What up, D?"

"We're ready to roll when you are." Footfalls thudding through the quiet, Denzeil pushed through the lab doors. As they flapped closed behind him, he said, "Sun sets in ten."

Spinning around to face his warrior, Ivar ass-planted himself on the lip of the counter. "Everybody clear on the plan?"

Halfway across the antechamber with an iPad in his hands, Denzeil nodded.

Ivar's eyes narrowed on the tablet. "What?"

"We may have a snag."

"With the female?"

"Yeah...an interview with KING 5 TV aired twenty minutes ago. Tania Solares up front and center."

Ivar growled, his hands curling into fists. "Shit. Let me see."

Denzeil handed over the tablet. Flipping it around, Ivar hit play and—

"Son of a bitch."

There she was...a dark-haired, burgundy-eyed female with more beauty than brains. How did he know? She was on fucking TV, drawing attention to herself...and her unbelievable energy. Jesus. She was power personified, so high-energy the Meridian's electrostatic current pulsed in her aura, rushing at him through the small screen.

The energy blast hit him midchest. Ivar sucked in a quick breath. Shit on a stick. Just his luck. No way the Nightfuries would miss her little sojourn on the network news. Which meant…what? Bastian and his band of bastards would be gunning for her. Would try to sweep her from harm's way before he got hold of her.

No fucking way. Lothair's death must be avenged. He needed the female to set the trap for the male responsible. So, yeah…the pain-in-his-ass Nightfuries were in for a surprise.

"Make the call." Ivar handed the iPad back to his warrior. "Triple our numbers."

Dark eyes gleaming, Denzeil's mouth tipped up at the corners. "Planning a little surprise party?"

Ivar returned his warrior's smile. "Dead Nightfuries as goody bags, okay?"

"My favorite kind."

His too. And although death didn't visit Bastian's pack often, tonight would be different. Ivar could feel it in his bones.

Chapter Seven

Turning the corner, Mac punched it, hauling ass as though his feet were on fire. The corridor's dead end loomed like a police barricade. Ancient stone blocks stacked one upon the next, the wall stood waiting like an angry ogre, Black Diamond's formidable energy shield standing guard right alongside it. Mac cursed through clenched teeth. Wonderful. Just terrific. Color him unhappy. Stupid frickin' portal and its pissy attitude. The thing was screwing with his plan, slowing his roll, getting in his way.

And oh goody, guess what?

He was headed straight toward the fucker, speed somewhere south of supersonic.

Baring his teeth, Mac upped the pace. The sound of his footfalls rebounding in the hallway, he roared toward the thick barrier. Fifteen feet out, he unleashed a spell, requesting safe passage through the portal. Magic whiplashed, warping the air as the shield denied him. Mac snarled at it. Jesus. He didn't have time for this shit. He needed the doorway to open. And open now. Otherwise he was in for a face full of granite and an inevitable pileup when the Nightfuries hammered him from behind.

Ten feet from the dead end. Now seven.

Mac slowed down. Taking a running leap at the thing never worked. He'd only get zapped with energy shards on the fly-through. The exact opposite of what he wanted right now. Especially with the beacon throbbing inside his head. He didn't trust his dragon half yet, and if he went into magical overload? He might lose Tania and the ability to track her. He couldn't let that happen. It was the only thing holding him together right now. She needed him, and for the first time since his change, so did the Nightfuries.

Thank God. The switch felt good. Felt right. Like he mattered—deserved to be included—for a frickin' change.

Sending another demand, he thumped on the door with his mind. Stone rippled. Mac growled, satisfaction ghosting through him as the wall moved from solid to wavy. A symphony of ass-hauling whistling in his ears, the boys pounding out a rhythm behind him, Mac employed his p's and q's and asked for safe passage into the LZ.

No sense pissing the contrary thing off.

The energy shield had a mind of its own and, more often than not, a bad attitude: whiplashing without warning, closing up fast, spitting males back out after chewing on them for a while. Sometimes it refused to open at all, leaving his new buddies stranded on the wrong side of the doorway, forced to sleep in the underground tunnel connected to the LZ until it decided to let them through.

Not that any of the guys complained about the occasional exile. They liked the pissy bastard. Praised the invisible force field that protected the lair. Revered it for keeping their home hidden from outsiders, both human and Dragonkind alike.

Three feet away.

Throwing his magic like a sidewinding pitch, Mac banged on the portal again. The shield hissed. His vision narrowed. Energy shards lengthened into a kaleidoscope of color, spinning around, zapping him with static electricity. *Come on...come on...*he thumped on it again...*don't fuck with me...*another rap with magical knuckles...*please, open up...I'll do any—*

The floor lights blinked off, plunging the hallway into darkness.

Rikar pinwheeled, circling his arms. "Holy shit."

"Fuck me," Bastian growled at the same time, his voice overlapping his XO's.

Skidding sounded, boot soles sliding on concrete as the Nightfuries put the brakes on behind him. Mac didn't slow. Frustration twisted his gut into a giant knot.

Reaching deep, Mac gathered his magic. Halogen bulbs sparked, electricity popping like popcorn before the light sputtered, flickering back on. His eyes on the portal, Mac watched the wall waver, shifting from milky white to clear air, opening into the cavern beyond the stone barrier.

Mac wanted to howl in satisfaction. He sped up instead, roaring through the archway into the LZ. The pungent smell of musty air and damp earth hit him. The roar of water echoed, rushing in from the tunnel mouth, bouncing off the uneven stone walls as light globes bobbed seventy-five feet above his head. Ignoring the crop of stalagmites, Mac sprinted for the edge of the LZ.

"Well done, lad," Forge said.

"Stop patronizing him, Scot." Wick's growled reply came over his shoulder like a softball pitch, floating on the thick air with deadly intent. Then again, that was Wick's MO. The guy never said much, but when he did, he meant every word. "Leave him the fuck alone."

Mac blinked. Jesus. What was that all about? Wick never defended anyone. Black Diamond's resident sociopath was a stone-cold killer: quiet, lethal, packing a helluva lot of vicious while he decimated Razorbacks. So his support... the fact he was ready to back Mac up? More than a little surprising.

Still running, Mac glanced over his shoulder. As he made eye contact with Wick, he murmured, "Thanks, man."

Golden gaze narrowed on him, Wick snarled, "Don't fuck it up."

Well, all right then. Back to normal on the antisocial front.

Mac nodded anyway. *Fucking up*, after all, wasn't part of his game plan. Not with Tania in trouble and the rest of the Nightfuries watching his every move.

Not wasting a second, Mac skidded around the beat-up Honda—the one Myst had arrived in after Bastian airlifted her off the road and brought her to Black Diamond. Not that he cared where the battered hatchback came from at the moment. The wreckage was the least of his problems. He needed to get airborne...right now.

Sure Wick might be on board, but the other warriors? Shit. They were playing for keeps, hauling ass across the LZ in fighting formation, acting like heat-seeking missiles instead of males. Mac snarled, struggling to get into position. His night vision sparked. It wouldn't be long now. He could feel the sun sinking below the horizon. A few more seconds and—

Halfway across the LZ, Mac shifted into dragon form: hands and feet turning to talons, body lengthening under his bladed spine, muscle, skin, and bone stretching beneath smooth blue-gray scales. His razor-sharp claws scraped granite. The lethal sound bounced in the vast space, sending a warning as sensation swirled around the horns on his head. With a growl, Mac spun to face his comrades and crouched low, the swing of his daggerlike tail slicing through thick, musty air.

His body language spoke volumes. No way was he going back inside.

The other Nightfuries put the brakes on, sliding to a stop on the uneven granite floor.

"Frigging hell." Ruby-red eyes shimmering, Venom retreated, granite crunching beneath his shitkickers. "Rikar, pull your head out of your ass and do something, man. Ice him up before he—"

The tips of his claws shrieked against stone as Mac unfurled his wings. Time to get airborne.

"Ah, hell," Venom growled. "Now we're in deep shit."

"Relax, Ven." Rikar jogged around the car's back bumper. He came in tight. Mac let him, wondering what the hell his XO was doing. Raising his fist, Rikar thumped him on the chest, rattling his scales. "It's all good."

B echoed the thought. "Let's go."

Mac's brows popped skyward.

Riding a shitload of pissy, Venom threw their commander an incredulous look.

"It's under control." Green eyes aglow, Bastian smiled at Venom.

"Control? Screw that." Venom pointed at Mac. "Does Boy Wonder look like he's in *control* to you?"

"Fuck off, dickhead." Tendrils of steam rising from his nostrils, Mac glared at the guy and mind-spoke, *"You've got two options. With me or against me…what's it gonna be?"*

The ruby-eyed SOB glowered at him. *"Pansy-ass fledgling."*

Ah, the sweet sound of acceptance. Yeah, Venom might like to call him names, but he wasn't an idiot. Like it or not, Mac knew the male was solid. Call it the warrior code of honor. Call it pack mentality. Whatever. Once called upon, commitment to a teammate couldn't be ignored.

With a huff, Venom glanced at Bastian. *"You really on board with this?"*

B nodded. *"All in."*

Mac relaxed, blowing out a pent-up breath.

"Hope you got a plan before he pulls another flash-and-fly and goes AWOL."

Leather creaked as B put his feet in gear. Skirting the male where he stood in the center of the LZ, he thumped Venom on the shoulder with a closed fist, then glanced at Mac. *"What the fuck are you waiting for? Get airborne."*

Venom dropped another f-bomb.

"Use your head, Ven." Bypassing his buddy, Wick leaped over the car. A second before his shitkickers touched down, he shifted. Black from head to tail, his gold-tipped scales flashed beneath the light globes. He landed with a thump, tossing stone dust into the air. *"Where do you think he's headed in such a hurry?"*

Venom's brows collided. A pause, then…the warrior sucked in a quick breath. *"Goddamn, the loft. His change… he's got the female—"*

Rikar piped up. *"Bingo."*

"Glad tae have you join us, Sherlock," Forge said, drilling Venom with sarcasm, confusing the hell out of Mac.

His gaze ping-ponged, meeting each of the warrior's gazes in turn. Unease shivered down Mac's spine. They knew something he didn't...a big something. Something none were ready to tell him judging by the looks on their faces. Mac frowned. Oh so not good. And the joke, it seemed, was on him. 'Cause, yeah, he remembered getting hauled off his boat by Rikar. Recalled the loft and the more painful parts of his change. But a female? What in God's name were they talking about?

"Brilliant," Wick murmured.

Bastian's mouth curved up at the corners. *"Glad you approve."*

"Hey, fledgling..." His gaze locked on him, Venom's expression went from worried to intense. *"Whatcha got? You locked onto something?"*

Locked onto something? Shit, he was practically throbbing with it. The beacon Tania threw off was so strong, Mac tasted her on his tongue. Still, suspicion lit him up, the cop in him asking questions even as instinct told him to go. To find her and bring her home.

He retreated a step. His back paw slid off the LZ's edge. Pebbles fell, pinging down the cliff face, splashing into the aquifer below. Bastian nudged him, urging him to take flight.

Alarm bells rang inside Mac's head. *"Rikar—"*

"Go, Mac." White scales flashed, winking in the low light as Rikar transformed, shifting into dragon form. He thumped Mac with the side of his spiked tail. *"Sun's gone down. You got the signal...track it. You lead, we'll follow."*

"Motherfuck." Where had he landed...Bizarroland? An hour ago none of the warriors would've signed off on his leaving the lair. Now? All of them were on board and

hanging back, waiting for him to take flight. Jesus. What the hell had Daimler baked into that roast beef? PC-fucking-P? *"What aren't you telling me?"*

"Go, man." Meeting his gaze head-on, his XO bumped him again, giving him a gentle shove. *"Tania's waiting."*

No arguing with that. No liking it, either. He'd solve the mystery later—beat the crap out of Rikar if he needed to—but for now, he spun on his back paws. The blade riding the ridge of his spine gleaming beneath the light globes, Mac launched himself from the ledge.

"Jeez," Venom muttered, claws scraping stone as he followed, his eyes trained on the tip of Mac's knifelike tail. *"Still getting used to that shit. Why couldn't we have adopted a normal fledgling...one without a water fetish and serious blade issues?"*

Wings spread in flight, Mac bit down on a grin. He couldn't help it. He understood Venom's reaction. The pack always did a double take when he shifted into dragon form. He wasn't Dragonkind's usual fare. No spikes along his spine or ridges on his scales. No sharp barbs on his tail tip, either. Just smooth, interlocking dragon skin, webbed paws, and a razor-sharp tail that could cut a male in half as he flew by. But what he considered ordinary, his new comrades marveled at every time he transformed.

Normal, he guessed. Despite living hundreds of years, the Nightfuries had never seen anything like Mac. Until him, Rikar had thought the existence of water dragons nothing but a myth. Which honestly should've set him back a step...made him feel like an outsider or less of a male. Somehow, though, it didn't. So he was different. Big deal. Mac liked the webbing between his talons, his smooth dragon skin, and bladed tail. All made him water-dynamic, able to swim with ease, and…yeah, there wasn't anything better than that.

Although he could've done without the tattoo.

Angela and Myst thought the swirling navy-blue lines that covered half his torso were cool. His opinion differed. *Cool.* Ha. Right. Like living with tribal ink he hadn't consented to getting and didn't want—or understand—was A-okay. Not that he could do much about it. The tattoo had arrived with his change and stayed.

Rikar believed it was a water dragon thing…some sort of magical connection to the element he controlled. The problem? His XO didn't know for sure. And no matter how hard he and Rikar searched in the ancient texts written in Dragonese, on the Internet, human mythology books, they both came up empty-handed on the answers front.

Beyond frustrating.

Rocketing around a tight corner, he led the pack, wing tips inches from the jagged side walls. The symphonic sound of rushing water roared through the tunnel. Mac hummed and, angling into the last turn, increased his wing speed. The waterfall lay just ahead. God, he couldn't wait to—

Flipping sideways, Mac went wings vertical. His night vision sparked, picking up trace, but it was the waterfall that interested him. Falling in a straight sheet, the cascade tumbled off the cliff Black Diamond called home. Three hundred and fifty feet of roaring perfection, it dove toward the river below, throwing up spray, shielding the tunnel entrance from intruders. He sliced through with a splash, relishing the cold-wet-and-delicious, and came out on the other side.

Without thought, he climbed, gaining altitude in the night sky, stars twinkling above him, the river and forest floor falling away below him. Forty minutes and some fast flying later, Mac leveled out over Highway I-5. Headlights blurring into a long tail, the highway snaked into the city of Tacoma. Almost there. A little farther now.

His sonar pinged, directing him in midflight. He banked north toward the Narrows Bridge spanning the narrowest part of Puget Sound. Storm clouds gathered behind him; heavy rains and the rumble of thunder rolled in his wake.

No surprise there.

The wild-and-wet thing always happened to him. Everywhere he went, water followed as though the element knew he owned it. Most nights, though, he controlled it better. Directing the flow. Dispersing the molecules. Condensation nothing but an afterthought. Too bad it wasn't working for him tonight. He was too distracted, all his attention focused on Tania, not the torrential downpour rushing in his wake.

"Bloody hell." Coming down out of cloud cover, Forge rolled in on his left side. He shook his head. Water flew, arcing off his dark purple scales. *"You mind getting a handle on the waterworks, lad? Otherwise, I'm going tae need windshield wipers installed on my eyebrows."*

Thunder boomed overhead. Mac threw his mentor an apologetic glance.

"No worries." Forge swiped at the water running into his eye. *"Just tell me you're still locked—"*

"Goddamn it." Green scales gleaming beneath the storm flash, Venom torqued into a full body spin, coming up on his other wing tip. He shook like a dog in midair, sending raindrops flying. *"Could you tone it down a bit, fledgling?"*

"Shut yer yap, Venom, and deal." Angling his head, his mentor glared at Venom over Mac's head. A second later, he snorted. Fire-acid flew, flaring bright orange against the night sky. With a curse, Venom ducked, avoiding singed scales and a trip to the lair's medical clinic with a bad case of ow-ow-ow. *"Unless you want a tidal wave tae go with that...knock it off."*

Mac's lip twitched. God love Forge. The protective SOB made him laugh. Was bang on too, 'cause...yeah, treating Venom to a face full of tsunami sounded like a helluva lot of fun.

"What do you say, lad?" Forge threw him a hopeful glance. *"You up for drowning the wanker?"*

Venom shut his yap in a hurry.

Mac swallowed his snort of laughter. Vindication in the form of silence. Sure, Venom might not trust him—might be convinced that he'd get one of the Nightfuries killed with his fucked-up magic—but at least Mac's ability as a water dragon backed the male up a step.

Mining Tania's signal, Mac banked right, heading away from Tacoma. True to their word, the other warriors stayed on his six, letting him set the pace. Which freaked him out. He'd never led a fighting triangle before and...

Fuck. There went suspicion again...getting inside his head, mucking up his flow until he couldn't wait any longer. The need to know was simply too strong.

"Hey, Rikar?"

"Here." Little more than a streak, Rikar rocketed out of the cloud cover. Water streamed across his white scales, turning to ice a second before it blew back in his wake. Frigid air turned frosty as his first-in-command tucked his wings, then flipped into position over Mac's bladed spine. *"You still got a lock on her?"*

"Yeah. She's on the move, though. Nine miles out, but..." The signal grew stronger, making Mac twitchy. Shit. That wasn't good. His scales felt like they were two sizes too small...as though he'd been shrink-wrapped or left to dry out in the sun. *"I shouldn't know that, should I?"*

Energy zapped him. The beacon throbbed through him, tunneling into sinew and muscle, torquing him into a full-body twist. He lost altitude, urban lights winking below him as he went topsy-turvy in midair. Forge cursed and dodged right, getting out of his way.

"Motherfuck," Mac growled, flinching as the pain moved from gut-wrenching to manageable. Leveling his wings, he exhaled long and smooth, combating the discomfort. *"Tell me what happened?"*

Silence met his demand.

Venom looped up and over, staying on task, following Mac's rapid descent toward human houses. Aligned in neat suburban rows, bungalows and two-story walk-ups sat together, coexisting peacefully, shoulder to shoulder on the edge of blacktopped roads and twinkling street lamps.

Nice. Normal. Nothing to get in a twist about.

Mac didn't care. He wanted to know everything no one wanted to tell him. *"Come on, guys."*

"Rikar...dish. No use hiding it," B said, the regret in his tone putting Mac on high alert. *"He'll find out eventually. Better now than later."*

"Shit," Rikar said, pale eyes glowing like twin spotlights above him. *"How close are we, Mac?"*

"Seven miles...give or take."

"B, peel off," Rikar said.

His commander nodded. *"Meet you on the flip side. Venom, Wick...you're with me."*

"On your six." Wick banked left, breaking formation to follow Bastian. Venom followed suit, taking the opposite wingman position.

Leading the kick-ass trifecta, Bastian turned south toward Gig Harbor. *"Sloan tracked her credit card to a hotel. We'll set up there. If you intercept her en route, give us a shout."*

Rikar um-hmmed. *"Holler if company comes calling."*

"Will do."

"What the fuck is going on?" Mac growled, his gaze ping-ponging between Forge and Rikar. *"Stop screwing around. Tell me why I can feel her. I've never touched her, so no way I should be able to track her."*

"Not true," Rikar murmured, his tone tinged with cha-grin—and something more. Shame, maybe? *"I...Christ, I know you don't remember. No male ever remembers going through his change, but..."*

As his XO trailed off, Mac's throat went tight.

"Fuck it." Rikar sighed. Frost shot from his nostrils. *"No easy way to tell you. You needed a female...would've died without one to stabilize your energy stream, so we used what we had and..."* Rikar glanced at him sideways. *"You can feel her because she fed you."*

"Jesus fucking Christ." Mac wobbled in midair before righting himself. Mother of God. Tania had fed him. *Fed him.* And he didn't remember? How in the hell could he have—

Wait a minute.

"The dreams." Mac's brows collided. *"I've been having dreams about her."*

Rikar shook his head. *"Residual memories."*

"Did you—"

"No one watched. We hid out in the bathroom until it was over."

"Did I hurt her?" Jesus, what an awful thought. *"Did I…?"*

"No." With a growl, Rikar glared at him. *"You didn't force her. She was willing…wanted you badly. We tried to separate you… had the escort Sloan called all lined up, but Tania wouldn't let you go. It was either injure her to get her to release you or let her have you."* His XO paused. Silence and more hung in the space where words wouldn't suffice. After a full minute of torture, his friend said, *"You needed her. She wanted you. We let her have you."*

Mac's heart throbbed in his chest. God help him. He'd never…hadn't ever…*Jesus.* How was he supposed to live with that? With the idea that Tania might not have been 100 percent—

"A rock and a hard place." Lightning struck overhead. Lit up by the flash, his mentor flipped up and over, rotating into a slow spin. As he settled beside him once more, Forge's brogue grew thicker as he said, *"Damned if you do…"*

"Damned if you don't," Mac rasped, finishing the sentence, his voice so hoarse it was almost nonexistent. *"Will she remember?"*

"B mind-scrubbed her afterward, but…probably. High-energy females have strong minds. Most recover the memory when a male touches them again. It happened to Angela and me," Rikar said, his tone as soft as Mac's had been. *"I'm sorry it played out this way. I know it's an ass-kicker, and I'm sorry."*

Sorry? Jesus, the apology didn't begin to cover it.

The problem? A catch-22 never came calling without leaving a load of trouble in its wake. It was always messy. Unwanted. Hard to clean up. And as much as Mac wanted to deny it—and kick Rikar's ass in the process—he understood his XO's dilemma. In the heat of that moment,

Rikar had made a choice...let him die or get him what he needed to live.

Rikar had made the hard call and saved his life. Thank God, but...shit. Mac despised the fallout. The aftermath that left him swimming in guilt, facing the possibility that Tania would hate him on sight.

Mac shook his head. How selfish was that? Very. Incredibly self-centered.

How he felt didn't matter. None of this was about him. It was about her. All about keeping her safe from bastards who wouldn't hesitate to hurt her. So fuck it. He could live with her hate, if it came to that. But man, he prayed he wouldn't have to. Hoped with all his heart that she remembered she'd wanted him too much to let him go... that she'd forgive him for touching her even though he couldn't remember his part in it.

Not clearly anyway.

The dreams weren't enough. All the heat and pleasure. All the yearning and relief; his need to please her, to touch and taste her until she came apart in his arms; the welcoming sounds she'd made, the way she'd moved against him, ridden him, her small hands in his hair. God. She'd been perfection in his arms, but as memory spilled through him, Mac frowned. The dreamlike quality persisted, muddying the water, mucking with his recall until—

Was any of it real...her response...his reaction? Or was his mind playing tricks on him, inventing things he wanted to be true?

Wrestling with self-recrimination, Mac thought back, replaying the scene, looking for clues. Shit. He wasn't sure.

He'd seen what happened to a woman when a male fed. Heat and need always turned to uncontrollable lust.

How did he know? Forge. His mentor believed in thoroughness, never leaving anything to chance. So, yeah, the male had taken him into town—to a Seattle nightclub one night last week—and taught him how to tap into the Meridian's electrostatic current...all while satisfying a female in the best possible way. Willingness was a prerequisite for a Nightfury. Woman were to be cherished and pleased, not used.

Still, an awful suspicion burrowed deep inside him, unearthing terrible questions. Had Tania really wanted him? Or had the Meridian surged, ensnaring her in a magical web...one too strong for her to resist?

Mac didn't know. Wasn't sure he wanted to, either. Especially since it painted him with a black brush. But as he flew over the narrows, watching whitecaps kick up as open water gave way to beachfront, then the dark green of an ancient forest, Mac knew he couldn't avoid the inevitable. He needed to know. Felt Tania with every breath he took, so...

No contest. He would find her first and somehow, someway, make it right for her again.

His heart aching so hard his chest hurt, Mac came up over a tall rise of weathered pine trees. Two lanes of asphalt, yellow lines reflecting in the weak moon glow, stretched out below him. The rural route snaked through rocky terrain, high bluffs reigning supreme along one side. A car engine whined, the smooth downshift of gears held aloft by gusts of frigid wind. Night vision pinpoint sharp, Mac's head snapped right. Red with white racing stripes, a Mini Cooper swung around an S curve.

His eyes narrowed on the car. Tania. The aura of her energy hummed, calling to him, washing the Mini's windows with soft blue light. The hue of the ocean, his favorite color in the world.

"Inside the car," he murmured, giving his boys a heads-up.

"The tin can with wheels?"

Forge snorted. *"It's vintage, Rikar. A fucking classic."*

"Looks like a death trap to me."

Mac hoped not, but conceded the point. The Mini might be beautiful, but it was tiny. Not something anyone wanted to ding up in a fender bender, never mind a crash. And looking at the terrain—rocky, inhospitable, thick redwoods and towering pines lining the narrow roadway—not a place he wanted to startle Tania, either. She might lose control and roll her car. Which would put him where? In Deepshitsville, playing the Jaws of Life with his talons as he pried her loose from a collision he'd caused.

Oh so not even close to what he wanted.

All his concentration on his female, Mac banked in behind her car. Gliding above the road now, he mind-spoke, *"Forge."*

"Aye?"

"Jam up the asshole in the truck. He's tailgating her."

"Do you want the prick dead or just damaged?"

Rikar huffed with laughter.

He glanced sideways at his mentor, then back at the truck. Mac wanted to say "dead." Lights off, practically riding Tania's bumper, the impatient SOB needed a lesson. He debated a moment, seriously considering it, but then...

The cop in him kicked in, hitting him with a damnable dose of the law and fair play. He drilled Forge with a look, one that said *behave.*

"Just saying." Forge shrugged and flew toward the pickup. *"Dead's a lot more fun."*

"Just keep him busy. Stop him. Mind-scrub him…whatever." His eyes glued to the car, Mac heard the engine rumble as Tania headed into another winding turn. He came in low, wings spread, adjusting his speed, and settled into a glide over her. He needed to time it just right. *"Heads up. I'm getting up close and personal."*

Frost dragon out in full force, Rikar rotated into a slow flip. The raindrops that followed Mac turned to snowfall in his wintery wake. *"Need any help?"*

Deep in the storm swirl, Mac shook his head, thunder rumbling behind him, snowflakes curling off his wing tips, a whole lot of "hands off" banging around inside his head. As stupid as it sounded, he didn't want another male anywhere near Tania. Not even Rikar, a guy he trusted with his life.

Tania was his. His responsibility. His to keep safe. His to hold if she let him.

But first he needed to reach her. And yeah, something told him she wasn't going to be happy when he dropped in and rained on her parade.

Chapter Eight

The clutch pressed to the floor, Tania downshifted into the next turn. As her car swung around the bend, she glanced out the side window. Something was, well...off. A little? A lot? She couldn't tell. Or place the odd feeling, for that matter. Sensation pricked the nape of her neck and intuition whispered, raising awareness, making her think...maybe...

Tania frowned, then shook her head. No. She was being ridiculous. No one was watching her. How could they be? She was in the middle of nowhere. Headlights eating the night gloom, washing over twin center lines. Miles of blacktop in front of her, the prison behind her, racing toward Gig Harbor and the telephone in her hotel room. J.J.'s letter burned a hole in her back pocket while hope did the same to her heart.

Parole. Unbelievable.

Her sister had a shot at a real life. A better one seeded in a second chance. And Tania refused to screw it up for her. She prayed the reporter agreed to stall the news station and put the interview on the back burner for a while.

All she needed was a month. A measly thirty days to get through the parole board hearing.

Big problem with that demand, though, and it had a name: Clarissa Newton.

Nibbling on her thumbnail, Tania racked her brain, searching for a viable strategy. One that would convince an ambitious woman to postpone an exposé that would no doubt make her career. Nothing came to mind. No clever argument. No aha moment or brilliant flash of clairvoyance.

She blew out a harried breath. All right, so it was a long shot. Tania knew it, but...damn it all. She had to try. J.J. was depending on her and—

A jolt of static electricity hit her.

Tania gasped, twisting in her seat, the tingle ghosting between her shoulder blades. Without mercy, the prickle collided with the base of her skull, then slid around to attack her temples. Ah, jeez. Another headache. The fourth one this week. She rubbed the sore spot between her brows. The throbbing sting was beyond strange. Especially since she wasn't prone to migraines. Had never suffered one until a month ago. The first had come right after visiting Myst's loft, and for a split second Tania wondered if the pain had something to do with the disappearance of her best friend. Worry and stress, maybe? The grief and psychological turmoil of heart-wrenching loss?

Check, check...and check to all of the above.

With a sigh, she pinched the bridge of her nose, combating the discomfort. Stupid cops. Double damn Detective MacCord. Tears welled in the corners of her eyes. She swiped at one, anger burning behind her breastbone. What the heck was he doing...besides not calling her back?

The pinpricks came again, slithering over her skin.

Frowning, Tania fidgeted, butt sliding on the leather seat, hands gripping the steering wheel as she leaned forward to peer outside. Nada. Nothing but her and a deserted stretch of blacktop. She looked harder, straining to see beyond her headlights in the dark. The muscles bracketing her spine stretched, pulling at the tension. Rain splattered her windshield and—

Huh. She sat back in her seat. Would you look at that? Snowflakes…mixed with fat raindrops, bizarre weather for November. Not that Tania minded.

She liked storms…of all kinds, the bigger the better. Truth be told, though, thunderstorms were her favorite. Something about the crash-bang, the absolute rawness of it, soothed her. She always pulled up a chair, poured herself a mug of hot tea, and stayed awake for hours when one of Seattle's finest rolled through. Just to watch it. Experience it. Be one with an elemental force greater than herself.

Weird, she knew. Most people hated the rain. Wanted sunshine and summer fun. And while that was all fine and good, nothing beat the rumbling sound of thunder.

As if on cue, the sky growled overhead. The wind kicked up, mixing the rain with swirling snow. She laughed a little, loving the combination. Snow and thunder. Who knew they went so well together?

Flicking off her high beams to see through the flurries, she flipped on her wipers. Gears ground into motion and the blades swiped, whisking the slush away. Headlights flared behind her, lighting up the back of her car. Startled by the sudden appearance, Tania glanced in the rearview mirror. She squinted to see through the glare.

Oh, snap. Where had he come from?

She frowned. The front grille looked like it belonged to a pickup truck. The brilliance of high, square lights confirmed it. A Ford F-150 perhaps. Or maybe a Dodge Ram.

The breath caught in the back of her throat. Oh God. Griggs. It had to be. His threats earlier hadn't been idle… he'd been pissed off and precise. And the engine that had cranked over in the prison parking lot? She now wondered if that had been him, lying in wait for her. Tania chewed on her bottom lip. All right…paranoid much? Maybe. But intuition yelled "no, you're not!" and as fear pulsed through her, Tania got the message. The one telling her to run, hide, and not come out for a while.

"Stupid…stupid…stupid," she mumbled, working the clutch like a pro, berating herself for not paying more attention. For being distracted. For letting J.J.'s good news overthrow her usual caution.

Tightening her grip on the wheel, Tania put her foot down. Her Mini might be small, but her girl had guts and a lot of horses under the hood. The engine whined. She shifted into fifth, burying the dial, and roared around the next corner. More cliff than bluff, a rock wall rose alongside her, hugging the right side of the road. The landmark reassured her. Not much farther now. Gig Harbor and safety lay less than a mile away. All she needed to do was hang on tight, drive faster, make it into town before—

The truck swerved wildly behind her. A second later, tires squealed as the driver hit the brakes. The pickup rocked beneath the sheet of rain, sliding across slick asphalt. Metal crunched. Glass shattered. The horrific sound cracked through the quiet as the vehicle whirled into a 180-degree spin behind her. The bright glow of headlights flashed against the sheer rock face, then disappeared from view.

Holy crap. What in God's name—?

Bang!

Tania yelped as something landed on top of her car. Steel bent inward, groaning as it caved toward her head. She ducked and, easing off the gas pedal, struggled to control the pitching sway of her Mini and stay on the road. Her heart in her throat, she held her breath and listened. Something scraped across the roof of her car.

What was *that*? A tree branch? A rock? Had the wind blown it loose from the top of the bluff and hit the truck before bouncing on her? Seemed like a logical explanation, if a little far-fetched, but that didn't change the facts. She needed to slow down and get off the road...

Right now.

She couldn't see the truck anymore. The pickup was gone. No lights. No discernible wreckage on the road. Nothing visible in her rearview mirror. Good God, Griggs must have driven right off the shoulder. And as much as she wanted to, she couldn't leave him there. What if he was hurt and in need of medical attention?

Tania slowed, intending to pull over. The scraping sound came again. Following the noise, she glanced toward the passenger seat. The door flew open, wind ripping it from the hinges. The Mini shuddered, pushing her into the oncoming lane. She glanced over her shoulder. Her mouth fell open as she watched her car door hurtling down the middle of the road behind her. An instant later, a man appeared in the gaping hole, long legs leading as he wedged himself inside her car. Fear shoved shock aside, hitting her with a shot of adrenaline.

Self-preservation riding shotgun, Tania screamed and lashed out. Her knuckles met bone. *Wham!* Pain screamed up her arm. She ignored it and let her fist fly again, aiming for the intruder's face.

His head snapped to the side. "Ow!"

"Get out!" She wound up a third time. Leading with her elbow, she cracked him in the temple.

"Jesus fucking Christ!" He reached for her, big hands blocking each punch.

Terror drilled her, narrowing her vision until she saw spots. "Don't touch me!"

"Tania...stop it!"

She paused midflail, sucking a quick breath. Wait a minute. *Tania?* The asshole knew her name? "Oh my God. Who are you? Who—"

"Mac."

"What...w-where...M-Mac?"

Holding the side of his head, he mumbled, "Yeah."

Breathing so hard she couldn't hear herself think, Tania stared at the man seated next to her. Her Mini shuddered, small tires bumping to a stop on wet asphalt. The windshield wipers slid back and forth, the squeaking squawk loud in the sudden silence. She opened her mouth, then shut it again.

Holy jeez. What did he think he was doing?

As the question banged around inside her skull, relief grabbed her by the throat. Not a serial killer. A cop. Mac was a cop. Out of air, she gasped, filling her lungs, trying to make sense of the invasion. Her eyes provided a quick snapshot, her mind, the context. Dark hair. Angular, too-gorgeous-for-words face. Aquamarine eyes. Big, muscular body with long legs, wearing nothing but jeans and a

T-shirt. A tremor rumbled through her, giving her a bad case of the shakes.

All right. All clear. No need to flip out, uh...again. Identification confirmed. It was definitely MacCord, the sexy-as-hell cop who never called her back.

"God, Detective, you..." Taking a breath, she trailed off. The adrenaline rush faded, pushing tears into her eyes.

"Hey, it's okay. It's me...Mac," he said, his tone full of reassurance. Reaching out, he caught her tear on the edge of his thumb and wiped it away. "You're all right."

"All right?" she repeated, incredulity spiking as her heart hammered. Concern in his eyes, he cupped her cheek, touched her skin, anchoring her with a gentle caress. Tania's brows snapped together. What the heck did he think he was doing? Soothing her? After scaring the crap out of her? Well...nah-uh. Not calling her back was one thing. No way he was getting a free pass for this one. Gasping in outrage, she whacked him, smacking his hand away from her face. "*All right!* Have you lost your flipping mind?"

"Tania—"

"You son of a bitch! Where the hell did you come from? And why haven't you called? You could've just picked up the phone, instead of tearing my door off." Yup. No doubt about it. Lunatics-R-Us had nothing on her, because...crap on a crumpet. Her car and the gaping wound in its side were the least of her problems. Her first clue? Mac and his flying squirrel act onto the top of her Mini. Add that to the fact he now sat scrunched next to her—knees jammed against the dashboard, taking up all her breathing room—and...

Jeez. The entire situation qualified as certifiable.

"You stupid..." Glaring at him, she punched him on the shoulder. He flinched and mumbled something she didn't quite catch. Unable to help herself, she wound up again…*whap!* "Idiot. You scared me!"

"I know, honey," he said. "I'm sorry."

Defending himself from her onslaught, he grabbed her arms. Heat rolled from his palms to encircle her wrists. God, he had big hands. Made sense. He was a big guy. At least six and a half feet of smell-good, feel-right sizzle with eyes the color of a tropical sea and…

Tania blinked. Jumping Jehoshaphat. What was her problem? He'd just scared ten years off her life, and what was she doing? Leaning toward him instead of away. Enjoying his warm, masculine scent as he wrapped her up, holding both of her hands in one of his. She should've felt trapped. Instead, his touch calmed her down, helping her heart slow and her nerves settle.

Which was completely deranged. In every way that counted.

Needing her sanity back, Tania tugged on her wrists. "Let go."

"You gonna hit me again?"

"Maybe."

Amusement sparked in his eyes. His mouth curved. "Honest to a fault. I like that about you."

Tania's eyes narrowed. *Enjoyed* that, did he? She gritted her teeth, determined not to be charmed. But wow… he was dangerous when he smiled. "So glad I could make your day. Now…let. Me. Go."

When he didn't move, she added a "please" for good measure. He held firm, ignoring her, the heat of his hands caressing her skin. Making her react and shiver…and want. Frickin'-frackin' guy didn't know when to quit. Or how to look ugly.

Too bad, really. She could've used the break. Especially since her pheromones refused to cooperate, cool off, and acknowledge that she was angry at him.

"I'm sorry I scared you." He took a deep breath, his expression moving from amused to serious in a heartbeat. "If I could've done it another way, I would have, but right now we need to go. It isn't safe here."

Unease skittered down her spine. "What's going on?"

"Drive, honey."

The rhythmic sound of the wipers whispering in the quiet, Tania hesitated. Should she trust him? Did she dare or even want to? The question circled, her uncertainty hanging between them as she tried to decide. He'd come out of nowhere. Landed on the roof of her car, for goodness' sake. Only an idiot would go anywhere with him, but maybe that's exactly what she was…a dum-dum, because he seemed solid to her.

Felt trustworthy. Felt right sitting next to her, as though he belonged there, as though she should accept him and his help…even though she didn't know why she needed it.

And oh boy. Had she said lunatic earlier? Put a capital *L* in front of it, a few exclamation points behind it and… ding-ding-ding. All she needed now were admission papers to the psych ward and a straightjacket to complement the *crazy*.

The pad of his thumb stroked over the inside of her wrist. Goose bumps rose on her skin as he brushed over her pulse point, back and forth, again and again. Time stopped, one second slipping into the next. Suspended with him, she held his gaze. An image flared in her mind's eye, one of him holding her, of her kissing him back; the intensity of heat and longing coupled with unbelievable pleasure.

A warm curl of sensation settled woman-low. Tania drew in a long breath. He mirrored her, inhaling deep, humming low in his throat, ramping up her reaction until it felt real instead of manufactured. Her brows collided. Impossible. She'd only met him once...she nibbled on the inside of her lip...right?

Yes. Absolutely. At the precinct when he'd questioned her about Myst.

Except with his hands on her, she couldn't discount the connection or deny the attraction. Not with the unmistakable throb of recognition stealing through her. Something strange had happened between them. All right, so she couldn't quite capture the memory or place it...at least, not all of it...but it was there, lying in wait, feeding her information, painting a picture of them entwined. On a bed. Him, surrounding her. Her, begging for more.

God help her. She knew him. Really *knew* him.

Tania swallowed, worry nagging at her. "Detective—"

"It's Mac," he murmured, uncurling his fingers from around her wrists. As his hands slid away, taking his heat with them, Tania tried not to mourn the loss. "I'm not a cop anymore."

Not a cop? "What happened?"

She needed to know. Wanted to make the right decision. Drive into town and drop him off? Or go with him? It was hard to know which way to jump. Away from him? Toward him? A tingle crept across the tops of her shoulders. She wanted to trust him. She really did, but a lifetime of hurt—of disappointment and betrayal, of watching her mother make mistake after mistake with men—squawked, warning her to be careful. To look before she leaped.

"Tania, trust me," he murmured. "We need to go... right now."

The deep timbre of his voice washed over her, chilling her out, ramping her up. But it was the urgency she heard in his words and the worry she saw in his eyes that got her moving. She put her foot on the clutch and pressed the pedal to the floor. "You're freaking me out, you know that?"

"Go." Palming the shifter, he put it into first gear, urging her to move the car from standstill in the middle of the road to rolling. "I'll explain later."

"Promise?"

"Cross my heart."

And just like that—with nothing more than his word and the steadiness of his aquamarine gaze—she tossed reason and a lifetime of caution out the window. But as she put her foot down and her faith in him, instinct spiked, telling her to watch out. Something wasn't quite right. Mac was different somehow: more focused, brutally intense, stronger in mind and body. Weird that she could feel it, but...

No doubt. She could absolutely feel the shift in him.

Sneaking a peek, she scanned his profile and swung around the last curve—speeding down the hill into Gig Harbor, city lights spread out like a carpet of glitter below her, wind blowing through the missing door to tug at her hair—and prayed she'd made the right decision.

Intuition told her yes. Logic said no.

Too bad she was already neck-deep and sinking fast. With an ex-cop turned...well, she didn't know exactly. But one thing for sure? She knew serious trouble when she saw it. An insanity-fueled, curiosity-driven mistake…that's what Mac was. And one Tania hoped she lived to regret.

———

Wind whistled in through the side of the car, blasting Mac in the face. His hair blew into his eyes. He stared at Tania through the strands before raking a hand through it, shoving the pain-in-the-ass load out of the way to improve his view. Shit. He needed to do something about that, like get a haircut…along with a new brain.

His was obviously malfunctioning.

The same thing happened every time he laid eyes on her. Okay. So he was exaggerating, but not by much. The first time he'd been at the precinct, watching her pace from behind the two-way mirror. Angela had teased him about his dumb-ass reaction. Too bad his partner wasn't around right now. He could've used a healthy dose of "you're an idiot." 'Cause, yeah, he was doing it again, gawking at her, reacting to Tania in ways that launched ridiculous into a whole new category.

Jesus. Just what he didn't need. A nasty-ass case of the stupids.

Too bad that seemed to be par for the course around her. He could feel the heat, smell his own need as desire ramped him into gotta-touch territory. His dragon growled, coming to attention, 100 percent focused on the woman seated beside him. He breathed deep, combating the urge to lean in and taste her mouth. The sweet curve of her bottom lip. The tender underside of her chin. The baby-soft skin of her throat. Any part of her would do, just as long as he got to linger and savor the beauty of her.

Mac shook his head, hoping to knock a few brain cells together. He needed to get a grip…in the next five seconds. Otherwise he would live up to the dumb-ass reputation, haul her out of the driver's seat and—

Umm, yeah. Right into his lap.

Oh so not a good idea. Especially considering he was hurtling down the road without a car door, nothing but air between him and miles of skin-grinding asphalt.

The thought sobered him fast. Now was not the time to become distracted, but even as his brain came back online, his attraction to her spiked. Wound tight, he absorbed every detail, his gaze drifting over her. Dark hair pulled back in a ponytail. Graceful hands on the wheel. All smooth skin and sweet curves. Her clutch-and-shift so smooth it gave him goose bumps.

Tania downshifted, propelling them around the next curve. Mac curled his hands into fists, the white-hot energy in her aura begging him to reach out. He glanced at the speedometer instead, trying to distract himself. Eighty-five miles an hour. Around a corner. His mouth curved. Man, she could drive. She was Formula One quality wrapped up in a pretty package, looking way too good sitting behind the wheel: in command of the helm, keeping it together when most women would've freaked out.

He smiled a little. Jesus, she was something. And he was in serious trouble, so impressed by her he was headed into dangerous territory. Collision inevitable with his lustier side and at complete odds with his commitment-phobe tendencies. Not something he liked, considering his love of freedom and playboy lifestyle, never mind a trap he ever fell into...at least where women were concerned. But with Tania, he wanted to take his time, explore, play with the idea of keeping her for a while and—

God. He was so fucked, way off his game and out of his mind. Conditions that needed to stop. Right now.

His mission didn't include a side trip into infatuation. He needed to get Tania to safety. Out of range if the Razorbacks came calling. An imminent possibility, considering the exposé responsible for plastering her face all over KING 5's nightly news.

The rogues weren't stupid. They were smart. Ruthless. Well acquainted with technology and human databases, Ivar navigated the information highway just as well as Sloan. So, yeah. Once the Razorbacks got a load of Tania...and made the connection to Myst? Sure as shit, the bastards would come out to play.

Which meant getting Tania the hell out of Dodge. ASAP.

Easier said than done. Why? Number one...his desire for her—and the overactive imagination that drove it— kept distracting him. And two? Tania wasn't anything like the women he usually dated...urr, rather, had sex with. She wasn't a fancy piece of fluff. Or accustomed to taking orders. She had a mind of her own and was accustomed to using it, so...

No. She wouldn't obey without question.

A lot of guys no doubt made that mistake—held her beauty against her while making a whole lot of asinine assumptions—but not him. He saw Tania for who and what she was...well dressed in skinny jeans, designer boots, and a curve-hugging fall sweater; sophisticated, smart, and sassy. Toss in her unrelenting determination along with a dash of curiosity, and yippee, he had a recipe for disaster. With a cherry on top. And no matter which way he sliced it, Mac knew she wouldn't be satisfied with half answers. He could see it, the formidable force of intellect shining in her burgundy-flecked eyes as she threw him another sidelong glance.

Locked and loaded, she took aim in his direction. Mac tensed as she made eye contact. Bull's-eye. She nailed him right in the rings...KO confirmed. It was only a matter of time now. The questions were a nanosecond away and—

"This has something to do with Myst's disappearance, doesn't it?" Shifting like a race car driver, Tania roared past the city sign into Gig Harbor. WELCOME! it said. Yeah, right. Something told him the next few minutes wouldn't be fun or anywhere near welcoming. Not with Tania gunning for information. "What's going on? Is she all right? Have you seen her?"

Mac opened his mouth to answer.

She jumped in, leveling him with a verbal hammer. "What is it, witness protection? Are they after me now to get to her? Is she testifying against someone? A serial killer...a mob boss?"

A serial killer? Mac's lips twitched. He couldn't help it. She was so damned adorable. No one would accuse her of lacking imagination. Or suspecting the truth. Thank fuck. He really didn't want to get into the truth. At least not right now. Introducing her to Dragonkind would come soon enough, but something told him Myst needed to be present when it happened. Otherwise Tania would freak out. And despite everything—or maybe because of it—Mac didn't want to frighten her. Kind and gentle was the better way to go...the only way he wanted to be with her.

Flanked by rows of town houses, Tania slowed down. The Mini lurched as she whispered, "Please just tell me she's safe."

Mac nodded as, unbidden, an image of Bastian surfaced. Like snapshots in a slideshow, the pictures flashed in his mind's eye: of B spoiling Myst, making her happy even as his overprotective nature reared its ugly head. Mac snorted. The male never said quit when it came to Myst. So…*safe*? Talk about a serious understatement. The Nightfury commander wouldn't have it any other way.

Holding Tania's gaze, he murmured, "In good hands."

She breathed out, the sound one of relief. "Can I see her?"

"That's where we're headed."

Happiness sparked in her eyes a second before it spread across her face. Flipping her blinker on, she turned right onto the town's main drag. Storefronts and the glow of neon signs kissing the illumination of streetlamps flashed past, and she smiled at him. His heart went jackrabbit, slamming the inside of his chest as his mouth tipped up, following her example. Goddamn, that felt good. Giving her what she wanted. Making her smile. Being the cause of her happiness. And as he shared the moment with her, Mac wondered if he'd found his calling.

"Yo, Mac?" Amusement in his tone, Forge mind-spoke, *"You're awfully quiet, lad. Having fun down there?"*

"Shut up." Breaking eye contact with Tania, Mac glared out the back window. *"Mind your own fucking business."*

Rikar snorted with laughter.

Ah, shit on a stick. He was in trouble now.

He should've kept his yap shut. Let the silence lead and made the dynamic duo flying in his wake believe there was nothing going on…that he wasn't starstruck by Tania. 'Cause Forge? The male was like a dog with a bone, and once he touched on something embarrassing he cranked the shit out of it. And that was before Rikar tossed his hat into the ring.

As if on cue…

"Nifty move, man," Rikar said, the rattle of scales coming through the mind-speak. *"She pissed about the door?"*

"Go fuck yourself."

"No thanks. I prefer my mate."

In other words? Angela…his self-declared little sister. *"I'm so kicking your ass when we get home."*

"You're welcome to try."

"Ask Forge about my kind of trying."

"Kung fu, Rikar," Forge murmured. *"Watch your arse."*

Mac clenched his teeth to keep from laughing. He couldn't help it. Despite the teasing, he loved these guys. Each made him feel as though he belonged with them, deserved to be inside the Nightfury pack. It felt good. Felt right. Felt like the rarest of gifts. One he refused to take for granted, even while getting razzed by his new buddies.

Blocking his friends out for a second, he tuned back into Tania. He frowned. What had she just said? Something about Ted Bundy? Jesus, she had a thing for serial killers. Or at least had the history of psychopaths down pat.

"So you see," she said, speeding by the drugstore, "he wasn't really a—"

A prickle ghosted across the nape of his neck, cutting off her monologue as his dragon senses tingled. Half listening to her, he latched onto the signal. More vibration than sensation, the buzz came again. The fine hairs on his arms stood on end. Alarm bells went off inside his head.

The static got louder. Mac's skin crawled, muscles fisting up hard.

Fuck him. Razorbacks. Coming in fast: locked, loaded, with a shitload of vicious riding shotgun.

Instinct and the territorial need to protect cranked into overdrive. He glanced at Tania. Still talking, the methodical sound of her voice reached him over the rush of wind. She'd moved on to the Green River Killer. His brows furrowed. Jesus H. Christ. How much did one female really need to know about serial killers?

Everything, obviously. The woman was a walking, talking encyclopedia on the subject. And judging by the static hammering his temples, she was about to get up close and personal with a whole new breed. Human killers, after all, had nothing on rogues.

"Motherfuck." The whole situation was headed south, and not in a good way. He'd hoped to break the whole dragon thing to her gently. But that wasn't going to happen now. Not with a boatload of fangs, claws, and scales riding their asses.

"Pardon me?"

"Nothing, *mo chroí*."

Tania threw him a startled look. "Mo…what? What did you just—"

"Forget it." He wanted to. Shit. Had he really just called her *my heart*…in Gaelic?

Mac gritted his teeth. Not the best time to remember his roots. Or the tough, trash-talking neighborhood he'd grown up in. But some things couldn't be exorcised. The Irish blood in him appeared to be one of them, the way he thought of her another. No matter how he sliced it, the truth reared its ugly head. His dragon half liked Tania…

way too much. And much as it chafed him, the endearment fit. Felt right and sounded good when directed at her.

"Hey, Mac?" Worry in her voice, her hands flexed on the wheel. "Could you just—"

"Hang on, honey." Eyes narrowed, he held up a hand, asking her to be quiet. He needed to concentrate to pinpoint the signal and...

Mac growled, cursing his fledgling status. He could feel the rogues, but thanks to his fucked-up magic, couldn't judge distances. Didn't know how far away the Razorbacks were or how much time he had to get Tania out of the line of fire.

Fear for her slammed into him. He hit up his XO. *"Rikar...how far out are they?"*

"Three miles. The first wave just broke through the fighting triangle."

"The first wave?" Motherfuck. That didn't sound good. "Tania, turn left."

"But—"

"Just do it. We've run out of time."

"What in God's name are you talking about?"

Holding her gaze, he said, "Trust me, honey, and... turn!"

Her knuckles went white a second before she cranked the wheel. The engine growled. The back of the Mini slid as she took the turn too fast. He curled his hand over the lip of the roof and, hanging on tight, reached out with his mind. He needed more information. Longs and lats of the enemies' approach. Direction and trajectory...the number of Razorbacks headed their way. Anything. Everything. Whatever he could scrape up to help him navigate the best way out of town.

His sonar pinged, casting a wide net. Like an invisible blanket, his magic settled over the terrain: trees and rocks, tall buildings and compact houses, shifting through all the electrical interference. He sorted through the intel rapid-fire, reading the smallest vibration, taking what he needed, tossing the rest.

Two minutes out. A measly 120 seconds before the rogues attacked en masse.

Calling on his magic once more, Mac conjured a matched set of Sig 40s. The ammo came next, landing in his lap. Not wasting a second, he flipped the cardboard top open, ejected the magazine clip from the first weapon, and started loading it.

"Jeepers!" The bullets rattled. Tania flinched. The car swerved, bobbing on the tiny tires. "Good God...what...how..."

As she trailed off, Mac finished with one clip and loaded the other. "Floor it, Tania. Head for the bridge."

"But the hotel. My bag. I need my—"

"Forget about your stuff." Ramping the second magazine home, he chambered a round in each gun. The clickety-click made her eyes widen another notch and... shit. He should apologize for that: for frightening her, for not explaining, for deliberately keeping the truth from her. And he would...later. Right now, all he wanted to do was get her out in one piece. "We've got bigger problems."

"Bigger..." She paused, her expression a combination of confusion and panic. "You don't understand. I need a phone. I did something stupid...an interview that will hurt my sister if it gets out. I need to reach the reporter and stop—"

"It's too late." Taking his eyes off her for a moment, he glanced out the back window, listening to the chatter on frequency Nightfury. The guys were airborne, flying in fast to protect them. Close. The enemy was way too close, and his brothers-in-arms still too far away. Night vision pinpoint sharp, he scanned the sky again. "It already aired...was all over the evening news. Why do you think I'm here?"

"Oh my God." Devastation surfaced in her eyes.

Mac's heart clenched. Jesus. He couldn't stand it or ignore her pain. Murmuring her name, he ditched one of his Sigs. Metal thunked against the center console as he reached out to cup her cheek. The softness of her skin grazed his palm. Stress made her energy spike. The powerful wave shivered through him and Mac swallowed, fighting his reaction to her. Tears welled in her eyes. He wanted to kiss them away, soothe her into comfort. He drew on her energy instead, took some of the anxiety to calm her. "Stay with me, *mo chroí*. Just a little longer. Trust me a little farther. I promise it'll be all right."

When she nodded, he murmured, "Atta girl" and, breaking eye contact, pinged his commander. *"Bastian... how many you got?"*

"A shitload," B growled, aggression and something more—worry, maybe—in his answer. *"Too many to track."*

Not good. The situation had just been upgraded from critical to goat-fucked. Bastian always acted as a sounding board, picking apart a male's abilities from a distance. The skill was a rare one and came in handy in a firefight. Thanks to B, the Nightfuries always knew what to expect—the age and skill of the rogues, what poison each breathed—before the enemy flew into range.

So, yeah, the outnumbered thing? Not good. If Bastian couldn't keep track of the bastards, it meant a platoon of Razorbacks could be headed their way. And seven against twenty-something males? Not great odds in battle.

Adrenaline hit Mac like a body shot. The need to fight amped him up, but...no way he could do that. Or leave the car to join his comrades in the fight. Tania was his responsibility. She needed his protection. He refused to leave her. Not until he knew she was secure.

"Listen up." Magic pounded through his veins as he connected to each one of his brothers-in-arms. *"New plan. We're heading over the bridge into Tacoma. Once we're in the city, I'll find a safe place for her and come back for you."*

Rikar growled. *"No fucking way."*

"Stay with your female," Bastian said, his tone brooking no argument. *"Get her out, Mac. We'll hold the line until you do."*

"Shit," Mac muttered as they reached the ramp onto the Narrows Bridge. Deserted, nothing but double lanes, concrete, and big-ass pole lamps, the bridge stretched out in front of them. "Floor it, Tania!"

She put her foot down. The car jerked, and his magic rolled. Thunder rumbled overhead. The smell of rain in the air, the first drops splattered the windshield. Almost there. Another five hundred yards and—

A fireball streaked across the night sky.

Orange flame roared, eating through the gloom. Ravenous, it hammered the center of the bridge. Asphalt and bits of steel exploded, mushrooming into a thick cloud. Shrapnel peppered the front of the car, blowing the hood off as the road gave way, caving in toward the water.

A red dragon, pink eyes aglow, materialized out of the darkness.

Wings spread in flight, sharp fangs flashed in the storm glow. Ivar inhaled, drawing air past his fangs. Pink flame gathered in the back of his throat. Tania screamed, feet churning as she tried to retreat. But neither of them had anywhere to go. Except...

With a snarl, Mac unclipped her seat belt and hauled Tania over the center console. The second she landed in his lap, he grabbed the steering wheel and cranked. The Mini swerved, tipping dangerously on two tires. Another fireball lit up the night sky. The inferno roared toward them. The car's front end hit the guardrail, twisted metal acting like a ramp and—

Fucking A. Mission accomplished.

They were airborne. Hurtling through thin air. In a Mini Cooper–cum–death trap. Heading straight toward the choppy surface of the harbor below.

Chapter Nine

"Ah, hell." On point and ahead of the others, Venom flew in fast, battling a case of WTF as a load of red with white racing stripes launched off the side of the bridge. *"He's overboard."*

Bastian growled. *"Shit."*

"Oh, for fuck's sake," Rikar said, white scales gleaming, snow flying as he rocketed out of thick cloud cover. *"Never a dull moment."*

"God love the lad."

Venom glanced overhead. He caught a flash of deep purple scales and glared at it. Frigging Forge. Trust that male to back up Mac's decision to perform a swan dive in a tin can with wheels. In a month, the two had become inseparable, the mentor–student racket forming an unbreakable bond between males. Not a bad thing. Optimal in many ways. Still, Venom couldn't get behind the become-a-projectile-in-a-Mini-Cooper thing. He seconded his commander's motion instead, ignored Forge's "atta boy," and jumped on the beat-the-hell-out-of-Mac bandwagon.

Stupid fledgling. The male had done that on purpose.

The car's front end dipped into a nosedive. He watched the free fall for a second, then scanned the bridge behind it. Nothing. No red dragon in sight. But he knew Ivar was here. He'd seen the bastard. Would recognize the pink-eyed SOB anywhere. Now all he needed to do was find and take him out. You know what they say: cut the head off the snake and the body died.

Kill the leader, destroy the movement.

Venom hoped that was true. That the Razorback organization started and ended with Ivar. No tentacles. No deep roots planted inside Dragonkind. No breach in his race's defenses for Razorback ideology to find a foothold. Just a rogue faction working on its own.

Somehow, though, he didn't think so.

The Razorbacks were hard-core. Motivated. Persuasive. Well able to camouflage their particular brand of crazy with patriotic love. And a lot of males—both powerful and inconsequential—fell for their bullshit all the time. How did he know? The proof was in the pudding, so to speak. In the number of rogues converging on his pack over the small town of Gig Harbor.

Someone was supplying Ivar's psychotic band of misfits. Someone with money and influence. Someone who wanted humankind as dead and gone as Ivar did. Genocide on a global scale. Extinction at its most lethal. All carefully disguised under the veil of an environmental agenda.

Brilliant. And oh so dangerous.

The trick now? Proving it.

Venom's night vision sparked. His eyes glowed, throwing a red wash out in front of him as he searched for his prey. Dark green scales glinting beneath the storm glow, he rocketed over the marina. Water churned in his wake.

Sailboat masts snapped like toothpicks, slumping over bows as smaller boats capsized in the fury of his wings' blowback. He didn't care. He'd trash the whole frigging place. KO every human in sight to protect his pack.

Even Mac, the inexperienced pansy-ass idiot.

Although…

Now that he thought about it, he had to admit the whole drive-and-dive idea was a pretty slick move. An insane one, for sure, but slick all the same. Especially considering the water dragon crap Mac had going on. Venom suppressed a super willy. Even after a month of trying, the ocean thing still unnerved him. Lit him up in ways he didn't want to contemplate, never mind examine too closely. But no matter how hard he fought it, he couldn't get the past out of his head. Or his sire's cruelty.

Which always happened when he got anywhere near water.

So screw the newest member of the Nightfury pack. He'd cling to his objections—his suspicion and mistrust—thank you very much. At least until Mac grew a brain and learned to control the element he commanded…one of the most destructive forces on earth.

Screwed-up fledgling bonehead. The idiot was going to get them all killed.

Venom went wings vertical, rocketing toward the bridge's support pillars. Or what was left of them. Blown wide open, the structure sagged, listing to one side, fighting gravity's pull toward the narrows of Puget Sound. A growl came from inside the car, swirling out across the chop and churn of water. The female screamed again. The long, terror-filled sound knotted the pit of Venom's stomach. Idiot male. Mac was scaring the hell out of her. Oh so not cool, but—

Rivets popped. The Mini's roof twisted beneath the pressure. Steel groaned, then rolled back and away. Mac emerged in dragon form, one talon cradling the female, eyes aglow, the razor-sharp blade along his spine opening the car up like a tin of sardines.

Venom blinked. Holy hell. Talk about a wicked move and, well…all right. Undeniably cool too. Who knew the blockhead could be used as a can opener?

Red scales flashed in Venom's periphery.

Already on the other side of the bridge, he tried to compensate, but…God. Ivar had the prime position, hanging over the bridge like a gargoyle, his gaze locked on Mac as he dove toward the ocean. With a curse, Venom put the brakes on. Wings stretched to capacity, he inhaled deep, desperate to unleash his poisonous exhale to incapacitate Ivar, trying to protect—

Mac flipped up and over. One razor-sharp talon curled around his female, the other gripping the car, he hurled the Mini like a baseball. Venom snarled, liking the plan, watching it unfold as he wheeled around. And wow. What a shot: pinpoint accurate with the velocity to match. Blockhead had an arm on him—he'd give him that—and it belonged in the big-time major leagues.

Right on target, the steel skeleton screamed toward Ivar. The rogue leader shrieked and, swallowing his fireball, dodged left. His spiked tail collided with a lamppost. Concrete crumbled. Steel buckled, and the mangled shaft went airborne. Venom cursed and banked left to avoid being stabbed by the flying projectile. The post whistled through the air, then touched down on the roadway, ripping up more asphalt. The Mini sailed past, missing Ivar by inches.

Too bad. Venom would've liked to see the rogue leader go splat…while plummeting from the sky with a face full of metal.

Swooping in behind, Venom attacked Ivar's flank, angling for a shot. His claws met red scales. Muscles along his side pulled as he raked Ivar on the flyby. The smell of blood joined the scent of rain, rising in the night air. Wheeling around, Venom went at the bastard again. No way would he let Ivar retreat behind the approaching wave of his warriors. The maniacal SOB always stayed on the sidelines, rarely coming out to play. And now that he had him in his sights? He planned to make the most of it before his lackeys flew in to save him.

Almost out of time, Venom bared his fangs and—

Splash! Well, all right then. Water dragon away. No need to worry about Mac anymore. Once in the ocean, no one—neither rogue nor Nightfury—could catch him. Which left the playing field wide open.

But it was too late.

The wave of rogues hit, collapsing the pocket around him. Cut off from Ivar, Venom tucked his wings and went supersonic, rocketing into a spiral. He broke through the Razorbacks' front line. Into the middle of the pack and away from his own.

Ah, hell. Not good. Not the brightest idea, either. Now he was cut off. No wingman. No one to watch his back. A thick wall of scaly muscle between him and his Nightfury brothers.

"Venom," Wick growled. *"Get the fuck out of there!"*

Great advice, buddy. Like he wasn't trying?

Ducking his head, he swooped beneath the underside of an oncoming rogue. Front talons spread wide, the asshole lashed out. Enemy claws flashed in the weak moonlight. Venom twisted into another spin. The rogue nailed him, ripping a bloody trail along his shoulder. Pain flared, then spiraled into an agonizing burn. Venom ignored it. He couldn't afford the distraction. Not with multiple rogues on his tail and more closing in fast.

Gritting his fangs together, Venom lashed out with his spiked tail. The barbs struck a bright blue rogue and sank deep. With a snarl, he flipped and yanked hard, ripping through rogue scales as he hauled the male sideways in midair. Thunder rumbled overhead. Raindrops fell, and more rogues flew in, frigid night air curling from their wing tips. With a curse, Venom dodged two more sets of enemy claws and, setting up his approach, calculated the best angle. It needed to be perfect. Just the right trajectory to inflict maximum damage.

One…two…three, and…

Go!

His fangs bared, he inhaled hard and exhaled smooth. Fast acting, filled with killer neuro-venom, green poison shot from his throat. Like a wave of luminous electricity, the contaminant traveled, spreading on a disastrous undulation of throbbing light. The rogues flying toward him squawked, wing-flapping to get out of the toxic path. One male dropped. Then another. Both clawed at their throats, airways closing up tight.

Hoorah. Anaphylactic shock had nothing on him.

Too bad it wasn't enough. The rogues were everywhere. Thick as frigging flies, engaging his brothers-in-arms, hemming him in, keeping the Nightfuries away as they fought to reach him. Wincing hard, Venom took a glancing blow. And then another. A third male hammered him on the flyby. His head snapped to the side. A cut opened beneath his eye and…

Goddamn-son-of-a-bitch. He was toast. In critical point-of-no-return territory without a lifeline. Talk about FUBARed. The situation had all the markings. And getting out alive? Pretty slim chance of that, considering—

"Venom…bank hard right," Mac yelled, voice wavering through salt water.

He shifted in midair, complying without thought. The Razorbacks adjusted, staying on his tail. Water roared. He glanced down and—

Good God. What the hell was that?

Venom's heart stopped, just hung inside his chest as an arsenal of kick-ass shot from beneath the surface of Gig Harbor. Three-pronged, the water spears hissed like rocket fuel, lighting his senses on fire. Venom ducked. The first one struck, skewering the rogue behind him like a shish kebab. As the asshole ashed out, dying in a flaky mess, four other sea javelins punctured scaled chests, taking out the Razorbacks surrounding him.

"Mac…"

More spears flew.

"Don't thank me," Mac said, voice muffled by water. *"Just get the fuck out."*

Another round of javelins.

Desperate to avoid Mac's carnage, the rogues parted like the Red Sea. Venom didn't hesitate. Blood streaming down his side, he flew hard and fast, picking through the violence, following the trail Mac left for him like bread crumbs. Breaking through the guard, Venom growled his relief and locked onto Wick. Outnumbered three to one, and still the male held his own: claws deployed and doing damage, black amber-tipped scales flashing as he took another body shot.

"Wick." Rounding a lamppost, he mind-spoke to his best friend, *"Right flank and coming in hot."*

"About fucking time."

Rikar seconded the motion. *"Dig in, Ven."*

With pleasure. Flying over Wick's spine, he latched onto a blue dragon's head. Sharp horns scored his talons. The male squawked. Venom showed no mercy. With a twist, he snapped the male's neck, severing his spinal cord. Ash blew into his face, and he rounded on another rogue. The bastard put on the brakes, trying to change course. Venom bared his teeth. The idiot. Hanging in midair. He'd just put a bull's-eye on his forehead.

Exhaling, he hit the SOB with a lethal dose of neuro-venom.

As the rogue plummeted toward the harbor, B said, *"Bug out, boys. There are too many of them."*

"The plan?" Wick asked.

"Lose the fuckers in the city?" Nothing but purple flash, Forge breathed out. Fire-acid flew from his mouth, lighting an enemy male on fire. The smell of burning flesh obliterated the fresh air.

"God, that stinks." Dark brown scales glittering, Sloan rounded on a Razorback. Low light played against the yellow-tipped spikes along Sloan's spine, then turned to glint off his multipronged, venomous tail. Putting the poisonous barbs to good use, he slashed an enemy dragon, sending the venom deep before grabbing another. Bone crunched against bone. His brother-in-arms twisted, ripping the male's throat wide open. Blood flowed, coating

his snow-white talons. *"Pair up…split into twos, divide their attention. Meet back at the lair at daybreak."*

"Sounds good. B…you're with me," Rikar said, frost crackling through mind-speak. *"Mac…how's your female?"*

"Freaking out, but alive." Mac hurled another water spear. Huh. Venom raised a brow. The fledgling's aim was a little off there. He'd only winged the rogue. *"I've got her in an air lock."*

Venom frowned. *"A what?"*

"Think air bubble with attitude."

"Bloody hell," Forge muttered.

"Keep her there," Rikar said. *"Swim, Mac…make a break for it. Find somewhere safe to hole up."*

Good plan. On so many levels. Especially since Mac couldn't cloak himself yet. Although that might've changed, because…hell. Venom couldn't see the male anymore. He'd gone invisible beneath the surface of the water. And if he couldn't track him, neither could the Razorbacks.

"I'll call in the longs and lats of our position once I've secured her."

"Good." Banking hard, B broke away from the fighting triangle.

As Rikar joined him, playing wingman to their commander, he and Wick headed in the other direction. Decision time, assholes. Which way would they go? Forge and Sloan peeled off in a third direction, bugging out, confusing the rogues, flying toward the forest. A moment of hesitation then…bam! The enemy faction split into groups, weakening the effectiveness of their fighting force. Strength in numbers, after all, wasn't a well-known expression for nothing.

"Later, boys," Mac murmured, the rush of water coming through mind-speak. *"Don't get dead."*

Venom snorted. Cocky pissant fledgling. Although maybe pissant didn't apply anymore. The newest member of the Nightfury pack had earned his stripes tonight. And as much as it pained him to admit it, he owed Mac. A thanks at the very least. A slap on the back at most.

And yeah, that was going to suck. Big-time. Almost as much as the deep slice to his abdomen.

Goddamn it. One of the rogues had done a number on him. He'd taken a serious hit somewhere along the way. Where and which rogue? Venom didn't have a clue, but now that he was flying away from the fight—playing hopscotch across building tops to camouflage his trail, losing the rogues one leap at a time—the pain reminded him.

Ah, hell. He was leaking like a sieve, his heart pumping plasma faster than his dragon DNA could stem the flow. Venom grimaced, flying hard, rogues sniffing in his wake as he and Wick searched for the next point of cover.

He needed to lose the rogues on his tail and land in a quiet spot. The sooner the better. Once he shifted into human form, he'd assess the extent of the damage. Put pressure on the gash and catch his breath. Before it was too late because...God. He was in trouble: losing muscle strength, vision narrowing to blurry pinpoints, talon tips tingling in warning.

Venom shook his head, forcing himself to function... to fly straight, see clearly, be strong. But as the Razorbacks fell farther behind, he knew he couldn't avoid the truth. Inevitability loomed, and with a wound this severe? He didn't know how much longer he would last.

Trapped inside a bubble deep underwater, Tania screamed her throat raw. Her awful cry bounced off the invisible, hard-as-steel walls to pound her temples. She slammed her palms against the barrier, searching for a way out. Seaweed whirled past, taunting her with freedom as its leaves clung to the curved walls for a moment.

She watched it wave at her. Tears welled and fell, each breath sawing in and out, making her chest hurt. Her prison didn't slow, the velocity supersonic as it sped out to sea. No match for momentum, the green string of flotsam let go, then disappeared, getting lost in the dark swirl of water around the globe's smooth contours.

Helplessness struck hard. Panic hit next, sending Tania sideways inside her own head. Hammering the barrier with her fists, she screamed again, "Help me! Somebody help!"

Surprise, surprise. No one answered. Not that she expected anyone to pipe up down here. She was miles beneath the surface. Miles from safety…and rescue. But worse—at least for her—was the absolute darkness.

And the fear that accompanied it.

God help her. She couldn't see much outside her transparent cage. Inside, however? She saw everything: the curved top of the ceiling, the crisp edge of the flat floor where it met the rounded sides of the interior walls. Double paned, filled with some kind of light, the whole globe glowed in the inky depths. The soft blue illumination only traveled so far, though, barely reaching out enough for her to see the air bubbles rocketing like a long-tailed comet in her wake.

Kneeling on the floor of the globe, Tania rocked backward. As her heels touched her behind, she cupped her hand over her mouth, trying to keep from screaming again.

Oh shit. Oh God. She was so screwed. And way too scared to think straight.

Out.

She needed out. Right now. Out of the bubble. Out of the water. Out of her own head and into a place where sanity lived.

With another hoarse cry, she slammed her palms against the barrier again. And again. Over and over, beating on the blue glow until exhaustion sapped her strength. As her muscles gave out, she leaned forward, pressing her forehead against the chilly facade, the boom-boom-boom of her heart a faint throb in her ears, arms hanging by her sides.

The stinging throb of her hands barely registered. Neither did the bruises. Nor the torn tips of her fingernails.

She was beyond rational thought, the ability to take a full breath nothing but a distant memory. Only one thing registered. The stupid snow globe—or whatever the hell it was—and the fact she couldn't get out.

Imprisonment complete. No escape feasible. Screwed with a capital *S*.

Deep in the depths, she sat on the ocean's equivalent of death row. Waiting. Watching. Locked deep inside a nightmare in which panic had already come and gone. Now terror reigned, raising its clubbed fists, beating on her without mercy.

Dragons.

She'd been attacked by *dragons*.

A sob rasped in the back of her throat. No doubt about it. She was going to die. Right here. Hemmed in on all sides. Buried under miles of seawater while she waited for her air supply to run out. No take-backs. No do-overs. No passing go or collecting two hundred dollars.

Blinking away another round of tears, Tania raised her head and stared out into the abyss. Ironic, wasn't it? She didn't even like playing Monopoly, and yet, in the waning moments before death came to collect her, her life didn't flash before her eyes (the way everyone always said it did). No cherished childhood memory full of summer fun surfaced. No great accomplishment rose for her to claim. All she could think about was that damned board game and the fact she would never roll the dice again. Tania's breath caught on a painful hitch as regret slid through her.

So many things left undone…unsaid and unrealized.

She wouldn't get to say good-bye to her sister. Never again see her best friend. Or get to design her masterpiece. No more landscapes bursting with bright flowers and beautiful trees. No more playgrounds, footpaths, or sunken pools to imagine or children to make happy. No more anything.

Just a cold, dark, watery grave.

And Mac. Whatever had happened to him, it couldn't be good. She'd felt the car explode around them. Heard her poor little Mini shriek as steel tore open and—

Wait a minute.

Pressing her bruised palms against the wall, Tania frowned. Something wasn't right about that memory.

"Think, Tania," she whispered to herself. "Think."

Hitting the pause button on her brain, she rewound the mental reel. Her eyes narrowed. He'd been right beside her in the passenger seat. Talking to her. Soothing and reassuring her with his beautiful voice. Had cupped her cheek while he promised everything would be all right. She remembered the hard turn, the screech of tires, the red dragon's sudden appearance, the explosion and—

Holy crap.

Tania sucked in a quick breath. Something about going over the side of the bridge wasn't right. Mac had done… something.

She closed her eyes to search her memory banks. Sifting deep, Tania rubbed her upper arms, combating the chill. Wet wool scraped her palms as she shivered in the dark, wishing for dry clothes and the answer.

Mac. Something about him. Something…

Her eyes popped open. "Oh my God."

Blue-gray scales. Aquamarine eyes. A big claw-tipped paw wrapped around her.

Shock clogged her throat for a second. A wave of relief followed. Which was just plain stupid. Mac was one of *them*. A monster with fangs and freaky body art. Yes, she'd seen the tattoo a second before they'd splashed down together. A swirling pattern like that was hard to miss. Especially with it shimmering against her cheek. Still…

Relief was a stupid reaction to be having. No way should she be happy about finding out Mac could turn into a dragon…or that the pink-eyed, red-scaled one didn't own the bubble she sat inside.

How did she know? Well, she didn't. Not really. But it made a certain amount of sense…in a freaky, crazier-than-crap kind of way.

Still kneeling on the hard floor of the bubble, Tania hugged herself and forced herself to think. Clearly. No fear blurring the truth. No panic clawing up her throat. Just clear, run-of-the-mill reason leading the charge into intellectual clarity. She took a deep breath. Then another.

All right. Good. Almost there.

She reached the point of no return fast. Maybe she'd lost her mind. Maybe she needed to be admitted for a round of drug therapy with antipsychotics, but the Mac/ dragon angle worked for her. She couldn't fault logic or what she'd seen. Okay, so she could. Eyewitness testimony wasn't the most reliable, but imprisoned inside a snow globe with two options—Mac or the scary red dragon coming to get her—she decided in favor of her own sanity, choosing door number one and the man behind it.

Mac, after all, was the better bet. He wouldn't hurt her...Tania blinked...would he?

Oh, snap. She hoped not. But a dragon was a *dragon*, and considering he'd trapped her underwater, she couldn't be sure...of anything.

Fear took another turn, circled deep to stir suspicion. As self-preservation reared its head, she shuffled forward on her knees. Running her hands over the smooth walls, she slid around the interior of her prison, checking for cracks, seams in the clear sides, any weakness at all. She didn't find one. The bubble was perfect, designed with one purpose in mind...to keep her in until whomever controlled it decided to let her out.

"Mac!" She glared at the domed top, then smacked the globe with the flat of her hands. The slap echoed, bouncing around the inside as her palms stung and her temper sparked. The big jerk. Who did he think he was... trapping her down here, scaring the hell out of her? "You nutbar...let me out!"

Calling the guy who held her prisoner names probably wasn't the best strategy. Tania didn't care. The chief idiot-in-charge deserved far worse—like a knuckle sandwich upside the head—for making her trust him. And as her terror morphed into anger, she yelled at him, "I mean it, Mac. Get me out of here, or I'll…I'll…"

Crap a frickin'-frackin' crumpet. She didn't know what she would do, but it wouldn't be good for Mac. Would be overflowing with bucketfuls of nastiness and involve her kicking his butt while she revoked the trust card she'd handed him earlier.

Trust. Ha. Like he rated as trustworthy? A lying homicide cop–cum–dragon guy?

God, she should never have made that leap of faith. Should've ignored instinct—the need to believe in him—and stuck to her usual aphorism…the one entitled *Never Trust a Man.* For any reason or any one thing. Hadn't she learned anything from her mother? From the jerk who'd called himself her father?

Men lied. All the time.

Tania curled her hands into fists as the certainty of conviction rushed through her. Her nerves settled along with it, then shifted, turning on a dime to fan her fury. The lying toad. The conniving jackass. He'd misled her on purpose…had jumped into her car (uninvited!), sat beside her (looking like a cover model and smelling like Calvin Klein cologne…the heavenly one she couldn't resist!), and used that smooth-as-silk voice to persuade her to go along without a fight (the knee-jerk ass-funkle!).

Well, she was done trusting. Sick to the gills of being scared. Tired of being stuck inside a stupid bubble traveling at breakneck speed while waiting to die.

So forget about denial and plausible explanation. Forget about possible versus improbable. She'd seen what she'd *seen*…crazy fire-breathing dragon stuff aside. Now it was time to buck up and be brave. She refused to ignore the truth and bury her head in the sand. Not now when her life depended on it.

And honestly? Being pissed off at Mac helped. It gave her a target, something to aim at. And somehow, that made all the difference: settled the dread churning in the pit of her stomach, stripped away the band of pressure roping her rib cage, allowing her to take a deep breath, making her feel more in control and better able to handle what came next, scales, sharp claws, and all.

And if she got it wrong and the red dragon showed up to kill her?

Tania swallowed the bile threatening the back of her throat. The awful taste lingered as terror flew in for another visit, forcing a brutal case of the shivers down her spine. Right. Wrong. Friend or foe. It was just a matter of semantics. Of who reached her first.

Either way, she would go down fighting. Courage, after all, was a better option than crying.

Chapter Ten

Deep underwater in the center of Gig Harbor, Mac watched his comrades bug out in different directions. Smart move. Divide and conquer. It worked like a charm too, forcing the Razorbacks to scramble. His eyes on the night sky, he saw the enemy split into smaller packs to follow the other Nightfuries. He conjured another water javelin. The smooth, weighted shaft settled in his talon, the urge to throw it and KO another rogue jabbing at him.

Patience, though, wasn't a virtue for nothing.

Ivar was still floating around, watching from somewhere. Waiting for the moment he broke cover. Too bad for the asshole, though. Mac wouldn't be coming out of the ocean anytime soon. Still he played wait-and-see, poised to strike the second the rogue leader took flight from his hidey-hole.

Mac swam in a circle, webbed claws and blade tail propelling him forward with more efficiency than a boat motor. Not surprising, really. He'd always been a strong swimmer, the best in his navy unit. Which was saying something. Especially since SEALs thrived in all things water. Tonight, though, he had an added advantage. For the first time ever, his magic worked with him, not against him, merging his two halves—dragon and human—into a whole.

And surprise, surprise. A wicked benefit came with the abrupt about-face. Invisibility. He'd gone silent under the surface of the water. Was 100 percent cloaked and more deadly than a nuclear submarine at DEFCON Delta. Locked. Loaded. Lethal amount of kick-ass at the ready.

Halle-fucking-lujah. It was frickin' about time.

Satisfaction ghosted through him. His tattoo tingled, throwing sensation over his shoulder and down his arm. Mac adjusted his grip on the water spear, wondering if maybe the tribal ink had something to do with his disappearing act beneath the surface. Not that he gave a rat's ass. Later would be soon enough to ruminate about the reasons. Right now he needed to make sure the Razorback leader stayed neutralized and off his trail. No way would Mac go after Tania until he knew for sure.

Splitting his attention, he kept his eyes on the night sky as he checked on her. Linked to her bioenergy, he scanned her vital signs. Elevated heart rate. Harried breathing. Pissed-off attitude. Mac blew out a long breath, relieved by the spike in her temper. Scared but okay. Thank fuck. Most women would've passed out by now…or had a heart attack from fright. But oh no. Not Tania. She reacted with a load of "I'm going to skin you alive."

Literally. He could hear her yelling that exact threat at him through the connection he shared with her.

"Easy," he murmured, pushing the word through mindspeak, hoping Tania would hear him. *"I'm coming for you, honey. Easy."*

More yelling. Then a slapping sound and—

Another round of swearing came back at him.

Mac's lips curved. He couldn't help it. Despite her fear, she came at him full throttle. Add in her incredibly inventive vocabulary and...Jesus. Had she just called him a maggot turd?

"Tania. Hold tight," he said, reassuring her the best he could from a distance.

He felt her go still, could almost see her tilt her head as his voice reached her. Propelling the air bubble out to sea with his mind, he checked its velocity. Stable and moving steadily. Next he tested the air quality, gauging oxygen levels and temperature. Too cold. He cranked the magical thermostat inside his head to keep her warm.

"Mac!" Muffled by layers of water, her voice wavered but still came through.

"You're safe, mo chroí. *You've got lots of air, and—"*

"Let me go!" The signal faded in and out, lengthening each syllable. "I w-want out."

Salt water washing over his scales, he cringed, regret sliding through him. Ah, God. He could smell her tears, feel her fear...and hated every second. The problem? He didn't know what to do about it. He hadn't liked sticking her in the air bubble any more than she liked being locked inside it. But keeping her off rogue radar was priority one. He needed her alive. Wanted her safe. Cared about her well-being more than he did his own. And whether she liked it or not, her happiness took a backseat to saving her life.

Still, his heart ached for her as he said, *"Just a little longer, Tania."*

"M-Mac..." She paused on a hiccup, and the hitch in her voice almost killed him.

"You're all right, love," he thought at her, asking for her patience. *"Give me a minute to make sure it's safe, then I'll come for you. I'll get you out...I promise."*

Static disrupted their connection, washing out her words. As it washed back in, he heard, "...donkey head... you can stick your promise up your—"

The signal faded out again.

But Mac didn't require a road map to read the signs. She yelled another threat. He cringed. Motherfuck. She was creative and...yeah, retrieving her wasn't going to be any fun. In fact, the antithesis of *fun* sounded about right. Particularly since she was now swearing a blue streak, piling on all the nasty things she planned to do to him when he came within striking distance.

Not that he blamed her.

"Mac," Rikar growled, interrupting his tête-à-tête with Tania. *"What the fuck are you doing? Move your ass."*

"Give me a sec," he said, staring up through 150 feet of water. *"Ivar's still here somewhere. I think he's laid up, waiting for me to break cover."*

"Christ."

Wind whistled through mind-speak, the sound all about ass-hauling as B said, *"We'll circle back."*

"Don't bother." His night vision sharp, breathing underwater, Mac flipped onto his back and stared at the thunderclouds overhead. The rippling swirl of whitecaps rolled on the surface of Gig Harbor, disrupting his view as he swam beneath the busted-up bridge. He murmured a command. The waves calmed and the bay went still, smoothing out into a glass-like sheet of dark blue. Better. He didn't have time for bullshit or one of Mother Nature's temper tantrums. He needed a clean sight line to check the other side of the

channel. One never knew. The asshole rogues might be hiding in plain sight, hanging off the structure like gargoyles or something. *"He can't see me down here. I'm cloaked."*

Silence met his announcement.

Bastian was the first to recover. *"Fucking A."*

Pride in his tone, Rikar murmured, *"You see anything?"*

"Not yet." His tail swishing in long, slow motions, Mac propelled himself through the water, cleared the underside of the bridge and—

"Motherfuck," he said through clenched teeth.

Would you look at that? Frickin' gargoyle was right. Make that plural, though—as in multiple bogies. He counted seven rogues, gazes aglow, all focused on the surface of the water. No doubt searching for him. Mac clenched his teeth as he found Ivar, pink eyes shimmering from the back of the pack. The lily-livered asshole. The Razorback leader was hiding behind his soldiers, using the bridge's twisted concrete and the rogue pileup as a living shield.

Typical. And fucking annoying.

No way could he get a clear shot at Ivar through all those bodies.

Mac searched anyway, looking for a hole. Nada. No opening. No chance of nailing the psychotic SOB without jeopardizing his own position. Which left him where? Pretty much screwed. If he hurled his water spear, the Razorbacks would hammer him...all at once. Yeah, he might be deep under a load of cold-wet-and-delicious, but that didn't mean the rogues couldn't blast him out of the water with the combined fury of their exhales.

Frustration lit him up as he mind-spoke, *"I've got a full fighting unit. And no shot."*

Bastian dropped an f-bomb.

"Mac…get the fuck out of there," Rikar said, his firm tone all about being his XO.

"Live to fight another day?"

"Something like that," B said.

With a growl, Mac rotated into a swirling flip. Cold water and ocean current slithered over him, wicking along his spine as he put himself in gear. Bladed tail working overtime, the water spear dissolving in his talon, he rocketed through the water. Leaving Gig Harbor—and Ivar the asshole—in his wake, Mac swallowed the bitter taste of defeat.

He disliked it. Immensely.

Retreat had never been his thing, but he knew his commander was right. He couldn't take out all seven by himself. He needed a boatload of backup, which…shit on a stick… wasn't available right now. The rest of the Nightfuries were a tad busy, playing hopscotch across Seattle with a horde of Razorbacks on their tails.

And him? His mission didn't include getting dead.

Tania needed him. She'd waited long enough, and he couldn't wait another second. Sonar pinging, he tracked her location, picking up the trace energy she left in her wake. The tingle slid around the horns on his head, and he growled, loving her vibe as it lit his senses on fire. God, he wanted to see her face. To make sure she was really all right. To soothe her fear, untwist her temper, and atone for her hurt feelings.

Sounded like an excellent plan. Only one problem with it, though.

Anger was unpredictable, and Tania's was beyond volatile. And he deserved every ounce of her venomous response. Mac only hoped she forgave him when he explained the reasons behind his actions. Otherwise he could kiss his ass—along with his balls—good-bye.

———

Out of breath from yelling threats, Tania paused to refill her lungs. Her chest inflated, renewing her resolve even as her stamina wavered. God, she was tired, aching so much from hammering the barrier that her muscles quivered. And no wonder. Being trapped inside an air bubble was the craziest kind of workout. One of champions, not for the faint of heart or someone who lacked upper body strength.

Frickin'-frack. She really needed to spend more time in the gym. With a tyrannical trainer and a handful of free weights, because her arms were giving out, along with her will to fight.

Muscles throbbing, her hands nothing but twin balls of pain, she swallowed the panic closing her throat. No way would she go there. The place called terror expanding deep inside her could go to hell. She refused to let fear win. Not again. She'd been there, done that earlier (and would have the T-shirt printed later if she survived to see another sunrise).

"Courage, remember?" she whispered to herself. "*Courage.*"

The pep talk didn't do much good. Time was slipping away, making her question her own mind. And the sound of Mac's voice. Had she really heard him talking to her? Had he really told her he was coming for her? That he was within striking distance…somewhere out there…swimming to rescue her from wherever she was in the middle of the godforsaken ocean?

Well, that had been…what? Five minutes ago? Ten?

Tania couldn't tell. Couldn't make her mind work well enough to count off the seconds to keep track of passing minutes. Blood rushing in her ears, she looked around, scanning the darkness outside the globe. Where the heck was he? She didn't think she could take much more without breaking down. Without starting to cry again. Or scream as anger lost its power and the soul-rampaging terror returned.

Tania started to shake, the trembling no longer about the cold. For some reason the bubble exuded warmth now, soothing her bone-deep chill one shiver at a time. And still she shook, physical exhaustion and mental fatigue taking a terrible toll. Combating the next quiver, she hung on, trying to be strong.

Her resolve lasted half a second before she shouted, "Mac!"

"Here."

His voice came out of nowhere, a beautiful, deep baritone full of promise. With a quick inhale, Tania spun on her knees in the center of the bubble, searching the abyss behind her. A glow cut through the darkness, coming at her like twin laser beams. Her breath caught. Shuffling to the other side of her prison, she pressed her injured hands flat against the curved wall. Ravaged by her rampage, her torn nails squawked and her fingertips throbbed. She ignored the agony as hope picked up her heart.

The air bubble's velocity slowed. Water whirled against it with white swirl. Tania swayed with the movement, feeling the bump as she stared into the inky depths, watching, waiting for—

A blue-gray dragon materialized next to her.

With a yelp, she sucked in a sharp breath and jumped backward. She landed with a thump, her behind now aching as much as the rest of her. "M-Mac?"

Aquamarine eyes aglow, he reached out with a huge talon. Tania cringed and scrambled, pressing her back against the opposite wall. But even as she put distance between them, she couldn't look away. Incredible. Weird. Astounding. He was power personified, a freak of nature with his horned head, webbed claws, and knifelike blade riding the ridge of his spine.

She sucked in a quick breath, dismay running hand in hand with fascination. Which was just plain stupid—the fascination part, not the freaked out part—'cause…holy crap. No way should she be looking at him and wondering about all kinds of inappropriate things. Like how he could breathe underwater. Or how he transitioned from a man to, well, *that*.

Tania frowned, her mind sharpening as she looked him over. Good lord. He was enormous, just flipping…*huge*.

Palming her prison with a webbed paw, he grabbed the bubble like a baseball, smooth scales glimmering in the near darkness. The curved points of his claws clinked against the globe. The sound echoed, pinging like silverware against glass. "Hold on, *mo chroí*. I'm gonna bring you up."

Up was good. A dragon talking to her? Not so much. Except…

She wasn't afraid anymore. A surprising reaction. Way off the wall considering all she'd seen tonight, but…God help her. She was so glad to hear Mac's voice, relief shoved fear aside. He'd kept his word and come after her, and, like it or not, that made all the difference. Needing more reassurance, she reached up and pressed her hand into the center of his talon.

Tania blinked. Yes, he was real. She wasn't imagining things. Or him...scales, fangs, and all.

With the thin barrier separating their palms, she rasped, "I want out...please, just get me out."

"Another minute and we'll be on the surface."

She nodded, her gaze riveted to him, taking comfort in the aquamarine of his eyes. Strange, she knew, but the color calmed her. Made her believe it was Mac instead of a stranger. Instead of a monster with every intention of harming her. And as he propelled her upward—swimming through ocean currents, blowing by schools of fish and the rocky side of a jagged reef, bladed tail swishing like an alligator's—Tania wondered when she'd lost her mind.

Somewhere between the bridge and here, certainly.

Proof positive lay in the fact she trusted Mac to keep her safe. To help her instead of hurt her. Crazy talk? No doubt. *Gentle* and *dragons*, after all, weren't normally synonymous. But as the surface of the ocean rippled above them, winking in the glimmer of Mac's gaze, Tania couldn't deny the truth.

Everything had changed in the space of an hour. Imploding her life. Sending her reeling. Catapulting her into the unknown.

One in which dragons existed.

Now she needed to decide which way to jump and where to go from here.

—⁓—

Tania hardly made a sound as he broke the surface of the water with her in his arms. Her shoulder blades bumped the wall of his chest. Mac hugged her from behind, drawing her in, keeping her head above the swelling pitch of ocean waves. Water streamed from her dark hair, smoothing the long strands flat. Gasping, she tilted her face toward the night sky. The long, indrawn breath sounded painful, more wheeze than actual inhale.

She filled her lungs again, shivering so hard Mac heard her teeth chatter. He wrapped her tighter against him, lending her his body heat, and summoned hot water. The warm flow swirled, then washed in, making Tania sigh. As her tremors lessened, satisfaction rolled through him, dragging pride with it.

Holy shit. He'd done it. Gotten the job done and her out in one piece, away from rogue claws and off Ivar's radar. No small feat. The unfortunate causality, however, was Tania. Regret lit Mac up like a war zone. His conscience dropped bomb after bomb until he imploded on a mental minefield.

Ah, who was he kidding? Good job, his ass. He'd scared the hell out her and…

Mac's brows collided. He hated that it had gone down that way. With her stuck in the middle: being driven off a bridge, screaming and crying while he trapped her in an air lock deep underwater, propelled her out to sea, toward safety and away from the fighting.

But no other choice had existed.

The mission was goat-fucked from the word *go*. And Tania? She suffered the consequences, a casualty in the ongoing war with the Razorbacks. Although she'd done well, all things considered. Most people would've curled up and died down there. Yet she'd yelled at him instead, threatening him with…

Well, a shitload of things. Not the least of which was damage to a certain part of his anatomy. Mac cringed, the male in him reacting to the imagery. He liked his package exactly where it was, thank you very much. No need to switch up the arrangement. So, yeah, he wouldn't be reminding her of that particular promise anytime soon. Or…ever.

Another soft swell rolled past, sending them bobbing on the surface. Tania twitched into a full-body quiver. He hugged her closer, using his voice—and a quiet tone—to soothe her. It didn't go well. She was too tense, her lungs locked down, working hard to draw each breath. With a murmur, Mac breathed in her beautiful lily-soft scent, cuddling her with an eye to her comfort, even as his body reacted to her proximity.

Par for the course with Tania around. But that didn't mean he would act on it. She deserved better from him.

A death grip on his urges, Mac shoved his arousal aside. He was stronger than that. The territorial beast inside him might not understand the difference between giving comfort and appeasing sexual need, but he did. No way would he add that insanity to the mental bag of WTF Tania no doubt already carried around.

So he held her instead…and waited. Tapping into her bioenergy, gauging her level of anxiety, he talked her off the ledge, using each murmur to ease her from frightened to calm and even. Little by little, her muscles unlocked, releasing the tight coil of tension, helping her to take deep breaths. Cresting another wave, Mac kept them buoyant, floating together inside the sickle-shaped cove of the small island. His gaze scanned the shoreline, night vision picking up trace along craggy outcroppings and the T-shaped dock jutting into the bay.

His mouth tipped up at the corners. Private. Beautiful. Remote. The island sat fifty-seven nautical miles from Puget Sound's outer marker.

He'd won it fair and square in a poker game from some rich asshole in Boston seven and a half years ago. Perfect timing as it turned out. With his honorable discharge from the navy rubber-stamped, he'd needed somewhere to go…a new place to make a fresh start. The deed to the island had given him the incentive to pull up stakes, head west, and lay claim to the only land he owned.

Home sweet home. One he came to every chance he got.

And now Tania was here…in the spot he loved most in the world. Fitting that she would be the first to visit what he considered his oasis. Not even his partner had rated a look-see. He'd kept Ange in the dark, refusing to invite her in. Which was how he liked it: part of his secretive, isolation-loving MO. No one needed to know where he went every weekend or how he spent his vacation time.

All that would change, though, when he pinged Rikar with his location.

His secret would be out, prompting an invasion in more ways than one. First the Nightfuries would show up. Second? Ange would hammer him with questions and encroach upon the privacy he'd tried so hard to maintain.

Mac sighed. Things changed. Some for the better, some…not so much.

Giving Tania a gentle squeeze, he raised his head from the curve of her neck. She was calmer now, able to breathe without the awful hitch in her throat, but—

She twitched against him.

The rolling shiver wound Mac tight, setting off his internal alarm system. Shit. She should be yelling at him by now. But contrary to his expectations, she hadn't said a word. Not one peep since he'd uncloaked and started dragging her up from the ocean's depths. Which scared the hell out of him. She should be on the rampage, pounding him with accusations along with her fists.

"Tania?" Cupping her shoulder, he turned her to face him. The smell of salt water swirled. He wrapped her up tight again and, his mouth pressed to her temple, asked, "Are you all right?"

Unresisting, she settled into his arms, tucking her head beneath his chin.

"Honey, I'm sorry I scared you. I can explain everything, but Jesus…please talk to me," he said, feeling her bioenergy dip into fatigue. "I need to know if you're hurt."

Still shivering, she drew her arms up. Her hands pushed against his chest. Stuck together, her lashes rose like dark spikes, and he got his first glimpse of her face. Jesus. She was so pale, and her gaze? Unfocused. Full of shock, which… God help him. Made his heart ache.

He cursed under his breath. It was his fault…the look in her eyes, the fear and uncertainty. All of it.

"My hands," she whispered, her hoarse rasp telling him all he needed to know. She'd screamed her throat raw down there. Choking on remorse, Mac massaged the tense muscle bracketing her spine. "I t-think…"

As she trailed off on a hiccup, Mac glanced down. Jesus H. Christ. He needed to get her inside his cabin right now. She required medical attention. Or at least her hands did.

Raw at the tips, her fingers were bleeding, nails torn to shreds.

With a muttered curse, Mac clenched his teeth, hating himself for causing her pain. Now, however, was no time to dwell on his stupidity. "Keep your hands above the water, okay? It'll sting less that way."

When she nodded, Mac hooked one arm under both hers. The Coast Guard lifesaving technique worked like a charm, his shoulder supporting her head as he towed her through the water. Powerful strokes took him across the cove toward the dock. Wispy clouds parted and moonlight glowed, glinting off inky waves, lighting the way toward the pier.

"How're we doing?" he asked, worry biting deep when she started to shiver again.

And no wonder. She was losing heat fast. He'd kept her warm while they floated, but with each hard draw and pull of his arm, cold water washed between them while frigid autumn air rushed over her damp skin exposed above the surface of the water.

Goose bumps broke across the nape of her neck. Mac growled, disliking the sign of her bone-deep chill. Shit on a stick. Next time he'd heat the whole frickin' bay, but...

His brows collided. Next time? Not frickin' likely. There wouldn't be a *next time*. Not if he could help it.

Each one of his strokes fast and true, Mac swam up to the dock edge. He didn't bother with the ladder. With a murmured command, the sea obeyed, bubbling beneath him. On a quick inhale, Tania panicked, squirming in his embrace. He tightened his hold on her and—

Splash!

The water thrust up, launching him skyward, up and out of the inky chill. Holding on tight, he swung Tania against his chest midflight, one arm hooked under her legs, the other supporting her back. She gasped. His bare feet touched down, contacting with the wide planks of the dock. Wood groaned as the pier went topsy-turvy, and the tendrils of water receded, releasing them one wet finger at a time.

The second he was free, Mac put his feet in gear and ran down the pier toward the limestone steps that climbed the steep embankment and led to the cabin overlooking the bay.

Twisting in his arms, Tania's teeth chattered. "I can w-walk."

"I know you can," he said, soothing her pride while refusing to let her go. She was out of luck, and he was out of time. No way could he put her down. Not with his dragon riding shotgun and his protective instincts up and running. "But this way's faster."

More efficient too.

Racing up the staircase, heart pounding, legs pumping like pistons, Mac reached out with his mind. His magic flared, rolling toward the cabin sitting at the top of the rise. Electricity crackled and industrial batteries—fed by the high-tech solar system—powered up. Interior lights came on, along with the LEDs flanking the footpath. He crested the last step. Another thirty seconds and he'd be inside.

Flipping open the double dead bolts with nothing more than a thought, he swung the front door wide. Within seconds, he crossed the threshold into his home, only one thing on his mind. Tania needed his care. And no matter how much she protested, that was exactly what she would get.

Chapter Eleven

Venom wobbled in midair, squad buildings and narrow alleyways blending into indistinct blurs below him. Circling overhead, looking for a safe place to land, he stretched his wings wider, trying to compensate. The north wind didn't cooperate, buffeting him into a downdraft, making him work harder to stay airborne. He bit down on a groan as pain took him for a ride, tearing at the numerous cuts crisscrossing his torso.

Goddamn, that hurt. But worse? The gash bisecting his abdomen.

Venom sucked in an agonizing breath. Trouble didn't begin to describe the situation. He was in crisis country, still bleeding like a sieve. Plasma flowed like rivulets of water, coating his dark green scales from lower belly to knee. Fatigue pulled at him. A sick wave of nausea joined the party, teaming up with the holy hell brigade already pounding on him.

Down. He needed to get his paws on the ground. Right now. Before he lost consciousness and kamikazied into the nearest building.

He had lots to choose from…unfortunately. The human ghetto was full of rundown-and-unlivable, the dilapidated housing units the norm instead of the exception. But worse, at least for him, no one seemed to have gone beddy-bye tonight. The street was way too busy: females working on corners, males milling around with heavy-duty bling displayed over dark hoodies pulling meet and greets, supplying product to customers. Music thumped too, bass pounding from stereo speakers as humans trolled, looking for drug action or asking a female's going rate in the predawn hours.

Frigging hell. Too many witnesses with camera-equipped cell phones. Too many humans to mind-scrub, never mind avoid after he face-planted into the side of a building. Which…God give him strength…was looking more and more plausible with each passing minute.

Another wave of weakness rolled through him. A terrible yearning followed. He wanted to go home to Black Diamond. Craved the safety of the underground lair and the medical facility that sat in the middle of it, instead of this BS. But that wasn't going to happen.

Not now. Or anytime soon, either.

He couldn't fly anymore. His body was failing. The injury he'd sustained too serious to fight anymore. And after roof hopping most of the night to screw with the enemy's head? The twenty-minute flight home through fresh mountain air and pine-scented forests wasn't doable. Not for him.

God. Talk about screwed with a capital *S*.

He'd always been the strongest warrior. Not in the magic department. B and Rikar took top marks for that, but physically he outdid them all. Was the biggest, fastest, the most deadly in a physical fight…in a pack renowned for its prowess. And that was before he tossed his stamina into the ring, in battle, while on covert operations…wherever. The other males in his pack admired him for it, counted on him in tight situations. So the fact his strength—the very thing he prided himself on—had abandoned him?

Not cool. Or even a bit fun.

He growled, grinding upper fangs against lower. The gritting noise sent his head sideways. As his brain ping-ponged, banging around inside his skull, another round of weakness hit. Blinking rapid-fire, Venom watched the flickering red glow of his gaze light up the gloom in front of him. Pain throbbed through his abdomen, dialing him down another notch.

No doubt about it. Time to land.

Throwing a Hail Mary pass in a losing game, he mind-spoke, *"Wick."*

Nothing came back. No answer. No growled response. No f-bomb or the rushing flap of wings.

Venom wasn't surprised. Wick didn't talk much…even to him. And hell, he was the male's best friend. Not that it mattered. He understood Wick. Knew what his friend had suffered and the conditioning that made him the way he was, so it was a no-brainer. His quiet nature and one-syllable responses never bothered Venom. But right now? He wanted to hear Wick's "fuck off, Ven" so badly his head hurt.

He hoped his brother-in-arms was all right. Was on his way back from leading the Razorbacks away. The second Wick had gotten a load of his injuries, the vicious SOB went supersonic, attacking four rogues to protect Venom. A wicked strategy. One that worked like a charm and was not only a testament to Wick's sharp intelligence and quick thinking but the enemies' stupidity. They'd taken the bait and flown after his friend, leaving Venom to escape in the other direction. Now, though, Venom worried his friend was injured.

Why the hell wasn't Wick back yet?

Forcing his sonar to work, Venom sent out a ping, trying to lock onto the magical signal Wick left in his wake. The energy signature was unique to the individual. Each male carried one, Dragonkind's equivalent of fingerprints. When nothing came back, concern lit him up, but...

He was just so damned tired. Too far gone to search via sonar, never mind go after his buddy.

With a reedy exhale, Venom let exhaustion take him and, tucking his wings, dropped through the thin space between rooftops. His paws thumped down. The rough landing made him wince and asphalt crack beneath his talons. Dumpsters jumped, leaving their wheels before coming back down with a clang. Shifting to human form, he used the last of his strength to conjure his clothes. As leathers settled against his chilled skin, Venom hugged one arm around his middle as his strength gave out. His legs buckled, knees connecting with the debris piled in the center of the alley.

The foul smell of garbage rose. He pinged Wick again. The cosmic connection they shared flared. Swallowing the bad taste in his mouth, he rasped, *"Wick."*

A heartbeat, then two throbbed past. Venom hung his head. His friend must be down or dead. Frigging hell. He'd sent his best friend to his death while he'd flown in the other—

"What the fuck?"

Relief grabbed him by the balls. *"I'm down."*

"No shit," Wick growled, the sound of wind coming through mind-speak. *"Where?"*

"Not sure." His brows drawn tight, he glanced around. Squinting at the mouth of the narrow alleyway, he fought to clear his vision. No luck there. His eyes were shot, leaving him unable to focus. *"In an alley. Between—"*

"Got you." A tingle lashed Venom as he sensed Wick connect to his signal. A second later a dark shadow flew overhead. His friend circled right, lining up his approach. *"Hang on."*

"The rogues?"

"Lost 'em."

Good job, Venom wanted to say. He nodded instead, then turned belly-up. As his back touched down on the blacktop, he flattened his hand over his belly, applying pressure to his wound. Blood spilled between his fingers. Oh man, he was so screwed. Deep in Holy-hell-ville and sliding fast. Taking a shallow breath, Venom stared up between buildings, his gaze on the narrow slice of night sky between rooftops. With the storm clouds clearing—thank you very much, Mac…the frigging fledgling was a freak of nature in the waterworks department—the stars came out to play, winking at him from their bed high above the earth. His mind drifted a little.

God, he loved flying. Wanted to feel the rush of air against his scales while he soared. Would he ever get to do that again? Seemed like a good bet to say no. And as anguish tightened its grip, twisting muscle and bone, he wondered if this was it. After eighty-seven years of living, had it all come down to here and now? A slow, agonizing death in a filthy human alleyway?

Calm acceptance drifted through him. Wow. He hadn't expected that, but…well, he was a warrior. Bred for war. Trained to fight. A killer in every sense of the word. The manner of his death—the violence in it—made perfect sense. Stood to reason he'd die in a cold, dark place, not peacefully in his own bed. And as the end came calling, Venom let his eyes drift closed.

The snick of claws sounded beside him. *"Oh no, you don't."*

"Let me go, Wick," he murmured, so tired he didn't care anymore.

"Fuck off. I'm taking you home."

"Not a good idea." Silence met that pronouncement. Venom broke through it by explaining, *"Myst and Angela are there."*

"Shit."

No kidding. A huge understatement.

Especially since the only thing that would save his life now was female energy. And lots of it. A high-energy female would be best, but any human woman would do. He needed to feed to sustain his life force. Was deep in energy-greed—a state all Dragonkind males feared—which meant if he got anywhere near a female now, he'd probably kill her. Drain her dry, take her life to preserve his own.

So you betcha. Going home wasn't a good idea. If he so much as looked at Angela and Myst the wrong way, his commander and XO would make him nothing but a memory. Zip-bang-gone…no discussion, no second chances, just deader than dead.

Venom swallowed past his dry throat. Not a bad way to go, all things considered. Quick and painless, at least.

Wick shifted into human form beside him. Air rushed at him, blowing his long hair off his forehead. Venom cracked his eyelids and turned his head. Gravel and broken glass bit into the back of his scalp as black combat boots came into view. Crouching beside him, he got a load of Wick's shimmering golden eyes.

"Hey," he said, coughing as he greeted his friend.

His gaze calm and steady, Wick reached out to shackle his wrist. The touch pumped heat through Venom, ghosting down his limbs in a soothing swirl. No surprise there. A fire dragon, Wick was a frigging furnace, his temperature always running hot. Applying pressure, his friend lifted his hand to examine the wound.

"Pretty, isn't it?"

A muscle flexed in Wick's jaw. *"Stay here."*

Venom blinked, a slow up and down. He tried to snort. It came out as a raspy exhale. Like he was going anywhere anytime soon?

"I'll get what you need."

Sure. Fine. No problem. Wick would get what he needed.

Venom frowned, trying to remember what that was exactly. He wasn't sure anymore. His brain was fried, mental acuity nothing but an afterthought as he floated on wave after glorious wave of numbness. He sighed. So nice. The absence of pain was so frigging good. All he needed before he ashed out and became nothing but a name etched into the Wall of Warriors deep inside Black Diamond.

A sharp clip-clop noise—almost like the clicking of high heels—invaded that lovely thought.

"Venom." Wick's deep growl sounded next to his ear. *"Open your eyes."*

He didn't want to. He wanted to float some more, to be air instead of muscle and bone.

"Come on, buddy."

The *buddy* prodded Venom's get-up-and-go. Wick never called him anything other than his name, so...

His eyelids flickered then slid open.

Sliding his arm around his shoulder, Wick sat him up. Pain lurched through Venom as his friend said, "Look... brought you a present."

"Hi, baby," a female said, husky voice coming through the mind-fog. A halter top, short skirt, bare midriff showing between the two strips of fabric, wavered into view. Venom's dragon half came to attention, pushing fatigue aside. "Your friend says you're looking for a flyer."

"Or two," a second female said.

A third giggled. "Make that one more."

"Straddle him," Wick said to the first female. Magic snapped in the rain-scented air, joining the smell of rotting garbage. "Get in close."

And well, well, well, would you look at that? Wick's telepathic prowess was out of the bag. A noteworthy occasion. Why? His friend hardly ever used the skill, but...

Hell. No one mind-controlled like his buddy. Most males needed to touch someone to control their minds and, by extension, their actions. Not Wick. True to his lifelong hands-off policy, he could manipulate without touching. The talent was rare among their kind, one none of the Nightfuries took lightly. Pissing off Wick, after all, wasn't smart. That kind of behavior would ensure a warrior woke up good and screwed, with no recollection of how he'd gotten wherever he'd landed.

Par for the course. Wick was just that good. Human. Dragonkind. Plant. Animal. Didn't matter. If the male wanted to mess with your mind, you got manipulated… hang on to your frigging hat.

"Wick, don't let me…" Venom trailed off, his voice so weak he didn't recognize it. But he had to make Wick understand. Energy-greed be damned. Screw his death. He would rather die than kill a female. "Don't let me hurt—"

"No one's gonna die. I got three for you. I'll switch 'em up quick," his friend murmured, reverting to mind-speak, propping him up as the first female slid into his lap. *"Feed, Ven."*

Full breasts brushed his chest. Warm thighs settled on the outsides of his. Under Wick's influence, she cupped the nape of Venom's neck. Small hands playing in his hair, she offered herself to him. An awful hunger rose, clawing at him, and with a groan, Venom dipped his head and set his mouth to her skin, the beautiful hollow of her collarbone.

The Meridian surged, whirling in an electrostatic stream that fed his kind. Energy flickered then flared, lighting her up from the inside out. Venom drank deep, pulling sustenance from her core into his own, and marveled at the irony. The situation was a total switch-up…Wick taking care of him for a change. Making sure he got fed instead of the other way around. But as the female raised his head and kissed him, swirling her tongue against his mouth, Venom left the hows and whys behind and opened for her. She tasted too good. He was so hungry. There would be time and more to unravel the mind-twist later.

Chapter Twelve

Tucking her face against Mac's shoulder, Tania curled her arm around his neck and hung on tight. Cradling her gently, he sprinted toward the cabin door, and she berated herself. She should be struggling to get away, shouting, cursing, or…well, at the very least, complaining. The problem? The pain wouldn't let her. She hurt every time she moved. And her voice? Shot to hell, so barely there her body went into executive decision mode, overriding mental firepower.

Tania huffed. So much for speaking up. Or defending herself.

From what? Him: his scent, his strength, the comfort of his arms around her. And the heat he radiated? God, it was the last nail in her coffin. She needed to get closer. To burrow in and take more. More warmth. More comfort. More closeness. Which was nuts to the next power. Mac was the reason she was here in the first place. In this condition too. But even as logic pointed out all the flaws, her body only cared about one thing.

He was warm. She was cold. He was helping.

End of story.

With a shiver, she called herself a fool—promised to yell at him later—but curled closer anyway. Just a little longer. She would push him away in a minute or two. After she warmed up. After he let her go. After her brain started to work again. But in the meantime? She'd take what he offered and hope more heat came her way.

Her face pressed to the side of his throat, she burrowed in, borrowing what she needed, drawing strength and more from him. A pleasant prickle ghosted through her. Hmm, that felt good, as though he shared something other than his heat with her. Alluring and powerful, the strange current flowed, drawing her along in its wake. With a sigh, Tania relaxed into the sensation, taking more when Mac murmured against the top of her head. The soft welcome tugged at her. His arms tightened around her, rushing the tingle along her skin, tugging at her tension until sleep called her name.

Tania let her eyes drift closed.

Bad idea. She knew it the moment her head lolled on his shoulder. Falling asleep in Mac's arms wasn't a part of the plan. Or at least shouldn't be, not after the hocus-pocus she'd seen tonight. But as the alluring tug and pull of sensation grew stronger, its familiarity struck her. She'd experienced the feeling before…somewhere, with some-one. Mac maybe? Tania frowned, trying to remember. No luck there. The heated draw intensified, messing with her head, cascading around her until she couldn't tell where she ended and he began.

Home. He felt like home…like warm comfort on a cold afternoon and—

Whoa. Time out. That was the wrong thought, ah… wasn't it? Probably. Too bad she couldn't get her body to agree with her. Her muscles kept ignoring direct orders, refusing to move, so...yup, cross fighting off as a viable option. It wasn't going to happen. Her strength—along with her priorities—were headed south into total compliance. A dangerous place to be with a guy she'd seen transform into a monster less than an hour ago.

"Mac...d-don't."

Something clicked and got bumped aside. "Shh, honey. Hang on. Almost there."

Tania frowned. *Almost where?* Good question. One she should've asked the second she'd surfaced with him in the middle of the bay. Knowing where, after all, was almost as important as knowing *what*. As in, what he intended to do to her?

Fighting the backward slide into oblivion, she cracked her eyelids. Bright light nailed her, tunneling through to the back of her brain. She flinched. Mac cursed and, with a whispered "sorry," flipped the lights off. Brushing the wet hair away from her face, he set her down on something solid. A table? A countertop? Seemed safe to say yes when her legs dangled, soggy boot heels banging into solid panels. The rush of water sounded, as though someone had just cranked on a shower. Tania blinked, seeing nothing but black spots. After a second or two, her vision cleared and—

She got a quick snapshot of Mac. Arm and shoulder muscles flexing, he bent and cupped her heel in his big hand. Her brows drawn tight, she stared at the opposite wall. Painted bright white, tongue-and-groove wainscoting gleamed in the low light. Mac tugged off one of her riding boots. As he dropped her footwear to the floor and attacked the other, Tania glanced at the claw-footed bathtub to her right. Long and deep, the thing qualified as a super-soaker, the modern-day version of an old-time design.

Her second boot hit the tiled floor.

She switched her attention to the oversize shower over Mac's shoulder. Enclosed by clear glass, gorgeous blue stone covered the back wall. Steam frothed and water droplets formed, streaking marble tile as the rainfall showerhead and body jets did double time, spraying out gentle arcs. All without Mac touching them, which honestly freaked her out more than just a little bit.

The hocus-pocus tightened her mental screws. Thank God. The rag doll routine wasn't doing her any good. Or helping her to ask the right questions, like, oh say…how Mac had gone from horned head and blue-gray scales to, well, *that*. Six and a half feet of ripped Irish American with an incredible tattoo. One she didn't remember seeing that night in the loft when they'd…

She frowned, questioning the memory. It flared anyway, defying reason, playing out each moment, shocking her with the details. Her cheeks warmed to a full blush. Dear God, she'd been out of control, so demanding and—

More heated images flashed in her mind's eye. Of her flat on her back while he…and oh boy. She squirmed on the countertop, forcing herself to reverse course fast. Only an idiot would go there. Thinking of that night—and Mac's part in it—wasn't a good idea. Particularly with him a heartbeat away, wearing nothing but skin and a pair of swim trunks.

Which reminded her. The tattoo.

No way he'd been inked when she'd…ahem…*collided* with him at Myst's place. She would've remembered. It wasn't something a girl forgot. Drawn with skill and care, the precise lines covered nearly half of his torso, then arched up to trail over one wide shoulder before continuing on to curve around his bicep. And the ink? Navy blue with a…Tania leaned in to get a better look. Yes, it was definitely shimmering. Not a lot, but enough for her to notice. Fascinating. Beautiful. Beyond strange.

"Hey, Mac?" Tania grimaced. Good lord, she sounded like a chain-smoker, one of those three-pack-a-day-ers in the vocal arena.

Crouched in front of her, Mac's head came up. His gaze on hers, he pushed to his feet and tossed her soggy boots into the tub. "Arms up."

She blinked. Arms…what?

"Up," he said, as though he heard the question without her voicing it.

Fisting his hands at the bottom of her sweater, he pulled. Her eyes widened. The wool gave, sliding up her body, carrying her arms toward the ceiling. She squawked in protest, but it was too late. With one last tug, the wet mess joined her boots in the tub, leaving her sitting in nothing but a lacy bra and skintight jeans.

"Hey!" She crossed her wounded hands over her chest. Blood oozed from a cut on her knuckle, rolling along the back of her hand. Tania ignored it, more interested in her modesty than her injuries. "What do you think you're—"

"Lift your bottom for me."

"No." Like she wanted to be bare-assed in front of him? Again!

Well, all right, so technically she wouldn't be naked. But as lovely as it was, the lingerie wasn't great cover in the assets department.

Good lord, why had she slipped on La Cirque today? Dumb question. She always wore her expensive stuff on important days: a big meeting at work, a difficult presentation to a client, visiting J.J. at the correctional facility. The fancy underwear gave her a boost. Made her feel prettier, more confident, able to handle the challenges life threw her way. Call it a quirk of character. Call it self-confidence in silk and lace. But whatever you called it, modest wasn't one of them.

And this set? One of her sexier numbers, pale pink silk trimmed out in black lace and bows. Oh so not for mass consumption. Or Mac. So…no. She wouldn't be *lifting* anything for him. Not now. Or any other time, either.

When Mac didn't argue, Tania exhaled in relief. The consolation lasted less than a second. Without looking at her, he leaned to one side and pulled a drawer open. Palming something, he pocketed it, straightened, then slid his hands beneath her butt and scooped her off the countertop. Which naturally sent her into Squawksville, but didn't affect him at all, because—

Holy jeez, he never broke stride.

Ignoring her struggles, carrying her in his arms, he walked into the shower. As the glass door closed behind them, water washed over her in a warm spray. Tania sighed. She couldn't help it. The warmth felt so darned good, rushing along her skin, streaming over her hair and down her back, chasing the last of her chill away. Giving up the fight, she tipped her chin up, closed her eyes, and leaned back against Mac.

Her shoulder blades bumped his chest. The smell of the ocean hanging in the air, the salt rinsed away, bringing relief to her battered skin. Relaxation took hold, releasing the tension along her spine. Encouraging her to settle against him, Mac's arms came around her from behind. A sharp snap. A quick tug and her jeans slid to the tops of her thighs. Tania tensed, but…nope. No good. He was too fast. Within seconds the denim was off, nothing but a dark pile in the corner of the stall.

She sucked in a startled breath.

"Easy." Pushing to his feet, he wrapped his arms around her. Her shoulder blades bumping his chest, he cupped one of her hands. She shivered, but not from the cold. God, he was so close. And she was so undressed. "I'm here to help, nothing more. Now let's look after your hands, okay?"

Surrounded by him, not knowing what to say, she nodded. A nail clipper made an appearance in his other hand. She shied, fighting his hold. Oh God, this was going to hurt. Her nails were so badly torn, the skin beneath them bruised and cut. And right now? She couldn't handle another round of pain.

She tugged to loosen his grip. When he held firm, imprisoning her hand with his much larger one, she said, "Don't."

"It needs to be done," he murmured, his mouth next to her ear. Warm water rolling over her, Mac's heat against her back, she went cold all over again. He gave her a reassuring squeeze. "I'll be gentle. It'll be over before you know it."

Her throat tight with dread, she shook her head.

"Trust me, *mo chroí*."

The deep timbre of his voice strummed through her. God, that was nice: the vibration, the sense of connection she felt with him, the endearment. *Mo chroí*. She liked the sound of it, giving the pet name more meaning than it deserved. But for some reason, she didn't care and couldn't fight it. Despite the craziness of the situation and all the dragon crap, it made her feel better to believe he cared for her. That she might be important to him somehow.

Tania blinked away tears. Oh, snap. Wasn't that a beautiful piece of fiction? Special. What girl didn't want to feel *special*? To be treated as precious and important. To be needed and cherished. To be front and center in her man's world. She swallowed the lump lodged in her throat. Heaven help her. She was a walking, talking cliché, one of those needy women who yearned for more than mere acceptance.

And as Mac clipped the first of her broken nails and she tried not to flinch, Tania wondered at herself. And when she'd become so incredibly weak-willed. Independence was a staple in her life. Like food and water, she needed it to survive. Depending on Mac to look after her wouldn't do. Was so dangerous on so many levels, and it scared her. Autonomy—the ability to take care of herself—was the only thing she'd ever truly owned. Her mother had never possessed it. Her sister didn't, either. She was the first in her family to go to school, to have a successful career, to make a life outside of poverty for herself.

No way should she be standing still while he cared for her. Giving it up without a fight. Or bowing to the will of a gorgeous man with a gentle touch and concern in his eyes.

As if attuned to her thoughts, Mac murmured, "Tania, honey. Everything is going to be all right. We'll figure it out. Get you what you need."

A lie. Boldly told and beautifully delivered.

Tania knew it the moment the words left his mouth. He could pretend all he wanted, but the dum-dum gene wasn't a prominent one in her family tree. She wasn't into lying to herself…and recognized the truth when she saw it. She was trapped in a cabin with a guy who could turn into a dragon. Nothing was going to be *all right*. It wasn't now and wouldn't be for a while.

———

Finished stacking logs in the fireplace, Mac clicked the lighter and set flame to paper. Fire curled, blackening the edges of year-old newspaper as the orange glow ate inward. A wave of heat pushed into the room, caressing his forearms and face, forcing the chill to recede. Tendrils of smoke rose, carrying the scent and sound of burning balsam into the damp air. Held by the hypnotic ripple, he stared at the flames, watching them leap upward toward the chimney flue, then pushed to his feet.

Check off job one. Now for task two.

One ear on the still-running shower and Tania, bare feet whispering across the wooden floor, Mac left the fire to its own devices and headed for the kitchen. He didn't have far to go, just a hop, skip, and a jump away across the living room. The open plan suited him to a T, the great room living large with timber-beam ceilings, rustic wood floors, and a shitload of new furniture. His favorite part, though, was the antique dining table. Long and wide, the thing fit the space behind the sofa to perfection, looking good framed by a wall of shutter-clad windows. Ironic in a way considering he never sat at the eight-seater. No need. He always ass-planted himself at the kitchen island when he came home, so…

Yeah. Not much use for the thing.

Walking past the stools sitting beneath the countertop's butcher-block overhang, he skirted the end of the kitchen peninsula and headed for the fridge. Not that there was anything in it. No fresh veggies or fruit, but true to his military roots, he always kept more on hand than he needed. Storms whipped up fast and died down slow around the island, and only a fool took Mother Nature for granted. So, yeah. Thanks to his solar panels, his freezer not only worked while he was away but was also well stocked. And his cupboards? Full of canned goods waiting to be used.

"No time like the present," he murmured, all his senses tuned to the activity in the bathroom.

The rush of water told him all he needed to know. He had time. Tania was still in the shower.

His lips twitched. Jesus, she was adorable, hiding in there, avoiding the inevitable while she struggled to pull herself together. He understood her desire for control, so no problem. Tania could take all the time she needed. Could pucker into a prune in there if she wanted. The limitations of his system didn't matter. His magic was up and running, feeding the warm water into the system to keep her well supplied.

And he refused to rush her. It wouldn't get him anywhere but frustrated. She needed to come to terms with her new reality. Dragons…in her tidy little world, a mindfuck of epic proportions. He should know. After a lifetime spent believing he was 100 percent human, he'd almost lost it when he woke up in dragon form the first time. So the whole lose your mind and freak out thing? Mac got it, was completely on board with her holy shit reaction.

What he didn't like was her silence.

Frowning, Mac grabbed the freezer handle and pulled. The door opened with a hiss. He stared at the load of food inside, seeing the assortment but not really. He was an idiot. Pure. Simple. No denying the veracity of the claim. He'd scared the hell out of her underwater, then been forced to hurt her again with a pair of frickin' nail clippers. His chest tight, he replayed her reaction: each flinch, every gasp, all the heart-wrenching whimpers. He hadn't wanted to do it, but her hands...both were...

Jesus fucking Christ. So much for the brilliance of his air lock idea. And keeping her safe. He'd done more damage than good and—

No. That wasn't true. Had Ivar gotten hold of her, things would be worse. For her. For him too. She'd be a prisoner at chez Razorback, being brutalized by bastards who considered rape a contact sport. The mere thought—the singular possibility—that Tania might be hurt that way put him into a tailspin. History wouldn't repeat itself. Not with Tania. Not ever or to any other woman if he could help it.

Angela's abduction and brutal treatment at the rogues' hands had been bad enough. His partner had come through with Rikar's help, but Mac knew she still struggled with what had happened. Having your will usurped, pride taken, and power rendered impotent—especially for a woman as strong as Ange—was no picnic. Healing took time. Rikar would help her with that, had already softened the impact of the emotional fallout, and yet Mac worried about her. Watched her closely. Waited for signs she needed him to step in and support her in the aftermath.

A big brother's prerogative, he guessed. But even as he watched and waited for Ange to fall apart, a larger part of him had already shifted focus. Now he fixated on Tania, refusing to allow the same to happen to her. He'd vowed to protect her. And he would, even if that meant protecting her from himself, but...

Shit. It had almost killed him to walk away. To leave her alone in the shower after clipping her nails and using his body to warm hers. Hmm, that had felt good. To care for her. To provide what she needed the moment she required it. Okay, so it had been hell too...being that close to her without touching while she wore nothing but racy underwear.

His heart thumped harder, hammering the inside of his chest. God, what a picture she made. Dark hair flowing, her head tipped back under a steady stream of warm water. Beautiful curves on display under pink satin and black lace. So relaxed in his arms, she turned into him instead of away, soaking up the heat, accepting his nearness, letting him wash her tension away.

Grabbing a bag of tortellini, Mac slammed the freezer closed and tossed the load onto the countertop. The frozen pasta landed with a bang and slid, plastic laying down a crinkle-crinkle-zzzz sound track as Mac flipped a cabinet door open. With a quick hand, he snagged a bottle of Ragu's finest and popped the sealed top. Tomato and the sweet scent of basil drifted. Usually the aroma was one of his favorites. Not tonight. He barely smelled the stuff. His focus was trained elsewhere...on a brainy brunette with burgundy-flecked eyes and a body to die for.

With a groan, Mac shifted, trying to ease the pressure behind his button-fly. It was a no go. He got aroused just thinking about her. Add one thought to another and—

Kaboom! Need and his libido went into orbit.

Mac swallowed. Shit on a stick. He was in so much trouble.

Rooting through the bottom cupboard, he found the right pot and set it on the front burner. Not that he needed the stove anymore. With a mental flick, he conjured water out of thin air. As the wet-and-wild hit the bottom of the pot, he brought the whole mess to a boil, ripped the bag open, and dumped the pasta in. Giving the contents a stir with nothing more than a thought, he leaned back against the edge of the countertop and stared across the cabin at the bathroom door. Jesus, he wanted to go back in there. She was probably naked by now, the lacy panties kicked into the corner of the shower stall while her bra hung over the—

"Stop thinking about it."

Sound advice, if somewhat problematic. His dragon was out in full force, telling him to claim what his territorial side believed belonged to him. *Belonged to him.* Curling his hands into fists, Mac rocked back on his perch. Holy shit. Arrogant much? He clenched his teeth as possessiveness clawed at him, urging him to wrap Tania up and lay her down. He wanted his scent on her, hers all over him, to please her so well she surrendered and then begged for more.

Just like she had the first time he'd made love to her.

Ah, fuck. Watch out. The threat level had officially been raised. Now he existed inside the red zone, struggling to keep a leash on needs that Tania wasn't ready to satisfy. 'Cause, yeah. Regardless of her compliance earlier, Mac didn't expect it to last. She was too smart—too strong, too stubborn—to accept without knowing everything, and once the shock wore off, she'd come at him with both barrels. Guns blazing, Wild Wild West style.

And honestly? He couldn't wait for it to happen.

He disliked the blank look she'd worn when he'd left her. Even though he understood it, her reaction worried him. Fear had no place between them. He wanted her back to her normal sassy self, to be hammered by questions and her anger. The quicker they got over that hump, the faster they could move on to the important stuff, like maybe...

Explaining the truth of his kind and the difference between good dragons and bad; about the war that raged between Nightfury and rogue; and that she was no longer safe in the human world.

Not with Ivar sniffing around.

The Razorback leader wouldn't quit. The bastard had targeted Tania for a reason. The *why* wasn't difficult to piece together. Hurt Tania, hurt Myst, and, by extension, the Nightfury commander. The strategy was poetry in motion, psychological warfare with flare. Myst would crumble if her best friend became entangled in the enemies' web. And Bastian? Shit, the male would disappear down the I-can't-stand-to-see-my-mate-suffer rabbit hole, then ramp into psycho mode. All to lessen her pain.

Not exactly a good place for the Nightfury commander to land. Bad tactical decisions always got made when a guy stuck his head up his ass. If that happened and B lost it, the fallout wouldn't be pretty. More than rogue soldiers would die. His brothers-in-arms would give their lives to protect Bastian. So no matter how much he hated frightening Tania, the air lock had done its job...been a necessary play to keep her away from the fighting and out of Razorback claws. Not only to preserve his own sanity but ensure the safety of the entire Nightfury pack.

His only hope now was that she'd forgive him.

A tall order? Probably. More than he deserved? Certainly. But even as logic said no-way-in-hell, Mac prayed she'd give him a second chance. Which in turn made him wonder what the hell was wrong with him. Somewhere along the way, a switch had flipped inside his head. Now he was off course, miles away from his usual self, not to mention his typical MO.

He was the independent one, for fuck's sake. The guy who thrived on the uncomplicated and a clear playing field. Angela accused him of being a commitment-phobe. Maybe he was...or at least had been until Tania tipped his radar in the wrong direction. Now all he could think about was her, and he didn't like it.

He enjoyed his lifestyle. The women he slept with did too, never complained about the one-nighters. Like him, they were one part free and easy, the other part escape hatch. Tania, though, wasn't his typical fare. She wasn't a no-strings-attached kind of girl...would expect kisses and cuddling in the aftermath. Mac knew it like he was standing there, bare feet planted in the middle of his kitchen, gaze glued to the bathroom door, ears attuned to her movements and the quiet rush of water.

With a sigh, Mac shook his head. Every instinct he possessed told him not to do it...to hand her over, make her Rikar's responsibility, then walk the hell away. But that wasn't going to happen. Not with his dragon fixated and the rest of him riveted on her. No way could he let her go. At least not without a fight. So screw talking himself out of it or denying what he felt for her. The bond they shared was simply too strong. Reason need not apply. Intellect could take a hike, 'cause now that she stood a mere room's width away? Need tugged on his chain, the steady stream of connection amplifying, winding him up just to watch him go.

Zip. Bang. Gone.

He was toast in the same way Bastian and Rikar were for their females. But unlike his comrades, Mac knew he wouldn't find relief anytime soon.

Rescuing the tortellini, Mac dumped the pasta into a strainer. As he grabbed a big bowl off an open shelf, the shower clicked off. Water slowed to a trickle. The glass door opened, then swung shut. He closed his eyes, keen senses picking up each minute sound, listening to the sound of Tania's feet touch down on the bath mat. His mouth curved. He loved everything about his new abilities, but more than anything? The capacity to perceive what should be imperceptible.

Case in point? Tania was now drying off with the towel he'd taken out for her. Soon she would surround herself in his scent—become more his—and slip into his clothes. The sweats he'd left on the vanity for her. He couldn't wait to see her in them. Strange, he knew, but providing for her nourished him somehow: having her wear his clothing, sleep in his bed, eat the food he'd prepared for her...man, he couldn't get enough of it.

Drawing a deep breath, he heated the jar of sauce with a whispered command. After pocketing two sets of utensils, he prepared two bowls and beat feet for the dining room. Tania would be out any second now and—

Hinges creaked. The bathroom door swung open.

Mac slid the meal onto the tabletop and glanced toward her. As his gaze got stuck on her, his heart fisted up tight. God, she looked good enough to eat, so adorable with his wide-legged pants pooling around her small feet and the oversize sweatshirt hanging off one shoulder, exposing smooth skin. He knew firsthand how soft she was…fit yet curvy, his favorite kind of female. The urge to close the distance between them hit him chest level. He wanted to touch her again. To take down her messy updo and run his fingers through her damp hair while he tasted her deep, tangled their tongues…made her crave him as much as he did her.

Grabbing on to the back of a chair, he clamped down on the need to move toward her. Proximity wouldn't help things. What he needed was a distraction. He scanned her face and found what he needed. She was still too pale. Less freaked out, sure, but still shell-shocked. An apt description. Particularly since her life had just imploded. And he was about to drop a few more bombs.

Compassion poured through him. The problem? Feeling sorry for her—about the shitty circumstances—wouldn't change a thing. The best he could do now was help her understand.

Holding her gaze, he murmured, "Hey."

"Hi," she whispered back, cradling her sore hands in front of her.

"You find everything you need in there?" When she nodded, he set the knife, fork, and spoon combo down next to each bowl, then pivoted and leaned back against the lip of the table. He kept his body relaxed and his posture unthreatening. The last thing he wanted was to frighten her. Or push too hard before she was ready. "You need anything else?"

"I don't know," she said, a rasp in her voice. "A lobotomy?"

His respect for her moved up a rung. Good for her. She was a drive-straight-to-the-basket kind of girl, direct and to the point. His kind of woman. "Don't think you need one. Prozac might be the better bet."

She huffed, the beginnings of a smile lighting her face. It lasted a second before she sobered. A furrow between her brows, she glanced away. Mac mourned the loss of her dark gaze and, heart aching for her, watched her curl her arms in front of her. The action was telling, a form of self-protection, a way to put up psychological barriers and shore up her defenses. He'd seen the same body language on countless victims—or as Angela liked to call them, survivors—as a homicide cop and...

He couldn't stand it. Hated that she felt compelled to put distance between them even as he understood her need to do so.

"Honey, listen to me." She flinched at the sound of his voice. He curled his hands around the table edge to keep from reaching for her. "I—"

"Your eyes are shimmering."

He blinked, hesitated a second, then said, "They do that sometimes."

"Are you going to turn into a dragon?"

"Only if you want me to."

Her head snapped back in his direction. "Don't be a jerk."

The warning gave him direction. Message received... no making light of the situation or teasing allowed. With a nod, Mac backed down. She wanted him to respect her boundaries. No problem. He could do that.

"You're safe with me, Tania. Despite what you saw tonight, I would sooner die than hurt you," he said, hoping to reassure her. She blinked rapid-fire, as though fighting tears, but didn't answer. He shifted course, traveling another route. "It's going to be all right, you know."

"How?" Her bioenergy flared, broadcasting her upset.

Her emotional response made him flinch. Anger and feminine outrage...the perfect storm. A lethal combo that packed serious punch.

Mac almost smiled, an "atta girl" poised on the tip of his tongue. He bit down on the response. She wouldn't appreciate it...wouldn't understand that his reaction was born of relief, not amusement. But as she glared at him, the urge to grin like an idiot poked him. Man, she was something, so fierce she made him proud. Even upended by circumstance and flattened by fear she gave as good as she got. Which was why he kept his mouth shut and waited for her to fill the void. Tania needed to vent: to let go of the fear, lay every card on the table and the blame at his feet. No way would he interrupt her before she got her groove on and lambasted him.

Pissed off and talking. That's how he wanted her.

"Please tell me, Mac...how?" Her eyes narrowed a fraction. "I mean, really, fill me in, 'cause...holy jeez, I was nearly killed by a whole contingent of frackin'-frackin' dragons!" Temper unraveling at the speed of light, she took a step toward him, a belligerent look on her face. Forgetting about her sore fingers, she pointed at him, then winced and shook out her hand. "And you! You're one of them. So, yeah. Sure. You go ahead and tell me. How the *hell* is it going to be all right?!"

"I'll keep you safe."

"You'll keep me...you'll..." She trailed off. A muscle flickered along her jaw. "You drove me off a flipping bridge. Wrecked my car...my beautiful girl...then buried me alive underwater. In a goddamn air bubble!"

Well, when she put it that way…

He cringed. Hero of the year wasn't a title he would be awarded anytime soon.

"I'm sorry," he said and meant it. "I didn't mean to scare you, but—"

"Oh. My. God!" Tania looked around, her gaze searching. She skimmed over the fireplace, then moved on to the living room before reaching the kitchen. "Do you have a gun here? I'm going to shoot you. I swear on my life, I am *so* pulling the trigger!"

Okay. This was good, if a little counterproductive.

Mac didn't mind. Despite the threat level, he was making progress. The more she yelled at him, the better she'd feel. And after she wound down? He'd get his chance to explain the how, what, and why of the situation. Good for him. Better for Tania. She needed to understand and accept the challenges of her new reality. Chief among them? The fact she wouldn't survive long without his protection. Not in a world where dragons ruled and high-energy females—like her—were targets for Razorback assholes.

Crossing his arms over his chest, Mac settled in to wait her out. More animated now, her mouth working overtime, she paced the length of the cabin. Round and round she went, bare feet pitter-pattering against the floorboards, tendrils of dark hair escaping her topknot to curl over her shoulders. His mouth curved as he listened to her rant. Sweeping around the end of the sofa, she hurled another insult his way, then marched past the fireplace. The flames reacted to the breeze-by, and sparks snapped as Tania called him a boneheaded doofus-face. Crackbrained whack-job came next, adding to the already colorful litany of name-calling.

All without swearing. Not once.

Pretty impressive, actually. Had the situation been reversed, he'd have dropped the f-bomb at least twenty times by now. Mac swallowed his amusement. Jesus, her creativity floored him, making admiration grow even as she scorched him with her temper. A spitfire, she was a hot burn with incendiary flare. Arousing as hell too, and…

Oh shit. That was absolutely the *wrong* thought. Mac drew in a calming breath, then let it out, forcing his brain into work mode. Strategy A wasn't working. Time to deploy plan B before he hopped back on the desire train.

For the umpteenth frickin' time.

One eye on Tania, he rolled his shoulders, tracking her progress around the end of the table. Close. She was so very close now. Barely an arm's length away, a piece of cake to stop her midstride. But reaching out would mean touching her. Not exactly the best strategy considering the level of I-want-her banging around inside his head at the moment.

She turned the last corner. Now or never. If he didn't stop her in the next three seconds, she'd put the hammer down and roar into another circuit around the room and—

With a fast pivot, Mac left his perch and planted his foot on a chair. Timing it to perfection, he pushed. The armchair slid, bumping across wood to shoot out in front of Tania. Quick reflexes helped her hop sideways, avoiding the collision. The pissed-off gasp stopped her tirade midstream. Mouth hanging open, she gave him an incredulous look before she sucked in a breath and—

"Sit down," he said, cutting her off before she came up with another inventive name to call him.

Pearly white teeth clicked together as she snapped her mouth closed. Pursing her lips, a mutinous expression on her face, Tania crossed her arms over her chest.

"It's getting cold," he said, lying through his teeth. The pasta couldn't get cold, not with him around. His ability to manipulate anything with water in it ensured the sauce stayed as hot as when he'd slid the meal onto the table. "Come on, *mo chroí*. Have mercy. I'm famished, and you can be just as pissed off sitting down as standing up."

"I'm not hungry."

"Yes, you are."

A standoff. One he won a moment later when her stomach growled.

"Oh, for heaven's sake," she said, disgust in her voice. "Just my luck. Foiled by flipping tortellini."

Mac laughed, adoring her poise under pressure. A scowl on her face, she pressed up on tiptoe to peer inside one of the bowls. He nudged the dish nearest her, hoping to tempt her. "Smells good, doesn't it?"

She grumbled something under her breath—probably another choice name for him—then bumped the chair with her thigh. With more determination than skill, she shoved it toward the table to avoid touching it with her sore hands. Unwilling to see her struggle, he skirted the table edge and cupped the backrest. Heat flared in her cheeks. He played the gentleman despite her chagrin: waiting for her to sit, scooting her chair in, leaning around her to straighten her utensils. As she murmured "thank you," he caught the fresh, heated scent of her. Like an addict, he dipped his head and breathed her in, wanting more.

Hmm, she was lovely.

And he should turn away. Right frickin' now. Take his seat and give her space while he gave himself a fighting chance to resist her. Instead, like a dummy, he opened his big mouth and said, "You smell like water lilies."

Shifting in the chair, she glanced over her shoulder. Her gaze met his, and the muscles roping his abdomen clenched. Still miffed, she muttered, "I smell like you."

Not really. Her natural perfume broke through, trumping his brand of body wash. "My soap."

On her. All over her, in places he dreamed about touching again. Heat coiled through him as he relived the sight of her in his shower.

Blushing brighter, she whispered, "Your shampoo too."

Unable to resist, Mac braced his palms on the arms of her chair and leaned in, surrounding her without touching. His mouth brushed her hair, and he breathed deep again, filling his lungs with her sweetness. Oh Jesus. He needed to stop…right now. Before he embarrassed himself.

"Tania?"

"What?"

"Do you need help?" Unlocking his muscles, he shifted out from behind her and headed for his own seat. Distance was good…really, really good. The farther he got from her, the better. "If your hands are too sore, I could feed you."

"You try, and I'll stab you with my fork."

Surprise made him blink. The threat made him smile.

Arching both brows, she reached for the utensil. "You don't think I will?"

"No."

Her eyes narrowed another notch.

Holding his hands palm up, he retreated, settling in the chair adjacent to hers, his grin widening by the second. "It was a good bluff, though."

Fiddling with her fork, she sighed. "I was never any good at poker."

Unfortunately for her, he was. A real student of the game, he was considered a master player in most circles. But the ability to bluff was the least of it. Patience had a hand in every round he played. Which...ding-ding-ding...was the reason Tania sat with him now, talking instead of yelling.

"I'll teach you." The *a lot of things* went unsaid. Just as well. Sex wasn't on the menu. At least not yet. Maybe not for a while, either.

A bite of pasta halfway to her mouth, she threw him a startled look. "How to play poker?"

Mac nodded, his attention riveted on her lips. He watched her chew for a moment, then glanced down at her hand, searching for safer ground. Her mouth was too frickin' tempting and...huh. A lefty. He would never have guessed that about her. Whether using her right or left, she handled herself well. Attacking his own food, he studied her a little more closely, observing her facility with the utensil, making sure she wasn't in any pain, absorbing every nuance. Yup. Definitely left-handed. Was she ambidextrous or something?

She speared another bite, twirling the fork above her bowl. "After we eat?"

He glanced at the round-faced clock hanging on the wall behind her. Three a.m. The equivalent of midday for him, but smack-dab in the middle of REM time for her. He returned his focus to Tania. Opening his senses wide, he tapped into her bioenergy, mining the bond he shared with her to gauge her fatigue level.

He frowned. "You should get some sleep."

"I'm not tired."

A lie, but Mac let it go. No sense arguing, but as she nibbled on her bottom lip, the urge to do something else—like taste her again—slammed through him. Leveling her chin, she met his gaze. Desire and need joined forces, hitting him like jet fuel, threatening to send him into orbit. With a death grip on his fork, he clamped down on the reaction.

"And Mac?" Soft inquiry. Big impact. Her tone was full of warning.

He swallowed. "Yeah."

"I have a ton of questions."

And there it was, the opening he'd been waiting for...an invitation to talk. And as her beauty spun into brainy, pride for her fortitude wound him a notch tighter. And what do you know? That aroused him too. Then again, everything she did made the male in him stand up and take notice. Shit, she could suit up in a clown costume and still turn him on. But no matter how much he enjoyed looking at her, Mac admitted her mind intrigued him more.

Gorgeous and smart.

It was a wicked combination. Lethal in more ways than one. And as she turned intelligent brown eyes on him, he prayed his Nightfury brothers showed up sooner rather than later...before base instinct shoved reason aside, took over, and made him do something stupid. Like strip her bare. Make her beg while he loved her hard.

Which wasn't even close to advisable.

Chapter Thirteen

Wings spread in flight, red scales flashing beneath the storm glow, Ivar swept over the Seattle shoreline, scanning left then right. Nothing. No sign of the Nightfury yet. Like the freak of nature he was, the male had gone deep underwater, though how the hell he breathed down there was a mystery. A real knock-down-drag-out in the mental sphere, and while he chewed on the puzzle, Ivar kept searching. Sooner or later the asshole would poke his head up. No one, after all, could refute Newton's law. Although in this instance, it was the opposite...a case of what went down must come up.

Somewhere. Someplace. Sometime.

And when that happened? Ivar would be there...waiting to blow the bastard sky-high. Or rip his head off. Either option would do.

He only hoped the opportunity landed in his lap faster than fast. Dawn approached and with it the deadly UV rays his kind couldn't tolerate. Which begged a question. Could the water rat survive a full day at the bottom of Puget Sound? Store enough O_2 in his freak-ass lungs to hold out until another night fell? The water was certainly deep enough. Would act like a natural barrier of sorts and—

Ivar snorted. He hoped not. Sunblock, dragon-style, wasn't what he needed right now. But the female? Oh baby, she was the ticket. The real deal, so high-energy just thinking about her made him salivate.

Hmm...Tania Solares. Yummy, yummy female.

He'd gotten a glimpse of her on the bridge in Gig Harbor. Her sojourn on TV had been a sampling, nothing compared to seeing her in the flesh. An incomparable specimen, her connection to the Meridian rivaled Bastian's female. Power personified, she was beauty electric. Hunger curled through Ivar. He wanted a taste of her, of the blinding heat that hummed in her blue-green aura. Proof positive she'd be not only an unforgettable fuck but a perfect candidate for cellblock A.

And his breeding program.

Five females had been imprisoned there so far. He wanted seven, and the number six would look good hanging around Tania Solares's neck. But only if he could find the pain-in-the-ass Nightfury and retrieve her.

He told himself it was for Lothair. For revenge and justice. To assuage his desire to get even. But now? After seeing her himself? His plans had changed. He wouldn't be using her to bait the trap that would bring Bastian running. He'd be tying her to his bed and making her his personal slave.

Banking left, he headed farther out to sea and swept over Puget Sound. The city sparkled jewellike in the distance as thunder boomed overhead. He ignored the warning. Didn't care that lightning forked through heavy clouds, threatening to down him with the electrical equivalent of a boot to the ass. His focus was absolute.

Pissant water rat.

Eyes narrowed on the choppy surf, Ivar scanned the surface of the bay again. Three of his soldiers followed, protecting his flank while keeping their distance. He didn't blame them. A smart male knew when to back off, and no one wanted to get in his way tonight. Not after the cluster-fuck over Gig Harbor.

Ivar ground his fangs together. What a mess. Four dead, double that injured with nothing to show for it. Oh sure, they'd hammered a few of the Nightfuries, but not hard enough. Put one down in the lose column, because, hey, Bastian and his band of bastards were still breathing. How did he know? The updates. Denzeil kept feeding the latest-and-greatest through mind-speak. The enemy was leapfrogging all over Seattle, leading his soldiers on a merry chase. One Ivar knew they couldn't win…even with superior numbers.

The Nightfury pack was too quick. Too efficient. Too damn smart. No way any of them would get caught in the open now. So like it or not, KOing the lone male protect-ing Solares was the only satisfaction he was likely to get.

With a snarl, Ivar called on his magic. Power rushed through his veins, then sparked, twisting into magical heat. Pink flame exploded down his spine. With a twitch, he hummed, loving the sweeping tingle as fire raced across his scales, setting him ablaze from horned head to spiked tail.

The wildfire thing happened to him sometimes. Extreme anger set him alight, turning him into a flying inferno. Right now, though, the extra bit of PO'd helped center him. His built-in radar cranked to full blast, his night vision sparked, picking up trace beneath the surface of the water. He inhaled, gathering a throat-full of fire, and—

Ivar growled. Fuck a duck. A school of fish, not the water rat.

The wind picked up, throwing cold mist into the air. Water wicking off his underbelly, Ivar's sonar pinged again, magic blanketing the swell and dip of whitecaps like a grid. A lone shark swam beneath his flight path. But other than that? Nothing. Not a goddamn thing. The male was gone, along with the female.

Christ almighty. What a night, never mind a waste of time.

But worse? The knowledge he'd been bested by a fledgling, a Nightfury whelp barely out of transition. Jesus, it was embarrassing. The male should never have been able to evade him. No way. No how. Not with his level of inexperience. Too bad the theory didn't hold water. Bastian's new boy packed one hell of a punch. Was smart too. Knew when to bug out and when to fight. The water spears were proof enough of that.

Inconceivable. A water dragon, one who possessed a strong throwing arm and pinpoint accuracy. Ivar shook his head. How was that even possible?

All right, stupid question. He knew it was *possible*. Hamersveld was proof enough of that. Ivar remembered meeting the male at the Archguard's festival. God, how long had it been…thirty years? Maybe a few more? Could be, but whatever the time frame, he'd never forgotten the male. Understandable. The warrior made one hell of an impression and packed an even bigger punch.

No one screwed with Hamersveld. Not even the Archguard's high council. Rumor held that the male preferred his own company and refused to swear allegiance to an established pack. Add that to his vicious reputation and the fact he claimed to be a water dragon?

Oh, the possibilities.

Ivar's eyes narrowed. Mind churning, he examined each idea from all angles, looking for pitfalls. Bastian had a water dragon in his corner—a powerful one, which qualified as an undeniable advantage. Hell, the pissant fledgling could already cloak himself underwater. Who knew what the Nightfury would be capable of given another week? Would the bastard be able to drown soldiers in midflight?

Ivar grimaced. The possibility didn't thrill him. Neither did going home empty-handed. He banked right anyway and, flying fast, headed toward 28 Walton Street. Time to hit Dragonkind's equivalent of the Internet and indulge in some reconnaissance. He needed to know more about Hamersveld. About his character and whether or not the male could be controlled.

With Lothair gone, Ivar required a new XO, one vicious enough to take his place. And Hamersveld? By all accounts, the warrior put the brutal in *brutality*. Toss in his propensity to unleash hell and...bingo. He had a match made in heaven. With an added bonus. Coaxing Hamersveld into the fold would boost morale among the Razorback ranks while backing the Nightfuries up a step.

Good plan. One he needed to put into action ASAP.

With Bastian's boy learning in leaps and bounds, he had limited time. And finding Hamersveld, never mind convincing him to join the cause, wouldn't be easy. But with the Archguard's festival in full swing, he might get lucky. If the warrior was in Prague, Ivar's contacts there would locate him.

Ivar doused the flames flickering along his spine. As his scales cooled in the frosty air, his soldiers closed ranks around him. Ignoring them, he rocketed over the warehouses sitting like steel-clad bricks along the waterfront, then turned northwest toward his city lair. The putrid scent of humans and furnace oil blew back behind him, curling like white froth from his wing tips. Ivar inhaled deep, sucking the disgusting smell into his lungs, satisfaction pumping through him.

Oh, he loved a clever strategy. And this one? His most brilliant yet. A battle plan with balls and a shitload of bite, because...oh yeah. It was time to fight fire with fire. Or rather, pit sea dragon against sea dragon. Let the water sports begin.

———

Nian, ascended male to the Archguard's high council, stood in the middle of the high archway, scanning the upscale VIP section. Cave-like, the gentlemen's club was all about soft jazz, comfortable booths, and strategically placed tables. A place where cigar smoke swirled, bow-tied waiters ruled, and Dragonkind came to unwind. His mouth tipped up at the corners. Prague's Emblem Club was a gem: hip, posh, with just the right amount of sophistication.

Right up his alley.

He sighed, unwinding one tense muscle at a time. After suffering through the heavy thump of bass one floor up where the Archguard held court amid erotic dancers and spoiled supermodels, the quiet was a welcome reprieve. As was the sight of the embroidered curtains that hung on either side of him, flanking the entryway.

Damask, probably…hand stitched and shot through with gold thread. Expensive, like everything else in the Emblem.

Not that he gave a damn at the moment.

Old-school gold lighter in hand, Nian flipped the top shut. A second later, he flipped it back open with the pad of his thumb. Click-click-snap. Click-click-snap. Worn by time, the warm metal settled like home against his palm. Habit made him repeat the flicking motion time and again. The sound brought soft comfort, reminding him of what he had done. Or rather, set in motion. A pleasant memory, but…whatever. The hows and whys of his sire's death didn't matter.

And neither did the club.

The dark interior of the upscale establishment didn't interest him tonight. He hadn't made the trip downstairs—slipped away, escaping the notice of the other members of the Archguard—for the decor. He'd come for the two Nightfury warriors sitting at the back of the dimly lit room. Decked out in expensive suits, the two looked like a couple of kingpins. Nian's lips twitched. The analogy wasn't far from the truth.

Gage and Haider, two formidable warriors from an equally formidable pack. Most called the pair "the Metallics," and for good reason. Liquid metal breathers, each exuded a lethal amount of hard-core and kick-ass. Gage was the more dangerous of the two, though. A bronze dragon with serious self-destruction issues and even less patience, the warrior would sooner kill a male than look at him. His strategy went something like…strike first and ask questions second. And only if his prey lived to see a new night.

A serious problem. Especially since Nian wanted to chat.

Which was where Haider came in. A silver dragon—a diplomat of sorts whose talent lay in the art of negotiation—the male was the more sensible of the two and would hear him out. At least Nian hoped. Nothing was certain. Haider might take one look at him and unleash Gage. His bloodline, after all, wasn't anything to boast about considering his family history…and the wrong his sire had done to Bastian.

He thumbed his lighter. Click-click-snap. Click-click-snap. Nervous tension fluttered through him. Proceeding with extreme caution seemed like a good idea. The Metallics exuded confidence like nuclear fallout did radiation. Catastrophic in so many ways.

Like a wraith appearing out of thin air, a waiter appeared at his side, crisply pressed tuxedo shirt gleaming under fancy wall sconces. With a slight bow, the Numbai held a round tray toward him. On it sat a humidor. "A Cuban from our collection, my lord?"

Nian shook his head. Despite the lighter he always carried, he never smoked. Fire, after all, wasn't good for a gold dragon. Glancing at the Numbai, he murmured, "A bourbon…neat."

The waiter nodded. "May I offer you a private booth, sire?"

"I'll take it at the bar."

"Very good, my lord."

As the servant turned toward the long mahogany bar at the back of the club, Nian returned his attention to the Nightfuries. The end stool sat just feet away from them. It was now or never. He might not get another opportunity. Not with the rest of the Archguard watching him so closely. The youngest member of the high council, he'd ascended to power three months ago when his sire had died in a duel. Now he headed one of the five dynastic families that ruled Dragonkind. A real player in a political landscape with the potential to influence the future success or failure of his race.

Nian took a deep breath, filling his lungs with air and his heart with courage. He could do this. He held the power in his hands, enough perhaps to—

"Thinking about making new friends, are we?"

Nian stiffened as the Norwegian accent washed over him from behind. Hamersveld. Had to be. No other male slithered in or out quite that quietly. Or possessed such bad timing. A quick glance to his left confirmed what he already knew. Big. Blond. Annoying. The warrior-cum-Viking had the irritant-from-hell market cornered.

He met Hamersveld's gaze, then shifted focus and...

Wonder of wonders. The bastard wasn't alone. Nothing new there. The male rarely went anywhere without Fen... his *wren*. A subspecies of Dragonkind, wrens were small, light, fast in flight, and wholly vicious; raptor-like with short dual-clawed forepaws. Able to take human form, loyal to the point of fatalistic, the miniature dragons didn't live in packs but bonded to a single male, swearing servitude until death separated him from his master.

But the true curiosity? Wrens were nearly extinct. Which begged the question: How the hell had Hamersveld gotten hold of one?

Not that Nian cared. The bastard could do what he wanted. As long as he left the club without mucking up his plan with the Nightfuries.

Feigning a nonchalance he didn't feel, Nian said, "Taken to following me around, have you?"

"You flatter yourself, whelp," the older male murmured, amused condescension in his tone and more. It was the *more* that concerned Nian. Hamersveld's cunning was legendary. Yes, the male might be antisocial, but he liked to play games. And if he could screw someone up in the process? So much the better. "I'm not the one looking for new playmates."

"The world is relieved."

"Question is…" Hamersveld paused for effect, no doubt searching for an angle. Nian's fingers curled, the urge to hit the male almost too much to resist. Almost, but not quite. Showing his hand before he was ready wasn't part of the plan. He stuffed the call to violence down deep as the Viking asshole leaned toward him. The scent of perfumed female flesh and seawater mixed, salting the air as the male said, "What do you need with more friends, Golden Boy? The Archguard elite not enough for you?"

The nickname wound him up another notch.

"Always good to know your enemy." Glancing over his shoulder, Nian made light of his interest in the Nightfuries by murmuring, "Don't you think?"

Shark-black eyes rimmed by pale blue met his. "Is it now?"

"Must be. I've been doing it with you for years, Sveld."

"You always were a smart whelp," the male said, amusement in his tone. "You ever wanna get your ass kicked, you know where to find me."

He sure did. In the gutter. Along with all the other rats.

His eyes narrowed, he watched Hamersveld walk away, the wren trailing behind him. He clenched his teeth. Brimstone and hellfire, the pair was headed in the wrong direction. He wanted the warrior gone, far away, occupied with a female, not planted inside the club with a bird's-eye view. But as Hamersveld settled inside a private booth, the futility of his strategy hit Nian chest level. So much for reaching out to the Nightfuries tonight. The Norwegian bastard might be antisocial, but he had a big mouth. If Hamersveld saw him talking to Gage and Haider, the head of the high council would hear about it before sunrise.

Which would put him...where? Under a cloud of suspicion. Mistrusted by the most powerful males of his kind.

Disappointment swelled inside him. He must find a way. Get word to Haider. Somehow. Someway. And soon. The festival would conclude in less than three days, and the Metallics would leave...jump the pond to make the trip home. He couldn't allow that to happen. Not without feeling them out first. He needed an ally to knock Rodin—leader of the Archguard—off his perch. The fact Nian planned to take his place was neither here nor there. His ambitions were his own concern.

And none of the Nightfuries'.

Calculating all the possibilities, Nian strode between tables on his way to the bar and his bourbon. Polished hardwood floors gleamed beneath the rasp of his designer shoes as melodic jazz piped through hidden speakers, drifting on wisps of cigar smoke. Fingering his lighter, Nian glanced to his right. Sprawled on the booth seat, tie loose, shirt collar open, big hand curled around a tumbler full of amber liquid, Gage narrowed his focus on him. Nian kept his expression neutral, satisfaction kicking his heartbeat into high gear. Good. Both warriors had noticed him. Were probably wondering what he was doing, leaving the comfort of the Archguard's company to invade the club they'd claimed as their own for the duration of the festival.

Very soon he hoped to tell them. Maybe even tonight. But only if Hamersveld buggered off and—

A scream ripped through the club, shredding the forlorn sound of a saxophone.

Zeroing in on the terror-filled cry, Nian pivoted toward the emergency exit. Too late. The Metallics were already on their feet. With a snarl, Gage hammered the handle locking the steel door in place. A band of bright light flooded the club, cutting a wide swath across the floor. He blinked, squinting against the glare as the Nightfury males roared over the threshold into the stairwell beyond.

Nian followed at a more sedate pace. No sense getting in the males' way. Not when a female was involved. He knew how much they hated to see the fairer sex hurt. The two would no doubt knock his teeth down his throat if he interfered. Not exactly the best way to forge international relations with the warrior pack he needed in his corner.

Chapter Fourteen

Fatigue tugging on her like a two-year-old, Tania rubbed her eyes. God, her head hurt. Maybe even more than her hands. Which was saying something considering the shredded condition of her nails. Even with Mac's patch-up job and the Polysporin, she still ached, the beat of her heart an echoing throb in her fingertips. The heels of her palms didn't feel much better.

Bruised. She was undeniably bruised, and not just on the outside. Her paradigm had shifted in a big way, making confusion her new best friend. Now she struggled to cope... to cobble together all she'd seen and not call herself crazy.

Which, honestly? Qualified as *crazy*.

She should be questioning her sanity. Or at the very least wondering when she'd been slipped the mind-altering drugs. Either option seemed a safe bet, an excellent explanation for why she sat playing poker with a man who could turn into a dragon. Tania frowned at her cards. Unbelievable. A frickin'-frackin' dragon! A creature that appeared in fairy tales (usually as the bad guy) to amp up the tension and frighten little kids at bedtime.

Tania wasn't immune. She *was* scared. Was still somewhere south of freaked out while riding a northbound psycho train called "trust him." Slipping the jack of spades in beside the ace of diamonds, she took stock of her hand and shook her head.

Right. *Trust Mac.*

As if she wanted to do that after all the crap he'd pulled tonight.

Too bad *want* didn't have a thing to do with it. Not with *need* leading the charge. He'd promised to keep her safe, and, despite everything, she believed him. No second-guessing. No doubting it. Just full-on faith. Which was full-on bizarre. She didn't trust easily. Evidence of that peppered her personal life: no boyfriend, many acquaintances, but few good friends.

But there was something about Mac. He was solid. Safe. Appealing in a way that drew her. Now she felt connected somehow, aware of him on a level she hadn't known existed, never mind experienced before.

Wedged into the corner of the deep-seated sofa, Tania peeked over the top of her cluster of diamonds and spades. She watched him for a moment. Aquamarine eyes on his own hand, he rearranged his cards, his big hands somehow graceful despite their size. What a puzzle he presented. Lethal in a fight yet always gentle with her. Gorgeous without knowing it. Confident without being arrogant. No denying it. He was a conundrum. One she itched to solve so badly curiosity took hold, nudging her in directions she didn't want to go.

Dangerous. He was dangerous. And she was out of her league.

Dragging her gaze away from his hands, Tania shivered. He could hurt her if she let him get too close. If she trusted too far, too fast. If she gave him the upper hand and allowed him to call the shots. She needed to stay even to figure it out…and get back to the real world. One that made sense and where she was in control.

Tonight, though, that seemed like a stretch. Beyond her reach, never mind her capacity to achieve.

Another shiver skated down her spine. She tugged the blanket higher around her shoulders. Soft fleece brushed her nape, keeping her warm, but as far as armor went it wasn't much help. She felt exposed…way too raw, unable to deny her dependence on the man sitting on the floor opposite her. With a sigh, Tania rubbed her eyes with the back of her hand. Ridiculous. Her. The situation. All of it. And she needed a distraction. Right now. Before she broke down and did something stupid, like leave the nest she'd made on the couch and hop over the coffee table to settle in Mac's arms.

God help her, but she needed a hug in the worst way.

Pressure built, rising like a storm inside her. As it squeezed around her chest, Tania swallowed the burn of tears and glanced toward the fireplace. Just beyond Mac, embers flickered on a bed of ash, casting a comforting glow, making shadows dance across the floor-to-ceiling wainscoting. The fire's hypnotic pull tugged at her, smoothing out the tension. She watched flames lick between the logs, her eyelids growing heavier by the second.

Mac cleared his throat.

Tania blinked and glanced his way. When he gave her a pointed look, she got back in the game, forcing herself to concentrate. It didn't go well. She was too tired, and everything about poker was too complicated. She could barely remember her own name, never mind what constituted a good hand.

She stared at her cards, seeing them, but not really. "Is three of a kind good?"

"Why?" Sprawled on the floor a few feet away, he raised a dark brow. "Is that whatcha got?"

His teasing tone rubbed her the wrong way. It shouldn't have. Not really. She understood what he was trying to do... keep it light by taking her mind off her troubles. Tania appreciated the effort—she really did—but knowing his intent didn't help. She refused to be an idiot and let him coddle her.

Leveling her chin, Tania glared at him.

Amusement sparked in his gaze. "Depends."

"On what?"

"On whether you've got aces or kings."

"In that case..." She laid her aces along with her jacks face up on the teak tabletop. Mac leaned forward to take a look. As he cursed, she said, "I just kicked your butt."

"Nice." A smile tugged at the corners of his mouth before he gave in and grinned at her. "You're a natural. When can I take you to Vegas?"

"Tomorrow," she whispered, unable to find her own smile. Winning almost always brought one to the surface, but not tonight. "But first you need to tell me this is all a dream. Just a bad dream. That I didn't see any dragons. That everything will go back to normal. That I don't need to be afraid anymore."

His gaze left the cards and landed on her face. Regret and something more—affection, maybe—shimmered in his eyes. "As much as I would like to, honey, I can't protect you from the truth. What you saw tonight is real. As dangerous as it gets."

"That's what I thought." Fear pricked through her. She nodded anyway, trying to be brave, but as her throat closed, she realized fighting was futile. She'd landed in a world where dragons lived, and happily-ever-afters happened in storybooks, not to her. "Hey, Mac?"

"Yeah?"

"I'm still really scared." Tania cringed, the shame of admitting it almost too much to bear. God, how embarrassing. She was such a wuss…a big, fat fraidycat for not being able to handle the news flash. And her new circumstances. "Guess that makes me a big chicken, huh?"

"No. It makes you normal."

Ha! Right. Normal. If only it were that simple. Plucking at the frayed blanket edge, she said, "I'm sorry I yelled at you before."

"I deserved it."

"Yes, you did." Chilled by more than the cold air in the cabin, she wiggled her toes to warm up her feet. "And I'm still mad at you for wrecking my car."

"I'll buy you another one."

"No, thank you," she said, her voice stronger, her tone surer. Thank goodness. At least she didn't sound like a crybaby anymore. "I can buy my own stuff."

"Think of it as a peace offering." His focus on her, he tossed his cards onto the table.

Tania watched them slide, and him shift, from the corner of her eye. As he rolled to his feet, Tania tightened her grip on the blanket. He skirted the end of the coffee table, raising her internal alarm. As the thing went ring-a-ling-ling inside her head, she squirmed on the leather cushion. What was he doing? An excellent question, one that got answered a moment later when he sat down beside her. The couch dipped, and Tania tensed, ready to let fly.

She didn't want to be touched. Not by him. Not right now.

He was too...too...well, *everything*. Big. Masculine. A smooth-talking charmer wrapped up in a too-gorgeous-for-words package. And if he laid a finger on her, she'd lose her cool, melt into a messy puddle of stupidity, and burrow into his arms. Ask for comfort. Demand he make it all better. Like a flipping child.

God save her from her own idiocy.

"Tania?"

"What?"

"It's okay to be afraid, you know."

"Easy for you to say." Back to staring at the fire, she whispered, "You're used to being attacked by dragons."

"Honey, look at me."

Feeling foolish, she shook her head. "I can't."

He stayed silent, waiting her out. She lasted all of five seconds before she cracked.

"God, you don't understand." And oh wow. She sounded awful, the vocal equivalent of a train wreck. "If I look at you, I'll fall apart. And I can't do that...I just can't."

"Why not?" He shifted on the couch, moving toward her inch by slow inch.

"I've always prided myself on being the strong one, you know? I always worry. I can't help that. Worrying, it's sort of...well, written in my DNA or something, but I never freak out. I'm the one who always fixes everything, but I can't fix this, so..." Her breath hitched as she paused, struggling to keep it together. She needed to prove—to herself and him—she was more than just a pretty face.

She was the strong one. *The strong one,* gosh darn it! But as tears pricked the corners of her eyes, she broke and curled inward, wrapping her arms around her knees. "Right now, I'm just…I don't know…pathetic or something."

"You are not." The edge in his voice made her look up. He captured her gaze, his so fierce she blinked. "You're nowhere near pathetic. What you are is exhausted. You need sleep and time to process, that's all. It'll all look better tomorrow."

Better? Was he nuts? No way would twelve hours of pillow time make it better. Not with a bunch of dragons running around, trying to kill her. But arguing the point wouldn't get her anywhere. Amassing more information, however, might.

Unlocking her muscles, Tania swiveled in her corner. Mac mirrored her movement, angling his body toward her. The couch arm pressing into her back, she settled sideways, chin resting on her bent knees and feet next to his thigh. Cool air rushed over her already cold toes. She hurried to cover them back up. He was faster. Reaching out, he cupped her heel in the palm of his hand.

His touch seared her. She got zapped by static electricity, and heat unfurled, curling up the back of her calf. Surprise made her flinch. The gentleness in his hands made her squirm.

She tugged, fighting his grip. "What are you doing?"

"Easy." Straightening her leg, he pulled her foot into his lap. "You're wound too tight. I can help if you let me. Let me, Tania."

His baritone washed over her in a coaxing wave. Oh so nice. He always sounded so darned amazing. And as he murmured her name again, tempting her to go along,

Tania stared at him, trying to guess his game. She knew he had one. Guys like him always did. She recognized the breed, a charming player who knew his way around women. So, uh-huh. No doubt about it. The whole let-me-help-you thing meant he was up to something. Too bad she didn't have the mental energy to unravel the mystery.

Her brain was gone, along with the capacity to argue. And the ache in her head? Almost unbearable now, thumping against her temples, making her teeth hurt. So like it or not, the Sherlock Holmes half of her personality wasn't making an appearance tonight.

She made a halfhearted attempt anyway. "How?"

"You're feet are like ice." Caressing the top of her foot, he tweaked the tip of her baby toe. "You need them warmed."

"So get me a pair of socks," she said, just to be contrary. "Problem solved."

"Don't have any." The devil in his eyes, his mouth curved up at the corners. "Besides, this is more fun."

"For whom?"

"Me."

"Figures," she said, feigning anger she didn't feel. And no wonder. Try as she might, she couldn't conjure up an ounce of pissed off. Then again, being upset with a man while he gave you a foot rub was a practical impossibility. She resisted anyway, putting on a good show. "It's all about you, after all."

He ignored the token resistance—thank you, God—and one-upped her, circling his thumbs in just…the right… spot. Tania bit down on a groan. He waited until she shuddered, then pressed in, rubbed deeper, nearly sending her into orbit. She sucked in a quick breath. Holy jeez. He knew what he was doing. She needed to add wicked-good massage to her running tally. The one entitled...Things at Which Mac Excelled and—

Oh boy. *That* felt unbelievably good.

Usually she couldn't stand to have her feet touched. Most women loved pedicures. Tania wasn't one of them. Her soles were too sensitive for that. Oh, she'd tried more than once, wanting well-groomed heels and pretty toenail polish, but it was always a no go. She couldn't sit still in the chair long enough for the esthetician to finish. She always spazzed out, then bowed out in a hurry.

But Mac's hands? Heaven on earth.

"Holy moly," she gasped, squirming as he stroked between her toes.

He chuckled. "Found the spot, didn't I?"

"Oh, be quiet," she muttered, unwilling to wave the white flag of surrender. She relaxed instead and, melting into the sofa, rested her cheek against the cushion. "Oh my...jeez. Do that again."

"Right here?" He rotated his thumb. Swallowing a moan of delight, she twisted in her seat. "I'll take that as a yes."

Under his spell now, she closed her eyes and slipped her unoccupied foot into his lap. As he continued to rub, heat rose, swelling into a blinding wave of oh-baby-please-don't-stop. The prickling sensation came next, rushing over her skin, drawing her deep only to keep her afloat on a bliss-filled swirl. And there she bobbed, cresting on gentle waves, lulled into total relaxation. God, he was warm. So very good with his hands.

He switched feet. Tania barely noticed. Immersed in pleasure, she snuggled into the couch, becoming boneless against the leather cushions. Time spun away, stretching out as fire crackled and the shadows on the wall grew longer. Seduced by the gentle rhythm of each stroke, she listened to the wall clock walk around its face, each ticktock calling softly in the quiet.

After a while—minutes…hours…she didn't know—the rubbing stopped. Battling through the mind-fog, Tania forced her eyes open. His gaze on her face, Mac studied her a moment, then shifted toward her. Setting her legs over his thighs, he slid his arm along the back of the sofa and settled in, one hand still warm on her toes, the other next to her head. When she didn't shy, he took it a step further and picked up a lock of her hair.

He twirled the dark strand around his fingertips. "You have beautiful hair."

So relaxed she couldn't move, she whispered, "My sister's is prettier."

"Impossible."

Tania smiled. Not a lot. A simple lift of her lips, but that was all the encouragement he needed. His fingers went searching, delving deep to stroke her scalp. "Hmm… that feels good."

"The bed's made." Sliding on the sofa cushions, he moved closer. His warmth curled around her as she breathed him in. Oh, he smelled good, like exotic spices and untold pleasures…exactly as a man should. "Let me tuck you in, *mo chroí*."

"Tell me about Myst first." Fighting a yawn, she asked, "Is she really all right? You said she'd be here."

"I know." His thumb brushed over her temple. With a sigh, she turned in to his gentle touch, asking for more. He gave it to her. Releasing her foot, he brought his other hand into play. As he cupped her nape, the current-like sensation increased, then swirled down her spine in a heated rush. "But the plan changed on the bridge. I brought you here instead of Black Diamond."

Her eyes drifted closed. Tania forced them open again. Shimmering aquamarine eyes met hers. Funny, but the glow didn't bother her that much anymore. Somehow it seemed normal now...part of the man, instead of a monster.

"The bridge," she said, trying to make her brain work. It was skipping all over the place, playing pinball inside her skull, scattering important puzzle pieces. Gathering up as many as she could, Tania struggled to connect each tidbit. "When the red dragon attacked?"

"Yeah. He's a really bad guy. Leader of a rogue faction of Dragonkind."

"Dragonkind?" She frowned. *Dragonkind.* That sounded weird, like a misnomer, not a real thing. "What are you? A different species or something?"

"Pretty much." He kept stroking her, his fingers working their magic. He skimmed the side of her throat. Moving down, he found the space between her neck and shoulder. He massaged with gentle hands, working out the kinks, and she purred. "I couldn't let him take you, Tania. He would've hurt you, and I...shit. No way I'm letting that happen."

Alarm pierced through some of the pleasant haze. "Did he hurt Myst?"

He shook his head. "Bastian got to her first."

"Who's that?"

"Commander of the Nightfuries...the pack I belong to now."

"Explain."

He did, and as she listened to him talk—about Razorbacks and Nightfuries, about dragon history, the ongoing war, and his transition into Dragonkind society—Tania didn't know what to say. Or how to react. And as words like *the Meridian* and *energy-feedings* got thrown around, Tania stared at him. It was all so bizarre. Not to mention confusing. A whole species of dragon-guys were flying around, blowing things up, and no one—at least as far as she could tell—knew a darned thing about it.

"So...you're not human."

"Half. My mother was human."

"But not your father."

"I was sired by a Dragonkind male," he said, watching her closely, no doubt waiting for her to freak out. But like a consummate poker player, he'd played his cards right, ensuring she was too relaxed to indulge in a mental meltdown. Now, instead of fear, curiosity took hold, making her want to know more. "Like all of my race, I can shift form at will."

Well, that was...kind of cool, actually. Then again, what did she know? The train named *Insanity* had pulled out of her station hours ago. "And at the precinct? When you hauled me in for questioning, did you know—"

"No." With a smooth move, he slid his arms around her and lifted. Before she could protest, he settled her in his lap, bum against his thighs, cheek nestled against his strong shoulder. Wrapping her up, he cuddled her close, using his warmth and scent to seduce her. And wow. She really should say something. Tell him to back off, put her down... *something*. But honestly? It felt too good to worry about. His hands were at it again, rubbing her back, caressing her calf. "Until a month ago, I didn't know dragons existed either. I thought I was one hundred percent human until I woke up in dragon form."

"Yikes." Another soothing stroke down her spine. She blinked, struggling to stay connected to the conversation. "Talk about a nasty wake-up call."

"You think?"

Tania smiled, then frowned. Something odd was happening. She felt the swaying pull—the drain and draw—as though she was linked in, aware of…everything. His heartbeat. The strength of his body and the power of his energy. The thoughts meandering through his head. Strange, but oh so easy. Her connection to him felt good… right in the best possible way. And as the current grew stronger, sensation crested, tugging her toward sleep's slippery slope.

Her head lolled on Mac's shoulder. Huh. She was sitting sideways in his lap. When had that happened? "What are you doing to me?"

His mouth brushed her ear. "Helping you fall asleep."

"Don't want to," she said, her words slurring.

"Yes, you do, honey."

One hand cupping her nape, he cuddled her close while the other flicked beneath the hem of her sweatshirt. His skin touched hers. She hummed, arching beneath the press of his hand. Fingers spread wide, his palm settled against the small of her back. He nuzzled her hair, then drifted down to kiss her temple. Surrounded by his scent, safe in his arms, something unlocked deep inside her. She heard the click. Felt the rush as the vortex picked her up, sweeping her along in its powerful riptide.

"Listen to my voice, Tania, and let go. Drift, honey. Nothing to do but drift."

And just like that, she did as he asked, let oblivion take her, and sank beneath slumber's warm waves. As she went under Tania thought…tomorrow. Tomorrow was a new day. Soon enough to gain some perspective and figure her way out of the mess.

Out of a world where red dragons were trying to kill her.

Chapter Fifteen

Ass-planted on the couch with Tania asleep in his lap, Mac wondered what the hell he was doing. And when he'd lost his mind. Gone AWOL. Whatever. 'Cause, shit. He shouldn't be hanging out in the near dark. Or listening to the sound of ocean waves roll into the shoreline beyond his cabin while he tortured himself with the warm, scented weight of the woman in his arms.

Motherfuck, he was deranged. A real candidate for the psych ward and electroshock therapy. Maybe if he got zapped a couple of times, he'd do the right thing. Pick her up. Walk into his bedroom. And put Tania to bed.

Alone.

But oh, not him. The longer he held her, the more he wanted to.

Mac sighed, mourning the loss of his moral compass, and cuddled her closer. A moment later, he compounded the idiocy by stroking her hair. He couldn't help it. He was too far gone…in Sapsville with no hope of backtracking. So he caressed her instead, loving how the dark strands clung to his fingers, each length an enticement he couldn't ignore. Jesus, she was beautiful. Soft and strong at the same time. And in the fading moments of the coming dawn, she was too much for him to resist. Everything he'd always wanted but knew he could never have and certainly didn't deserve.

He must be a masochist or something. An idiot without the sense God gave most people.

Clearly he didn't own any at all. If he possessed half a brain he'd tuck her into bed and then do what he did best. Get gone. Disappear for a while. Put as much distance between them as he could before he did something stupid.

Like what? Oh, he could think of a few things. Or twenty. All involved getting naked. Which...yeah. Was *not* going to happen.

He'd already overstepped his bounds and taken without her consent. Had tapped into the Meridian while putting her to sleep and fed on her energy. And oh man, good didn't begin to describe her. Frickin' amazing fit better. Perfection worked too. Mac bit down on a groan, combating the urge to taste her again. Drink so deep satiation took hold.

Which made him a first-rate jackass.

He should've explained first. Should've told her what he took each time he touched her, instead of skirting the issue and telling half-truths. She deserved to know how he staved off hunger and stayed healthy. About the power of the Meridian, her value as a high-energy female, and what that meant for her. For him.

For them going forward.

To indulge or not to indulge, that was the question. Yes, he wanted her. No question about that, but was seducing her—keeping her around for a while—the smart thing to do? The *right* thing to do? His conscience said no. Tania deserved the best, a better male than him. One willing to go all in and commit to her without hesitation. One ready to offer her his love. Too bad he didn't know how to give her that. Jesus. He hadn't seen the better side of himself in years. He excelled at the sex stuff, not intimacy. Didn't know the first thing about loving a woman, never mind showing how much she meant to him.

His heart sank like a stone in the center of his chest. He was an asshole, cuddling her close while he yearned for more. Everything. Her love. Her passion. The same kind of commitment Bastian and Rikar had found. And yet with his next breath, he questioned whether he wanted to love her in return.

Fan-fucking-tastic. His commitment-phobe tendencies were out in full force, messing with his ability to think straight.

Mac shook his head, then gave in and kissed the top of her head. Not that Tania noticed. Curled around him, she'd fallen into a deep sleep, each breath long and even. He gave her a gentle squeeze, enjoying her heat, reveling in her trust, wanting to get horizontal with her even though he knew it was a bad idea.

Making love to her wasn't in the cards. At least not tonight. Tomorrow, however? Man, he hoped so, but that would be up to her. Given his uncertainty, he refused to push her. But if she wanted him and initiated sex? Call him a first-class bastard, but she wouldn't have to ask him twice.

With a sigh, Tania shifted against him, nestling her bottom into his groin. He bit down on a groan. Okay. Time to go. Self-torture proclivities aside, he couldn't hold her much longer without touching her. In serious ways.

Sliding his forearm beneath her knees, Mac pushed to his feet with her in his arms. She grumbled in her sleep. He murmured an apology and, keeping each stride smooth, carried her across the living room. Desire hummed, streaking through him as she rubbed her cheek against his chest. Mac shoved his arousal aside. Now was not the time or… well, okay. It *was* the place. His bedroom, after all, lay just ahead, but no way he would do that to her. Or himself. When he made love to her, she'd be on board, 100 percent into the sexual play, giving as good as he gave her.

With a mental flick, he opened the double pocket doors to the left of the fireplace and crossed the threshold. Pushed against the far wall, his bed took up most of the room, usually a king-size oasis for him. Tonight, it would be hers. The place he would tuck her beneath feather down and leave her to dream.

After which he'd haul ass. Get as far away from her as possible.

It was either that or suffer the consequences when she woke up with him wrapped around her. Not exactly the best way to start a new relationship. He was already in clusterfuck county as it was, considering the problem with his memory bank. The lapse bothered Mac more than it should. The memory loss wasn't his fault, after all. His *first shift* into dragon form had kicked his ass, obliterating all but bits and pieces of Tania's role in it. But that didn't mean she would understand. She'd no doubt rip him a new one when she discovered he couldn't remember making love to her.

Women were funny that way. They tended to get irate when a guy confessed to not remembering their name, never mind sharing a mattress. Or a pool table. Or the coat check in a—

Okay, then. No need to go there, but…

Mac frowned. What was he supposed to be doing again? Oh, right. Putting her to bed.

Good plan. Now all he needed to do was stick with it. Especially since he now stood beside the bed, muscles twitching, his dragon rebelling, refusing to lay her down. His mouth brushing the top of her head, Mac cursed. Terrific. Just what he didn't need, his base instincts riding shotgun.

Fighting to stay on an even keel, he leaned down, supporting her with one arm, and grabbed the corner of the duvet. He flipped it aside, revealing the expanse of white cotton. The territorial beast inside him went into lockdown, wanting to keep her in his arms. Mac shook his head. Jesus, it shouldn't be so hard. All he wanted to do was take care of her, do right by her, but…

Sometimes the right thing wasn't the easy thing. And as he stood there, heart thumping, bare feet planted, need rising, he waged an internal battle. Stay. Or go. Be the good guy. Or the needy one. Forcing himself to unlock, he laid her down. The sheets rustled. Tania grumbled, an adorable pucker between her brows. Mac murmured, hoping the sound of his voice would compensate for the loss of his body heat.

Her dark eyelashes flicked.

He froze, his arms still half around her.

"Mac?"

Ah, fuck. He was so screwed, wanting to get away, but unable to leave. "Shh, it's all right. Go back to sleep. Everything's all right."

"No." The denial slurred by sleep, she turned toward him, wrapping both her arms around one of his. Mac sucked in a quick breath. "Don't."

Brushing the hair away from her temple, he caressed her cheek. "Don't what, honey?"

"Go. Don't…go."

Another gentle stroke across her superfine skin. Another sigh from her. "It's okay. I'll just be in the other—"

"He might come back," she whispered, her eyes drifting closed.

"Who, *mo chroí*?"

"The red one."

Mac closed his eyes. Shit. *The red one.* She meant Ivar. Even in her sleep, the bastard chased her, making her afraid. "You're safe. I won't let him get you."

She shook her head, panic making her breathe faster.

"No one knows where we are, Tania," he murmured to reassure her. It didn't work. She was too worked up, and as she whimpered, his heart sank. And he ached for her. For the fear she suffered now and the changes to come. Life as she knew it was over. No more landscape design firm. No more apartment in Seattle. Good-bye, human world. Hello, Dragonkind. A total frickin' makeover was in order.

"I'll keep you safe, Tania. He can't find us here, I promise." He retreated another inch.

She clung to him. "Please…don't."

Her plea wrecked him, just leveled him where he stood and…ah, fuck. He couldn't do it. Couldn't leave her knowing she needed him. Which meant more torture. He really must be a masochist. A sadist or something because, without a doubt, holding her without making love to her first would kill him. Yet even knowing that, he slipped in beside her. The mattress dipped. He settled on his back and reeled her in, pulling the duvet back into place, cocooning them in feather down. She snuggled into his side, her head on his shoulder, one leg thrown over his thigh and her hand—

He jumped like a jackrabbit as she caressed his skin. Oh so not good. He was already set to go off. So damned sensitive her touch made every single one of his skin receptors fire…at once. Sensation flooded him, ratcheting him into the danger zone.

Clenching his teeth, Mac stared at the ceiling, counting the planks of Douglas fir tongue-and-groove paneling to distract himself. Her hand coasted over his belly, moving beneath his T-shirt before she laid her palm in the center of his chest. Tense muscles twitched in protest. He inhaled, filling his lungs to capacity to keep from exploding, hoping she was done with the renegade hand routine.

When she settled deep, relaxing completely against him, he released the breath he'd been holding. Okay. He was up and over hurdle one. Now all he needed to do was leap over all the others in his path between now and nightfall. Mac frowned. Or maybe not. Maybe salvation was just minutes away.

Firing up the connection he now shared with his brothers-in-arms, Mac reached out with his mind. *"Rikar. Where you at?"*

Static buzzed between his temples, then…jackpot. The connection flared, his kind's cosmic equivalent of a cell phone opening the channel between them. Wind whistled inside his head, the sound one of ass-hauling as his XO mind-spoke, *"Nowhere good. Got multiple rogues on our tails."*

Concern lit Mac up. *"You need backup?"*

"Nah, B and I got it covered." A pause, then, *"You safe?"*

"Yeah," he said. *"Holed up in my cabin."*

Bastian chimed in. *"Where?"*

"On an island off the coast of Seattle."

Silence met that happy bit of news. Static filled the radio waves, stretching out, making Mac wonder if he'd lost the connection.

"Jesus fucking Christ," Rikar grumbled. *"Couldn't you find somewhere a bit closer to home? Somewhere without a shitload of ocean between here and there?"*

Bastian laughed. *"Water dragon syndrome. The more ocean, the better."*

Mac guessed that was true. It hadn't occurred to him to find somewhere in the city to keep Tania safe. He'd wanted to be in the water, out to sea, as far away from Ivar and his band of assholes as possible.

"How long will it take us to get there?" Rikar asked.

He gave his buddies the location of his weekend getaway, then estimated the flying time. *"A couple of hours... give or take."*

"Not happening tonight," B said. *"Sun's up in forty-five."*

Huh. Was it really that late? Craning his neck, he looked over the top of Tania's head. She snuffled, nestling her cheek against his shoulder. He caressed her back, soothing her while he glanced toward the dresser along the far wall. His cloak radio glowed from its perch on top of a stack of books. The red numbers read 5:03 a.m. Wow. Guess time really did fly while you were having fun. Or rather...teaching a gorgeous brunette how to play poker.

"Stay put," Rikar said. *"We'll come for you at sundown."*

Mac nodded, even though neither male could see him. He required the self-reinforcement. With no cavalry on the horizon, he was, well...FUBARed. Trapped by daylight, he'd be stuck inside with Tania for the next twelve hours. No buffer. No relief. Just torture central on the desire front, waiting for his brothers-in-arms to show up. Mac suppressed the urge to squirm. How the hell was he supposed to resist her that long?

And not do something stupid?

Mac dropped another f-bomb. Now more than ever, he despised his fledgling status. 'Cause, yeah. If his magic worked the way it should've, the ability to cloak himself would be nothing but an afterthought. Just business as usual as he flew for the safety of Black Diamond. But, oh no...not him. He never did anything the easy way.

The manner of his change was proof enough of that. His *first shift* had been anything but normal. Most Dragonkind didn't need female energy at the moment of transition. A male required two things. One...to have reached physical maturity. And two? A strong male to connect through mind-speak and guide him through the brutal shift into dragon form.

Mac was an exception to the rule.

He'd been raised outside the Dragonkind community. Had never benefited from being surrounded by members of his own kind. From the moment of his birth, a male fed from the collective energy emitted by his pack, siphoning the excess until he reached a magical threshold. The second a male finished growing and his energy tank read full, his dragon DNA ground into motion, catapulting him into the change.

Too bad his upbringing hadn't been quite so idyllic.

Abandoned by his father in the human world, Mac had never gotten that kind of nourishment. Which meant his dragon half had lain dormant until he'd gotten zapped, blown through the one-way mirror in SPD's interrogation room by the Razorback XO's nasty-ass exhale. The magical onslaught triggered his change, causing the Nightfuries to scramble. Rikar and Bastian had chosen the path of least resistance, hoping an infuse of female energy would stabilize his levels enough to save his life. The gamble had worked, topping him up, doing in a few hours what took most Dragonkind males eighteen or twenty years to accomplish.

Which had put Tania on the hook. And him in the hot seat.

So here he was. A thirty-four-year-old fledgling with fucked-up magic and a soon-to-be-pissed-off female. One he couldn't protect properly, because…shit. He couldn't cloak himself or her while in flight yet. And that left him with an inescapable truth. One that chafed his pride and made his heart ache. He was 100 percent inadequate. Not man enough for the woman he wanted so badly she twisted him into knots.

Mac hugged her tighter, desperation taking hold.

Sensing his disquiet, Bastian asked, *"How is she?"*

"Sleeping now."

Rikar snorted. *"With you?"*

"Fuck off," he said, resenting his XO's teasing tone. It kicked up all kinds of mental debris. Guilt? Inadequacy? Self-loathing? Take your pick. Mac owned them all. *"She was scared…needed to sleep, but couldn't settle down. I drew off some of her energy to help her."*

The guys remained silent. An unusual occurrence, one that spoke volumes.

"Motherfuck," Mac growled. *"What else was I supposed to do?"*

"Nothing. You did what was best for her. No one's faulting you for that." Static interrupted the connection for a second.

B's voice faded out, then back in as he said, *"But she may not think so when you explain everything later."*

Didn't he know it. Tania was going to kick his ass when he opened that can of worms. Started the conversation in which he confessed all and hoped she not only understood his reasons but forgave his selfishness.

And still he turned in to her instead of away, wrapping both arms around her. As he snuggled in, he kissed her softly. Not much. A simple brush of his mouth against the corner of hers, nothing more, telling her without words he was sorry. Thanking her too. For what she had unknowingly given him, for the gift of allowing him to hold her.

The sound of the wind picked up, the increased velocity coming through mind-speak. His sonar pinged, and, closing his eyes, Mac reached for his magic, tracking the flight path. And what do you know? His dragon came online, charting his brothers-in-arms' course, giving him the longs and lats of their location. East of the city, flying fast toward the Cascade Mountain range.

"You free and clear yet?"

"Looks like it." Rikar's scales rattled in flight. The sounds echoed inside Mac's head. *"The rogues are bugging out."*

"Fucking pansies," B said.

Rikar growled, the lethal sound full of agreement. *"Mac?"*

"What?"

"Get some sleep. It'll all wash out...look better in the evening."

Uh-huh. Right. As if that was going to happen. Sleep and him weren't the best of friends. Mac snorted. Enemy was more like it. Insomnia always beat on him with brass knuckles, disrupting his ability to rest, keeping him wide-awake most days. But even as he signed off, severing the link between him and his friends, he felt the tug...the slow slide into exhaustion.

His head on the pillow, his face tucked into Tania's shoulder, the duvet up around their shoulders, Mac allowed his eyes to drift closed. Up, then down. He fought to stay awake. He failed, losing the battle as his muscles uncoiled one taut thread at a time, rushing him into relaxation.

Wow, that was weird. He hadn't been sleepy in ages. But with Tania nestled against him, oblivion beckoned, drawing him into a dark fall down a long tunnel. As he succumbed, surrendering to dreams, he wondered if she was the cause. The thought drifted a moment before he let it go. Stopped trying to figure out why and simply thanked God for the effect she had on him instead. 'Cause, umm-yeah, it felt so good to be in her arms.

———

The smell of blood propelled Nian through the Emblem Club's outer door, over the threshold and...

Straight into a load of lethal.

A dark blur hurtled though the air, coming at him like an inbound missile. With a curse, Nian ducked and dodged right. The Dragonkind male smashed into the solid wall behind him. A sickening crack echoed, bouncing around the stairwell, ricocheting off steel and ancient stone. His brows snapped together as he watched the bloodied stranger turn belly-up on the floor with a groan. The door clicked closed, thick mahogany blocking out the smell of cigar smoke and soothing croon of jazz music. The sound of knuckles meeting flesh replaced it, cracking through the foyer of the Emblem Club's back entrance.

Nian's attention snapped toward the foot of the stairs. Good Christ. What the hell was going on here?

Jaw gone slack, he took in the scene. He shut his mouth, then shook his head. Well, so much for decorum. Or a modicum of decency. A full-on brawl was in progress. Fists and feet flying. Grunts and groans rebounding up the spiral staircase to reach the upper floors. Although, come to think of it, maybe *brawl* wasn't quite the right word. *Beat down* was a more apt description, because holy God...

He'd never seen anything like it.

Gage was a force of nature. A sight to behold...unleashing hell, taking on five males at once. Nian's brows popped skyward as the Nightfury bashed two males' heads together. The pair crumpled. Gage lashed out, kicking a third one in the face. Swinging around, his bronze gaze aglow, he locked on the final two. The pair squawked and retreated. Tuxedo tails flapping, they scrambled up the stairs. Gage snarled and, with a quickness that defied reason, went after them, hauling both back into the foyer. Within moments his adversaries lay unconscious in a bloody heap on the floor next to their brethren.

Surprise still circling, Nian glanced at Haider.

Standing off to one side, a sobbing female in his arms, the male shrugged. "Gage doesn't like rapists."

"I can see that," he murmured, reading the rage in Gage's eyes. Breathing hard, the warrior pivoted toward him. Nian tensed and got ready to sidestep. Getting in the Nightfury's way wasn't a good idea. Especially considering the devastation he left in his wake. "Does he like anyone?"

"Not really." Haider made a soothing sound and rubbed the human's back. "I'm an exception to the rule. Most days, anyway."

"Bully for you." His focus shifted to the light-haired female. Tucked up against Haider, he couldn't see her face, but...

Nian's heart clenched. Her dress was ripped. One stiletto on, one off, her stockings were wrecked too, huge holes in the nylon along both thighs and knees. But that wasn't the worst part. Clothes could be repaired and shoes replaced. The bruises on her upper arms, though, turned his stomach. His hands curled into fists as he stared at the angry marks on her pale skin. The bastards. They'd held her down, torn her clothing...hurt her without a moment's hesitation.

Nian growled low in his throat. "Is she all right? Did they—"

"No," Haider said, holding her slight form close, comforting her with gentle hands. "We intervened in time."

Thank God. He couldn't stand the thought of a female being raped. Not anywhere, but certainly not in one of the clubs he owned. Stinking Archguard festival. Had the situation played out differently, he would've refused the high council's request. Never let them darken his doorway, never mind use his establishments as ground zero for festival parties. He hadn't wanted to, but having eyes and ears on the other members of the council was useful. Intelligence-gathering at its best. As the newest member of the Archguard, he needed to make inroads into the group. Trust, after all, was earned, not freely given.

Hence the offer to use his clubs. Situated in the city center, Prague rose majestic and true around his night-clubs and the upscale cigar bars he favored. Perfect for the festival. The constant stream of female clubbers kept the Dragonkind males who'd made the trip to honor the traditions of their kind not only satisfied but content.

Still, Nian disapproved of them playing fast and loose with the rules. He hated his race's disregard for females. Low-energy. High-energy. It didn't matter. Women, regardless of their capacity to feed his kind, ought to be treated with respect. Valued. Granted every kindness. The fact his counterparts on the high council disagreed simply cemented Nian's wish for real, sustainable change.

Which meant knocking the leader of the Archguard off his perch. The sooner, the better.

The glow in his gaze subsiding, Gage stepped around the unconscious heap of male bodies and approached on silent feet. Holding out his arms, he met Haider's gaze. "Give her to me."

Haider didn't hesitate. Turning her gently in his embrace, he nudged her toward his comrade. Still frightened, the female clung, shying away with a flinch, mascara streaking her cheeks. Her breath hitched on another sob. With a murmur, Gage calmed her, and she settled, curling against the massive male's chest. He gathered her up and pivoted, carrying her toward the security door that would take them outside into the alley beyond.

"It's all right, *talmina*. You're safe now," Gage said, deep voice full of gravel, his mouth brushing the top of her head. "Let's get you home."

She nodded. And Nian marveled. *Talmina*…"little one" in Dragonese. Incredible. Not the word so much, but Gage's gentleness. The Nightfury had just creamed five males without breaking a sweat and yet was able to treat the female with a caring that belied his aggressive nature. Witnessing it was like watching a spectacle, one with a twist at the end you never saw coming. Unexpected, but welcome all the same.

No doubt about it. The Nightfury pack would be excellent allies.

Which meant he needed to put his feet in motion. If he didn't act fast, Gage and Haider would disappear into the night. Leave him behind to return the female home, and he'd miss his chance. To chat. To make his argument and present his case. He must do it now. With the festival coming to a close in a couple of days, the Nightfury males wouldn't be around much longer.

Moving ahead of the pair, Nian grabbed the metal handle and cranked down. The reinforced steel door swung wide. Chilly air rushed over the threshold, hitting him in the face, bringing welcome respite from the heat of the club. His night vision sparked, and he looked both ways, scanning for any threat from outside. Empty but for a row of dumpsters, flanked by brick walls down both sides, nothing jumped out at him. Well, other than Prague's inhospitable November wind.

Nian stepped out into the alley. Ignoring the snowy bluster, he pivoted in the middle of the narrow thorough-fare and slipped out of his tuxedo jacket. "Here...take my coat. It's too cold out here for her dressed like that."

The Nightfury's eyes narrowed. Nian didn't retreat. Instead, he stepped up to wrap Armani's finest around the female, surrounding her with his warmth as Gage shifted her in his arms.

The crunch of footfalls sounded behind him. The soft voice came next, slithering like poison and just as deadly. Nian tensed, preparing to be bitten as Haider said, "What do you want, Nian?"

He glanced over his shoulder. Pale silver eyes met his. "What makes you think I want something?"

"Stop fucking around," Gage growled, the impatience in his tone tangible. "Or I'll stomp your skull and be done with it."

Well, now. Nothing like skipping the formalities to get straight to the point. "I want you to take a message to Bastian."

"Really?" Raising a brow, Haider shook his head. Straight, long hair followed the movement, brushing the male's shoulders as silver strands shot with dark gray and black shimmered beneath snowflakes and the moon glow. "And just what would it say: sorry my father tortured and almost killed you?"

"I am not my sire."

"Could've fooled me." Giving Nian a once-over, Gage snarled, then sidestepped, brushing shoulders with him. "You look a lot like the bastard...right down to your fancy fucking shoes."

Reaching into his trouser pocket, Nian palmed his lighter. Instant relief from the tension. The gold settled him down, sent his nerves from frayed to rock steady. He needed to stay calm. The second he rose to Gage's bait, the pair would assume he was just like the male who had sired him and walk away. Or worse yet, slash his throat, *then* walk away. "I am a member of the Archguard, Nightfury. There are certain expectations that must be met. And appearances can be deceiving."

"Um-hmm." Dress shoes scraping over cobblestones, Gage strode toward the mouth of the alleyway. Halfway down, he turned to glare at Nian over his shoulder. "Haider, you deal with the asshole. I'll see the female home."

Trust. Had he said it was earned earlier? A huge assumption. Particularly since Haider and Gage didn't appear to have any. So getting in their good graces and winning them over? A distinct impossibility. Unless, of course, he got lucky, phrased his argument just right.

"I'm fed up, Haider," he said, being honest for once. "Tired of all the power mongering."

"You've been a member of the Archguard...for what? A month?"

"Three, actually." Nian knew what the male was getting at. A few months was nowhere near long enough to be fed up with the instability. With the nonsense that went on day after day, year after year. "I haven't been in power long, but I've spent a lifetime watching my sire pull strings from the sidelines. Time enough to see the need for change."

Interest lit in the Nightfury's eyes. Good. The male was listening.

"What are you proposing?" Haider asked, reaching into his breast coat pocket.

The Nightfury pulled out a slim silver cigar case. With a pop, he took off the rounded top and extracted an expensive cigar from its confines. The work of seconds, the male prepared the Cuban, clipping the end with a cutter before setting it in his mouth. Quick with his hands, Nian put his lighter to good use. The small flame flared. The cigar burned bright orange, releasing the smell of burning tobacco into the night air. Haider leaned back and away. Nian clicked his lighter closed as smoke curled from the male's mouth, obscuring his face a moment before floating upward to meet the snowy sky.

The cold air licked deep, attacking the thin material of his silk shirt. Nian suppressed a shiver, refusing to show any weakness. Not in front of a male who was nothing but strong. "I propose an exchange."

"You don't have anything we want."

"I'm on the inside…right at the top of the inner circle."

"So what?" Taking another puff, Haider blew out a smoke ring. "You want to be our minute man?"

"I'm invited to all the private parties. Am privy to all the council does and says inside and out of chambers. Are you?" When the male remained silent, Nian raised a brow, pushing his advantage. He had eyes and ears everywhere. Was welcomed in places where, as Nightfuries, Haider and Gage would never be accepted. "Rodin's neck-deep in nothing good. You know it, and so do I. I could be your friend, Nightfury. An asset to your pack."

"At what price?"

"A very small one."

"Lay it out."

"Support from Bastian and the entire Nightfury pack," Nian said. "Protection and backup when I need it."

Haider's mercury eyes narrowed. Nian could almost see the male's mind turning, ferreting out the facts, calculating every possibility. Smart with a whole lot of cunning. The Nightfury might be a diplomat, but he wasn't a politician. Impossible to bribe. Hard to fool. Even more difficult to manipulate. Which meant keeping his cards close to the vest. No sense giving away the game before it even started.

"Think about it, Haider." Nian flicked the top of his lighter. Open. Closed. Click-click-snap. The sound ringing in the silence that grew between them. "Best friend or adversary. Your choice."

"I'll take it to my commander." Flicking ash from the end of his cigar, Haider pivoted toward the street. To where Gage was helping the female into a taxicab. Halfway between him and his comrade, the male glanced over his shoulder, and he got nailed with shimmering pale eyes. "No guarantees, though, Nian."

Nian nodded. That was all he asked. A chance to win Bastian's favor. Now all he needed to do was wait...hope and pray the powerful male took the bait and agreed. He required a powerful ally, one of the Nightfury commander's caliber. One that would set Rodin on his heels and the rest of the Archguard running. He couldn't, after all, overtake the high council and rise to power without a little help from friends.

Ambition, he thought, watching Haider walk away. His cross to bear. Then again, he was his sire's son, and his father had taught him well.

Chapter Sixteen

Weak sunlight broke through the cloud cover, caressing the tops of J.J.'s shoulders. The beginnings of a new melody flitted through her mind. The chorus had a one-two beat. The main instrument? An acoustic guitar. It always happened that way. The drums came first, gifting her with the rhythm before the musical layers filtered in to take shape and form. Eventually it would become what it was meant to be...a song, complete with lyrics. The ones she scribbled down inside the notebook she kept stashed under the mattress inside her cell. Getting to that point might take her fifteen minutes or a few days, but...

Eventually. The piece would come together. A beautiful marriage of rhythm and music notes. Something she could sing while lying in her bunk at night, listening to the prison whisper around her. Soft comfort in a harsh place.

Tania called her gift for music genius. Marveling at her ability to pick up any instrument and learn how to play it in less than two weeks. J.J. didn't agree. Her talent was nothing special. Just more normal in a life filled with routine. Ho-hum at best, but at least her songs kept her company.

Humming the tune, J.J. tipped her face up toward the sun. Meager warmth caressed her skin, tempting her to stop, stand still, and soak up more. She kept moving instead, the soles of her shoes scuffing against worn pavement, walking the fence's perimeter, chain link topped by barbed wire to her left, the wide-open expanse of the prison yard to her right. Day in. Day out. It was always the same. She stuck to her chosen path, to the regular routine that sustained her.

Today, though, it wasn't about survival. Or her self-imposed exile into the land of loneliness. It was about strategy. About preparing for what was to come.

Excitement prickled through her. Nervousness tempered it, spinning hope toward caution. She couldn't afford to mess up. But neither could she wish too hard. Danger lay in that direction. Disappointment the main dish at the dinner table called life.

Burrowing deeper into her prison-issue jacket, J.J. kept walking, each of her strides eating the ground, covering the distance. Round and round she went, one lap turning into another. Guitar notes and drumbeats melding, her mind flipped through the possibilities. All the likely questions the parole board would ask. And how she would answer each one.

She finished her fifth circuit, ignoring the desolate gray of the fenced-in area. Huddled together, inmates stood in the middle of the large yard, hands buried in their coat pockets, wool toques on their heads to ward off the chill. Their voices rose and collided, sounding more like birds chattering than grown women talking. The mental snapshot made J.J. picture a flock of flamingos standing one-legged in a pond. The noisy result would be about the same. Clusters of birds clucking versus groups of women chatting. The only real difference? Color, and the fact flamingos were free to fly away.

Anytime they wanted.

Nodding to a cluster of friendlies, J.J. strode on and, looking skyward again, worshiped the sun, pretending for a moment she was...

Free.

Taking an afternoon stroll in downtown Seattle. Window-shopping instead of stuck here...on the inside. The mental picture was a powerful one. But the yearning that drove it? Even more so.

A month. Just thirty days—a measly 720 hours—and it might actually happen.

Might was a pretty big word, though, wasn't it? It left so much unsaid...undetermined and up in the air, leaving her to wonder which way Father Chance would throw her when the time came. Ah yes, hope...a very dangerous thing. A grand illusionist with too many tricks up its sleeve. The sleight of hand, however, was the least of her problems, and belief, the most. She recognized a smoke screen—a pipe dream—when she saw one.

And yet J.J. couldn't turn away from its allure. Couldn't slow down long enough to allow reality to burst her bubble. She didn't want to be reasonable. To look at the facts and admit her chances of getting parole were slim. She wanted to dream, if only for a little while. And as her low spirits spiraled into lightheartedness, opaque emotional skies moved to light-filled and airy.

Her lips tipped up at the corners. Insane. Ironclad certifiable.

But oh, the possibilities. Tra-la-la-la-la.

J.J. huffed, laughing at her own stupidity.

"What's so funny, Injin?"

More rasp than substance, the voice coiled around her like a venomous snake. As the insult to her Cherokee heritage—to the father she'd never known and didn't share with her sister—sank deep, the song she'd been composing died a quick death. Anger bubbled up in its wake, blistering the inside of her soul. Griggs. It couldn't be anyone else. None of the other guards called her *Injin.*

The racist podunk.

Wrestling with her temper, J.J. wiped her expression clean and glanced over her shoulder. She blinked, two things surprising her at once. One, she'd gotten too close to the yard's outdoor gym, her nemesis's playground. Oh, and speak of the devil, Daisy (a misnomer for the butched-out, heavyset woman if there ever was one) was now eyeballing her from behind a pair of free weights. And two? Griggs looked like a train wreck. Or rather as though he'd gone toe-to-toe with one...and lost. Big-time. The two black eyes he sported told the tale. The white butterfly bandages above one eyebrow and the cut across the bridge of his nose finished the story. Someone had unleashed hell on the guard, using his fists to mete out some serious punishment.

Bully for him. Or umm...

Her.

Ah, crap. Had Tania finally lost it and put up her dukes? Taken all her kickboxing lessons and hammered Griggs like he deserved? J.J. frowned, playing with the idea. It took her less than a second to decide. Her sister wasn't the culprit. As much as Tania complained about Griggs, she knew the price for losing her temper with the guard...J.J.'s butt in a sling. So, no. Her sister would never risk her that way.

Too bad, really.

She would love for her sister to go ballistic. Could handle the repercussions—endure the idiot guard's vengeful payback—to see Tania put the hammer down and clock the jerk. Just once. Okay, so that was a big, fat lie. One fist to his face would never be enough. She wanted to witness the whole kit and caboodle. A handful of knuckle sandwiches. A flurry of solid kicks until he folded like a bad poker hand.

Griggs had earned it, after all...and then some.

"Well?" he said, his tone sharp with authority.

"Nothing, Officer," she said, looking skyward. The clouds shifted, hiding the sun behind a blanket of thick, white, and fluffy. Figured. The second Griggs showed up, all lightness vanished. "Just enjoying the fresh air."

"Fitting, I guess. Especially since you won't be enjoying it much longer." His smug tone put her on high alert. What the heck did he mean by that? Unease skittered deep. J.J.'s focus snapped back to him. Victory in his bloodshot eyes, he murmured, "Interesting personal file you got there, Injin."

J.J.'s heart dipped, then rebounded. Oh God. He knew. Had seen the letter from the parole board in her file and now...he *knew*. Fear sent her sideways, closing her throat, locking her lungs until she couldn't breathe.

"Better talk to that sister of yours. No one else needs to know about your appointment with the PB. Certainly not Daisy." A knowing gleam in his awful eyes, Griggs smirked, threatening her with Daisy the Destroyer. A woman doing time for a triple homicide and known for her brutality to other inmates. "You could turn it all around. An encouraging word or two from you and..."

A gust twisted through the yard, blowing stone dust across the pavement. The smell of stale grass whipped in its wake, mixing with Griggs's corrupt stench as he trailed off, letting the implication of sexual favors lie. And J.J.'s stomach rolled, disgust joining terror on her top two hit parade. As it beat on her like a drum, she looked away to stare across the yard.

It wasn't fair. Not to her. Not to Tania, either.

They were so close. So amazingly close to winning. And Griggs…the goddamned asshole…threatened to ruin it all. But no matter what he said—or how hard he pushed—she would never give up her sister. Would risk death to protect Tania. She'd done it before and would do it again without a moment's hesitation.

"Your life for one night with her." Utility belt creaking, Griggs leaned toward her. J.J. fought the urge to cringe. She refused to give anything away, but fear took its pound of flesh anyway as he whispered, "Not too much to ask, is it?"

She didn't answer. Simply walked away without a single word or backward glance. Time for a new plan. One that included calling the lawyer Tania retained on her behalf. She needed out of general population and into protective custody…lightning fast. Before Griggs made good on his promise and sent Daisy after her. Before she ended up with a shank between her shoulder blades.

Chapter Seventeen

The voices came from far away, traveling through a pain-filled tunnel. Agony flicked through Venom and grew sharper, lighting his skin on fire. As sensation burned across his abdomen, sound warped, funneling into a long, vicious hiss. Fighting through the sensory static, he struggled to open his eyes. A no go. Nothing worked right. Not his body. Not his mind. Not even his eyes listened to the commands he gave them. But goddamn, he needed to snap out of it and get mobile...right now.

Staying still wasn't an option.

Not while Razorbacks circled. Hunted. Searched for an opening to deal the deathblow.

Planting his palm, Venom pushed up, fighting to get himself vertical. The ground beneath him squished inward, feeling...well, kind of spongy and soft. He managed to crack his eyelids. Bright light burned the backs of his retinas. A wave of black spots screwed with his vision. Something crawled over his belly, poking at a sore spot.

Pain rippled through him.

Venom bit down on a curse. Silence was imperative. The second he screamed the bastards would find him. Finish the job. Leave him ashed out in a pile of nothing special.

Another tug at his wound, this time along his hip. Anguish splintered, driving the needles of pain deeper. Raising his arm, he grabbed a fistful of the fabric beneath him and pulled, desperate to find a safe spot to hide, to wait the rogues out, but...

God, that hurt. Everything hurt: his head, his body, the red-hot poker burning a hole in his stomach.

The prodding contact came again. He shoved it away.

"Venom, don't." The soft voice sped toward him, tying him up with confusion. Who the hell was that? He went still. The person spoke again. "Hold still, honey. I'm almost through."

Venom and *honey*. Two words that never went together. At least before now.

But the combo was a good sign. He frowned. Wasn't it?

Someone brushed the hair back from his forehead. Venom turned his face into it, testing his theory. Another soft stroke and...

Yeah. Definitely a friendly. He wasn't alone. Didn't need to be afraid, which meant one thing. Black Diamond. He was at home, safe inside the lair.

Relief sent him sideways, and, fighting a bad case of dry mouth, he croaked, "Myst?"

"Hey, welcome back."

"Where'd I go?"

Shoes squeaked against the hospital-grade floor. "You've been unconscious for over twelve hours."

"Doesn't sound like me."

Myst snorted.

Trying his vision again, Venom opened his eyes. His focus wavered a second and then sharpened. Eyes the color of violets met his, anchoring him in the here and now. Myst's domain. He was safe, laid up inside one of Black Diamond's recovery rooms. The white walls, glossy cabinets, and stainless steel countertops were a dead giveaway. The only sure thing that pierced through the mind-fog. Except…

After a moment that cleared too. Memory rushed in, replaying the battle over Gig Harbor, the brutal hit he'd taken and—

Holy Christ. Wick. Where the hell was his best friend?

Worry spun him into action, giving him strength. With a groan, he propped himself on his elbow and looked around. Nothing but medical equipment, Bastian's female, and…Sloan. Oh thank God. The male would know if Wick was AWOL or okay.

He pegged his buddy with a glare. "Where is he?"

"Around." Dark eyes collided with his. Sloan rounded the end of the bed and unloaded his weight, making the mattress dip as he sat down. With a grunt, he swung his legs up, planted his big-ass boots on the coverlet, and crossed one over the other. "He brought you in, stuck around while Myst sewed you up, then fucked off."

"Smart guy," Myst said. "I wanted to do the same near the end."

"Gave you a hard time, did I?"

"You're a freaking pain in the butt to patch up, Venom. Swearing. Kicking. Being a regular pansy about getting stitched up." Picking up a role of tape, she tore off three strips and, smoothing his bandage down, taped it in place. "So now you owe me one."

Ah, hell. That didn't sound good. "My penance?"

"You stay off your feet for two days. No sudden movements, which means…" Holding up one of her hands, she ticked off her fingers with the other. "No wrestling. No fighting. No active play video games. Or—"

"Ah, come on," he said, sounding like a whiny brat.

"—hall hockey, either. In fact, go back to sleep for a while. It'll help you heal." He opened his mouth to object. She nailed him with one of her no-nonsense looks. "If you don't listen to me, I'll sic Bastian on you."

All right, then. Game over. No way he wanted B riding his ass. About anything, but especially not for upsetting Myst. Nothing but a serious beat down lay in that direction, and…goddamn it. No video games? Seriously? What the hell did she expect him to do all day?

Oh, right…sleep.

Terrific advice. Too bad he didn't feel like taking it. He was wide-awake now, nowhere ready to go back to la-la land. He wanted to move, stretch his sore muscles, and test his strength. Not lie in bed and stare at the ceiling. He was already bored, and he'd only just opened his eyes.

Myst's eyes narrowed on him. "I mean it, Venom."

Venom grumbled but settled back against the sheets. No sense arguing with her. He was a fast learner, and watching Bastian the last couple of weeks had taught him plenty… like females rarely—if ever—lost an argument. Hell, Myst would eat him alive if he tried. Just KO his ass before he even got out of the gate.

"Good boy." Myst patted him on the shoulder.

Sloan snorted in amusement.

Which, naturally, made Venom want to kill something. And since it couldn't be B's female, Sloan jumped to the top of his hit list. "Traitor."

"You'd do the same for me," Sloan said.

Myst rolled her eyes. Giving him one last love tap, she tossed the tape on the side table and headed for the door. "I'll be back in an hour to check on you. Behave while I'm gone."

"Yeah, yeah," he said, glaring at his buddy.

Grinning, Sloan watched Myst retreat. As the door opened then closed behind her, his buddy's gaze settled back on him. "You hungry?"

No, he wasn't. But if it meant getting rid of Sloan? He was 100 percent on board with that plan. "I could eat."

"I'll grab you something."

A "thanks," twenty seconds later, and—

The door to the recovery room closed. Silence descended, and Venom sighed in relief. Alone at last. With time and plenty to disobey a direct order. Myst wouldn't be happy, but that was too flipping bad. He refused to stay flat on his back in the recovery room. Not while his own bed awaited in the aboveground lair. At least there he had books to read and...yeah, an Xbox to keep him busy while he waited for the dragon DNA to get with the program and heal him up tight.

Looking forward to a round of *Halo*, Venom conjured a pair of track pants. An instant later, he flipped the covers back and pushed himself upright. Weak from blood loss, his arms shook as he swung his legs over the side of the bed. Pain spiraled around his rib cage, then took a side trip up his spine. With a muttered curse, he gripped the edge of the mattress, searching for steady in a sea of topsy-turvy. It didn't go well. His brain kept sloshing around inside his skull, making the room spin. Round and round. One revolution after another. A mental roller coaster without end.

His stomach heaved, trying to crawl up his throat. Tasting bile, Venom swallowed the burn, refusing to throw up. He was tougher than that. Was warrior strong. Would sooner punch himself in the balls than surrender to the knifelike pressure in his belly or to the—

Ah, hell.

Venom lunged for the trash can next to the bed. The second his hands curled around the lip, he gagged, dry heaving over the basket. Then groaned. His belly wound squawked, elevating agony to new levels. Sweat beaded on his skin, sliding between his shoulder blades as his brain turned into an Olympic gymnast, doing cartwheels inside his head. And his stomach? The frigging SOB was in full revolt, trampling his esophagus, evacuating a load of bile…and nothing else. But then, there wasn't much else the bastard could do, considering he hadn't eaten in a while.

On his knees, one hand planted flat on the wall, he hugged the round can and hung his head over the lip. He dry heaved again. This time, though, he breathed through it, pulling air in through his nose before exhaling out his mouth. Better. He continued with the in-and-out routine, enriching his body with oxygen. After a minute or ten, his stomach settled enough for him to push to his feet. Which, of course, made the gash across his abdomen holler even louder. Propping his shoulder against the wall, he peeled back the bandage and—

Holy God.

The wound started at the underside of his rib cage, then slashed across, bisecting his entire torso to reach the top of his right hip. Venom grimaced. Jeez, talk about a close call. Good thing the Razorbacks didn't have good aim. A few inches lower and his days of pleasing females would've been over.

Folding the gauze back into place, Venom set the trash can on the floor. As he stood upright, he swayed a little, weakness attacking his thigh muscles, making him quiver. He steadied himself and turned toward the door. Bare feet silent, he made his way out of the recovery area, ignoring the utilitarian white walls and green hospital-grade floor, and walked into the underground lair's medical clinic. More bright light hammered him. He squinted against the glare, scanning the space. Empty. Excellent. Nothing but a bank of wall cabinets, medical equipment pushed up against the back wall, and a stainless steel operating table.

One hand pressed to his belly wound, Venom stared at the table a moment, then frowned. He remembered being up on the thing last night, getting held down as Myst stitched him up. A twinge of embarrassment rolled through him. He owed her an apology. He'd said some things; been too pissed off, in too much pain to censor himself, and—

Yeah. No doubt about it. She'd gotten an earful. And wasn't that something to be proud of?

Raking his hair back, he shuffled across the clinic, careful to keep each stride short. The last thing he wanted was any more trouble. And if he tore the stitches, Myst would scold him, and he'd get the eye evil from B. So not on his list of things to do tonight. Neither was finding something to eat, but that wouldn't fly. Despite the rot-gut he had going on, he needed the fuel. Food equaled energy. And energy equaled fast healing, so, yeah, it looked like he'd be eating whatever Sloan brought him.

The motion sensor above the sliding glass door went active. As the thing opened wide, Venom gimped his way into the corridor. The main point of passage in the underground lair, the double-wide hallway saw a lot of traffic every day. Good thing it was quiet now, though. Otherwise he would get turfed, tossed back into the recovery room while Myst padlocked the door.

Tucking his left elbow into his side, Venom spread his hand across his belly and, reaching out, used the wall as a crutch. The solid support along with the added push helped propel him up the slight incline toward Sloan's computer lab.

The cool tones of a sexy saxophone drifted toward him.

Venom's brows collided. Nowhere near Sloan's style. The male never played stuff like that. Hard-core rap. Heavy-duty death metal. Not…

What was that? A little R & B in the evening. Sade maybe?

Coming even with the doorframe, he glanced inside the com center. Ah. It all made sense now. Rikar's female had set up shop. Red hair bright beneath the overhead lights, file folders spread out on the conference table behind her, Angela stared at the opposite wall. His focus shifted, taking in the photos of five missing females…the ones she suspected had been imprisoned by the Razorbacks. The sight made him sick all over again.

Asshole rogues. Heartless bastards. Ivar needed his head ripped off in a big way.

Leaning on the jamb, he cleared his throat to avoid startling her. She glanced over her shoulder, and he got nailed by intelligent hazel eyes. "Whatcha doing down here, Detective? Daimler kick you out of the dining room?"

"I left my gun on the dining room table again." She fingered the Glock strapped to her thigh. "He wasn't happy."

"The M25?" A gift from her mate, the sniper rifle was a beautiful piece. More so for what Angela could do with the thing. A crack shot, she took out moving targets from eight hundred to one thousand yards away. Astonishing by any standards. Kick-ass useful by his. "You scratch the table?"

Angela grimaced, then held her thumb and forefinger an inch apart. "A little bit."

"Ah," he said, fighting a grin. Made sense. Their resident go-to guy was picky about stuff like that. A real neat freak, Daimler liked rules and woe betide anyone who didn't toe the line. Guess Angela had just found that out the hard way.

Venom's focus jumped back to the wall behind her. Glossy eight-by-ten pictures glinted in the low light. He tipped his chin. "How's it going? You find anything yet?"

The questions put Angela on high alert. Her eyes narrowed on him, and Venom saw her mental wheels turning. She was trying to decide whether to share the information or hold on to her grudge against him.

Venom didn't blame her.

He hadn't made it easy for her to like him. She loved Mac, backed the male up at every turn. And as far as the newest Nightfury was concerned? Venom was the Antichrist, so…no question. It was only natural for Angela to resent him. He and Mac had issues; calling each other names wasn't the least of them. They were like oil and water…constantly divided. Although after last night's performance—the one in which Mac saved his noodle… goddamn it—Venom knew he needed to cut the fledgling some slack.

Holding her gaze, Venom gave in to the urge to explain. "You know the thing between me and Mac?"

"The thing being…what? You acting like an ass?"

His lips twitched. He couldn't help it. Rikar's female was strong, as direct as a sledgehammer to the head.

"Maybe," he said, conceding the point. "It isn't personal. This is my pack. Has been for the better part of sixty years. Rikar and the others are my family…mine to protect and keep safe. I take that vow seriously. A weak male in the mix will get one of us killed. I can't allow that."

"You haven't given him a chance, Venom." Adjusting her gun, she leaned back against the lip of the table. "How long did it take you to get your crap together after your *change*?"

Venom flinched, not liking the reminder. Or his sire's role in the memory. "A while."

"Mac's been Dragonkind for just over a month. Add that to the fact his transition was anything but normal and—"

"We're at war, Angela. I don't have time to coddle a male," he said. "He's either an asset to our pack or he isn't. No leeway there."

"So stop being a naysayer and"—giving him the stink eye, she pointed at him with her pen—"help Forge get him up to speed."

Flexing his hands, Venom examined his bruised knuckles, vacillating, wondering whether he should give in and back off. Capitulation wasn't his favorite thing. Once he decided something…he *decided*. But when Angela stood strong, refusing to retreat, he folded like a dirty shirt. Pleading hazel eyes could do that to a male. And Angela… God love her…wasn't above playing dirty.

"All right," he said, the words tasting sour. Venom swallowed the burn. Giving in was the right thing to do, no matter how much it stung his pride. "You win, Detective. I'll lay off."

"And help him too. Teach him a few tricks along the way."

Okay. Now she was just pushing it. "Maybe."

Nowhere near humble in victory, she grinned at him. "Truce, then."

Thank God. It was about frigging time.

He needed to take a load off. And standing around arguing with her wasn't helping him. Pushing away from the doorframe, he limped into the room. He glanced at Sloan's ugly purple chair. Ugh. What a travesty. The thing belonged in a dumpster, but it looked solid enough, so...

Steel groaned as he gripped the armrests and lowered himself into the seat.

"Are you all right?"

"Never better," he murmured, lying through his teeth, pain twisting his muscles into knots. Venom bit down on a grunt. Shifting in the chair, he tried to get comfortable. But comfort wasn't in the cards. Not tonight anyway.

Boots scuffed the floor. "I'll get Myst."

"Don't bother." Agony settled into a throb, beating against his abdomen. Venom released a pent-up breath and shook his head. "It's nothing time won't heal. And painkillers don't work on me, so...no point."

"So last night?"

"No anesthesia." Just straight-up surgery without the relief of drug-fueled oblivion. Hell on earth.

"Ouch." Angela grimaced. "Why doesn't it work on you?"

"I'm a poison breather. Full of toxins in and out of dragon form. Anything foreign enters my bloodstream, it gets killed. Instantly."

"Guess that makes flu season a breeze for you, huh?"

Venom snorted, then cursed under his breath. He pressed his hand to his side. Frigging hell. Laughing with a belly wound…not a good idea.

"Pretty much. But forget about me." Sliding into a slouch, his nape touched down on the seat back. He pointed to the white board screwed into the wall—and the collection of pictures taped to it. "Whatcha working on?"

"The missing women." Her attention snapped back to her handiwork. In red marker on one side of the board, she'd written a name, the date, and time of abduction under each female's picture. On the other side, she'd tacked newspaper clippings, all kinds of notes, and a dog-eared map of Seattle. "These women fit the pattern. All in their early to midtwenties. All highly intelligent. Huge overachievers."

She paused to chew on her bottom lip.

Venom murmured, encouraging her to continue.

"Every single one, without exception, was abducted from or close to Seattle U's campus." Her pen jogged in midair, pointing to each female in turn. "The victimology suggests they're all high-energy females."

"Young. Bright. Good candidates for the Razorbacks' breeding program."

"Exactly," she whispered, the strain in her voice unmistakable.

But when she turned to look at him, the shadows in her eyes almost killed him. Goddamned Razorbacks. The bastards had hurt Angela so badly, and for that alone, Venom wanted to rip every single one of their heads off. Losing his temper, though, wouldn't help her. Not now. Not ever, really. Only time and Rikar's love would heal that wound. Still, as he watched her struggle to contain the pain, the compulsion to help her lit a fire inside him. A slow burn.

A dangerous one that would fuel him when he went back out to hunt the enemy.

Slice and dice. Torture time with a rogue, here he came.

Angela cleared her throat. "All were taken about the same time...just before midnight. I've read through the reports...all the eyewitness accounts, hoping to find something...*anything*...that might tell me where to start looking for—"

"Ivar's lair."

She nodded, then turned toward him. "Venom, we need to get those women out of there."

The hitch in her voice cracked him wide open. His predatory instincts flared, dragging his need to protect up front and center. Not surprising, really. Female or not, she belonged to his pack now. Was his to protect and safeguard. And family always looked after and shielded their own. No matter what.

"Maybe I can help."

Surprise at his offer winged across her face. "How?"

"Wick and I busted into one of the rogues' old lairs a while ago. About the same time Mac went through the change." Frowning, Venom thought back, doing some mental inventory. "We were chasing their XO, so we didn't stop to look around, but...I saw other stuff there."

Angela perked up. "What kind of stuff?"

"Boxes. Things left behind in a hurry. There could be information...a paper trail...maybe some clue as to—"

"I need to go there. Walk the scene."

Venom hesitated, wanting to help without putting his own life on the line. No way could he take Angela outside the lair without Rikar's consent. The energy-fuse/mating stuff was serious business, and that kind of interference would get him squished faster than an ant under a boot heel. Well, that, or his balls handed to him on the end of a blade. Either way, he refused to step into that powder keg...with a frigging frost dragon. He'd end up in a cryogenic ice block.

So strategy time. He needed to figure out a way to let her down gently without—

"Venom?" The hopeful note in her tone zapped him. "Will you take me there?"

"Take you where, angel?"

The disembodied voice drifted in from the corridor. Shitkickers thudding on polished concrete, Rikar followed, crossing the threshold, pale eyes locked on his mate.

Venom blew out the breath he'd been holding. Saved by the bell. Or rather, the timely appearance of his XO.

"To the Razorbacks' old lair." Expression set, Angela met Rikar head-on. "I need to take a look around...see what they left behind."

"No fucking way," Rikar growled, then turned to glower at him.

Venom quelled the sudden urge to skedaddle. Jeez, like it was his fault? Rikar was mated to the detective, not him. But considering the PO'd look on his XO's face, only one thing left to do. Shifting in Sloan's chair, he tossed Angela back in the hot seat. "Don't get the wrong idea, man. I offered to get her the info, not take her with me."

"Ah, come on." Giving Venom an exasperated look, she crossed her arms over her chest. "I'm trained for this... know how to work a crime scene. I'll notice and remember things you guys won't."

Rikar scowled at her. "No."

"Please?"

Venom blinked. Oh-ho. Trouble wrapped in a gorgeous, hazel-eyed bundle with a *pretty please* on top. Rikar was so cooked. Venom could see it just by looking at him. Yeah, the male had dug in to hold the line—desperate to back up his big-ass NO—but Angela knew how to handle her mate. Smiling softly, she approached on silent feet, got in nice and close, and laid her hands flat on Rikar's chest. Venom shook his head. Holy God. The bonded male crap was some serious stuff. Why? Rikar—one of the strongest males he knew—was folding, his I-must-please-her gene kicking in with the force of nuclear fallout.

"Look, Rikar." Snuggling in, she encouraged Rikar to return the embrace. His XO didn't waste a second. He wrapped her up, closing his arms around her before pressing a kiss to the top of her head. "You and the other warriors will be with me. I'll be armed and—"

The computer dinged.

Dragging his attention from the lovey-dovey couple, Venom's attention snapped toward the wall-mounted computer monitors. Bright blue, a video chat box flashed in the center of the middle screen. Not liking his delayed reaction, the ping turned into a squawk, sounding like a bad version of a fire engine.

"Christ," Rikar muttered. "What the hell is that?"

Venom snorted. Frigging Sloan. Trust him to give a conference call an annoying ringtone.

Paddling with his bare feet, swiveling in the ugly chair, Venom turned to face the desk that stretched wall-to-wall beneath high-tech computer screens. Hell, another travesty. Burned and blistered in places, with hatchet marks cutting into the wood, the work surface was more than ancient. It was a disaster. Sloan really needed to get a clue. The male was two for two in the design no-no department.

Venom reached out, ignoring a twinge of pain, to palm the mouse. He double clicked on the link, expecting to see one of the Metallics. Too far away to use mind-speak—the cosmic connection required two things…consent between males and no more than five hundred miles between them to forge the link—Haider had been forced to set up a computer to relay messages from Prague.

The video chat opened.

Bronze eyes narrowed on him. "Where the fuck is Sloan?"

Standing behind the chair, Rikar laughed. "Good to see you too, Gage. What's up?"

Never one for niceties, the male said, "Shitloads."

"Any of it good?" Venom asked, wanting to make sure. One never knew with Gage. Violent to the point of self-destruction, the male considered what the rest of them labeled FUBARed as fun. "We get any nibbles yet?"

"Yeah. A big one."

"Oh goody," Venom said, glad his buddies' trip to Prague had borne fruit. That had been the idea…drop the hook, see who swam out to take the bait. His commander was smart that way. A consummate chess player, Bastian was always fifty moves ahead…a strategist without equal. And the Archguard's stupid festival? Perfect cover for some serious reconnaissance. Gage and Haider had gotten the job. Smart move on B's part. Haider was cunning, a smooth talker with wicked diplomatic skills. Hell, the male could charm the ears off an elephant if he wanted to. Anticipation gripping him, Venom shifted in the chair. "Who?"

"Nian."

Rikar's mouth fell open. "Jesus fucking Christ."

Yup. That about summed it up. Nian was a big fish, with even bigger family history. One that included his sire murdering Bastian's father—and becoming sole guardian of B before his change—to take control of the Archguard. Not that anyone could prove it. The sly male had been careful, leaving no trail of evidence for anyone to follow. Supposition upon supposition, that was all they had. Not enough to go after the head of one of the dynastic families that ruled Dragonkind.

And certainly not now. Nian hadn't even been born when that crap went down.

"You need to tell Bastian." One hand planted on the desktop in his hotel room, Gage leaned in, getting so close to the webcam Venom saw the stubble on the male's cheeks. "Protection in exchange for info. That's the bastard's game."

"Is he legit?"

"Fuck no," Gage said. "The little prick's power hungry. Wants to be top dragon, just like his sire. Haider's sniffing around. I'll let you know what he turns up."

"Good," Rikar murmured, one arm wrapped around Angela. "Next check-in?"

Gage glanced at his Rolex. "Forty-eight hours. Make sure B's in on the call."

As they nodded and Gage signed off, Venom's eyes narrowed. Well, well, well. What a very interesting turn of events. Nian...in their back pocket. How serendipitous, not to mention fun.

Venom hummed, the sound full of satisfaction. The set of circumstances almost made him wish he was in Prague...where he could witness firsthand the payback every Nightfury itched to deliver. And as he stared at the black computer screen, mind churning over the facts… heart filled with vengeance…he could hardly wait for the moment Bastian gave the order, and Gage ripped the Archguard idiot into tiny little pieces.

———

The digital clock read 5:47—p.m. or a.m.? Tania didn't have a clue. She was still fuzzy around the edges. Sleepy and warm. A gritty-eyed mess cocooned in cotton cling and fluffy feather down. Curled on her side in bed, she sighed and snuggled deeper, enjoying the soft covers and radiating heat, content to stay put and dream. To do something she rarely if ever did…

Relax and be lazy.

Hmm, yes. Without a doubt. Heaven. Angel clouds must feel exactly like this.

With another sigh, she let her eyes drift closed. A few more minutes. Just a little longer, then she'd force herself to get up and face the day. Or night. Whatever. The time didn't matter. Tackling her to-do list, however? Yup. That needed doing. Letting things slide wasn't her style. So five more minutes. After that, she'd do what she did best. Brave the chilly air and cold floors outside the nest of feather down to check her e-mail. Call her clients. Keep everyone happy while she made all the problems go away.

The thought made her smile.

She loved her job. Adored creating beautiful gardens and intricate landscapes. There was something about seeing her designs go from paper to reality; the pride, the joy, the sense of accomplishment never got old. She made a difference in someone's life every time she went to work. Tania snorted, the sound soft against the sheets. A *difference*. All right, maybe that was overstating it a bit. She wasn't a brain surgeon, after all. Didn't save people the way doctors did, but she improved their lives just the same, giving each of her clients a retreat. An oasis where stress took a backseat and happiness restored the balance a busy schedule obliterated.

Sort of a game changer on the health front. Restorative in a way everyone needed...right?

Tania yawned, then indulged in a mental nod. No question. Psychotherapy via backyard redesign. Her lips curved. Hey, she might be onto something there. A new marketing strategy to try at the next board meeting. She harrumphed. Uh-huh. Sure. And wouldn't all the suits and ties get a kick out of that one?

No doubt. But Tania didn't care. She felt too darned good right now to worry about what they thought. Which was, well...odd. Especially since worrying was her go-to game. And she excelled at it. Little. Big. Concern knocked the ball out of her park every day.

Home run. Round the bases. Go! Go! Go!

Like an addiction, the vicious cycle never quit. Part of her makeup, she knew. A condition brought on by growing up hungry and never having enough. Well, boo hoo. Whatever. The therapists could slap all the labels they wanted on her. She'd survived: her father's abandonment, her mother's string of scuzzy boyfriends, J.J.'s fall from grace. Now she was stronger than she'd ever been, so...

Tania took her psychological temperature one more time. Yup. Definitely lukewarm. No worries today. The realization made her giddy as the urge to jump up and yell, "Free at last. Free at last. Praise God, I am free at last!" streamed through her. She smiled, laughing at herself. Good Lord, she really had lost it. Well, either that or getting the recommended number of Zs really was a cure-all.

Hurrah for her GP. He'd nailed that prediction.

With a mental eye roll, Tania shook her head, then took a deep breath and got ready. Time to brave elements outside in No-covers-ville. Ugh. This was not going to be pleasant. The cold air told her so, nipping at her nose. She grabbed the edge of the duvet anyway, girding herself for the chilly rush, and—

Something shifted behind her.

Tania flinched as a low growl curled against her ear. Glorious heat followed, radiating along her spine. Another rumble rolled over the quiet. She froze, afraid to move, refusing to breathe, never mind look over her shoulder...

Just in case.

'Cause, God. She wasn't 100 percent sure, but that felt like a man snuggled up against her. One she couldn't remember. At all. Which meant...what? One word. Tequila. Too much Jose Cuervo always resulted in bad decisions. Although, she'd never ended up in a stranger's bed before. Had never wanted to, either, but...

She shifted, wiggling to confirm her suspicions. Solid and warm, the body nestled closer and...oh, snap. Not good. That was definitely a guy. A big one with long limbs roped by a serious amount of muscle. Tania cursed under her breath. She was so screwed, way out in deep six territory with no idea how to handle the situation. Should she make a quick getaway? Slip out of bed? Hope he didn't notice? Put her clothes on and—

Wait a minute. Hold everything. Clothes?

She scissored her legs beneath the sheet. Relief hit her in a blinding wave. Definite separation. No skin on skin, just blessed too-big sweatpants and a thank-you-God hoodie covering her from ankles to chin. Hurrah for her modesty. It was easier to make a mad dash for the door, after all, when you had clothes on.

Releasing the lockdown on her lungs, Tania exhaled and, preparing to move, opened her eyes. The clock face glowed, staring at her through the darkness, illuminating the edge of the bed. One hand flat on the mattress for leverage, she slid toward it, praying she didn't wake him. Her slight shift jostled him. Whoever-he-was hummed, the sound half growl, half purr. Tania froze, simply stopped breathing to bargain with God.

Oh please, let her make a clean getaway.

All she needed was thirty seconds…flat. That was it, and she'd be gone. Halfway home before Mr. X woke up and—

A big hand settled on the curve of her bare belly.

Heat flared. Static electricity zapped her. She jumped, shock wreaking havoc as his hold firmed. With a quiet snarl, he reeled her in, pulling her back into his arms. Flush against him now—bum to groin, back to his chest—his calloused hand roamed, moving up beneath her shirt. She gasped and made a grab for it. He whispered her name. Her breath caught, the sound of his voice dragging recall front and center.

She twisted to look over her shoulder. He blocked the movement, imprisoning her against him. A tussle ensued as she tried to turn in his arms. She lost. He won, controlling her completely. His fingers slipped beneath her waistband, teasing the sensitive skin on her belly. Tania swallowed, each breath coming harder and faster. God, she knew him. Recognized the hard body spooning hers now: the calloused heat, the wicked sensation, the way he made her nerve endings stand at attention while she waited for him to move lower. And his scent...oh jeez, someone help her. He smelled clean, spicy, more exotic than skinny-dipping at midnight.

"Mac?"

"Mine." Edged by slumber, his voice came out low and deep...possessive.

Tania blinked. *Mine?* What kind of answer was that? Not a very good one. Especially since his hand was on the move again. She twitched as he dipped into her belly button, then reversed direction. His palm slid up, pushing her sweatshirt above her rib cage. Pleasure licked through her. Tania tensed and told herself to do the right thing. To wiggle free and give him hell, but...oh crap. Sound the alert. The ship had already landed. Or rather, Mac's large hand, curling around her breast, brushing over her nipple, arousing her so fast surprise took a nasty turn into disbelief.

Oh boy...oh boy, oh boy. He was...was...

He stroked her again.

Sucking in a quick breath, she arched against her will. Ah, nuts. Rampaging attraction. Pitiful willpower. Beautiful ever-loving bliss. He felt so good. And she was so cooked, unable to deny desire as she pressed her bottom against his groin. She bit down on a moan. Oh, but he was incredible: long, hard, so ready to please her. Memories of the first time—the pleasure of having him deep inside her—nudged her, egging her on. Red-hot need seconded the motion, and—

What the heck was wrong with her?

She should be stopping him, not encouraging him. But even as her internal alarm bell clanged and she told herself to stop—to shove out of his embrace and get the heck away from him—Tania shifted, rolling her hips with erotic precision. He groaned, responding so well and...oh yes, please. Full-on contact: his hands beneath her shirt and on her bare skin, his erection pressed against her bum, the heat of his mouth on the side of her neck.

She swallowed past her sudden case of dry mouth. "Mac?"

"More," he said, the word slurred, his voice husky and sleep filled. "All...everything."

Tania frowned. He sounded odd, not at all like his usual self.

A quick twist. A tidy shift, and...bingo. She turned the tables, loosening his grip, and spun in his arms. He retaliated by taking control. With rough hands, he pushed her onto her back and into the mattress. Cotton sighed. Tania moaned as he shackled her wrists with one hand and settled between the spread of her thighs. Mac pressed in, erection to core, and circled his hips against her. And she lost her mind. Just a little bit, 'cause, holy jeez, he knew what he was doing. Turning her on. Holding her down. Dominating her the way she liked...craved. Needed him to.

She'd never been into BDSM. But with Mac? The idea of being tied up and made to submit took on new dimension. Silk bonds and fur-lined handcuffs? Oh baby. Bring it on.

With a gasp, Tania arched, prolonging the contact, so sensitive already each coil and release of his hips shoved her closer to the edge. Both hands trapped above her head, sweatshirt riding beneath her breasts, she gazed up into his face and...

Froze.

Good God. He was fast asleep. Deep in the grips of a dream, eyes closed and moving rapid-fire behind his lids. Whispering his name, Tania tugged against his hold, hoping to wake him up. A no go. He was enthralled, so far under he responded with heat, rolling his hips, pushing her into pleasure one wicked thrust at a time. A purr locked in her throat, she struggled to stem the bliss-filled flow. It didn't work. The body rush was too strong. And he was too damn good, cranking her so high temptation urged her to let go. Give in. Accept the orgasm he was about to give her and thank God.

But oh, that was just so wrong. Bent in a very serious way considering he wasn't quite himself. God, she'd heard of sleepwalking before, but...sex while fast asleep? How ridiculous was that? Very. Way beyond abnormal.

"Mac..." Another wicked wave of delight washed through her, interrupting her good intentions, filling her with bad ones. Desperation spiked, and riding a wave of oh baby just...like...that, she gasped, "Holy God...wake up! Mac, you need to wake—"

"You'll take me," he said, ordering her around in his sleep, giving her shivers. "All of me."

Blessed be the saints. Yes. She would. Forget right. Wrong felt way better, and she was diving in...headfirst. No holds barred. No safety net.

Watch out below!

"Sorry," she gasped, apologizing while wrapping her legs around his hips.

The rub and tease through her pants—the scent and feel of him—pushed past her limits, and chained by his hands, Tania submitted, gave herself up to him, and closed her eyes. Tipping her head back on the pillow, she matched him thrust for thrust, pressing up, egging him on. Greedy. Beyond the pale of good behavior. She berated herself with each pulse-pounding stroke of pleasure. But after weeks of waking up needy—of living with the frustration—she couldn't stop him. Refused to say no. Took all he gave, half praying he woke up, half hoping he didn't.

"I'm sorry. S-sorry, but I need it…I…God, I need it."

Cupping her bottom with his free hand, he murmured to her, controlling the tempo, riding her so well tears formed, then fell. A pleasure cry. Something that never happened to her. At least not before. But ecstasy overload was par for the course with Mac. He stroked, and she cried, begging for release. He didn't deny her, pressing deep, circling hard, the rub and tease through her clothes hitting all the right notes. And as the tears streaked over her temples, glorious oblivion came. With a hitching sob, she exploded, tensing around him, his name on the tip of her tongue, guilt for taking advantage like a thorn in her heart.

God forgive her. Because she had a feeling Mac never would.

Chapter Eighteen

Tania was crying. Begging. And Mac didn't know why.

Which cranked his screw the wrong way. Someone was hurting her. And he was going to tear their fucking limbs off. One by one. Without mercy or conscience. Until they lay in a bloody heap at his feet.

No one touched his female. *No one* but him.

Still half-asleep, aggression sparked through him. He needed to wake the hell up. Right now. Lethal intent pumping through his veins, he clawed at the mind-fog, fighting to break free. She sobbed again, her breath hitching on his name. Mac surfaced hard, rocketing into wake-up mode with gut-wrenching velocity. Primal instinct ignited. His dragon responded, coming alive with a silent snarl. Magic exploded, fusing muscle over bone, rushing down his spine as he tapped into the connection they shared.

Tania's bioenergy flared, lighting him up from the inside out. Mac mined it, searching for the threat. He didn't find one. No pain. No distress. Nothing but a powerful wave of...

White-hot need.

Mac's brows collided. What the hell? Was he reading that right?

He accessed the threat again. A load of sexual energy sucker punched him. Sucking wind, confusion got shoved aside. Awareness flickered, flipping Mac's brain to the ON position. As all systems went from fucked up to functional, he opened his eyes and lost his next breath. Holy shit. He was deep in the zone, and even deeper between Tania's thighs, holding her down, making her moan and...

Yeah. Cry beneath him.

Dark lashes pressed to her cheeks, legs gripping his hips, she arched, tipping her head back on the pillows. More tears rolled from the corners of her eyes.

Breathing hard, he watched the droplets disappear into her hairline, struggling to grasp what his body already knew. He was on autopilot, still fully clothed, working her so hard she undulated beneath him while he pushed her toward orgasm. Surprise made him flinch. The desire to please her made him move. Gauging her need, he upped the pace, the last of the mind-fog vanishing. Like pieces of a puzzle, the facts clicked into place. Him. Her. In bed together. A shitload of I-want-you and...

Jesus fucking Christ.

He wasn't dreaming. Not this time. Which meant he was doing it...*again!* Making love to her while practically comatose.

He growled.

She sobbed. "Oh God, I'm...s-sorry, but I...oh yes, *please*. I need it."

Motherfuck. Forget the apology. He needed it too. Wanted to see her come. To feel the explosion. To reap the benefits as she came apart in his arms. His satisfaction didn't matter. Not now. Maybe not ever again. All that mattered was her. That he pleased her while watching it happen.

Poised above her, he adjusted their fit and, circling his hips, released her wrists. Bringing her arms down from above her head, she latched onto his shoulders and rode the wave: each rhythmic roll of thrust and retreat. One hand beneath her bottom, he cupped her cheek and turned her face toward him. As he thumbed another tear away, Mac dipped his head. He couldn't wait a second longer. He needed to be inside her, any way he could. Licking deep, he took her mouth without mercy. He groaned as she responded, opening wide, inviting him in, kissing him back with a ferocity that matched his own.

Umm, God. She tasted so good...like decadence and delight. A heavenly combination that surpassed sinful, throwing him into the fiery pit of desire. The burn nourished him, and memory sparked. Flashes of their first time together exploded across his mind: of her beneath him, of him deep inside her, the loft, his *first shift*, and her wicked, welcoming heat.

Man, he wished he could remember more of it.

Not that it mattered now. She was in his arms, and he was wide-awake, all synapses firing. Hyperalert and ready to please her, he registered her every response. And oh baby, she moved like a dream. Drove him wild with the flex and release of her hips against his. Reveled in the arch of her spine and taut curves of her breasts. Loved each soft gasp, all the sexy sounds she made, he listened to her beg him for more.

With a growl, Mac gave it to her. No holding back. He craved the heart of her, the heat of her skin against his, the exquisite pleasure of being deep inside her. Wanted to experience it all...again. Recall everything as Tania came apart beneath him.

But not like this. Not without making sure first. He didn't want either of them incoherent this time around. He needed to know she was 100 percent on board before he took her hard and loved her long.

A death grip on the urge to strip her bare, he backed off, lifting his hips from between her thighs. "Tania, honey...look—"

"Oh no...no, no." Her eyes closed, she twisted beneath him, raising her hips and...

Mother of God. She stroked him good and hard, rubbing against his erection. Heat lightning zapped him, screwing with his resolve, shoving him toward blind lust instead of controlled lovemaking. With a curse, he clamped down on his reaction and her. Gripping her hip with one hand, he held her down, pressing her into the mattress, lifting himself away to keep his cool. But shit, it almost killed him. He wanted her so badly his body didn't care how it happened...just as long as he ended up buried to the hilt inside her.

Fighting the lockdown, she gasped, "Mac, don't... please. I'm close. So close."

"I know, love." He retreated a little more. She snarled at him and tugged at his shoulders, trying to pull him back. When he didn't move, she nipped the underside of his chin. He twitched and clenched his teeth. "I'll give you what you need—"

"Now!"

"In a minute. I promise, but first..." He kissed her softly, keeping each caress light, hoping to soothe her while he slowed himself down. It would be so easy to take her this way. Forget right, embrace wrong, and love her without thought to the consequences. While need rode roughshod over reason. But he refused to do that to her. Not again. The first blind loving had been bad enough so...yeah. This time would be different: slow, measured, all she deserved, not the incoherent scramble she didn't. "Tania...look at me."

She shook her head, the movement sharp with denial.

"You wanna come?"

"Yes!"

"Then look at me."

Short nails biting into his biceps, she shifted beneath him and grumbled, "Mean. You're just plain mean..." Breathing hard, she shivered before her eyelashes lifted. Dark brown, burgundy-flecked eyes met his. She blinked, and Mac felt her mind sharpen as she gazed up at him. "And, ah, wide-awake now."

Watching her closely, he propped himself up on one elbow. "Is that a problem for you?"

"Are you going to stop now?" Color stole into her cheeks.

"Depends."

"On what?"

"Whether or not you want me to."

Flat on her back beneath him, one of his thighs pressed between hers, she hesitated. Mac held his breath. Shit. What was he doing? He should be inciting her to make love with him, not giving her an out. But now that he had? He couldn't deny it was the right thing to do.

Chewing on her bottom lip, she glanced away. "Sorry."

"For what?"

"Taking advantage," she whispered, breaking his heart with her apology. God, she was adorable. And way too honest for her own good. Thank fuck. It made reading her a whole lot easier. Tania would never leave him guessing. Clobbering him with what she thought and felt along with the truth was more her style. "I didn't realize you were asleep when you started, ah, touching me. But by the time I figured that out I was…well, it was too late. I'm not usually so…umm…"

She trailed off, embarrassment in her tone.

Mac's lips twitched. *Taking advantage.* Jesus. He hoped she took advantage of him every damned day. Still, he couldn't resist teasing her a little. "Not usually what? So hot to trot?"

"Shut up." She scowled at him. "It's not my fault. It's yours or my stupid subconscious…whatever. I've been having these dreams. So when I woke up and you were…well, I just…I don't know…went with it."

Her admission popped his brows skyward. Naughty dreams. About him. Mac opened his mouth, then closed it again. He didn't have a clue what to say, other than "thank you, baby Jesus." 'Cause, holy shit, what a compliment. Not to mention a wicked turn-on. Especially since he dreamed about her too. All the time. So much he couldn't get her out of his head. Awake. Asleep. It didn't matter. She was always there, taunting him with her sweetness. And now? She lay spread beneath him, aroused, relaxed, already halfway home. All she needed was a little encouragement to take him the rest of the distance.

Fucking A. He was so on board with that. Couldn't wait to feel her come around him.

Holding her gaze, Mac shifted his hips and pressed in. As he settled deep between her thighs, her eyelashes flickered. Oh yeah. She was still really sensitive, needy from being so close to orgasm without going over.

He rolled against her, keeping the action light. "You wanna go with it again?"

"Depends on the conditions."

"Skin to skin this time. Me deep inside you."

"Demanding, aren't you?" She shifted beneath him, the move one of welcome.

"Honey, you have no idea," he said, more growl than actual words. "So what's it gonna be? If I leave you, it's gotta be now, Tania. I won't be able to pull back later."

"Here's the deal." Dark eyes serious yet still full of need, she cupped the nape of his neck. The caress turned desire incendiary. Mac's heart jumped like a jackrabbit, pounding hard as he waited for her to lay out the conditions. She took her time, fingers playing in his hair, cranking him tight, grazing him with her short nails. Unable to stop himself, he arched into her next stroke, pressing deeper between her thighs. With a hum, she kissed the corner of his mouth, then nipped him gently and whispered, "You make me come in the next fifteen seconds? You can do anything you want to me after."

Mac's breath caught. *Anything.* God, that was a big word. "Done."

Her lips curved. "Thought so."

Enthralled by her, he cupped her face and traced her cheekbone with the pad of his thumb. Brushing her hair back, he drew soft circles on her temple, memorizing every detail: the thickness of her eyelashes, the softness of her skin, the lush pink of her lips, the gentle arch of her eyebrows. Man, she was beautiful, but more than just skin-deep. Hers was a beauty that traveled inward, touching every part of her, and he responded to that truth. It made him want her more, to touch all that goodness, possess her in every way...physically, emotionally, body, mind, heart, and soul. And as he reveled in the desire in her eyes, wasting precious seconds, he couldn't deny what he wanted.

Her. Forever.

So screw the time factor.

He yearned to spend hours blissing her out. Wanted to explore every inch of her and—

"Ticktock," she said, devilry in her eyes.

Mac huffed. "You asked for it."

"Yes, I did."

Stretching her arms above her head, she settled in, waiting for him to start. Mac shook his head, even as his mouth curved. Remarkable. She was the most remarkable woman he'd ever met, and she blew him away. With the heat and want. With the vulnerability she showed and her willingness. But most of all? With her trust. Even after he'd scared her half to death. Even after seeing him in dragon form. Even after all the shit that had gone down with the Razorbacks last night. She placed herself in his hands, *trusting* him not to hurt her.

Mac's throat went tight. Jesus, she turned him inside out. Made him ache with the compulsion to please her. To keep her close and protect her always. "Tania, *mo chroí.* You are a gift."

Her breath caught. Whispering his name, she tipped her chin up and offered him her mouth. He took it without hesitation, kissed her deep, delivering his taste, getting a contact high from hers. And as he tangled their tongues and listened to her moan, he shifted right and slipped his hand beneath the waistband of her sweats. She wanted to come. He would make her.

Guaranteed. And more than once if he got his way.

Spreading his fingers wide, he caressed her belly, then pressed down, filling the space between her hip bones. Her hands twisted in the sheets above her head. She raised her hips, demanding more. He gave it to her, watching the rise and fall of her breasts, listening to her moan. He purred in answer and sucked on her bottom lip, knowing exactly what she needed. He could hear the frantic beat of her heart. Was connected to the fever in her blood and the scattered thoughts tumbling through her mind.

More. Harder. Faster. *Right now.*

Mac growled. Sir, yes, sir. Her wish was his command.

Clamping down on his own need, he controlled the pace...and her. Making her pant and beg. Using every ounce of his skill to drive her wild, closer to the edge and orgasm. And yet he held back a little, wanting Tania so high she fell long and hard, plunging into ferocious pleasure. It would be better for her that way. More intense. More explosive. Bone-melting good if he forced her to ride the razor's edge.

With a practiced touch, he caressed her in light passes, played with teasing strokes, dipping in her belly button until she sobbed. Her breath rasping in her throat, she released her death grip on the sheets. Grabbing fistfuls of his hair, she tilted her hips, begging for his possession. He grazed her curls between her thighs and—

Holy God. She was hot. So incredibly wet. Such a snug fit inside she took his breath away. His balls fisted up tight, making the tip of his erection throb. Jesus, he wanted inside, but...

Not yet. Not until he stripped her down.

He always kept his word. He'd said skin to skin, and he meant it. He'd have her naked—exposed, 100 percent bare beneath him—before he rode her hard. But that wouldn't happen until he kept his end of the bargain.

And speaking of which?

Night vision sparking, Mac glanced at his watch. Time was of the essence. He only had a few seconds left to make her explode. No way would he miss that deadline.

Anything, after all, lay like a promise on the other side of her pleasure.

———

The streets were awash in lamp glow as Nian flew over Old Town, wings extended in full glide, his ear attuned to the chatter below. Prague at midnight. Party central...the magic hour when all kinds—both human and Dragonkind—came out to play. Too bad he wouldn't get the chance to join them. At least not for a while.

Maybe not at all tonight if Rodin stayed true to form.

Gifted with a bird's-eye view, Nian watched a group of drunken humans stumble out of a club and spill into the narrow, cobble-paved avenue. He snorted, fine golden mist rising from his nostrils, and shook his head. Never a dull moment. Never a quiet one, either. Perhaps, though, that was a blessing tonight. He needed the distraction. Time enough to settle his nerves, and watching the imbeciles stagger around? Amusing, to say the least, which...

Yes. Kept his mind busy. An absolute blessing, considering where he was headed.

Angling his wings, he flew east, following the main drag out of the city. More laughter rose in mirth-filled snatches, rising between pale building facades to meet stormy November skies. As the cold air flowed, rushing over his scales, Nian danced with the north wind. The night current whirled into an updraft, lifting his bulk. With a growl, he rotated into a slow flip, music drifting up to meet him. Different genres mixed, the big bass of the nightclubs intertwining with the soothing tones of more sophisticated establishments.

Nice. A real collection of sounds. Some soft with smooth undertones. Others savage, a jarring conflagration of vicious guitars, brutal beats, and violent lyrics.

Fine by him. The lethal mix suited his mood, preparing him for the meeting to come. Thank Christ. It wouldn't do to show weakness in front of Rodin and his crowd. He needed to be picture-perfect when he walked into the Archguard's private party. Bang on in the political sphere. Calm. Cool. And collected. Otherwise he wouldn't make it out alive.

The urge to bank hard and fly home pricked through him. Nian ignored the warning. Self-preservation was all fine and good, but it wouldn't get him what he wanted. Rodin dead, nothing but a messy pile of dragon ash blown away on a brisk wind. But it was far too soon for that. The groundwork must be laid first. Which meant strengthening his position within the high council before he knocked off the top dragon.

The sooner Rodin kicked the bucket, the better for him.

Why? The sick bastard was up to no good. Again.

The summons to his pavilion proved it. The arrival of the gold-leafed invitation (and the fact Nian had never been included on the guest list before) an hour ago confirmed his suspicions. The who's who of Dragonkind— the much-lauded elite, the wealthiest, most powerful of their kind—would be in attendance tonight. Doing what?

Backroom deals, no doubt, but mostly? Rubbing elbows while indulging in Rodin's specialty…

Debauchery of the highest form.

Normally Nian didn't mind. He enjoyed getting down and dirty as much as the next male. But not now. And certainly not at Rodin's. The leader of the high council had a reputation, one no one ever talked about. Not if they wished to be invited back, never mind stay alive. Rumors, however, abounded. Part myth? All truth? Nian couldn't be certain, but anything was possible.

Especially with the Archguard involved.

Red-tiled roofs flashing beneath him, Nian increased his wing speed, flying fast toward the Vltava River. Bitter wind whistled, rattling over his scales, hiding the moon behind heavy cloud cover. Errant snowflakes frolicking in his wake, he crisscrossed a cemetery, tombstones nothing but pale slices in the darkness, then circled into a holding pattern over the Grecian pavilion below. He scanned the manicured gardens, searching the frozen landscape for the landing pad. The second he found it, Mozart's *Requiem* started up, spilling out of the house to drift between ancient trees, the skeletal branches doing little to muffle the melody.

Nian growled. Terrific. Trust Rodin to play a masterpiece at an orgy. All right. So maybe that was overstating it a bit. He didn't know for sure, after all, what Rodin and his cohorts engaged in down there, but…

He had pretty good idea. Could smell the sex already, and he wasn't even on the ground yet.

Tucking his wings in fast, he set down softly on the lawn. Sculpted shrubs swayed, brushing the sides of his shoulders as frosted blades of grass sighed beneath his talons. The sound whispered, rushing up to meet the Grecian-style front entrance. Standing guard between massive marble columns, two males whirled in his direction. A second later, they left their post and trotted down the wide, fluted staircase.

A wind gust blew across the circular driveway, throwing dust into the air. The bigger male's footfalls crunched on the gravel that kissed the base of the stone steps. His eyes narrowed, swept the area...right past Nian, whose mouth curved. Nice try, hotshot. The guard would never see him. A master illusionist, Nian could disappear into thin air. His skill went beyond simple cloaking—the way in which his kind hid from human eyes—entering into a whole new category. One that made him 100 percent invisible, impossible to detect even to his own kind.

Nian frowned. Well, at least most of the time. Haider was the exception to that rule.

No matter how strong an illusion spell he cast, the Nightfury saw through the smoke screen, detecting him without delay. Troubling as much as it was annoying. And let's not forget frustrating. Every time he tried to follow the male and gather intel on the Nightfury pack, he got outed, then warned to stay "the fuck away unless he wanted his balls ripped off." Gage's words, not Haider's.

But as far as threats went? Pretty damn effective. Particularly when one considered Gage's violent nature and the enjoyment he gained from unleashing it.

His gaze leveled on the two guards, Nian decided to test his skill. Just in case. His failure to hide from Haider worried him. Maybe he was slipping...the stress of the last months messing with his ability to control the magic. Maybe he wasn't. Either way, he needed to know for sure.

Lifting his paw, he scraped the tip of a single claw along the base of a marble statue. Like nails on chalkboard, the awful shriek made him grimace as it ricocheted around the garden.

Guard number one spooked, jumping out of his skin. "Did you hear that?"

"Uh-uh." Dropping his cigarette to the ground, the second guard crushed it beneath his boot heel. Gravel crunched. Smoke swirled around his dress shoe. The male scanned the shadows, searching for the source of disturbance. "You see anything?"

"Nothing."

Nian hummed. Excellent. His skill was...

All right. Maybe not perfect. It wasn't, after all, Haider proof, but at least his ability to conjure illusions was intact. So enough with the game.

With a mental flick, Nian uncloaked, allowing the pair to perceive him. Startled, the guards hopped backward, tripping over themselves, recognition in their eyes. Fear swelled, then poured, corrupting their scents. In tandem, they bowed their heads in deference, then knelt in the dirt.

Hmm, power. It never got old.

Walking out from between two topiaries, Nian's claws clicked on the flagstone path. His gaze leveled on the pair, he waged an internal war and debated. Put them at ease with a few words? Or stay silent and crank the hell out of their discomfort? He wanted to do the second. A loner by choice, he didn't often get the opportunity to see another's reaction to his dragon form. But oh my...he hadn't lost his touch.

And no wonder. He was a rare breed: majestic, powerful, as stunningly beautiful as he was lethal. He acted the part and prowled toward the subjugated males, the burnished gold of his scales and his jet-black claws gleaming in the lamplight. The triple-pronged spikes along his spine moved with him, the bloodred tips rolling as his barbed tail snaked out behind him. The guards tensed and curled inward, becoming more uncertain by the moment.

Nian purred, the deep sound one of satisfaction. He loved the way he looked. Gold with black and dark red embellishments. An unusual combination, and more deadly for the fact he breathed yellow acid (aka liquid gold). Corrosive and fast acting, his special brand of poison fused scales—turning males into living statuary—if his target didn't wash the acid off within minutes of getting hit.

Lawn sculpture dragon-style. Always fun to watch.

"Gentlemen," he murmured, stopping ten feet away.

"My lord Nian," both males said at once, heads still bowed and napes exposed. The position was a vulnerable one—a compliment to his elevated station and their subservient role. "Master Rodin is expecting you."

Shifting to human form, Nian conjured his clothes. As the silk shirt and slick tuxedo settled against his skin, he tied his shoelaces with a mental twist. Stone dust scuffing the bottom of his new Berlutis, he approached the two guards while he studied them. Big. Strong. Not too bright. Soldiers who took orders but never questioned authority. Exactly the type of male Rodin appreciated and used as guards dogs on a regular basis.

Nian swallowed his disgust. Some things never changed. Good on a number of fronts—the behavior was predictable, at least—but depressing too. Dragonkind would never evolve with Rodin at the helm.

Brushing past the kneeling males, Nian tugged his shirtsleeves and, adjusting his gold cuff links, jogged up the marble steps. At the top, he paused on the landing, glanced over his shoulder, and said, "On your feet and to your posts, *zi kamirs*. I will tell Rodin you greeted me well."

He waited just long enough to register their relief, then turned and made his way through the open door into the pavilion. Mozart morphed into Jay-Z, big bass replacing violins as he walked down another set of steps into the central corridor. His shoes skimming over mosaic floors, his gaze ran the gauntlet. Vaulted ceiling, three large crystal chandeliers strung at precise intervals down its center, a round antique table beneath each one. And dressing the walls? A smattering of erotic art. Opulent, and in very bad taste, the colorful canvases hung between pale marble pillars, occupying both sides of the hallway. Studying each depiction, Nian's mouth curved at the corners. Every category was represented: male on male, female on female, threesomes...ah, make that four- and fivesomes...of every sexual combination and variety.

Well, bully for Rodin. The prick might be a sadist, but at least he didn't discriminate.

Coming abreast of a closed door, Nian slid his hand into his pants pocket and palmed his lighter. His thumb brushed over his family crest engraved into the golden side. He took a deep breath. Showtime. Good thing he'd never suffered from performance anxiety. Why? Something told him the next few hours would not only get out of hand but be exhausting as well.

He reached for the door handle.

From out of nowhere, a Numbai appeared at his elbow. Tray in hand, a single glass filled with amber liquid upon it, the servant bowed and offered him the drink. With a raised brow, Nian palmed the crystal tumbler. Ice clicked against his teeth as he took a sip. Decadent and welcome, the cool burn slid down his throat. Well, well, well. Surprise, surprise. Bourbon. His favorite brand too. Rodin, it seemed, paid attention.

Good to know. Even better to remember.

"My lord," the Numbai murmured, a healthy dose of respect in his tone. With a quick shift, the male grasped the handle. He twisted the knob, pushed the door open, and waved Nian through. "Welcome."

Tumbler in hand, Nian nodded and, putting his expensive shoes to work, crossed the threshold into—

Christ be gone. Because hell, *He* wasn't anywhere near here.

Nian blinked. Had he said debauchery earlier? Brimstone and hellfire. Take that up a notch, then times it by a hundred. Females were everywhere—dressed, half-dressed, not dressed at all, engaged in all kinds of pleasurable pursuits—outnumbering the males in the room three to one. Sexual energy hummed in the room. Arousal twisted his balls up tight.

Nian took another pull from his drink. As the bourbon washed into his mouth, he scanned the crowd over the rim of his glass. He spotted Rodin right away. Over in the corner, sprawled on a chaise longue, enjoying a dark-haired female while two others waited in the wings for a turn. Dark eyes shimmering in the low light, the leader of the Archguard raised his glass, toasting Nian from across the room. He tipped his chin, returning the greeting, and watched Rodin signal to someone behind him. A moment later, small hands touched down on his back. He glanced over his shoulder. Sultry blue eyes met his.

"Hi." Caressing him through his suit jacket, the female explored his shoulders, then hooked the collar and tugged. Nian shrugged, helping her undress him. "I'm Purity."

Wearing nothing but skin, a second female joined the first, stopping in front of him. Certain of her skill and his welcome, she loosened his tie, then turned her attention to his shirt. Nimble fingers slipped the buttons free. "And I'm Chastity."

His lips twitched. Interesting names...considering their busy hands. "Twins?"

"Identical," both said at the same time. With identical voices.

Yum. What fun. He hadn't shagged a pair of twins in a while. Years, really. Identicals were hard to come by. And despite their low-energy status, he wanted each one. Would take them both multiple times. Wouldn't stop until he pleased them so well the females forgot who they were, never mind where they lived.

Raising his glass, Nian tipped the rim in Rodin's direction, thanking the bastard for his gift. The male grinned, then got back to being busy. Nian followed his example and, tangling his hand in one of the females' hair, invaded her mouth. With a hum, he deepened the kiss, tasting her tongue as her sister unbuckled his belt. Shirt half-on and half-off now, he allowed the twins to pull him into the curtained alcove beside the door.

Three hours and a pair of blissed-out females later, Nian rolled off the daybed and onto his bare feet. Fun time was over. Not because he wanted it to be. He could go another hour or two, but the twins couldn't. He'd worn them out.

Made them come so often and so hard, their bioenergy lagged, pulling them into a deep sleep.

God, he loved a good fuck. And the twins had been better than most.

Running his gaze over their naked bodies, he reached down and scooped a throw blanket off the floor. He tossed it over their sleeping forms to keep them warm and ensure their comfort. It was the least he could do. They'd fed him well, taking the edge off his hunger. Now his magic writhed, sharpening his focus.

Brushing aside the green-and-gold-tasseled curtains, he stepped out into the main room. Some males were still engaged, kissing each other, pleasuring yet another female. Most, however, sat propped up on plush daybeds, relaxed and comfortable, the frenzy sliding into the blissful aftermath of sexual release.

"Enjoy yourself?"

The voice came from his left. Conjuring his clothes, Nian glanced in that direction. Propped against a marble column, Rodin smirked, the predator in him banked but still burning beneath the surface.

"Twins," Nian murmured, holding his nemesis's gaze. "Good choice."

"I know you like it hard-core."

"Go hard or go home. Always the best policy."

Rodin laughed, white teeth flashing against his olive complexion. "Next time, I'll get you triplets."

Next time. A good sign. There would be other invitations. Time and plenty to slither under the older male's guard.

Nian quirked a brow. "So…what now?"

"You always were a quick study," Rodin said, tone full of appreciation.

"Old habits and all that."

"You are smarter than your sire was, Nian."

A true compliment, one he took as Rodin pushed away from the column. Slighter built and not as tall, the leader of the Archguard gazed up at him from a few feet away. He could almost see the wheels turning inside Rodin's head. The bastard was assessing him, no doubt ticking off boxes inside his head, trying to decide whether he was worthy of joining his innermost circle of friends. Nian held the line, refusing to back down. Or abandon his plan. Everything hinged on gaining Rodin's approval and trust.

And he was close. So very, *very* close.

He could feel the victory. It sizzled in the air as the silence expanded.

After what seemed like forever, but was only a few moments, Rodin huffed. A smile playing at the corners of his mouth, his elder rolled his shoulders beneath his tuxedo jacket and tilted his head toward the door. "Come with me. I wish to show you something."

And just like that, Nian was in. Walking away from his old life to step into the new. All for the price of following Rodin down the deserted corridor. Quiet reigned in the house now, no more classical music or pulse-pounding rap. No more cries of ecstasy or growls of triumph. Just smooth-as-silk silence.

Taking him through a series of doorways and back halls, Rodin stopped in front of a section of wainscot paneling. The male's magic flared, crackling around them an instant before the wall retreated and slid sideways, opening into a passageway beyond. Right on his host's heels, Nian strode over the threshold and down a set of narrow steps. Gears whirled into motion, the hum echoing in the small space as the false wall closed behind him.

His night vision sparked, orienting him. Smooth marble walls. Stained concrete floor. The smell of human blood.

Muffled shouts came through the thick stone walls. And Nian's stomach clenched. He knew that sound and what it meant. Had been to enough illegal Dragonkind parties to recognize the signs. A fight club, one in which the males of his kind bet on their favorite human fighter.

None of whom were willing to fight at all.

Captured for this very purpose, the slaves had one chance at survival. Keep winning. Losing meant death, and not always a merciful one, either. Remain the victor eleven times in a row, however, and a human bought the right to ask for his freedom. Whether or not he gained it depended on his owner. Not everyone liked to cut a champion free.

An ancient way of being entertained. In the tradition of the Roman gladiators.

As disgusting now as it had been then.

Dread congealing in the pit of his stomach, Nian crossed into the club. He expected to see adult males. What he got was far worse. Children. The bastard was using boys as gladiators, forcing them to fight and spill each other's blood. The pair fighting now, though, were Dragonkind. Orphans, no doubt, without sires to protect them…maybe ten years old, perhaps a year or two older. Knives raised, the two circled each other on the raised stage in the center of the room. Sitting as though watching a boxing match, some of the most powerful members of his kind shouted, egging the boys on.

Rage clouded his vision.

"Boys," Rodin said. "Such a profitable business."

The satisfaction in the bastard's tone rolled over him. Nian's hands curled into fists. Just once. He wanted to hit the sadistic asshole…just once. That's all it would take to bash Rodin's brains in. After that? He'd find shelter for the boys, mow down the rest of the sickos, then burn the pavilion to the ground.

But he couldn't. Not tonight. His hands were tied. He was outnumbered thirty to one in Rodin's territory. Here to gather intel and make inroads, not get himself killed. But as he watched the fight, the pressure built, turning his skull into a pressure cooker.

The sick son of a bitch. The spineless, perverted—

Rodin slapped him on the shoulder, acting like a friend. Nian swallowed a snarl.

The older male pointed to another door across the room. "But come, *zi kamir*. You may return here after and place a bet on a boy, if you choose. I have another event in mind for you."

Another event? Something as sick as what he bore witness to here? Christ help him. He wasn't going to make it. Would tear Rodin limb from limb before the night finished and he could escape the depravity.

Chapter Nineteen

Flat on her back beneath Mac, a death grip on the sheets, Tania moaned his name. Blind, deaf, and dumb, all she knew was Mac: his taste on her tongue, the skill of his hands, and the pleasure he gave her. Pushing her thighs wider, he slipped a second finger deep inside her, stretching her gently while his thumb...

Oh mercy. "Mac!"

Shoving her sweatshirt up with his free hand, he bared her breasts and dipped his head. The heat of his mouth scorched her. He suckled, and she gasped, hips rolling, head thrown back, body straining to reach the pinnacle. His low growl amped her up. His pace made her pant while he pushed her toward delight. Oh so good. And she was oh so close. A nanosecond away from implosion, but...

God. He wouldn't let her. Kept her on the edge, backing off the second she threatened to go over. A breath away from orgasm, she begged him for release, her world narrowing to...just...one...thing. Him. His spicy scent on her skin. His delicious taste in her mouth. And his hands. Hmm, she loved the roughness of his calloused palms, the gentle way he delivered each white-hot lash of pleasure. He was a wide-shouldered, hard-bodied dream, so skilled he made her burn with the need to have him deep inside her.

"Give it to me, honey." He flicked over her nipple, then nipped at the tip. "Now, Tania."

His tone brooked no argument. Tania obeyed and, riding the wave, exploded, a scream locked in her throat, tears rolling from the corners of her eyes. Mac kissed them away as she throbbed, clenching hard around him. He groaned in answer, cradling her close, feeding her more delight where an overload of ecstasy already existed.

Each breath coming on top of the next, she sobbed, coming a second time. And then again, each bliss-filled wave more intense than the last. Her hands knotted in his hair, she held on, taking all Mac gave while he stroked her into submission. Over and over until she sighed and went boneless in his arms. He brushed his mouth over hers. She accepted the gentle caress and listened to his voice, hung on each murmur as he talked to her. Called her beautiful. Told her she was special. Made her feel loved. Tania hummed, pleased with herself, but mostly with him. He was a force of nature. God's gift to…

She frowned. No, not all *women*. To her. Mac belonged to her. And woe betide anyone who—

Wait a second. Back up a step. She needed an attitude readjustment.

Deep in the pleasure fog, Tania swam for the surface, one called sanity. 'Cause, yup. Staking a claim on him was a bad idea. And second on her do-NOT-do list? Become a jealous idiot, one ticked off by the thought of him with someone else. Nothing good would come from wandering into that mess. She needed to stay in the here and now where serious took a backseat, leaving fun and mutual pleasure to ride shotgun.

Tania bit down on her bottom lip. Right?

Wrong, a voice inside her insisted. Just one word. A single syllable. But the conviction behind it sent her reeling. Worry picked her up, spun her around, then flung her headlong into confusion. Her internal alarm system started to howl. Oh boy. Not good…at all. Somehow, in the last few hours, she'd become attached to Mac in a major way. She sensed her connection to him and knew…just *knew*… it wasn't normal. How could it be? She didn't know him all that well. Sure, she liked him. It was easy to do. But the need she felt for him surpassed sexual chemistry, rocketing her into compulsion. Left her wanting something she'd never had before…

Commitment.

Her throat clogged with panic. Forget the dragon stuff. Tania didn't want a man of her own. She enjoyed her independence. Liked her job…was fulfilled and happy with her life. But even as she insisted, pushing the feminist agenda, a pang echoed inside her. The hollowness expanded and a lifetime of hurt slipped through her defenses, making her yearn for something more. Acceptance and love…common ground with a man she could trust to never betray her.

Oh dear. She'd outpaced crazy. Now she lived inside a world called Certifiable.

"Hey," Mac murmured, slipping his hand from between her thighs. Tania mourned the loss of contact for a moment, then forced her eyes open. He met her gaze, his full of concern. Her heart flip-flopped, sending her into a messy emotional tailspin. God, what a man. After all he'd just given her, he was worried…about her. "You okay?"

"All good." A lie. But it was the best Tania could do under the circumstances. She didn't want to talk about what she felt or why. Not yet. Not until she figured out what it meant. So she deflected instead, diverting him with a compliment. "Holy jeez, Mac. You're good at this."

He grinned. "You have no idea."

"Arrogant jerk," she said, teasing him, loving every second of being in his arms. Umm, he was delicious. A sexual dominant with no off switch in sight. Perfect. Exactly what she needed to take her mind off her troubles while he had his way.

After all, what could it possibly hurt?

She enjoyed his brand of hard-core in bed. And the fact he could coax her into submission? Oh baby...not much better than that. So, yup. She was all in, past the point of no return with Mac in the driver's seat.

Touching her fingertip to his bottom lip, she raised a brow. "You've had lots of practice, haven't you?"

A wicked gleam in his eyes, he answered with action. Smoothing his hand over her hip, he tugged her waistband. She lifted her bum, willing to let him strip her. He didn't hesitate, pulling the sweats down and off before tossing them over the side of the bed. Attacking her shirt next, he sent the hoodie to join its better half on the floor and...

Tania held her breath and stayed perfectly still. As his gaze skimmed over her, her heart picked up a beat, then another. Did he like what he saw? Most men did, even though they never got to touch. She'd kept them all at bay. Had never encouraged intimacy of any kind beyond her first experience or two. Why? Fear of losing herself, maybe. Lack of pleasure, certainly. But mostly? No one had ever made her feel the way Mac did.

Caressing her with a light touch, he trailed his fingers over her collarbone. Awe played in his expression, and his mouth parted on a rough exhale. "I love your body, Tania. You're so soft and curvy. So sweet."

And there it was. The approval she craved. Silly, she knew. It shouldn't matter what he thought, but somehow it did. More than she wanted to admit, and as he turned his hand to cup her breast, she welcomed him. Pushing her hands into his hair, she played with thick strands and tipped her chin, asking for his kiss. The devil in his eyes, Mac shook his head. She tugged. He retaliated by deviating, moving away from her lips.

Her breath caught as his mouth touched down on her breast. Playing the tease, he flicked her with the tip of his tongue, taunting her with the promise of possession without giving her any. She growled at him. He smiled against her skin, blowing on the damp patch, cranking her higher before settling in to suckle her...hard. Heat lightning streaked through her, arching her off the bed, making her gasp his name.

He chuckled. Tania moaned and tried to move him. An impossible endeavor if ever there was one, but...oh, how she craved his taste. Wanted to dip inside his mouth and appease the hunger.

"Mac!"

"Uh-huh?"

"I want your mouth."

He nipped her gently, causing her to squirm. "Where?"

"On mine."

With a snarl, he lifted his head from her breast and invaded her mouth. She met him, opening wide, tasting his tongue, needing more. Yum. Perfection wrapped up in a kiss. He was the addiction she would never kick. Tantalizing. Drug-like. Undeniable. Tania knew it and didn't care. He was so good, and she was too needy. Ready to take everything he gave her and beg for more. To hell with her pride and doing the smart thing. Later would be soon enough for recriminations. To screw her head on straight and unravel the mystery of her reaction to Mac.

Yes, absolutely. *Later.*

Right now, the primal urge to satisfy him took over. A slave to his kiss, she drank him in, reveling in the way he possessed her. The kiss lasted forever, yet nowhere near long enough. And as he withdrew to suck on her bottom lip, Tania protested, not wanting to let him go. With a hum, he met her gaze and, shackling her wrists, loosened her grip in his hair.

Following his retreat, she raised her head off the pillow. "Come back."

"Behave and I will."

Tania blinked. *Behave?* What kind of request was that? Not a very good one, considering neither of them had a stitch on. Add that whopper to the fact his thigh was pressed between hers and…fat chance. No *behaving* would be happening anytime soon.

Reading her right, he warned, "Behave or I'll make you."

"How?"

He laced their fingers and shifted to straddle her. His knees on either side of her hips, he pressed the backs of her hands into the mattress. "I'll tie you down."

"Oh," she whispered, surprise and interest mixing. Anticipation broke through the passion barrier, busting her wide open, making her want to yell, "Oh yes, please. Tie me up!" Which was…Tania shivered…ridiculous. Completely ludicrous. And so arousing she could hardly stand herself. But now that the seed had been planted, she couldn't deny that she wanted him that way. Hated to admit it, but being dominated by Mac sounded, well, delicious.

Way beyond exciting. Except…

How did one go about admitting that kind of thing? Should she blurt it out and hope for the best? Maybe. Tania really didn't know. But honesty seemed like the better policy. What was the worst that could happen? He'd walk away. She'd cry and then get over it.

"I'm not…" She paused to shore up her courage. Feeling her cheeks heat, she said, "I mean you can…if you want."

Rapt interest sparked, sharpening his focus, making his irises shimmer. His hands flexed around hers. Tania swallowed. Watching her closely, he drew her arms above her head. He held her there and waited, listening to her pant as excitement and ravenous need intertwined.

His nostrils flared. "You like being held down, don't you?"

Mouth gone dry, Tania couldn't answer. Her mind had flown, leaving her vulnerable beneath him. And her heart? God, the thing pounded so hard her pulse hammered her temples, taking up all the space inside her head.

"You ever been with a dom before, Tania?"

She shook her head.

"I'll be your first then."

And last. He didn't say it. Didn't need to either. Tania sensed the conviction in his tone.

Shackling her wrists in one of his large hands, he leaned in and nipped her bottom lip. Another light pass with his teeth. A heated flick of his tongue at the corner of her mouth. More titillating tease before he raised his head to look at her. With slow, deliberate movements, he spread her thighs and, cupping her bottom with his free hand, adjusted their fit as he settled against her core.

She moaned in delight, and he asked, "How do you want it, *mo chroí*...silk bonds, handcuffs, or leather?"

Her breath caught, and she tried to decide. Go all in or start slow? Errant urges piped up, telling her to be brave. She licked over her bottom lip, swallowed her apprehension, and—

"Yo, Mac. Where you at, lad?"

The thick brogue drifted in from the living room. Tania tensed, her eyes widening. A second voice joined the first. "You sure this is the place, Rikar?"

"Yeah. He's here, B. I can feel him."

"Motherfuck." Mac's grip tightened on her wrists. With a growl, he twisted to glare at the door. "I'm going to *kill* them."

"Who?" she asked, a little slow on the uptake.

And no wonder. Desire still had her by the throat, and after the excitement of nearly being tied up and dominated by Mac? Well, her lack of mental acuity was understandable...mandatory, even. But as more heavy footfalls sounded outside the bedroom door, Tania forced herself to get a grip. A fast getaway was definitely in order.

Unhooking her calf from Mac's hip, Tania tugged on her hands. Freedom and finding her clothes seemed like a good idea. No way she wanted to be butt naked when whoever was out there walked in on them. Murmuring Mac's name, she yanked harder. He got the message, uncurling his hand from around her wrists. "Is it your dragon-thingy?"

He blinked, then threw her a startled look. "Thingy?"

"Pack? Or whatever you call it."

"The Nightfuries."

"Oh, right...of course," she said as though it made perfect sense. But it didn't...not by a long shot.

The whole thing was downright hinky. Shimmering eyes. Magical air bubbles. A gaggle of dragon-guys showing up out of the blue. The bizarro list went on and on into never ending, but the weird thing? The absolute crazy part? She wasn't that alarmed by any of it. Sometime in the last few hours, she'd accepted Mac for who and what he was and understood that he would protect her.

From all comers.

And oh boy. Call the loony bin. She needed a serious injection of drug therapy.

"Tania, honey, I'm sorry, but..." With a sigh, Mac shifted to lie alongside her. Propped up on his elbow, one of his muscled thighs between her own, he cupped her cheek. "We'll have to do our *anything* another time. When I get you home, I'll show you—"

Metal squeaked as the knob turned.

Mac's focus snapped back to the door. "Come in here and I'll cut your balls off."

"Bloody hell," the Scottish guy said.

Someone else chimed in. "Ouch."

The wince in the guy's voice provided Tania with a mental snapshot. One of Mac's friends with a pained look on his face, both hands cupping his package. The picture struck her funny bone. She snorted, amusement tightening her chest. More grumbling came from beyond the door, giving her a bad case of the giggles. Covering her mouth, she tried to hold it in. Mac scowled at her. And she lost it, laughter spilling from between the press of her fingers.

"Shit," he muttered.

"Sorry," she gasped, her eyes watering. "I know it's not funny, but…I just…you gotta admit it's pretty—"

"Frickin' frustrating?"

"Hilarious." Caressing his shoulder, she traced the swirling lines of his tattoo. The ink glimmered, warming beneath her fingertips and…God. It was fascinating. Beyond cool. And as he relaxed beneath her touch, she marveled at him, wanting to know more about the magic in his blood.

"Easy for you to say. You got off three times already."

"Four, actually."

"Hurrah for you." His lips twitched, ruining his dejected tone.

"Poor baby," she said, smiling at him. She held his gaze a moment, then turned and kissed the taut curve of his biceps. "So hard done by."

"Not really." Dipping his head, he brushed her mouth with his. Lingering over her, expression dead serious, he whispered, "Holding you…pleasing you…is enough."

Tania drew in a soft breath. Oh wow. What an incredible thing to say. So very…unselfish. Her heart dipped, flipping into a somersault inside her chest. And just like that, she was in serious trouble. Neck-deep and sinking fast with the man in her arms. She wanted to respond. Say something… anything…to lighten the mood and set herself back on the right path—the one called self-preservation. But for some reason, she couldn't. His courage was too precious a thing to disregard. And as surprise circled into wonder, deep appreciation raised its fist and knocked on the door where love lived.

Before she could stop it, the portal she guarded so closely swung wide and invited him in. A split second in time, and it was over. She was done. Falling hard, so deep and fast that when Mac slipped from her arms and rolled to his feet, it hurt to let him go. She released him anyway. Watched him walk away, her throat aching as he stole her heart and took it with him.

Halfway across the bedroom, Mac glanced over his shoulder at Tania. He wanted to see her reaction. Needed to be sure what he'd seen in her eyes was real, not a figment of his imagination. Trust. Acceptance. Maybe even a little love. Or a lot. He couldn't tell. Wasn't sure how to interpret the "look" she gave him, and honestly? He wasn't sure he wanted to.

Hope, after all, was a slippery slope. One full of icy terrain, jagged cliffs, and long falls if he allowed it to push him over the edge. 'Cause, yeah, a man reading a woman wrong? It had been known to happen. Mac stifled a snort. Shit. What an understatement. Women eviscerated men on a regular basis. Which was why he always stayed away from serious entanglements. Commitment equaled pain squared.

Period.

Sex and pleasure, however? Sure. No problem. When a female wanted him that way, he never said no. Until now. His playboy, have-any-woman-he-wanted days were over. Mac knew it as he stood there, naked in front of the female he yearned to make his own. What differentiated Tania from all the rest? Fuck if he knew, but she was special. Screw the reasons why. None of them mattered.

Mac huffed. Sweet Jesus, he was messed up. Way out in the middle of Deepshitsville with no chance of getting back. Knowing that, however, didn't solve the problem. Neither did looking at her. The sight of her wrapped in his sheets—long hair a messy tangle around her bare shoulders—just made him want her more. His gaze met hers, and—

Ah, shit. Might as well get it over with, throw up his hands, and admit defeat.

He was a goner. No question. No fighting it. No denying his need for her or the territorial half of his nature. And as his dragon fixated on her, picking up body cues, reading her bioenergy, Mac wanted to own her...possess her so thoroughly she never questioned to whom she belonged. What he got instead, though, was almost as good: the spike of her scent, the desire in her dark eyes, and...oh yeah. There it was. Genuine liking that defied reason and crossed boundaries, flirting with love's outer edges.

Good news? Bad? Mac didn't know, but he was game to find out. To explore the connection they shared and decide what the future held later.

But first things first.

She needed to know a few things about him...about Dragonkind and what the magic allowed him to do. Telling Tania wouldn't be enough. Curious by nature, she required proof, all the cold, hard facts before accepting or believing. So his plan went something like...show her first, survive the barrage of questions second.

Issuing a silent command, Mac conjured his clothes. Worn to perfection, his favorite Levi's settled at his waist. On her knees in the center of the bed, Tania's eyes went wide an instant before her mouth fell open. A second passed, then ticked into more before she snapped her teeth together and pointed at his jeans.

He bit down on a grin. "Get dressed, *mo chroí.*"

"But…you…" An adorable pucker between her brows, her gaze ran the length of his body, making his balls fist up tight. Oh man, he liked her eyes on him, relished the sweet ache of anticipation, knowing he'd have her spread beneath him again soon. But while he burned for her, she shook her head. "How did you do that?"

"Magic." Grasping the antique handle, he swung the door wide and gestured to the living room. "Meet me outside, all right?"

Not waiting for an answer, he crossed the threshold and—

"Motherfuck." Mac stopped short, getting nailed by four sets of very interested eyes. He tensed, muscles flickering beneath the scrutiny. Jesus, it was like being plugged in the chest with a .44 magnum. No flak jacket in sight.

"About fucking time," Wick growled.

"Give him a break, lad." Forge breathed deep, no doubt picking up Tania's scent on his skin. A wicked gleam in his eyes, the male grinned. "He's been a busy boy."

Bastian snorted. "You're just jealous."

"Damn right I am," Forge said. "She smells good…like water lilies."

Mac's eyes narrowed on his mentor. "Stop scenting my female. Or I'll beat the snot out of you again."

Ass-planted on the kitchen counter, shitkickers swaying in the breeze, Rikar laughed.

"Shite." Forge cringed and rubbed his knee. "I'll stop."

"Uh-huh." Mac glared at the Scot a moment longer, then shifted focus, scanning the room.

Huh. Wick without Venom. A rare occurrence, one that raised Mac's internal radar. What the hell was going on?

Yeah, he and Venom might not get along, but for the male not to have made the trip out to the island? Something was way, way off.

His attention landed on Wick. "Where's dickhead?"

"Healing."

Rikar's heels banged against the cabinet doors. "He took a hit last night."

"How bad?"

"Enough to ground him for a couple of nights." Taking a seat on the sofa, Bastian propped his feet up on the coffee table. "Myst sewed him back together. It wasn't pretty."

Concern lit Mac up. "It wasn't me, was it? I didn't hit—"

"No. That water spear shit got him out of trouble." Standing beyond the dining room table, Wick crossed his arms over his chest and leaned between two tall windows. The storm shutters protecting the glass rattled, vibrating as wind gusts rushed in from the ocean. His golden gaze, usually raptor flat, flickered, and...holy God. Mac frowned. Was that emotion...from Wick? A disgruntled look on his face, the warrior bent his leg and, planting his booted foot against the wall, grumbled, "You have my thanks."

"Christ," Rikar murmured, sounding surprised.

Twisting in his seat, B glanced over his shoulder at Wick.

And Mac understood. Gratitude from their resident psychopath. That was something new. Maybe even something he could leverage. He heard Tania now: feet hitting the floor, clothes rustling, the bed being made. A second later, she was on the move. Bare feet whispering over the floor, she approached the door. The urge to shield her cranked Mac tight. His brothers-in-arms weren't like any military unit he'd had the privilege to be a part of. A bazillion times more lethal, the Nightfuries looked like a bunch of serial killers. Honed. Focused. Brutal. None of them pulled any punches, and the last thing Mac wanted was to frighten her.

"Look, guys," he said, meeting each warrior's gaze in turn. "Go easy on her. She's a bit skittish and—"

"Am not." The door creaked open behind him. "I'm freaked out. There's a difference, you know."

Holding up the fireplace mantel with his shoulder, Forge's lips twitched. "Contrary, isnae she, Irish?"

"The best ones always are." After lifting his size four-teens off the coffee table, B let his shitkickers hit the floor. He stood and, shoulders rolling, leather trench coat creaking, stretched out the kinks. "Myst is like that."

"Angela too." Rikar hopped off the countertop. "Wicked challenging."

Wick nodded in agreement.

Forge snorted. "High-energy females. Naught but trouble."

Not quite. Mac could think of a number of things to do with his H-E that didn't have anything to do with *trouble*… like, oh, say, serve up some domination with a healthy helping of bondage. Not that Tania cared at the moment. She was too busy glaring at him. Swallowing a smile, he grabbed her hand and tugged her out of the doorway into the living room.

Time for the meet and greet, Nightfury-style.

Her hand clasped in his, he laced their fingers and turned back to the boys while he pulled her in close. She settled alongside him, body touching his, her cheek brushing his upper arm. Hmm, so sweet. And a little unsure. Yet she stood tall, chin level, shoulders back, daring to be unafraid. Which cracked his heart wide open. His dream girl, trusting him to keep her safe, nestling against him as though she belonged there...as though she'd been by his side all his life.

A nice thought, if somewhat fucking ridiculous.

The past was *the past*. No changing it, and Mac didn't want to go back. Didn't want to think about it, either. The here and now was much better, and as he looked at the warriors crowding his cabin, he thanked God for them. For steadfast loyalty, and yes...even their love. They'd flown over a shitload of ocean—their least favorite thing in the world—to bring him home. And now, he had what he needed. A kick-ass fighting force, one that would help him get his female to Black Diamond safely.

Tania's eyes widened as she got her first look at them. Her gaze ping-ponged, sweeping the group. A quiver rolled through her. Mac gave her hand a gentle squeeze to reassure her and made the introductions. Each warrior nodded, greeting her with a murmured "hey" or a "what's up?" Well, all except Wick. He just stared, his expression back to emotionless.

Tania shuffled closer to him—and farther away from Wick. He pointed to B. "And Bastian. Commander of the Nightfury dragons."

"Commander. Right," she whispered, focused on Bastian. "He's the one, isn't he?"

"Yeah."

Her dark eyes narrowed on his commander. "Where's Myst?"

"At home." An amused glint sparked in Bastian's eyes, making the green shimmer. "Waiting for you."

"Oh, well...all right then," she said, her tone tough, her hand trembling in his. "As long as she's okay...?"

She trailed off, letting the statement (disguised as a question) hang in midair, the implication clear. If her best friend was hurt, Tania would kick the Nightfury commander's ass and—

Ah, fuck. Mac sighed. There he went again, getting aroused by her moxie.

"She's good, *kazlita*." B grinned, no doubt enjoying the threat, paying Tania a huge compliment. *Kazlita*...fierce one in Dragonese. Mac knew the word. He'd been studying the language of his kind for over a month, picking up bits and pieces. Now he understood most of it when the guys talked in their native tongue. Bastian met his gaze and nodded, approving his choice of female, then looked around at the others. "Now, we headed home or what?"

Grunts of agreement met the inquiry. The mass exodus came next. Four sets of boots pounded across the wooden floorboards. Thirty seconds later, the last one filed out the door, leaving the small cabin feeling huge.

Tania nudged him. "Hey, Mac?"

He glanced at her sideways.

"Can I just...?" She pointed toward the bathroom.

"Go. I'll wait for you outside."

Cheeks tinged pink with embarrassment, she whispered a thank-you, released his hand, and skirted the end of the sofa. The second she disappeared inside the bathroom, Mac followed her across the cabin. Prowling at a sedate pace, he fiddled, straightening the furniture his brothers-in-arms had knocked askew. In the hallway now, he headed for the front door. Hinges squeaked, and Mac stopped short. Tania stepped into the hallway and bumped into him.

"Oh jeez!" Trying to avoid the run-in, she hopped backward.

The bundle of clothes she held in one hand wobbled. He cupped her biceps to right her balance. Paper crinkled between them, and Mac glanced down, catching a glimpse of a letter folded into four quarters. Curiosity made him reach for it. With an indrawn breath, Tania shoved the white paper into the front pocket of her hoodie, hiding it, denying him.

"Ready?" she asked, her tone a little too bright.

Hmm. And wasn't that interesting? A mystery. His female was keeping secrets. A dangerous proposition. For her. Not for him. 'Cause, shit, he loved a good puzzle. Like his partner, he thrived while in investigation mode. So Tania's evasion and the problem that made her so desperate to keep it?

Fair game. Oh so on his list of things to do.

But for now, he would let it go. The other Nightfuries were getting restless outside, and Mac couldn't wait any longer. He wanted her to see him in dragon form again. To gauge her reaction and know true acceptance. Sure, she might be willing to sleep with him—allow him to rule her in bed—but did her desire for him cross into commitment? He needed to know and understood the gamble better than most. The stakes were high and the odds piss-poor, but he refused to hide who and what he was from her. Disaster lay in that direction. And true acceptance always came at a cost.

Chapter Twenty

Right on Mac's heels, Tania padded across the front porch.
Staying close seemed like a good idea with a bunch of
dragon-guys milling around. Except…

The scary foursome was nowhere to be seen.

Glued to Mac's backside now, she leaned left to peer
around his shoulder. Nope. Not there, either. Nothing
but the smooth top of a bluff stretched out in front of the
cabin. A cool draft of air blew across the nape of her neck.
Tania jumped like a jackrabbit, bumping into Mac, the urge
to leap onto his back and yelp, "Help, the boogeyman!"
stuck in her throat. God, she was losing it. Scared straight
as she waited for the other shoe to drop…or, ah, dragons
to fly overhead.

Spooky. And totally idiotic.

Dragon stuff notwithstanding, Mac would keep her
safe. She swallowed. Wouldn't he?

"Relax, *mo chroí*," he murmured, glancing at her over
his shoulder. "It's all good."

Relax? He was frickin'-frackin' nuts. And obviously not
paying attention. If he had, he would've noticed the way

Wick had stared at her. Jeepers. Serial Killers-R-Us had nothing on that guy.

Hooking her finger through his belt loops, she whispered against his back, "They don't eat people, right?"

Mac blinked, surprise lighting his eyes. "Not that I know of."

"Terrific," she muttered, unease circling. Her gaze bouncing around, she rechecked the open ends of the porch. Moonlight glowed a moment before ghosting back behind cloud cover. Wonderful. Nothing like the pitch-black of midnight to camouflage a dragon's movements. A shiver ran down her spine. "You could've just said no, you know."

"And lie to you? Thought you told me never to do that."

"Shut up. These are extenuating circumstances."

Fighting a grin, he shook his head and led her down the steps. Wood creaked, creeping her out even more. It was the sound an ax murderer made before he attacked; she was sure of it.

"No serial killers in sight," he said, surprising her, making her wonder. Was he reading her mind? Seemed plausible. Especially considering he kept doing that... repeating almost word for word what she was thinking as she thought it. "Come on. The others are already airborne."

"All right." Trailing him onto a smooth outcropping of rock, she glanced skyward. "But if I get eaten, I'm blaming you."

He chuckled. She scurried to catch up, scanning the area and...

Tania's breath caught. Oh wow. What a view. Stretched out for miles, the ocean dipped and swelled, rolling onto the craggy coastline below. It was incredible in a lot of ways, dangerous in others, but wholly beautiful...the power of Mother Nature at her best.

"Tania." Mac's deep voicc rumbled, lapping at her like gentle waves. Dragging her attention away from the water, her gaze landed on the man she yearned to know without understanding why. Well, all right. The *why* wasn't hard to figure out. Any woman in her right mind would want him. He was just that hot, but her *want* went deeper than the physical, crossing into must-have territory. And as he made eye contact, she gave up trying to resist. "I want you to watch."

"What?"

"Me."

Not hard to do. Standing shirtless in the moonlight, the ocean a magnificent backdrop behind him, he looked like a Greek god. Powerful. Irresistible. Golden skin poured over hard muscle and long limbs. Gorgeous with a capital *G*, even now with his glowing gaze fixed on her.

Electricity crackled, raising the fine hair on her nape. Mac transformed, shifting into a blue-gray dragon. Her jaw dropped and shock bit deep, clipping her reflexes. With a yelp, Tania scrambled backward and lost her footing. Her butt collided with solid stone. The stinging thump barely registered. She was too busy staring...mesmerized by the man-to-dragon switcheroo.

"Holy jeez," she whispered, taking in his scales, horned head, and killer claws. A dragon with Mac's aquamarine eyes. The stuff of fairy tales and little girls' dreams. Surprise circled into awe, making her forget to be afraid. "Mac... you're...wow, just beautiful."

He snorted. Steam rose from his nostrils. His mouth tipped up on one side, revealing a razor-sharp row of teeth and one huge fang. "I prefer lethal."

No kidding. And he was that...deadly with an extra helping of vicious. The moon came out to play again, making the blade along his spine gleam like a razor-sharp sword edge. Tania pushed to her feet. Flexing her fingers, she chewed on the inside of her cheek, wondering if... maybe...she could...

Screw it. He looked too incredible standing there, and she was too curious not to ask. "Can I touch you?"

"Please."

He rolled his massive shoulders. Smooth scales clicked together as she approached. Heart hammering, each breath coming in a frosty burst, she swallowed her apprehension and stopped in front of him. Warm, mint-flavored breath rushed over her, ruffling the hair on top of her head. Tania smiled a little. Jeez, it really was Mac. He smelled the same, like the man she'd woken up with, not the dragon she stood next to. Moving slowly, she raised her hand and, reaching up, laid her palm flat against his scaled chest. He growled. She jumped but stayed true, lifting her other hand to join the first, spreading her fingers wide to touch more of him.

Incredible. "You're so warm."

"Dragonkind is hot-blooded."

"No relation to the reptile family then, huh?"

He huffed. More steam rose, flirted with the breeze before drifting away. Shifting his weight, he turned one of his paws palm up, showcasing the tips of his claws. "Ready?"

She hesitated. *Ready*. Huh. Really good question. One she wasn't sure she could answer. At least with any amount of intelligence. The strange factor was just too, well...let's put it this way. She was touching (and talking to) a dragon. A *dragon*! So, yup. *Strange* and surreal qualified in the screwed-up situation department.

Ocean waves crested, rushing sound up the cliff face. His chest rose and fell beneath her hands. Chewing on her lip, she glanced up. Familiar aquamarine eyes met hers. "We're not doing the air bubble thing again, are we?"

"No. I'm going to fly you home."

Oh. Well, all right then. Flying was good. Much better than—

Tania blinked, cutting off that thought. Good lord, she really had lost her mind. Hello, Crazytown. Goodbye, sanity. But even as the realization registered, Tania pushed it aside. Despite his rapid change, the man-dragon (dragon-man…whatever!) was undeniably Mac. And she trusted him. To keep his word. To keep her safe. And take her to Myst.

So instead of fighting, she added faith to her list of accomplishments and slid into the middle of his paw. Huge talons closed around her. She squeezed her eyes closed and held on tight as he unfurled his wings and dove over the cliff edge into the night sky.

———

Shitkickers planted in the middle of Black Diamond's driveway, a protein shake in one hand, half a toasted bagel in the other, Venom watched Bastian's female pace. He cursed under his breath. Goddamn, she was fast. The one-minute mile had nothing on her. Up. Down. Back and forth. Round and round she went, nervous tension lighting her up from the inside out. Her aura flared bright white then streaked in her wake, the abundance of energy making her look like a long-tailed comet.

Or a supernova.

Whatever. The analogy didn't matter. Myst's upset, however? No question. That mattered, bothering Venom more than he liked. All that agitation couldn't be good for her. Shoving the rest of the bagel in his mouth, he frowned. Could it? He didn't know. Had never been anywhere near a pregnant female before, never mind one that belonged to a male in his pack. Seemed safe to say her anxiety wasn't the best idea, though, and...

"Ah, hell," he muttered around the mouthful.

Bastian wouldn't be happy when he got home. Not good for anyone, but especially not for him. His commander would take one look at his mate's current state of distress and flip out...go ape-shit crazy on his ass. And B in a snit? Oh so not advisable. No male with two brain cells to rub together wanted to be in that situation.

No getting around it, though. Venom knew he deserved the ass kicking coming his way. Hands down. Without a doubt. Break out the ibuprofen, 'cause, oh yeah, he was going to need a crateful when B finished reaming him out.

As the last of his snack hit the bottom of his stomach, Venom grimaced and, following Myst's movements, wracked his brain. He needed a new angle, the best way to calm her down. He'd tried talking to her. A no go. He'd threatened her. She'd flipped him the bird and just kept pacing. Next he'd turned to pleading, which...you guessed it. Got him absolutely nowhere.

Goddamn it. He never should've told her Bastian was on the move...with Mac, Tania, and the rest of the crew in tow. Now Myst couldn't stay still. And while she waited for her best friend to show up, she stomped around Black Diamond's front yard, charting a route that went something like...march up the flagstone walkway, take a sharp left at the third shrub, hustle down one side of the driveway, then up the other in front of the garage doors.

She completed another circuit, arms swinging, gravel crunching beneath her small, booted feet, the rhythm of her footfalls nonstop. His eyes narrowed on her, he wiped his buttery fingers on his shorts. Time for another try.

"Myst," he growled at her as she approached, skirting between two shrubs. "Reel it in, female. You're driving me frigging nuts."

She glared at him on the flyby. "Where the heck are they?"

"Any minute now," he said, repeating the same thing he had the last four go-rounds.

"Why is it taking so long?"

"She's safe, Myst. Mac's got her. Says she adjusting just fine, so—"

"Shut up. *Fine* by your standards means butt-fuck crazy by mine. I did this with Bastian five weeks ago, remember?" An abrupt about-face put her nose to chest with him. Violet eyes intense, she pointed at him. Venom flinched as the tip of her index finger stopped an inch from his nose. "Got airlifted in my goddamned car, for God's sake! So don't you dare tell me she's *fine.*"

Venom opened then closed his mouth. Jeez, the language. He'd never heard Myst swear before. Talk about out of character, and even more shocking for the fact she spent most of her time scolding the warriors about dropping f-bombs inside the lair. Well, at least around G.M. (aka Gregor-Mayhem, Forge's biological son and Myst's adopted one). A furrow between her brows, she dropped her hand and circled around behind him. She paused to kick a rock across the pathway, and Venom held his breath. Was she stopping now? He hoped so, because—

Ah, frig. There she went...stomping up the driveway for another go-round.

He sighed, then glanced toward the front entrance, hypersensitive senses registering the sound of footfalls. A moment later the handle clicked and the door swing wide. Red hair flashing beneath the porch lights, Angela emerged and, with a slam, closed the heavy cedar monstrosity behind her.

One hand pressed to his belly, he limped up the path toward the steps. Pain sawed along his side and then—oh goody, just his luck—paused to chew on his leg. Biting back a curse, Venom stopped at the bottom tread. He tipped his chin at Angela and said, "Help. Crazy female at three o'clock."

Her palm closed around the gun holstered on the outside of her thigh a second before she saw Myst. Her gaze ping-ponged back to him. She snorted. "No way. I'm not touching that one."

"Ah, come on. Talk her down." Using his ruby-red eyes and thick eyelashes to effect, he gave her his best pleading look. "I'm injured."

"Suck it up, flyboy."

Venom blinked. *Flyboy?* "Heartless wench."

"You know it," she said, grinning at him.

He returned her smile, thankful for the truce between them. Ange was cool, a tough female with a wicked vibe. Right up Rikar's alley and exactly what his XO needed. Thank God. The male had been more relaxed lately, less of a hard-ass, more of a buddy. Good all the way around and—

Speak of the devil.

Sensation tingled along Venom's spine, telling him his XO was coming in hot. A second before his claws clicked down on gravel, Rikar uncloaked. Poised on his back paws, white scales gleaming in the moonlight, he wing-flapped, sending stone dust rising in the frosty swirl. The temperature dropped and Angela purred, trotting down the steps to greet her mate as he shifted to human form.

"Hiya, gorgeous." Meeting Rikar at the end of the walkway, she hugged him. An instant later, she popped up on her tiptoes and gave the lucky SOB a firm kiss. "The others?"

"On my six." Rikar met his gaze over the top of his female's head. He tilted his head in Myst's direction. "What the fuck?"

"I tried," Venom said, shrugging.

Forge and Wick came in next, landing in tandem at opposite ends of the driveway. As each transformed, boots crunching on gravel, B rolled in like a thunderstorm. The wind picked up, gusting over the treetops. Thick trunks bent nearly in half, wood creaked, and Bastian tucked his wings. He dropped like a stone. Huge paws thumped down in front of the garage doors, making steel clank and the ground tremble as the midnight-blue spikes along his spine rattled. Baring his fangs, he snorted, then shook his horned head.

"Bastian!" Moving like an inbound missile, Myst ran toward her male. Green eyes aglow, his commander's focus landed on his mate. With a snarl he shifted, leather trench coat settling across his shoulders. Stepping up, he caught Myst midleap. As B wrapped his arms around her, she asked, "Where are they? Is Tania okay? Please tell me—"

"It's all good, *bellmia*." Kissing the top of her head, Bastian pointed to a spot above the tree line.

Venom's eyes narrowed, sweeping across the sky. What the hell? He couldn't see—or detect—a frigging thing. No spike in energy. No fledgling vibe coming his way. Nothing but the pine-scented night air as his brothers-in-arms joined him by the front steps. Except...

Hold everything. Venom inhaled, putting his nose to good use. Brine. The ocean. He smelled salt water.

A second later Mac appeared from out of nowhere. He flew in fast, coming in like a blue-gray viper. Venom's brows collided. Holy Jesus and a bread basket. Blockhead could cloak himself. When the hell had that happened?

"Oh, how our laddie has grown." A feigned hitch in his voice, Forge pressed his hand to his heart and pretended to wipe a tear from beneath his eye. Venom scowled at him. The warped Scot chuckled. "Get ready, dickhead. Mac learned a few things while away."

No kidding. The ability to cloak was a big deal. It meant Mac could fly out on missions. Would be paired up with a more mature male to complete his dragon combat training in the field. Live and prime-time action. Mac was about to see a crapload of it. He locked gazes with his commander. B raised a brow. And Venom got a bad, bad, *bad* feeling. He hoped he was wrong, but...

Hell. Bastian was just that smart—or cruel...Venom couldn't decide which. His commander liked a tight-knit group, expected all the Nightfury warriors to get along and present a united front in a firefight. So no question... that look—the one B hammered him with right now—told Venom all he needed to know. Blockhead was about to become his new best friend…the third warrior in his and Wick's fighting triangle.

Venom clenched his teeth as he watched Mac land, a pale-faced female in the palm of his paw. Lord help him. Looked like he'd be keeping his promise to Angela after all and making peace with their resident water rat.

Which would suck…in every way that counted.

Chapter Twenty-One

The second Mac touched down, Tania squirmed inside the scaled paw that held her. She wanted out. Right now. To be on terra firma again, her feet planted on a whole lot of normal-nothing-special, not hanging in midair, clouds bathing her in mist while treetops galloped beneath her. Still a few feet from the ground, Mac's paw jogged. Her heart dipped into her rib cage, stirring her stomach, throwing bile up the back of her throat.

Tania gagged but breathed through the heave-ho. She refused to lose it now and embarrass herself. Again. For oh, she didn't know, maybe the gazillonth time in less than twenty-four hours? Well, no thank you. She was done being a scaredy-cat. Done with her body's insubordination too. She wanted it to get with the program. But her muscles? Nothing but Jell-O, wibble-wobbling as she tried to make her limbs work.

Another tremor rolled through her. Tania clenched her teeth. Lovely. Just what she didn't need…a physical meltdown to go along with her mental one.

Forcing her arms into compliance, she wedged her palms between her breastbone and one of Mac's talons. As she pushed, he put her down feetfirst and opened his dragon paw. Suffering from a crapload of *holy shit* and a smattering of *dear God*, her knees buckled. Mac caught her and—

Tania looked up. Oh thank heavens. Mac…back to looking like a man, wrapping his very human arms around her. She shuddered and, unable to help herself, nestled deep. Slipping her arms under his leather jacket, she pressed her body against his and her face into the side of his throat.

Holding her close, he rubbed circles down her back. "You okay?"

"I don't think I like heights anymore."

"And you did before?"

"I wasn't sure, but now I am."

He smiled against her temple. "Heads up, honey. Incoming."

Incoming? Tania frowned. What the heck was he—

"Tania! Oh my God…oh thank God!"

Turning in Mac's arms, she glanced over her shoulder. And the tears—the ones she'd been battling for over a month—surfaced in a heartbeat. As the first pair slid free, rolling over her bottom lashes, she shoved out of Mac's arms. He let her go, and she spun. The soles of her bare feet digging into gravel, she ignored the sting and ran toward her best friend. They met each other halfway, colliding in the center of the driveway, wrapping each other up in a hug and…

Let the blubber-fest begin. Which went something like…laugh, cry, talk at the same time and over one another. Pause to take a breath. Rinse, repeat, start all over again.

Coming up for air, Tania wiped both eyes with the backs of her hands. Then hugged her best friend again and whispered, "Holy jeez, I'm so glad to see you."

Myst sniffled. "Me too."

"I totally thought you were dead."

"Via serial killer?"

"And wood chipper."

"Gross." Her best friend made a face, then grinned through her own tears. "Nothing quite so spectacular, though."

"Yeah, right. If a gaggle of dragon-guys isn't spectacular, I don't know what is," she said, and...uh-huh. There it was, the understatement of the century. The memory of Mac bumping down on top of her car winged through her mind. A pang for her Mini Cooper throbbed through her. It was stupid, really, to mourn its loss, but...she'd loved that car. Had spent hours in the body shop with her mechanic fixing it up, taking it from rust bucket to beautiful. And honestly? When she thought of her girl at the bottom of Puget Sound, well...she glared over her shoulder at Mac. "Who like to kill cars."

"Motherfuck," he muttered. "Thought we settled that."

Myst blinked. "They wrecked your car too?"

Tania frowned. *Too?* She opened her mouth to ask, but didn't get the chance. In her typical take-the-bull-by-the-horns fashion, Myst grabbed hold and, dragging her past a cluster of gorgeous boxwoods, hustled her up the wide-faced steps. "Come on. I've got a *ton* of stuff to tell you."

And just like that, Tania was through the front door and into the house, being towed behind her best friend like a water-skier behind a powerboat. A minute later, a kitchen came into view at the end of a hallway. Myst streaked into the room. Glossy white cabinets and marble countertops flashed beneath halogens. Beautiful. The decor was right out of one of those fancy design magazines: sophisticated with a hint of homey.

Skirting the huge center island, her friend yelled, "Hey, Daimler!"

A door flapped open at the opposite end of the kitchen. With a joyful hop, a guy popped over the threshold, a spatula in one hand, a cupcake in the other. "Yes, my lady?"

Myst hit the pause button on the dash-and-tow routine. "Meet my best friend, Tania."

"Oh, how lovely!" Exuberance plain to see, he clasped his hands together. The icing-smeared spatula dipped dangerously a moment before he righted it and smiled. His gold front tooth winked at her. "Welcome to Black Diamond, Lady Tania."

Swallowing a laugh, Tania thanked him. It was impossible not to…he was just too adorable for words with his "my lady, this…and my lady, that" attitude. And that was nothing compared to his obvious pleasure at meeting her. But even as she returned his smile, she looked at him a little closer, picking up details. Weird, but…did he…were his ears really, ah…

Nudging Myst with her elbow, she whispered, "He's got pointy ears."

"Elf," her friend whispered back.

Tania's brows popped skyward. Oh. Well. Why not? Color her unsurprised. A gaggle of dragon-guys and an *elf.* What could be simpler?

Tossing her an amused glance, Myst squeezed her hand. "Daimler, would you mind whipping up something for us to eat?"

"Cupcakes?"

"With chocolate icing?" Both she and Myst's attention sharpened on the spatula.

The elf nodded.

"Perfect." Myst smiled at him. Daimler beamed at her in return, and Tania shook her head. Give her friend an hour, and she could make anyone like her. Give her five weeks? And yup, adoration became par for the course. "I'll be in my room. Oh, and keep Bastian busy, would you? I'm due for some girl talk."

Oh yes…please. Girl talk sounded better than good. And after weeks of going it alone—without the daily phone calls, coffee shop pit stops, and window-shopping while yakking—Tania needed an infusion more than a caffeine addict needed a shot of espresso.

After repeating her friend's "thanks" to the elf, Tania pivoted and, following in Myst's wake, beat feet out of the kitchen into another corridor. Wider than the last one, the hallway was another study in sophistication: dark hardwood floors, twin tracks of halogens marching down twelve-foot ceilings, white walls flowing behind a chunky chair rail, and—

Gad. The art. She'd never seen anything like it. Well, all right. That was a lie. The Louvre in Paris might beat what she saw with each passing canvas…by a scooch and not much more.

"Holy jeez," she murmured, not wanting to talk above a whisper for fear a museum curator might jump out of the woodwork and shout "Quiet!" A huge painting of ballet dancers rolled by on her right-hand side. Tania's jaw dropped. "Is that a Renoir?"

"Yup."

Tania pointed to the next one. "Vermeer?"

"Nailed it."

"Good lord."

"I know, right? Crazy expensive," Myst said. "Wick likes art."

Oh, of course Wick liked…what? Were they talking about the same guy? The one that had given her the stink eye back in Mac's cabin? Seemed like a bit of a stretch—from psychopath to art lover—but really, how many Wicks could there possibility be at Black Diamond? She hoped no more than one, because…wow. One nut job was more than enough for any girl to handle.

Reaching a pair of doors at the end of the corridor, Myst flipped the handle, pushed it wide, and ushered her into—

A man cave. Nothing else came close to describing it. Walls the color of eggplant. Big antique sleigh bed with a light-gray duvet. Charcoal accents. No frills. No muss. The room was a serious, masculine space.

Tania swept the decor again, picking up a few more details. Like the ratty old Barcalounger set in front of the stone-clad fireplace. Her lips twitched. Well, at least some things were normal at Black Diamond. Only a guy would keep something that ugly around—and needed duct tape to keep it together. "Bastian's room?"

"Mine now too."

Halfway across the room, Myst glanced over her shoulder. As their gazes met, Tania shook her head. None of it made sense. Just over a month ago, her friend had been entrenched in her life. On a career track that might've taken her all the way to the top of the hospital administrative hierarchy. Now? She played house with a guy who commanded a warrior clan—pack…whatever!—of

Dragonkind. All under the noses of human authorities the world over.

But worse? Her friend seemed perfectly okay with the situation. She was content, happier, and more settled than Tania had ever seen her.

"God, Myst," she said, not understanding. "What the heck happened? One minute we're going for lattes. The next? You're gone and—"

"Kidnapped, actually. In my car with a newborn baby screaming a blue streak."

"What is it with these guys and cars?"

"I don't know, but Bastian airlifted me right off the road."

Well, since they were comparing notes. "Mac landed on mine, ripped the door off, then drove us off a bridge."

Myst's mouth fell open. A moment later, she laughed. "Okay, you win that one."

"Wanna go for round two?"

"Hit me."

Padding across the room, Tania followed her friend and hopped into the middle of the big bed. Settled on a sea of cool gray cotton, she sat Indian-style and, grabbing a pillow, plopped it in her lap and started to talk. And as the litany streamed out of her, her tension eased. God, it felt good to get it off her chest, to have someone understanding all the freaky dragon stuff. But mostly? To stop the tilt-a-whirl of worry eating her alive inside.

And Myst? Thank goodness for her friend. She nodded in all the right places, asked questions in others, and Tania got bolder, moving into more personal territory. Namely, Mac and how she felt about him. The intensity of her reaction didn't make sense. It was bizarre and scary, and yet somehow magical too. Two opposite ends of the spectrum. And honestly, she didn't know which way to jump: toward Mac or away.

Picking at a stray thread, Tania mangled the corner of a pillow. "So I guess you love Bastian, huh?"

"I really do." With a quick shift, Myst reached out and grabbed her hand. "He's the one, you know. The guy I've been—"

"Waiting for," Tania said, finishing her sentence. God, how many times had she heard that? *If only*—the hoping, the wishing, the dreaming—had always been a running theme with them. Well, at least for Myst. Tania had never quite trusted that far. Men were tricky creatures and her independence an absolute must. Forever, after all, was a very big word. "So…"

"You gonna spit it now?"

Tania laughed. ESP had nothing on her friend. Myst knew how to read her. "I've been trying to figure something out."

"What's that?"

"How could I have slept with Mac and not remember?"

Myst sucked in a quick breath. "When did this happen? Last night?"

"No. A month ago…in your loft." Tania cringed. Yikes, that didn't sound good. Nothing like telling your best friend you had sex with a guy in her bed. Without her permission. "Sorry. I didn't mean to, but…it all happened so fast. I went to your place to find you. Next thing I know, Mac walks in and…kapow. We kinda collided." Chewing on her bottom lip, she threw Myst an apologetic look. "It's the funniest thing, though. I didn't remember any of it until I saw him again last night."

"I'm going to kill him."

Tania blinked. "Who? Mac?"

"No. Bastian." Her eyes narrowed on the door, Myst tossed the pillow over her shoulder. Its fluffy body hit the headboard with a thump, and…oh dear. Tania knew that look. Someone was in very big trouble. It didn't, however, appear to be her. Thank God for small favors. "Oh. My. God. He is so dead when I get a hold of him."

Well, all right then. Suspicions confirmed. Her best friend was inbound on a train called PO'd. Why? No clue, but at least she wasn't pissed off about the whole sex-in-her-bed thing. That could've gotten messy…fast. Especially considering Myst's current state of mind. It took a lot to make her friend angry, but when the pot boiled over?

Oh boy. Watch out world.

"Freaking guy," Myst growled, scooting toward the edge of the bed. "Trust him to gloss it all over."

Frowning, Tania watched her go. Alarm mixed with surprise. Good lord, what the heck was going on? She opened her mouth to ask. Myst cut her off.

"Routine, he said." Myst huffed. Looking like a gymnast, she flipped off the mattress. Her feet hit the floor with a thud. She cursed again and plunked her hands on her hips, outrage in her eyes. "And Sloan! Oh, I'm gonna kill him too."

"Why?"

"He told me they used a hooker to stabilize Mac's energy levels before he went into his *change*. Except he neglected to tell me *you* were there." With a growl, Myst spun away from the bed and headed toward the door. "And then he erased your memory afterward. *Mind-scrubbed* my best freaking friend!"

"Excuse me?" Confusion set up shop inside her head, obliterating her ability to follow. Not surprising, really. With Myst gone berserk, descending into meltdown mode, not even a Mensa candidate would be able to understand. "Mind what?"

Halfway across the room, her hands balled into fists, Myst ignored her. "Holy crap, I'm living with a bunch of liars. *Liars*, I tell you! Just wait until I—"

"Time out!" Tania yelled, interrupting the temper tantrum.

Myst swung back toward her. Tania made the time-out sign with her hands and hopped off the bed to land on the floor. Persian rug warming her toes, she stared at her friend, all the questions she planned and wanted to ask sidelined. One thought circled, blotting out all the others.

A hooker. With Mac.

Fury ignited so fast it singed her. Surprised her. Made her want to throw something...right at Mac's head.

"A little clarification here, please," she said, fighting to keep her tone even. But boy, it was hard. She wanted to let loose, find Mac, and do some serious damage. Crazy much? Absolutely. Mac didn't owe her a thing. Hadn't promised her forever or even broached the subject. But imagining him with another woman, kissing, touching, loving someone else? Well, the idea struck her as danger-ous...for the other woman. "What in God's name are you talking about?"

With a long sigh, Myst stopped pacing and pivoted to face her. "How much do you know about the Meridian and how it works?"

"Just what Mac told me," she said. "Something about electrostatic bands ringing the planet and Dragonkind's connection to it. But honestly? I was so tired when we talked about it that I just...I don't know. Didn't retain much."

"Okay, then." Tucking her blonde hair behind her ears, Myst nodded. "Here's how it works."

Thank God. Finally. Viable information. From a reasonable person, one she trusted to give it to her straight. But as her friend laid it on the line—explaining the cosmic connection to the Meridian and how a male fed from female energy via touch to receive the nourishment he needed to keep him not only healthy but alive—dread circled deep. Mac had used her as an energy source. Had touched and fed from her in the way Myst described...in the loft, yes. But also last night while he rubbed her feet on the couch.

Tania pinched the bridge of her nose, thinking back, remembering, putting a label on the siphoning rush of sensation. Heat. Pleasure. Comfort. Yes, all that qualified, but then so did *theft*. Except...

Was that really fair?

She didn't know. Wasn't sure how she felt about feeding him, never mind the whole mind-scrub, memory-tampering thing. It wasn't an easy thing to figure out. Especially since she liked Mac. All right, so maybe *like* was too tame a word. *Craved* was no doubt a better one, but still...

"Do you enjoy feeding Bastian?" Tania asked, needing to know the ins and outs from a woman's perspective. "I mean...is it something you do because he needs it and you have to or...?"

"I love it. He's...incredible." Myst sighed, looking worn out all of a sudden. "But that doesn't mean I won't nail him for not telling me about...jeez, Tania. He offered you up as Mac's main meal."

"Well..."

"Well, what?" Myst snapped, then muttered, "Oh, just you wait, Bastian."

"I wasn't exactly unwilling." Tania cringed, feeling her cheeks warm. "In fact, I may have been, ah…the aggressor."

Her friend threw her a surprised look.

"I seem to remember Rikar trying to separate us, but I…then Mac, he…" Tania pursed her lips. "Let's just say it didn't go well."

"Oh. All right then," Myst murmured, her eyes twinkling. A second later she gave up trying to hold on to her amusement and laughed. "I guess you want him, then."

"From the moment I saw him at the police precinct."

"When you filed my missing person's report?"

Tania nodded. "But you know, I'm scared of him too. He's so intense, and I'm just…ridiculous or something, because I want him. Even though I know it'll change everything, Myst. *Everything.* My life. My work. Me. But when I'm with him I don't want to be anywhere else. It's as though there's some weird connection between us, like he's a planet, and I'm stuck orbiting him. And well, that's just plain nuts. I hardly know the guy!"

"It isn't crazy," Myst said, her voice soft with understanding. "At least, not to me. The connection is real, Tania. Dragonkind calls it energy-fuse…a magical bond between mates. I did the same dance with Bastian five weeks ago."

Energy-fuse. Fused to Mac. Tied up in irrevocable ways, unable to get away. Uh-huh, that sounded about right.

Leaning back against the bed, Tania rubbed her temples, trying to head panic off at the pass. It didn't work. Uncertainty cranked her tight one notch at a time. The urge to run and never look back poked at her. Tania locked it down. She wasn't a coward, and fear or no fear, she needed to see the situation through. Exploration, after all, was mankind's great gift to itself. So, no, she couldn't walk away. Not yet. Not without giving what she felt for Mac a chance.

He deserved better than a fast lay and an even faster good-bye. And so did she.

Inhaling through her nose, she exhaled through her mouth. The in-and-out routine helped, and as she evened out, the knot in the center of her chest unraveled. She could do this. Be as brave as Myst. Explore a brand-new world. Give Mac the benefit of the doubt and herself time to decide whether to stay or go.

She glanced at her friend. Patient as always, Myst stood a few feet away, watching her, waiting, allowing her to come to terms with the scary thing called Dragonkind.

Tania rolled her eyes.

Myst laughed before her expression smoothed into serious lines. "So I have something to ask you."

"Go for it."

"Will you be my maid of honor?"

"Holy jeez!" With a hop, Tania leaped away from the side of the bed. "Really? A wedding?"

"Yes…Dragonkind-style."

"God help you." Tears in her eyes, laughter in her voice, she gave Myst a hug. Call her idiotic—or a hopeless romantic—but she loved weddings. All the love-fueled chaos and fancy hairdos, glamorous gowns, and oh happy day…the shoes! The only hiccup in an otherwise excellent plan was the future groom. She didn't know Bastian at all, and, well, let's face it. The whole dragon thing held the potential to blow up in her friend's face.

And per usual? That worried her.

But Myst wasn't stupid. She loved Bastian. Tania could see it in her eyes, and only a fool stood in the way of true love.

Grinning like an idiot, she asked, "When?"

"Any day now. Daimler's getting everything ready, but we'll need to…umm…" With one last squeeze, Myst let her go, stepped back, and rubbed her forehead. Tania scanned her face and frowned. Whoa. Something was wrong. As in no-color-in-her-friend's-cheeks-now *wrong*. "I have a list and…"

Covering her mouth with her hand, Myst swayed on her feet.

"Hey, are you all right?"

Dumb question. Tania knew it the moment it left her mouth. No way her friend was all right. She looked as though she was about to throw up.

Pale as death, Myst shook her head. "It happens about this time each night. Just give me a minute. I'm sure it'll settle."

Well, wasn't that cryptic? No doubt, but now was not the time to unravel the mystery. "What can I do?"

"Get Bastian. I need him. Get…"

"Okay. Hold on. Let's just…"

Her friend's eyelashes fluttered. A second later, Myst collapsed, becoming a deadweight in her arms. Adrenaline hit her like rocket fuel, pumping fear through her. Tania tightened her hold and sank to the floor. Oh jeez. Oh crap. She hated situations like these. Her brain always shut down, leaving her blank, mind deep in panic and floundering to think straight. Breathing hard, her heart thumped, roaring like a runaway freight train.

And only one thought surfaced. Call for help. Right now.

She drew in a lungful of air, preparing to yell Bastian's name and get Myst what she needed. But when she opened her mouth, she screamed for Mac instead.

Chapter Twenty-Two

Venom was acting strange. Mac recognized the signs. Could smell trouble a mile away as the guy ass-planted himself on a stool at the kitchen island, sticking around while he foraged for leftovers in the refrigerator. His internal alarm system pinged, sending warning bells ringing inside his head.

Jesus, that wasn't good. Something was up. Wrong. Inside out and backward, 'cause...

Dickhead didn't do random.

Wicked smart and armed with a lethal vocabulary, the male never pulled any punches. He aimed to kill and usually did. Mac gritted his teeth, wishing the male would piss off...slither back into his hole and leave him the hell alone. Condescending dickheads weren't his favorite thing. Neither was being ragged on. So, yeah. Venom settling in at his back? Bad news, all the way around. Nothing fun was headed his way.

Mac tightened the screws on his temper, waiting for the barrage to start. A full minute passed and...nada. No derogatory comments. No teasing quips or jabs about his lack of ability. Just the hum of the refrigerator and the faint rumble of male voices. He listened harder, hyperacute dragon senses picking up...

The first voice belonged to Bastian. The second and third, Rikar and Forge. Thank fuck. He didn't want to tangle with Venom tonight. And the trifecta of kick-ass yakking it up in the outer foyer? The boys gave him the perfect out if shit went critical in the kitchen, allowing Mac to keep his mind where he wanted it. On Tania and the mystery of where she would sleep inside the lair.

Daimler would know. But no way would he ask. He had made a promise to himself not to pressure her. So hands off...keep it locked down. It was Tania's choice: sleep alone in her own bed or wrapped around him in his.

White-knuckling the top of the fridge door, he scanned the top shelf again, then glanced at dickhead from the corner of his eye. Venom shifted in his seat, first left, then right. The movement spoke volumes. Nervous. Restless. Way out of his league on the how-to-start-a-conversation front.

Terrific. Just what he didn't need. A Nightfury with an agenda.

Pushing a jar of mayonnaise out of the way, Mac dug deeper, working his way to the back, looking for protein. A whole chicken would be good. Roast beef, though? Even better.

His stomach grumbled, eating away at his insides. A fledgling's curse, he guessed. But whatever. He didn't care about the *why*. Mac simply wanted it to be over...to be out helping his brothers KO rogues without having to worry about the body drain. Or subsequent dip in energy and loss of firepower when hunger gnawed on him.

Damned annoying. But no bigger a problem than the SOB perched at the island, clouding the air with, well...Mac didn't know. Toxic waste in the form of a serious attitude problem, maybe?

Venom grumbled something under his breath. Mac threw the male a perturbed look. Too bad Venom didn't get the memo. He was too busy frowning at his knuckles as a muscle twitched along his jaw. Jesus fucking Christ. What was his problem? The male was hedging, struggling to find the right words. And by the looks of it? It wasn't going well.

Venom cleared his throat and opened his mouth. No sound came out.

Mac growled at him. Venom blinked and looked up, away from the self-examination of his fist. Slamming the fridge door, Mac plunked a container on the countertop. Glass hit marble, clunking in the quiet.

Ruby-red eyes solemn, Venom met his gaze. After half a minute of staring, he cleared his throat and said, "Listen, I—"

"You want me to make you a plate?" he asked, hopping on the asshole bandwagon, deliberately cutting the guy off. Juvenile, Mac knew, but he couldn't help it. The urge to prolong Venom's discomfort was just too much to resist. After all the BS and trash talking, he wanted some payback. Besides, the mouthy jack-off deserved a little of what he excelled at dishing out. "I got roast beef and gravy."

Dickhead frowned.

Mac ignored him and, leaning to one side, reached for a couple of plates sitting on an open shelf. "How much do you want?"

"Frigging hell," Venom murmured. "You're enjoying this, aren't you?"

"What?"

"Screwing with me."

He shrugged.

Venom sighed. "Look, about last night, I—"

"Forget about it," Mac said, picking up the reason behind Venom's discomfort. "Wick already thanked me."

A silence-filled pause. No fidgeting. No rustle of clothing. No movement whatsoever and then, "He did *what?*"

Cracking the top off the roast beef, Mac inhaled hard, drinking the decadent aroma right out of the air. Umm-umm good. Daimler was *da bomb*, a culinary wizard bar none. His mouth watering, he tossed the lid aside and glanced over his shoulder.

Surprise creasing his puss, Venom looked like he'd been hit upside the head...with a hatchet. Sharp side up.

Mac clenched his teeth to keep from laughing. "I know. Fucked up, right?"

"That's one way to put it." Staring at the countertop, Venom shook his head and muttered, "When he decides to talk, he *talks*, I guess."

"You've known him a long time?"

"Almost from the beginning. I got him through his change...like Rikar did you." Tracing a swirl of gray embedded in white marble with his fingertip, Venom's brow furrowed. And Mac waited, amazed by the information and Venom's peace offering. They'd never really talked without sniping at each other, so...yeah. The sincerity in the male's voice qualified as boot-to-the-balls surprising. "Hell, I was only a couple of weeks out of transition myself. A fledgling without the maturity or strength to control the energy and...Jesus. Still amazes me either of us made it out alive."

"Tough times."

"The roughest."

"Not everyone gets a fairy tale," Mac murmured, understanding better than most.

His upbringing had been a train wreck, and he'd been messed up in a lot of ways until he'd met Angela. She'd straightened him out in a hurry, bringing stability into his life, accepting him without hesitation, becoming his friend. And as he held Venom's gaze, Mac understood something else too. None of them were immune. Pain and suffering came to the best of them, and he and the warrior struggling to make peace were more alike than different.

Go figure. A peace treaty inked over a couple of sentences. The United Nations had nothing on them.

Pulling a drawer open, Mac grabbed a fork and, stabbing the beef, dished out equal portions on each plate. "Hey, Ven?"

"Yeah."

"Enough with the fledging BS. I'm done with it."

"No more calling me *dickhead*, then."

"Deal," Mac said and thanked God. He was tired of the conflict. It took way too much energy to fight with a guy meant to be your brother. "So…we good now?"

"Goddamn, I hope so," Venom growled. A twinkle in his eyes, he rapped his knuckles against the countertop. "Otherwise we're gonna end up having a love-in, and quite frankly? I'd sooner beat you unconscious than hug you."

Mac grinned. "Ask Forge about that."

"About what?" the Scot said, walking into the kitchen with Bastian and Rikar on his heels.

"Kung fu."

"Oh shite." His mentor threw Venom an alarmed look. "Doonae go there."

Sitting up a little straighter, interest flared in Venom's gaze. "I got some time. Let's hit the gym and—"

"Mac!"

The scream echoed, making his heart jackrabbit inside his chest.

"I need help...Mac!"

Holy shit. Tania. Sounding terrified.

Adrenaline hit him like a nuclear bomb. Muscles cranked tight, he exploded around the end of the island and rocketed into the corridor. The raging beat of his shitkickers rang out, hammering the silence, joining the din of the males hauling ass behind him.

Skidding to a halt in front of Bastian's door, Mac unleashed and kicked the fucker open. Wood splintered, shattering inward as he roared over the threshold. He scanned the room, searching for the threat.

"Good Christ," he said, taking in the scene. Tania on the floor. Myst unconscious. Tears in his female's eyes. Crossing to where she sat, he ran his gaze over her, then reached out and cupped her cheek. "Are you all right? What happened?"

"She fainted," she whispered, her face ashen. "One minute she was just fine, and the next—"

"What the fuck?" Bastian rolled in like an electrical storm, violence shivering in the air around him. A vicious growl and two strides later, his commander reached them. Green eyes aglow, he shoved Mac out of the way and, with gentle hands, scooped Myst off the floor. When Tania clung, not wanting to let her friend go, he murmured, "Let me have her, *kazlita*. She needs me."

"That's what she said." So shaken her hands trembled, Tania released her friend and pushed to her feet. Her gaze trained on Bastian, she followed his progress across the room. Reaching the bed, his commander sat down with Myst in his lap. "What are you going to do?"

"Feed her."

Shock flared in her eyes an instant before Tania threw him a questioning look. "He's not gonna—"

"Hurt her?" Mac shook his head and, needing to soothe her, moved in close. His heartbeat evened out, thumping just for her when she turned toward him, accepting the comfort he offered. Drawing her closer, he laced their fingers together. "B would rather blow his own head off than hurt her."

The side of her shoulder bumped his chest. She shuddered. He gave her hand a gentle squeeze, watching her watch Bastian cup the nape of Myst's neck and slip his hand beneath her T-shirt to palm the small of her back. "Then what's he doing?"

Closing his eyes, Bastian dipped his head and nestled his cheek against his mate's. With a sigh, Myst curled into him, snuggling closer, murmuring B's name.

Tania frowned. Mac's mouth curved as he explained, "The energy exchange, remember? He's sharing his life force, connecting to the Meridian to stabilize her bioenergy and ease her discomfort."

"Oh, well…" She paused, glanced up at him, and…pow! He got hit with burgundy-flecked eyes and a shitload of smarts. Oh man, he was in for it now. She was doing the math, putting the complicated equations together so fast Mac swore he could see her mental wheels turning. "You held me like that. At the cabin and…before. When we were, umm, together."

Mouth gone dry, he swallowed, wondering what to do. Come clean or lie his ass off. Lying would be easier. The problem? He didn't want to lie to Tania. "Yeah, I touched you like that, but…I didn't feed you. I, ah…"

She raised a brow.

Ah, fuck. Time for the reckoning.

Nervous as hell, he cleared his throat, searching for the right words. None came. And as the blankety-blank-blank clouded over mental acuity, Mac decided on the direct approach. "I connected to the Meridian through you and fed."

"Lucky for you."

Mac blinked, surprise giving him a major case of the stupids. "What?"

"'Cause if you'd lied to me just now? I would've been forced to kill you." The corners of her mouth tipped up, but not with amusement. The expression was half self-deprecating, half-sad. "I can handle a lot of things, Mac, but lying? Not one of them."

"Consider me warned."

"So…" she said, her gaze probing. "Anything else you want to tell me while we're at it?"

So many things. He wanted to crack himself wide open and confess all. The uncertainty he harbored for his—and their—future. The fact he couldn't remember making love to her the first time. His need for her. The yearning to claim her as his own, to share himself so completely he lost sight of where he ended and she began. And as he held her hand along with her gaze, the pressure inside him geysered, pushing him toward honesty and away from self-protection.

Bizarre. Beyond scary. But more real than anything he'd ever experienced.

Taking a deep breath, Mac shored up his courage. Time to go. To get her alone. To sit down and talk…really *talk*. No bullshit or hedging, just honest-to-God truth shot straight from the heart. "Tania, honey, can we—"

"Hey, Mac?"

Dragging his gaze away from his female, his head snapped toward Bastian.

Wrapped around Myst, but lying in the center of the bed now, B murmured, "Find Daimler. Tell him to get everything ready."

"For the energy-mating?"

"The ceremony just got moved up."

With a nod, he tugged Tania toward the door. "How soon?"

"The second my female is back on her feet."

Which wouldn't be a minute too soon. With Myst's pregnancy advancing, she needed a permanent connection to her mate, a magical one that would keep her bioenergy stable even when B couldn't be with her. But beyond that, Mac didn't know much about it. Good thing Forge did, though. His mentor understood all the ins and outs of the Dragonkind marriage ceremony. Had memorized every detail from an ancient text at the behest of his sire, in the hopes of one day mating a female of his own.

So far, that hadn't worked out. And after the birth of his son, which had resulted in the death of his child's mother, Forge swore he'd never try again. Time would tell the tale. But as much as Mac wanted the Scot to be happy, he didn't hold out much hope.

For himself, either.

Jesus. He sucked at relationships. The evidence lay in the trail of women left in his wake over the years. Love 'em and leave 'em fast. His motto until meeting Tania, but as he opened the door and pulled her into the hallway behind him, Mac wondered if anything had truly changed. Was she just another in a long line of lovers? Was he capable of permanency and fidelity? Would he make her a good mate?

Tough questions. Ones he didn't like. Each forced him to examine who and what he was. And that made his heart ache and his throat go tight.

A leopard never changed its spots. Fact. Not fiction. But as he led Tania down the hall toward the kitchen and Daimler, he prayed he could change for her. That he could become all that she needed, everything she deserved, and strike a chord.

The one called happily-ever-after.

Hope circled through him. Pragmatism pushed it aside. He wanted to do the right thing by Tania. He really did. But sensible said the past often dictated the future, and Mac knew his track record spoke volumes. None of it good.

* * *

Kneeling at the base of the marble steps, Tania fussed, adjusting the folds at the back of her best friend's dress. With a critical eye, she tweaked each fold into place, even though the vintage Versace didn't need it. Perfection in motion, the gown's deep purple hue complemented Myst the way roses did Valentine's Day.

Simple. Elegant. Gorgeous. Just like the girl she'd known since fifth grade.

Tania fluffed out the silken hem, playing until it pooled on the floor just right. The movement was nervous, more busywork than necessary, but...God. It was almost showtime. Within minutes, Myst would climb the steps, walk into the rotunda, and marry the man she loved.

Dragonkind-style.

Picking at a piece of fluff, Tania frowned and wondered—was it just her, or did the idea of exchanging vows with someone a month after meeting seem a bit, well... nuts? She couldn't decide. Was torn between two opposing schools of thought. The first went something like...marry a man you loved? Excellent idea. Check that bad boy off the to-do list and get it done. The second, though, whispered in her ear, urging her to toss Myst into the nearest trunk, put the hammer down, and peel out of Black Diamond so fast she left rubber in the driveway.

Which was where crazy came in. At least on her part. Because marrying into a pack of dragon warriors seemed counterintuitive. Maybe even pathological.

In a flurry of movement, Tania refluffed the train of her friend's dress. For the fifth flipping time.

"Would you stop fussing?" Myst threw a perturbed look over her shoulder. The gown's hue picked up the lavender in her eyes, making them more violet than blue. "You're making me crazy."

The rumble of masculine voices drifted in from the rotunda. The quiet echo cranked Tania's tension up another notch. The groom was there, along with the other Nightfuries, waiting for the ceremony to begin.

Another readjustment. Myst scowled at her. She ignored the scolding by glare and asked, "Are you sure you're okay in those heels? You're not gonna—"

"No, I'm not going to fall over...for the zillionth time." Her friend sighed. The white roses woven into her updo shivered under the strain. "Or faint again. I'm pregnant, Tania, not sick. Now come up here before I take off my glass slipper, bash you over the head, and leave you lying unconscious on the floor."

With a huff of amusement, Tania pushed to her feet. "Glass slipper?"

"I'm feeling a tad Cinderella-ish at the moment."

"The violent version?"

"Cinderella 2.0...Murder Becomes Her in Fairy Tale Land."

Lacing her fingers with her best friend's, she grinned. As Myst returned her smile, Tania got serious again. "Are you sure about this? About Bastian and Dragonkind...all of it?"

"I love him. I want him more than I want my next breath," Myst said, voice soft yet somehow full of unrelenting certainty. "I can't go back. I don't want to live without him now."

"Worth the sacrifice?"

"Every single one."

Throat gone tight, holding on to her tears, Tania nodded. God love her best friend. She was the bravest, smartest, most incredible woman she knew. And as she gave her hand a squeeze, she envied Myst's certitude, the unwavering conviction that sent her friend toward love instead of away. "Good enough for me."

"I hope so." Shifting her weight from one foot to the other, Myst grimaced. "We need to get the show on the road. These shoes are *killing* me."

"Worth every sacrifice, remember?" Tania smoothed her hand over her own skirt. The bloodred silk clung, caressing her palms. Pleasure erupted, swirling through her on a wave of oh-thank-you-God. Beautiful, after all, was just that...*beautiful*. "Vintage gowns and three-inch heels. Like PB and J. Can't have one without the other."

"God help me," Myst grumbled. "Let's go before I start cursing like a trucker."

With a laugh, Tania started for the stairs. Three steps up and she stood at the top, on the edge of the rotunda between two massive pillars, in plain view of the men standing beneath the dome. Illuminated by soft light thrown upward by the standing candelabras, the ceiling fresco glowed, highlighting colorful dragons in flight.

All conversation stopped.

As silence drifted on the scent of hyacinths and yellow tiger lilies, she scanned the room. Off to one side, Angela stood in a shimming gown of ice blue, Gregor-Mayhem cradled in her arms, Daimler by her side. Tania acknowledged each with a nod, then turned her attention to the Nightfury warriors. Her breath stalled in her throat. Dear lord, taken as individuals, each was gorgeous. But gathered together? They were a visual feast for the eyes, a tall, wide-shouldered, hard-bodied collection, and every girl's wet dream.

Nerves getting the best of her, Tania twitched her skirt. Each warrior responded by bowing his head. The ceremonial navy robes they wore rasped against the floor, flowing around their bare feet, as each placed a fist over his heart and knelt, lowering to one knee on the limestone tile. Bastian alone stayed standing, his green eyes fixed on her, waiting for her to begin.

Her gaze lingered on Mac's bent head. The sight of him helped her floundering confidence. Tania gave herself a mental nod. She could do this. Could remember everything. The right words. The proper place to stand. All the fine details of protocol. And no matter how much she disliked the scrutiny, she refused to screw up her best friend's wedding. Myst was counting on her—had chosen her to officiate the ceremony—so…no question. She would deliver; remember everything Forge had explained, drilled her on, and made her memorize all afternoon. Be the best darned *lyzemai* (master of ceremony) Dragonkind had ever seen.

Leveling her chin, Tania assumed the mantle of responsibility and, tone full of authority, said, "By right, I enter unto this ceremony. The keeper of the female you wish to claim." Her voice echoed in the vastness, whispering over the round walls before escaping through four identical archways. She held Bastian's gaze, prolonging the moment as Forge taught her, then swept over the warriors kneeling behind their commander. "Defender of her honor. Protector unto the ages. Supreme unto this chamber and all in it. Who denies me?"

"None," the Nightfuries said as one, deep voices intertwining into acceptance.

"So be it. The rite of passage is mine."

Having claimed the position of *lyzemai,* she locked gazes with Bastian again. Her stilettos clicking against stone, she broke eye contact with the groom to complete the mandatory circuit around the room. Passing the marble columns and the mosaics of individual dragons depicted between each, she strode behind the kneeling Nightfuries, then crossed to the large disc embedded in the floor. In the center of the room, the crest sat beneath the vaulted dome, an intricate inscription in a language she didn't know woven into its outer edges.

Stopping at its center, Tania held out her hand, palm up in invitation. Myst took the cue and, like a vision in purple silk, mounted the steps. She came forward to take Tania's raised hand. Tania turned her to face the man she meant to marry.

Bastian's breath caught. "*Bellmia.*"

"Are you worthy of the female I give unto your care?"

"No." Bowing his head, Bastian adhered to the ritual and said, "I am unworthy."

"And so you are." Releasing her hand, she moved in behind Myst to unclasp her cape. With a flick, she removed the velvet and bared her best friend's shoulders. As Daimler stepped up to take the heavy throw, she said, "But you have been chosen by this female and have now been accepted by me. Come, warrior…claim what is now yours by right."

"*Mervais, zi lyzemai,*" Bastian said in Dragonese, thanking her for the privilege. Without hesitation, he stepped over the ancient inscription and into the heart of the crest.

Tears in her eyes, Myst reached for him. With a murmur, he accepted and stepped in close. The air stirred, and electrostatic current rising, he slipped his right hand into hers and cupped her cheek with the other. "My love… almost there."

Tania's chest grew tight as she watched them. Amazing. Heart-stopping. Beyond beautiful. She'd never seen anything like the love they shared…or their commitment to one another. She saw the way Bastian looked at her friend. Felt their connection with every breath she took. Recognized forever in Myst's eyes and the rush of awe in her own veins.

Meant to be. These two were undeniably meant to be.

Her own tears rose. Tania pushed them away. She didn't have time to cry. Not right now. Later would be soon enough to turn into a blubbering idiot. To rejoice in Myst's good fortune and let the tears of happiness fall. To become her best friend again and leave the role of *lyzemai* behind...for good.

"Rise all," she said. "Gather round to bear witness to this male and this female."

Taking a calming breath, Tania paused to collect her thoughts as the Nightfuries obeyed and rose. Their bare feet whispered in the silence, and she dug deep to remember the words. Nothing surfaced. She blinked. The big blank expanded, wiping out memory. Panic grabbed hold. Mac moved into her line of sight, taking his place on the outer rim of the crest with the other warriors. His gaze met hers. He nodded, encouraging her, steadying her, the confidence in his eyes absolute.

The words popped back into her head. With a shaky exhale, she sent a silent thank-you Mac's way, then raised her arms, held them wide, and said, "Let the covenant begin, and so to the vows, the strength of which will bind hearts, marry souls, ring throughout this chamber and upon the ages...*iazen.*"

The final amen echoed, rising toward the dome, and Daimler stepped forward. His head bowed, the Numbai presented her with a length of yellow ribbon. As it slid through Tania's fingers, she approached the bride and groom and, with careful precision, threaded the silken length over and around their already intertwined right hands.

Finished tying them together, Tania stepped back to take her place outside the circle.

The second she settled, Bastian spoke, holding his female's gaze, reciting his vows in the language of his kind. His deep voice rose and rang inside the rotunda. The inscription embedded in the floor began to glow. Like moonbeams, the illumination spread, rising up from the letters, bathing each of them with soft white light. Between one heartbeat and the next, the brilliant tendrils twisted, blew inward, ghosting across the floor to surround Bastian and Myst.

Tania's breath caught, the beauty more than she could bear. The tears resurfaced, filling her eyes. Uncaring, she let them come and, pressing her hand over her heart, listened with profound gladness as the Nightfury commander's vows came to a close and Myst's began.

Strong and proud, her friend's voice rang out, "Fate of my fate. Light of my light. Kindred of spirit without shadow or slight. You are mine. And I am yours. Two hearts intertwined, forevermore."

As the last word was spoken, the light flared, rushing up to surround their bound hands. The ribbon ashed, falling into a wispy gray pile on the floor. Wind gusted through the room, tugging at Tania's unbound hair. Lightning forked overhead, fracturing the gloom. Myst gasped and, wide-eyed, watched the white-hot glow encircle her index finger, then travel across the back of her hand. Intricate lines formed, an ancient tattoo inked in shimmering silver on Myst's skin. A muscle twitched along Bastian's jaw as identical lines burned across his knuckles.

The mating mark.

Forge nodded, a look of satisfaction on his face.

Thunder boomed, shaking the rotunda. One more crack of lightning and...

All went quiet.

Frowning at the pale lines of his new tattoo, Bastian flexed his fist. With a laugh, Myst shook out her hand, joyful tears in her eyes.

"And you may kiss the bride," Tania said, interjecting a human custom into the Dragonkind ceremony.

The baby cooed as Angela jostled her with an elbow and grinned. "Good one."

"I thought so." Returning the smile, Tania reached out to stroke G.M.'s cheek. Waving his chubby fists in the air, he squawked, talking to her baby-style. She smiled and murmured back. He was so cute: dark mohawk sticking straight up, making happy sounds, tiny feet peeking out from beneath the navy-blue outfit that matched the Nightfuries' ceremonial robes to a T. Unable to resist, Tania rubbed the baby's belly. "Hello, beautiful boy."

"Lads arenea beautiful. We're tough." Stopping next to them, Forge held out his hands. Angela rolled her eyes but obliged, transferring G.M. into his arms. "Isnea that right, laddie?"

His focus riveted to his father's face, the baby gurgled in agreement. A moment later he stuck his fist in his mouth and sucked on his knuckles.

"Och, now." Cradling his son, Forge patted his small bottom and turned away, the love in his eyes unmistakable. "Hungry, are we?"

The baby kicked his legs, pumping his knees like pistons, and Tania's chest started to ache. God, what a sight...a loving father caring for his child. What a gift. One she'd never had the privilege of experiencing, but as Forge walked away, gladness filtered through her. G.M. would never know neglect, not with Myst and the Nightfuries in his corner.

Rubbing her hand over her heart, Tania watched the pair retreat and—

A gasp sounded behind her.

Tania glanced over her shoulder and suppressed a grin. Good lord. Bastian was on the rampage, in full "just married" mode: kissing Myst deep, swinging her into his arms, heading for one of the archways.

Just before he descended the stairs, Bastian relinquished her friend's mouth and glanced over his shoulder. "Don't wait up. We won't be around for a while."

"Us, either." Scooping Angela up, Rikar tossed her over his shoulder and headed for the exit.

Tania blinked, then swallowed a laugh, listening to the detective squawk in indignation. Funny thing, though? She noticed Angela didn't struggle. Was actually fighting a smile as she got carted off like a sack of potatoes.

From the opposite side of the rotunda, Forge said, "Yo, Daimler. You got anything cooking?"

"Oh yeah," Venom said, hot on the Scottish guy's heels. "I could eat."

Daimler came to attention with a happy hop. His mouth as quick as his feet, he scurried ahead of the Nightfuries, a long litany of everything he'd prepared for the "mating feast" trailing like a ticker tape behind him. Tania watched them go, a smile threatening. After a moment she gave in and, with a grin, put her pretty footwear to good use and—

A big hand curled around her wrist, stopping her midstride. "Where do you think you're going?"

The deep growl sent her pulse thrumming. Oh boy, he sounded good, like a hot-blooded male with only one thing on his mind. His touch confirmed it—soft, seductive, a decadent slide up the inside of her arm. Pausing at her elbow, Mac stroked over sensitive skin, cranking her tight, and moved in close. His chest bumped her from behind. She shivered as he gathered up her unbound hair, twirling it around his hand. With a gentle grip, he tugged her head back, raising her chin, giving himself access. She arched under the pressure. He took advantage and dipped his head. His whiskered cheek prickled her a second before his mouth brushed the side of her throat.

A soft kiss. A gentle nip. The tease and tug on her hair. That was all it took for her to lose her way. Sensation swirled in a heated coil, making her tingle.

Fisting her thick strands a little tighter, he growled, "You stay with me."

Better than any rope, he tied her up with his words. But even as she surrendered, wanting what his closeness promised, she refused to go easily. He liked her feisty. Tania liked herself that way too, and with Mac? Shyness wasn't an option. Neither was backing down.

Anticipation whipped through her. Oh yes. This was going to be so damn good.

"What if I don't want to?" Stepping back, she bumped him, then settled, her back to his front.

"You promised me *anything* earlier." Pressing his free hand flat against her belly, he claimed all the real estate between her hip bones. Wrapped tight to his muscled length, Tania bit down on a moan. He smiled against her throat, then drifted up to nip her earlobe. "I'm here to collect."

"Payback?"

"The best kind."

No argument there. She couldn't wait to have him inside her again. To ride him hard and be ridden in return. To hold him skin to skin and have his taste in her mouth.

Twisting in his embrace, she tugged on her hair. Mac growled in protest. Tania insisted, applying pressure until he let her go. The instant his grip loosened, she turned in the circle of his arms. Face-to-face now, she reached up, traced the contours of his lips before sliding her hands into his dark hair.

Meeting his gaze, she whispered, "You gonna show me?"

His nostrils flared. "You gonna let me?"

Playing the tease, she scraped her short nails along his scalp, holding him on the razor-sharp edge of desire, heightening her anticipation, forcing him to wait. After what seemed like forever, but was only a moment, she asked, "You want me to let you?"

"Motherfuck, yes."

"Say please."

His eyes narrowed on her. She held her ground, refusing to back down. He needed to give to receive, and she wanted it all. Every last piece of him before he laid her down.

"I'm going to make you pay for it," he murmured, warning in his tone. "Make you beg again."

"You first."

A muscle twitched along his jaw. "Please, *mo chroí*."

Caressing the tops of his shoulders, Tania smiled. "I'm all yours."

And she was. As much as she wanted to deny it, she *was* his. Logic and all the dragon stuff be damned. Intuition ruled, and the truth hit home. She belonged with Mac in every way that mattered. But even as she acknowledged it and offered him her mouth, fear slithered through her. He would hurt her in the end. Tania knew it deep down, no need to explore further.

She was headed for a fall. Heartache inevitable.

She wanted him too much. Couldn't deny herself the pleasure of his company, the heat of his body, or the decadence of being held in his arms. And as he accepted her invitation and kissed her—tangling their tongues, tasting her deep, making her moan—Tania gave up the fight. She couldn't say no, never mind walk away. That would take bucketfuls of willpower, and right or wrong...

She simply wasn't strong enough.

Chapter Twenty-Three

The irony of the situation wasn't lost on Ivar. He'd always suspected he would lose Lothair, in one manner or another. The inevitability had been written in the stars. The sands of time…whatever…fate turning its indestructible wheel. He saw that now. His best friend had been too reckless—his temper too volatile, his personality too obsessive—for him to survive long inside the Razorback ranks. In a war that took no prisoners.

Still the loss hurt like a son of a bitch.

And therein lay the irony.

He never felt. *Anything.* And yet weeks had passed. Over a fucking month, and no matter how hard Ivar tried he couldn't let it go. The pain stayed with him, swelling like a balloon inside his heart and mind, pushing at the edges of his control, and…he mourned. Grieved for a male lost too soon. Raged at the unfairness. Wanted to level the nightclub—and every soul in it—as he folded his wings and touched down in the parking lot behind Deuce's.

Streetlights flickered, reacting to his magic as his claws clicked against asphalt. He shrugged, flicking the condensation from his bloodred scales, and, shifting to human form, conjured his clothes. The expensive suit fit him like a glove, settling across his shoulders, folding with precision around him.

Quick. Easy. No fuss, no muss. Ivar tugged at his shirt sleeves, adjusting his favorite cuff links. He didn't have time to mess around. Not tonight. Or any other, for that matter.

Skirting a row of dumpsters, he ignored the foul stench of human waste, blocked out the crunch of broken glass beneath his shoes, and strode toward the back entrance. The moment he reached the concrete steps, the human bouncers snapped to attention. In a flap of movement, each picked a door and wrenched the glass sliders wide, saving the fuckers from the smash-bang routine Ivar yearned to deliver.

Just as well. Wrecking his own club held little appeal. Especially since he'd be on the hook for the bill when he finished ransacking the place.

Never a good idea. You didn't cook the golden goose. You nurtured it, and Ivar was nothing if not astute. Deuce's provided a healthy revenue stream. One he needed if Rodin severed all ties after learning of Lothair's murder, cutting off the steady flow of capital to the Razorback coffers. Ivar hoped not, but the Archguard asshole was unpredictable, as volatile as his son in some ways, more dangerous in others.

Which meant dumping plan A—capturing Tania Solares—in favor of putting plan B into effect. The entire purpose of his visit to Deuce's tonight.

Hamersveld was in town.

Satisfaction shoved grief out of the way. With a soft growl, he crossed the threshold and entered the club. Jesus, Hamersveld was quick on the trigger. One message, a politely written, hand-delivered note by one of Ivar's associates in Prague...that was all it took to tempt the male into hopping the pond. Then again, he always dangled the right bait. And a water dragon within the Nightfury ranks—one Hamersveld didn't know existed? Pretty irresistible stuff. Enough to get the lethal male to come and take a look-see.

Now Ivar had the Norwegian exactly where he wanted him. Curious in Seattle. With no allegiance or love for the Nightfuries. Which was where option two came in. He needed to execute it to perfection. Flipping the powerful warrior—bringing him on his side and into the Razorback camp—wouldn't be easy. Maybe even inadvisable.

A prickle of unease ghosted between Ivar's shoulder blades.

From all accounts, Hamersveld was a lone dragon. Uncontrollable. Without friends. Loyal to none, an entity unto himself. Not the kind of male another trusted, never mind allowed close under normal circumstances.

But these were anything but *normal*. Dangerous and out of bounds was more like it.

Bastian had a sea dragon at his command. A fucking water rat, a male of unknown skill but unprecedented power. No way could Ivar let that stand. His soldiers would get drowned right out of the gate. He must fight fire with fire...or rather, water with water.

And where did that lead him? Right back to Hamersveld. The unpredictable, prickly SOB currently enjoying the finest BDSM club in Seattle.

Ivar's pride and joy. The best-kept secret in the city.

Deep in the cool confines of his home away from home, Ivar walked past the private rooms situated in the back of his establishment. Senses attuned, he picked up all kinds of trace. Some females moaned in bliss, others screamed as the pleasure-pain was delivered, but all performed (both the professionals he paid and patrons he didn't), servicing the collection of males who frequented the club, Dragonkind and human alike. The smell of sex and leather, the sharp tang of alcohol, and the subtler, underlying scent of blood mingled, tightening the muscle over his bones.

Ah, yes. The sweet sting of anticipation.

Not that he would indulge tonight. His pack, and the safety of his lab and the experiments he conducted there, took precedence over pleasure. And as he listened to a variety of different music drift from behind closed doors—heavy metal, classic rock, R & B, and even a little jazz—he left the private playrooms behind and walked into the main part of the nightclub.

Standing in the elevated section of the mezzanine, he stopped at the fancy wrought iron railing and looked down on the scene. Hmm, a full house tonight. Good. He needed the business. Could practically see the money flowing as waitresses, dressed in black leather bustiers, microminis, and lacy garters, moved between the tables, taking customer orders and delivering those already placed. Ivar scanned the twin bars flanking either side of the room. Antique glass glittered on the back walls behind each long snakewood-clad length, reflecting the selection of alcohol in colorful bottles of all shapes and sizes.

Ivar's eyes narrowed. Bartenders working at a steady pace. Check. Everything neat and tidy. Double check. No need to kill anyone for slacking off. Excellent. Just the way he liked his club run.

His pace unhurried, Ivar strolled down the stairs and into the fray.

Standing post at the bottom, Denzeil glanced up at him. The male tipped his chin. "Boss man."

"Where is he?"

"In a booth. Back right-hand corner."

"Best spot in the house," Ivar murmured, another round of irony hitting him full force. Deep, comfortable, with curtains that could be drawn for privacy, the booth had been Lothair's favorite spot at Deuce's. He stepped off the last stair to stand shoulder to shoulder with his warrior. "Hamersveld's got good taste."

"Eclectic too," Denzeil murmured, dark eyes flicking over the crowd.

Ivar raised a brow, asking without words.

"He's sampled more than his fair share of females since arriving...all shapes, sizes, and skin color. No straight-up preference or pattern I can detect."

"Good."

And it was. A relaxed Hamersveld worked to his advantage. Was better than the alternative. An amped-up male would be harder to read, less inclined to talk and be controlled. So screw the male's preferences. The warrior could fuck every male and female in the club, and Ivar would've gotten him more if needed.

No questions asked.

Hanging a left at the base of the stairs, Ivar headed toward his quarry, skirting patrons and a few tables, making his way across the bar. Denzeil stayed on his heels, offering backup even though it wasn't necessary. The likelihood Hamersveld would start something inside a club peppered with humans was slim to none. The intel he'd collected on the male suggested he was coolheaded, cunning with a sharp edge, more inclined to think things through than act rashly.

Excellent on every score. It meant he'd get to say his piece.

Ivar came abreast of the corner enclave. Shaped like a horseshoe, the booth's plush burgundy upholstery glinted in the low light, framing Hamersveld's Norwegian beauty to perfection. Black eyes trained on the female astride him, big hands locked on either side of her hips, he encouraged her to ride. Ivar's gaze flicked over her face. His lips curved. Even half-dressed and arched in orgasmic pleasure, he recognized the bleached-out blonde from TV, one of KING channel 5's up-and-coming stars.

How...interesting. Serendipitous even. Reporters, after all, could be useful upon occasion.

The warrior's focus shifted, his gaze cutting through Ivar like twin laser beams. He clenched his teeth, suppressing a flinch. No way would he show an ounce of weakness. Not to a shark like Hamersveld. Like respected like. The second the male in front of him smelled vulnerability, he'd move in for the kill. So Ivar smothered his reaction instead, his expression one of pure amusement.

"Give me a minute, Ivar." Breathing hard, the male held his gaze and increased the pace, making the female moan. "Unless you want in?"

The invitation temped him to a dangerous degree. But he hadn't made the trip downtown for a fast fuck in one of his club's corner booths. "Another time."

"Suit yourself."

"Always do," he said, turning to prop his shoulder against the side wall.

With a good view of the club, Ivar ignored the couple—tuned out the reporter's moans of pleasure—and flicked his fingers at the nearest waitress. She came toward him through the crowd. He pushed his drink order into her mind. Her eyes glazed over a moment before she spun toward the bar, one thought ruling her…get Ivar a drink, right now. A minute later, he held a tumbler full of Jimmy Beam and Hamersveld's full attention as the female stumbled out of the booth, blouse hanging wide open, a blank look on her face.

Good riddance. Arrivederci, sweetheart.

Tipping his glass in salute, Ivar slid into the opposite side of the booth. "You fuck like a world champion."

"Three hundred years of living does that to a male." Picking up his Heineken, he took a pull from the bottle. "Nice place you got here."

"I have particular tastes."

"I am aware of them. So is Rodin," Hamersveld said, his expression thoughtful. "Have you told him his son is dead yet?"

Refusing to rise to the bait, Ivar stayed cool under fire. "What the asshole doesn't know won't hurt him."

"I like your style, Ivar. I really do." A dangerous glint in his eyes, the male held his palm up in front of him. Magic flared, slithering on a wet curl of air. The condensation rings made by his beer bottle formed a straight line on the tabletop. A second later the water leaped, flowing into Hamersveld's palm. "You've got some slick moves, not the least of which was getting me over here."

"You think I'm lying?" Settling in a comfortable slouch, Ivar sipped his drink. Ice clinked against his teeth and the JB bit, sliding down the back of his throat.

"Have you seen him...up close?"

"Close enough to see the fucker's tattoo."

Hamersveld's interest sharpened, clouding the air inside the booth. "He has tribal markings?"

"Navy-blue ink."

"Slifer's balls," the male muttered, taking the dragon god's name in vain. "Another of my kind."

Blond brows drawn tight, the warrior picked at the label on his bottle. Ivar remained silent, watching, waiting for...

Ah, and there it was. The reaction he'd hoped—and needed—to see. Anger. Blazing, unsurpassable rage from the warrior sitting across from him. To be expected. Accustomed to being the only water dragon in existence, another male encroaching on his territory (aka the entire planet) wouldn't be welcome news to a bastard with narcissistic tendencies.

A fortunate turn of events for Ivar. Not so lucky for Hamersveld.

The male enjoyed his uniqueness and the status it gave him among his peers. That an upstart Nightfury might take that away? Shit, Ivar could almost hear the warrior's mind churning, running through all the possibilities. And as Hamersveld glanced up, Ivar almost smiled. Fury vibrated through the Norwegian, increasing by the moment, making him twitch. He nailed Ivar with the directness of his gaze.

"So I guess that leaves us with just one question, Hamersveld..." Ivar paused, preying on the male's insecurity, wielding his disquiet like a weapon. "Is there room enough inside Dragonkind for two of you?"

The male hesitated less than a heartbeat. Raising his bottle in silent appreciation, he said, "Call me Sveld. Looks like we'll be working together."

"Thought you might feel that way."

"You always right?"

"Most of the time."

Hamersveld laughed. And Ivar thanked God he *was* right the majority of the time. That facts, data crunching, and precise predictions were his forte. Otherwise he wouldn't have a sea dragon in his corner. And Bastian's water rat wouldn't be in for a shitload of trouble.

———

Heat lightning in his arms, Tania bared her teeth and nipped Mac's bottom lip. Need met desire, then went apocalyptic. Caught in the passionate explosion—and his female's crosshairs—Mac's internal compass twisted. Due north? Where the hell was that again? Nowhere near where he stood, that was for sure. And as the ground beneath his mental feet shifted, he wasn't sure which way to go. Head for safer water? Or dive in and let have Tania have her way?

Diving in sounded good. Very, *very* good.

One small problem with that, though. He was the dom and—

Tania kissed him hard, sending her tongue deep into his mouth. Pleasure scorched him, swirling down to surround his balls. Already taut muscle flickered, flexing up tight, and he tried to remember. What the hell was he…?

Oh, right. Dom. He was the dominant one. The one who controlled the pace, dictated the play, gave the orders, not her, but…

She slid her hands under the lapels of his ceremonial robe. Mac purred, arching into her touch, heart slamming as she drew circles across his chest.

Umm, *anything.*

Shit, he loved that word. Couldn't get enough…of her taste, her touch, the way she felt in his arms and fit against him. She was heat lightning in a bottle, incendiary yet somehow contained, driving him closer to the edge and out of control.

It's what she wanted, he knew. No limits. No mercy. Just him, her, and a whole lot of down and dirty. And they would get to that, but not yet. Maybe not for a while. He yearned to love her properly first…to go slow, be gentle, give her everything she deserved while he got all he needed.

Love and trust. Decadence and delight. Tenderness disguised by dominance. Perfection. Just like Tania… everything he wanted, and all that he feared.

Confusion circled deep. It didn't make any sense. How could he want her so badly yet be afraid to commit to something long term? The whole thing mystified him. Which was…well, no great surprise considering who he held in his arms. 'Cause, yeah, his ability to think straight while anywhere near Tania? Two things that didn't go superwell together.

Especially while she wore a scrap of silk she liked to call a dress. But God help him, he adored her in it. Another paradox, but as Mac cupped her shoulders, stroking his hands over her bare skin, he couldn't bring himself to care. So he was confused. So he didn't have a clue what he was doing or where the hell their relationship would go. He was here now. So was she, in a barely there, strapless dress. Umm-umm good. Sexy and demure, all at the same time. His favorite combo, and matching her caress for caress, Mac wondered if she'd known that. Had she worn the gown with him in mind? Hoped to turn him on and make him lose control?

Good strategy. Effective too.

And beneath the domed roof, cocooned in candlelight and surrounded by colorful dragon art, Mac understood his peril. Tania would burn him alive before she was through. Lock him down. Tie him up inside his own head. Rule him so well she conquered him completely. Mac knew she could do it. Shit, he'd barely touched her yet, and he was already there. Ready to stomp on caution. Throw a lifetime of autonomy out of his mental locker room and surrender.

Become 100 percent hers...in every way a male could for his woman.

Raking her hands through his hair, she strung kisses along his collarbone, and Mac pushed the worry aside. The future would wait another day. God knew his female wouldn't. She wanted what she *wanted*...preferably right now.

Tracing her silk-clad curves, Mac bumped her cheek with his. She got the message and, raising her chin, offered him her mouth. He hummed, parting her lips, making her open wide for him, and walked her backward across the rotunda. A bedroom. He needed one. ASAP. Before he did something stupid, like strip her down and make love to her here...where anyone might walk in and see them. One problem, though. He couldn't stop touching her long enough to jump-start his brain. He knew he needed to pick her up, carry her under the archway, down the stairs, and get good and gone, but...holy shit. Tania wasn't cooperating. She enticed instead, amping him up with her sweetness, whispering his name between kisses, stoking him with her busy, clever, beautiful hands.

And oh man, liquid heat. Passion incarnate. Way beyond good.

Breathing hard, he dragged his mouth away from hers. She protested and, tightening her grip in his hair, tried to bring him back. He shook his head, desperate to hold the line. "Tania, you...we should...oh Jesus! Don't do that. Don't—"

She didn't listen. Showing him teeth, Tania nipped the underside of his jaw. Mac lost his train of thought. He groaned, loving her mouth on his skin, and she attacked the belt holding his robe closed. Her hands brushed over his chest. He cursed, muscles twitching as she reversed their positions, turned him, then pushed backward, forcing him against the wall. Her smile one of wicked delight, she grabbed his lapels and yanked. The heavy material parted, then slid from his shoulders, down his arms, and—

"Drop it."

Mac obeyed and let the robe fall. It pooled around his feet, leaving him without a stitch on. "Honey, we can't stay here. Let me take you to—"

"You want me?" Licking over his pulse point, she sent her hand south.

His breath seized inside his chest, fracturing his good intentions. And he waited, craving her touch so badly he couldn't think straight. "Oh fuck...baby, come on."

"Do you?" Her fingers danced across his abdomen.

"Yes!"

"Then my way first," she said, her tone soft, her touch electric. Kissing her way across his chest, she flicked one of his nipples with her tongue. When he groaned, she raised her head, met his gaze, and dipped her hand. With a gentle touch, she explored the head of his erection. She played a moment, circling the sensitive tip, prolonging his pleasure, making his hips curl toward her. "I want you here, Mac… in the rotunda. You deep inside me, your spice on my skin, and the scent of tiger lilies in the air."

Thrusting into her palm, he struggled to hold the line. To tell her no, but God, she was persuasive. And as she stroked him, adjusting the rhythm to give him maximum pleasure, he rode the razor's edge. The one called Tania. His female. Glorious in her passion. Unrepentant with need. Determined to have her way.

"I'll be quiet." Cupping his nape with her free hand, she set her mouth to the corner of his and whispered, "No one will hear us."

"Motherfuck, I…" She upped the rhythm. Unable to deny her, Mac tipped his head back against the wall. "Oh God, yeah. Just like that, Tania. Don't stop…don't stop."

"I won't."

Under her spell, lost to everything but her, Mac growled and invaded her mouth. Burying one hand in her hair, he fisted the other in her skirt. Jesus, it wasn't right. Not any of it. Was so fucked up, Mac didn't know how he'd ended up naked in a public place, pushed up against a wall while Tania dictated the play. Things like that didn't usually happen to him. At least not unless he made it happen. So, yeah. No question. She should be the one without a stitch on, stripped to the skin, 100 percent under his command, subservient while he dominated.

Too bad he couldn't bring himself to care. Not while she kissed him. Not while she teased and tempted, making him yearn for more. Her grip tightened around him, and Mac lost his ability to breathe. So much for moving to a bedroom. To hell with decency and decorum. Screw the possibility of discovery. All he wanted to do was please her. In whatever way she demanded.

Right fucking now.

"Tania, where's the…" Running his hands over her back, he tugged at her gown. "How do I get this off?"

"Zipper…left side."

He found the clasp on the first try. Thank fuck. He couldn't take much more. Not without raising her skirt and…

The zipper slid down. She shrugged. He yanked. The strapless dress resisted a moment, then slid to her waist. His breath caught. Oh thank you, God. No bra, just smooth-as-silk skin poured over pink-tipped breasts and unbelievable curves. The sight of her pushed him over the ragged edge. It was the only explanation. The only viable reason he snarled her name and spun her around.

She gasped as her shoulders touched the wall. Controlling her completely, he held her there while he shoved her skirt up, the red silk rose, and he caught her scent. Ready and willing. So hot for him he tasted her arousal. "Spread your legs."

"What?"

"Playtime's over." Cupping the back of her knee, he hooked her calf over his hip. "Spread 'em."

Shock flared in her dark eyes. Mac showed no mercy. He caged her with his body, using the wall for leverage, pushing her thighs wide, settling into the cradle of her hips. His mouth a hairbreadth from her, he held her gaze, moving slowly, daring her to stop him, and slid his hand beneath her skirt. He skimmed her thigh, caressed the lush curve of her bottom, loving the softness of her skin. Desperate for more of her heat, he reversed course. His fingers dipped deep, slipping beneath her panties to find her core.

And oh God. Slick. Hot. So fucking wet.

She took his breath away, then stole his mind while she moaned his name. The urge to take her hard—do her right, make her scream—bombarded him. Mac clamped down on his need, struggling to keep it together. But each gasp, every shiver, the way she moved against his hand cranked him so high there was nothing left to do but fall.

And still he played in her heat. Torturing himself. Unable to deny himself the pleasure of watching her...of listening to her beg him for more.

"Oh yeah, that's so..." Tipping her head back, she writhed against him, lips parted, need in her eyes. "Oh. My. God. Mac, you need to...I'm gonna...oh, please, now... please!"

Circling his thumb against the bud of her sex, Mac sent one finger deep. He set a pace designed to drive her wild: slow, sure, one delicious glide after another. She tightened around him. He backed off, wanting her on edge, nowhere near ready to let her come. When she exploded into orgasm, he would be buried to the hilt inside her, experiencing it all: the feel and sound, the unbelievable scent of her while he stroked deep between her thighs.

"God, please." Her plea echoed against the high dome, shattering the quiet.

"Thought you were going to be quiet?"

"Shut up! And just—"

"Who's begging now, *mo chroí?*" Sliding a second finger deep, he upped the pace, making her ride each rolling thrust. "Tell me. Who?"

"Me. Just me." She met his gaze head-on. Honest need. Explosive desire. Incredible trust. Mac saw it all, every bit of what he wanted in her eyes. Slipping her hands into his hair, she kissed him softly, tenderness personified. "Please, Mac. I need you."

I need you too.

Like a confession, the words streamed through his mind, but he didn't say them. He couldn't. Each one got stuck in his throat. All he could do was show her, and so he did. Murmuring her name. Caressing her just the way she needed. Telling her she was beautiful, how much he wanted her, how precious she was to him.

And as she responded to each truth, he withdrew from her core. A sharp tug, and the lace covering her ripped. Unable to wait a second longer, he set himself at her entrance and pushed. Mac bit down on a shout. Mother of God. She was fucking perfect. So tight, her slick heat resisted as he worked himself inside.

Squirming against him, Tania cried out his name. He didn't stop. She'd asked for him, just…like…this…and so she would take him.

Every last inch.

One hand pressed flat against the wall, the other cupping her bottom, he buried himself to the hilt, listened to her gasp, filled her full, possessing all of her. When she twitched, Mac adjusted their position, waiting for her to relax against him. He was a tight fit, and Tania needed time to accept his invasion. And so he stayed still, held back, forcing himself to be patient even though it almost killed him.

He wanted her to move first, and—

Oh yeah. There it was...her sigh, the gentle shift, the welcoming warmth. Opening her eyes, she looked at him.

He smiled at her. "Hold on, honey."

"Maybe you should do the same." Her warning came with a kiss, soft and sweet, a second before she nipped him...hard. "Now move."

Sir, yes, sir. His pleasure...entirely.

Starting the ride, she rolled her hips into his. He followed her lead, letting her control the pace, watching rapture gather in her eyes. Her lips parted on a long-drawn moan. Mac took advantage, kissing her the way he always did in his dreams, mating their tongues, taking her higher with each stroking flex and release of his body. Raking her nails over his shoulders, she purred, and Mac read her like an open book. Gauged her increasing urgency. Thrust deeper, giving her all she asked and more. Slick skin sliding against hers, he circled his hips, worked her hard, each breath a rasp at the back of his throat, only one thought in his head.

Tania.

So beautiful. So right. Made solely for him.

She was so close now. So very close. All she needed was a little push...a tiny shove...the right move to send her over.

Leaving her mouth, he growled, "Give it to me, Tania."

The sound of his voice sent her over the edge.

"Oh fuck yeah. Come on...come on, love."

Squeezing him tight, she clenched hard around him. He snarled her name. Gripping his hair with twin fists, she threw her head back and came undone, exploding into bliss. Her cry bounced, tearing through the rotunda. Energy throbbed in the air, buffeting him with wave after wave of intense, all-consuming power. The territorial beast inside him growled in satisfaction, and still Mac rode her, the air sawing in and out of his chest, moving between her thighs, propelling her into another round of delight.

Glory, glory hallelujah.

She was incredible. So amazing in the throes of ecstasy Mac lost control, let her drag him under, and surrendered to her mastery. Became weak to her strong, wrapped her against him, tucked his face to her throat, and rocketed into the devastating pleasure she gave him. But as his legs gave out and he sank to the floor with her cradled in his lap, one last thought circled...

Oh how he loved Tania's *anything*.

And yet as the bone-melting aftermath of bliss took hold and his guard came down, Mac realized something important. His uncertainty about the future didn't seem quite so uncertain anymore. He closed his eyes, unable to deny the truth any longer. Somehow, someway, Tania had wormed her way into his heart. And that scared him more than a full squadron of rogues ever would.

Chapter Twenty-Four

Wearing nothing but skin, Tania lay gasping in the center of the big bed. In Mac's room. Hands bound with red ribbon. Arms stretched above her head and secured to the headboard. Cracked wide open, vulnerable to Mac and his special brand of domination.

Oh God, how she loved him.

And what he did to her.

The intensity was incredible. But the pleasure? Unbelievable. So catastrophic Tania didn't know how much more she could take.

Holy jeez, he knew how to please her. How to ensure maximum effect while he held her hostage. Broke her down until helplessness blurred into bliss. The heat of his touch, the scent of his skin on hers, the way he controlled and made her submit…all of it pushed her toward the pinnacle, into an experience she hadn't known she was missing.

Tied-up Tania.

Uh-huh. That sounded about right. And she allowed Mac to do it all, any way he wanted…and usually ended up begging for more.

Strange, really. She hadn't known she had it in her. Had never been interested before, but with Mac? Well, the lines blurred, leaving her with nothing but the truth.

She thrived under the spotlight of his dominant nature. Got off when he controlled her so completely. And as he spread her beneath him for…what? Maybe the fifth time in as many hours, she accepted everything he gave her. Moaned his name. Parted her thighs. Wrapped her legs around his waist as he stuffed a pillow beneath her bottom, angled her hips up, then rode her toward oblivion.

Her grip tightened around the ribbon binding her. Soft satin and intense lovemaking, a decadent combination. One that sent her over the edge so fast, Tania forgot to breathe. Suspended in pleasure, she heard Mac's shout, felt his body stiffen and the warm throb deep inside her. Hmm, yeah. There he went, losing control, giving Tania her due, coming apart so fast she reached orgasm again, throbbing hard around him.

"Fuck me," he groaned against the side of her throat.

Heart hammering like runaway voodoo drums, she gasped, "Thought I just did."

He huffed, the sound half laugh, half moan a second before he went warm and heavy against her. With a sigh, Tania followed his lead. As she softened beneath him— cradling him between her thighs, her knees up around his hips, holding him the only way she could—the relaxing curl of afterglow took hold.

Minutes (or hours later…Tania didn't know), Mac raised his head. Cool air washed in, prickling along her shoulder and neck as his skin left hers. She grumbled in protest, wanting him to come back. He shifted instead, making her hum, pressing deeper between her thighs to prop himself up on his elbows. Languid, suffering from a serious case of fuzzy-brain syndrome, she forced her eyes open.

The color of turbulent seas, his gaze met hers. Hmm, so nice. Not to mention a huge switch. At the cabin, his glowing irises had freaked her out. Now? She loved it when the Mediterranean blue shimmered like that.

Now it roamed, warming her face as he brushed the hair away from her temples. "You okay? I wasn't too rough?"

"Nah-uh. Sheer perfection."

Satisfaction stole into his expression. Reaching up, he tugged at the satin knots securing her hands. A moment later she was free, and Mac went to work, unwinding the ribbon from around her wrists, massaging the marks on her skin, then the palms of each of her hands before moving on to treat her fingers.

She sighed. "So nice."

He murmured in answer. When he was done taking care of her, he caressed the undersides of her arms, encouraging her to bring both down from above her head. She took the hint and, twining them around his neck, pushed her fingers through his hair. With a soft growl, he arched into her touch, enjoying her foray across his scalp. She gave him more, playing in the soft strands at his nape.

"God, unbelievable. You're so fucking good, honey."

Tania's heart swelled at the compliment. It was one of many she'd received throughout the day. He liked to talk while he loved her into a pleasure coma, and she couldn't get enough of him...or the wicked timbre of his voice every time he whispered something naughty in her ear.

Everything he said made her feel worthy.

Desired. Important for a change. More than just the pretty face men saw but never looked beyond. No one cared that she was smart, that she had feelings, ambitions, and needs of her own. All they saw was a curvy brunette. Not her. Never the real her.

But not Mac. He liked her sense of humor. Enjoyed her brain as much as her body. She could tell by the way he looked at her. How he laughed at her jokes and asked all kinds of questions: about her life, likes and dislikes, her favorite color. Nothing was out of bounds. And she'd answered them all. Which, of course, prompted the use of her two favorite things...

The color red and fancy ribbon.

"You're a wild one, Tania Solares," he murmured, twirling a lock of her hair around his fingertip.

Another compliment. At least by Mac's standards. "So are you."

"No question," he said. "I just...didn't expect you to want it like that."

"Me, either. I'm not very experienced with—"

"The dom stuff?"

"With the sex stuff." His brows rose. Tania swallowed, trying to decide. Go all in and be honest? Tell him she'd been with a total of one guy (which had been decidedly unfun) or gloss over the truth, distract him while she protected herself? But as she met his gaze, the damnedest thing happened. She didn't want to lie to him. "I have a hard time trusting men, so I've never let any of them close, well... until you. You're different. You make me feel safe. I know you won't hurt me, and that makes me...I don't know... bold, willing to experiment or something. I honestly don't know what I like in bed."

"I found a few things today."

"Yes, you did." Appreciation for his skill prickled through her. She wiggled beneath him, pushing her hips into his. "Question is...will you be able to find more?"

The smile reached his eyes a second before it curved his mouth. "Count on it, but not right now."

"Ah, come on. One more round."

"Night is falling, *mo chroí*. The others are already gathering, so..." He pulled out, leaving the cradle of her thighs. Supersensitive from all the loving, Tania sucked in a quick breath. A muscle flexed in his jaw. Hanging his head, he groaned through his teeth, gave her bottom a gentle slap, then slid toward the mattress edge. She threw him a look of feigned outrage. He grinned and, shackling her wrist, tugged her across the crumpled sheets. "Up and at 'em."

"I need a shower."

"Fucking A," he said, his tone full of anticipation.

And oh boy. *Bleeping A* was right.

Showering with Mac was an experience, a frickin'-frackin' fantastic one. So fun Tania didn't want playtime to end. He was better than a water park with a gigantic wave pool; more intense, one hundred times more scream worthy, and an excellent surfer too. And as he whipped up minicyclones with his magic inside the oversize shower stall, she splashed around like a naked water nymph...enchanted by his awesomeness, getting carried away, asking him to do the tidal wave thing *again*.

Half an hour and another slap on the butt later, though, they were out, dried off, and Mac was all business. While he did the magical get-dressed thing, she wiggled into the pair of borrowed jeans, then pulled one of Myst's T-shirts over her head. Unwrapping her towel turban, she padded across the multicolored Persian carpet, tossed the terry cloth over the end of the four-poster bed, and stopped in front of the dresser. The glimmer of the antique mirror did its job, picking up her reflection. She shifted through the mound of hair elastics. Thank God for Daimler. The elf was a freak of nature, all knowing or something. He kept leaving stuff outside Mac's bedroom door: food, clothes for her, and now hair stuff.

She grabbed a red band, then paused. J.J.'s letter. Warped by its swim with her at the bottom of the ocean, it sat beneath the pile of barrettes, the folded corners curled up and looking at her. Staring back, Tania looped her hair into a messy bun on top of her head.

Mac appeared behind her, his reflection dwarfing her own. "Ready?"

A mighty astute question.

It could've applied to anything, but Tania chose its direction. Honesty required commitment, the kind that crept into every corner of a person's life. J.J. had made a terrible mistake, sure, but Tania wasn't ashamed of her sister. And as she looked at Mac, Tania knew...just *knew*...she needed to tell him. To open up, trust him completely, and admit to something she'd only ever spoken about with Myst.

There were no happy mediums. Not with him. All or nothing. That was the way she wanted it to be.

Deciding on something, however, didn't make it any easier to talk about. Mac was a cop at heart, ex-SPD. No telling how he'd react when he found out she had a felon in the family. Tania grimaced. Jeez, that sounded bad, and she hadn't even said it out loud yet.

Nerves got the better of her, twisting her stomach into knots. She took a deep breath, reset her courage, and reached for the letter. Paper rasped against her fingertips. The barrettes jingled, clicking together as she dumped them into a new pile on the dresser. Raising her gaze, she met Mac's in the mirror. A solid, silent presence behind her, he tipped his chin, asking without words. Her heart picked up a beat, then another, pumping her full of uncertainty. She murdered her unease and, swallowing hard, handed him the letter over her shoulder, trusting him with her secret.

Holding her steady with his eyes, he accepted her offering. The smell of salt water rose as he unfolded J.J.'s letter. Tania watched him read it. He reached the end, then started again, scanning it from top to bottom.

"My sister...the convicted criminal," she whispered, unable to stand the silence any longer. "How's that strike you?"

"Doesn't bother me at all, honey." Wrapping his arm around her from behind, he settled his chin on the top of her head. He tossed the letter, aiming for the dresser top. The paper fluttered, seesawing in midair before it touched down. "But it bothers you, doesn't it?"

"I hate that she's in there, but not for the reasons you think," she said, close to tears, the if onlys rising to taunt her once again. If only she'd been a better big sister. If only she'd paid attention and gotten J.J. help. Gone to her rescue...whatever...before things escalated into an extreme life-and-death situation. *If only...if only...if only.* Two little words. A huge cross to bear. "J.J.'s a free spirit...a beautiful bird. She needs to fly."

"But got a cage instead." When she nodded, he asked, "What's she in for?"

"Manslaughter." He arched a brow. She leaned into his embrace, resting the back of her head against his shoulder. "Jerk-off boyfriend. She left him. He didn't like it and—"

"Shit. He came after her, didn't he?"

"Threatened to kill me first, then go after her."

"The fucker," he growled, his eyes darkening with fury.

"An asshole of the first order," she said, holding his gaze. "But here's the thing...J.J.'s parole board hearing? I need to be there. I'm all she has. Her only family. No one else will stand up and speak for her. She's my baby sister, Mac. I need to get her the hell out of there."

"I hear that," he said, tying her in knots with his understanding.

Astounding, incredible, beautiful man. Instead of judging her as she feared, he listened and accepted, supporting her without hesitation. Holding on to her tears, she whispered a heartfelt, "Thank you."

"No need." Brushing aside her gratitude, he gave her a gentle squeeze. "Before we decide anything, though, let me talk to Sloan."

Tania frowned. "Why?"

"He's good with computers. He may be able to hack into their system...give us an edge on your sister's proceedings and—"

"Oh my God!" she yelped as what he offered struck home. A miracle...a real chance at victory and securing J.J.'s freedom. Joy made her heart hitch. With an exuberant hop, she spun in his embrace. "Holy jeez, I love you. I love you!" Planting a kiss on his mouth, she threw her arms around him. "Thank you...thank you... thank you!"

Expecting to be hugged in return, Tania frowned when Mac went stone still against her. A nanosecond later he stiffened, his arms loosening around her. She pulled back to glance at his face. He looked, well...*stunned* was a good word. *Panicked* was another. What the heck was wrong with him? Confusion met concern, then shook hands and—

Ah...what had she said to him?

She replayed her reaction and resulting tumble of words. *I love you.*

Oh, snap. She hadn't meant to say that. But now that she had? Tania refused to regret it. Or take the words—and the unrelenting truth behind them—back.

Too bad for her.

'Cause sure as she stood there, staring up at the man she loved, Tania knew she'd pushed too far, too fast. And sent Mac into a tailspin while she was at it.

———

Standing under the blistering spray, Nian tossed the soap into its holder. Sudsing up a fifth time wouldn't help. No matter how hard he scrubbed, he couldn't get clean enough. Washing the ugliness away was an impossibility. So was the ability to forget. Psychological filth, after all, was a tricky beast. It stuck with a male, pervasive, persistent, but above all...

Unforgiving.

Planting his hands against the shower wall, Nian hung his head and with a mental flick dialed the temperature up another notch. Hot water scalded him, streaming over his shoulders, down his back to rush over the tops of his bare feet. He relished the burn and craved the pain. He deserved it, and far worse, for what he had allowed to happen tonight. For standing by while others suffered. For abandoning the innocent souls trapped inside Rodin's pleasure pavilion to return to the comfort of his home.

God forgive him. He'd watched and done nothing.

Nian frowned at the colorful mosaic tiles between his feet. Well, not quite *nothing*. He'd managed to save one female, a blonde-haired beauty caught in an untenable situation. Drugged into compliance. Shoved up on stage. Forced to stand on an auction block while males of his kind bid for her favors…for the right to own her in the way humans did their dogs.

The depravity turned his stomach. And yet he'd played his part to perfection. Made Rodin nod in approval as he dropped forty-five grand to possess one of the females on display.

Go along to get along. Wasn't that the saying? Probably, but…

Nian closed his eyes. He despised himself for it. For staying his hand and allowing the slave auction to proceed without objection. Now he paid the price. The cost? His honor. So here he stood, dirtied by shame and trapped by circumstance. One in which an innocent female would pay with her life.

Goddamn Rodin and his sick games.

Revulsion made Nian reach for the soap again. As the slivered bar slid into his palm, a soft voice called, "My lord?"

Opening his eyes, Nian pushed away from the wall. Obscured by steam, a dark shadow stood on the other side of the shower door. Lapier. As usual, the Numbai's timing was impeccable. Plugged into every aspect of Nian's life, the male never missed a beat, was always Johnny-on-the-spot, his thumb firmly pressed to the pulse of his master's mood.

Tonight was no exception.

Steeling himself for what lay ahead, Nian flipped the faucet off with his mind. The steady stream of water lessened to a trickle. He palmed the handle and opened the door, accepting the towel Lapier handed him. After drying off, he straightened and stepped out of the shower. The Numbai's raptor-sharp gaze met his. The paternal look struck deep, hitting a nerve. The pang of conscience arrived next. Nian ignored it and, looking away, headed for the other side of the room. Smooth-faced mosaic set in intricate patterns brushing the soles of his feet, he passed beneath the Arabic-inspired archway. Vaulted ceiling soaring overhead, he stopped in front of a long vanity and stared at his reflection in the mirror.

Appearing behind him, Lapier held out a comb.

Nian used his hands instead, raking the jet-black hair away from his face. "Is she awake yet?"

"Just, my lord," the Numbai said, accepting the damp towel Nian unwrapped from his waist. Folding the terry cloth length in half, Lapier hung it over a gilded wall rack, then smoothed it out with long-fingered hands. "I have acquired what you requested. The sum of its entirety is on the hall table outside your bedchamber."

Nian nodded, his mind straying to the list he'd written hours ago.

"My lord." Consternation sparked in Lapier's pale eyes. His hands fluttered. Light arced, bouncing off the rows of golden rings he wore on each finger to wink across the tiled walls. "Are you certain—?"

"I am." With a frown, Nian conjured a pair of pajama pants and a short brocade robe. Knotting the belt, he pulled it tight and went over his plan again. "I have considered all the possibilities, my friend. Until I lead the Archguard, there is no other way. I must play for keeps or not at all."

Bowing his head, Lapier murmured in agreement.

Turning away, Nian left the bathroom and crossed into the wide central corridor of his home. Or rather, his home away from home. Although he owned it now, he never slept inside his sire's mansion on the edge of Prague. Too many memories lived there, not many of them good. And so he stayed in more humble accommodations. Built by a duke over a century ago, the house boasted the best of Arab architecture: extraordinary ironwork, amazing tile work, domed entrances, and curved doorways. But the absolute best part? Nestled into the mountainside, it perched on the edge of a sheer cliff face, high above the verdant valley below…halfway between heaven and earth.

Close to God. Far from his old life. Perfect in every way but one.

It hadn't been built as a prison. And if he didn't hurry? His captive would take a wrong turn and a dangerous tumble.

Even from thirty feet away and through the thick walls, he could hear her fiddling with the window locks, checking all the doors, searching for a way out. Another antique knob jiggled. A muttered curse followed. Nian's lips tipped up at the corners. Persistent little she-devil, wasn't she?

Not a bad thing, considering what was to come.

Turkish rugs beneath his feet, Nian approached the round table in the middle of the hallway. A tidy black duffel sat atop it, waiting for him to grab hold. He didn't hesitate, swinging the bag from its resting place and over his shoulder. As he turned toward his chamber door, a laminated card winked in the low light, drawing his attention. He paused and, sliding the document toward him, flipped it open.

A driver's license complete with picture.

Nian's heart sank as he ran the pad of his thumb over the typewritten text. *Grace.* The blonde's name was Grace von Ziger. Not that it mattered. After tonight, she would no longer need it.

Drawing a deep breath, Nian took a moment to center himself and then strode toward his bedroom door. He stared at its worn face a moment, the pale wood at once familiar yet somehow different. Nian felt different too, as though he stood at a crossroads. Go one way and save the world. Go the other to save himself. And despite everything—his misgivings, the self-loathing, and disgust—it wasn't a difficult choice.

Survival of the fittest...self-preservation always won out in the end.

With singular purpose and a magic-driven thought, Nian flipped the lock and swung the door wide. Startled by his sudden appearance, the female spun away from the window. Surprise flared in her eyes a second before fury sparked in their depths. Demonic rage fueled by fear took hold. She raised the fire poker she held in her hands like a samurai sword, warning him to stay away without words.

"Easy, *talmina*," he said, his tone soft, hoping to soothe her. With a flick, he closed the door behind him, blocking her avenue of escape. "I'm not here to hurt you."

"Where am I?" The demand carried weight, her accent, a hint of Austria. White-knuckling her weapon, she shifted left, putting a low couch between them. "Who are you?"

"Nian. The male who saved your life."

Each breath harried, her chest rose and fell, rasping in her throat. Her hands trembled, forcing her to readjust her grip on the poker. "What h-happened?"

"What do you remember?"

"The last thing?" The whispered question smacked of bewilderment. Her brows snapped together, and Nian saw her focus shift as she thought back. "Three guys grabbed me in the marketplace. I'm always so careful, but...I didn't see them coming. All of a sudden they were just *there*, forcing that awful drink down my throat and..." Tears filled her eyes. "No one helped. I screamed and screamed, but no one helped me!"

No surprise there. None of the humans had been able to hear her cries for help. The ability to cloak—to go dark and silent in any situation—was one of Dragonkind's specialties, a defense mechanism used to keep their race hidden in a world where humans outnumbered them thousands to one. Using the skill while kidnapping a female, however, broke every rule in the book, all the laws set down to govern their kind.

Any female would be defenseless in the face of such power. Grace was no exception, and as he watched her struggle to understand, he bled for her. It shouldn't have happened, not to her or anyone else. The reality, though— the one he couldn't ignore any longer—was that it was happening. On a regular basis to women in Prague and, perhaps, all over the world.

The thought tightened his throat. He cleared it, banishing messy emotion before he felt too much. "Do you remember what happened after?"

She shook her head. And Nian thanked God. Grace didn't need to know that she'd been stripped bare and put on display in front of a room full of strange males.

Holding her gaze, he strode past the end of his bed and into the room. When she shied, he stopped, setting the duffel down on the coffee table. The metal buttons protecting the underside of the bag clinked against glass, a sharp echo in a quiet space. "I want you to listen very carefully to me, *talmina*. That's over now. You're safe here."

"You really won't hurt me?"

"I promise not to touch you," he said. "But we need to talk about what happens next."

She sidestepped around an armchair. He followed her progress, watching her move toward the fireplace. Cold from disuse, the grate sat empty but for a pile of gray ash. The hem of her robe brushed over the hearthstone, then fluttered around her feet, parting to reveal one shapely thigh. Molten attraction blindsided him. Nian swallowed and clamped down on his reaction, fighting the sudden surge of lust. Not good. Oh so not good. He didn't need the complication. Was in too deep as it was, but, umm, she was something. So sweet and curvy and—

Holy God. What was his problem? Desire never got the best of him. But looking at Grace revved sexual longing into overdrive. Which didn't make any sense. She wasn't high-energy, so he shouldn't be fixating on her like—

Her energy flared, then exploded. The corresponding blaze filled out her aura. Nian flinched as the effervescent light expanded around her. The tip of the fire poker dipped an instant before she came out of her fighting stance, relaxing, daring to trust his word and...

Strike that last thought. Not high-energy, his ass.

The more relaxed she became, the brighter her connection to the Meridian burned. Which meant...improbable as it seemed...she was the rarest of the rare. A *zinmera*, a female able to alter her energy stream the same way chameleons changed colors, blending into the surrounding terrain, instinct urging her to camouflage herself as a low-energy female in the presence of his kind to avoid detection. Nian knew females of her caliber existed. He'd seen one as a boy, in his sire's harem, but...

Nian shivered, fighting the prickle of sensation ghosting over his skin. No wonder he'd wanted her the second he saw her at the auction house. Without knowing it, his skill at illusion had sensed hers, making it impossible for him to ignore her, never mind leave her for another male to claim.

"What do you mean...*next?*" Back to being wary, her energy dimmed.

As her aura downgraded from brilliant to somber, relief arrived, unlocking his lungs, allowing Nian to take a deep breath. He fingered her driver's license, then tossed it onto the tabletop beside the bag. "You can't go home, Grace. The life you knew is over."

"Wha—why?"

"The thugs who kidnapped you work for a lethal male. One who enjoys brutalizing females," he said, deploying vicious honesty, leaving no room for doubt. "The moment you resurface...go back to work or your home...they will find and take you again. And the second time is never a charm, *talmina*. You will be used by multiple males, day after day until your life force ebbs, after which your body will be disposed of like trash."

As intended, his graphic description hit her where it counted, driving home her peril.

Fear spiked in her scent a second before it flared in Grace's eyes.

Nian clenched his teeth. Unfair. For her, not him. He hated to scare her, but one fact remained indisputable. Her terror gave him the upper hand. And he needed every advantage to win the silent war he waged with Rodin. If that included frightening Grace, so be it. He wanted her gone, to ensure she left Prague and never came back. Her exile equaled his salvation. The Archguard would be watching, waiting for him to make a mistake. And freeing Grace—leaving her untouched and alive—would amount to a serious one.

The action jeopardized his position. Rodin would believe him a weak fool, and the rest of the Archguard would follow suit.

"What am I supposed to do?" Her already pale face grew ashen. "I don't have any money or anywhere else to go. I—"

"You will take the new identity I have secured for you and leave Europe." He flicked at the duffel's handles. "Inside this bag is everything you need…clothes, an untraceable cell phone, information for the bank account I set up for you in America. My servant, Lapier, will drive you to the airport where you will board a plane under your assumed name and never come back."

"But—"

"Never, Grace," he growled, the aggression in his tone making her jump. "You get low and you stay there. Nothing familiar. No calls to friends or family. No vacations that bring you home. Understood?"

"No."

Well, at least she was honest. He couldn't fault her for that.

"Do you wish to live, Grace?" When she whispered "yes" she nearly broke his heart. And all of a sudden, he wanted to keep her…to lock her away inside his mountain lair and make her his. The urge circled a moment, tempting him, stoking his imagination before Nian shoved it aside. He didn't have time for nonsense. Or room in his life for a female. *Zinmera* or not, she needed to go…and do it now before he lost his head and decided to claim her in the way of his kind. "Then do as I say. Take the bag and go."

She hesitated a second, then broke eye contact with him to set the poker down. A tremor in her hand, she leaned the makeshift weapon against the end of the couch and approached him on silent feet. Nian tensed, every nerve ending alive as Grace's energy flared again, electrifying the air around him. Hunger dug a hole in the pit of his stomach. He swallowed, the movement compulsive, belying his thirst for the female he yearned to draw close even as he pushed her away.

Grace reached for the bag. The need to know made him reach for her. As he curled his hand around her wrist, pleasure zapped him. She gasped. He growled and, with a gentle tug, brought her close. The work of a moment, he cupped the back of her head and set his mouth to her temple. Connected at three points—wrist, nape, and temple—he tapped into the Meridian and drank deep, drawing the nourishment he needed through her. His knees went weak as, drunk on sensation, she overloaded him with need, satisfying his hunger in ways he never imagined.

Invigorated. Captivated. Beyond denying his reaction, Nian drew more, increasing the powerful flow even as shame surfaced. He ignored it, glutting himself. Grace tensed and recoiled, fighting his hold. But it was too late. He'd already damned himself with the bounty of her taste. With the press of her lithe curves and the decadent scent of her skin.

Which forced him to let her go. In a hurry.

A mistake. He'd made a terrible miscalculation.

Grace didn't belong to him. He didn't want her to, either. His position—and the power play he was neck-deep in—demanded 100 percent of his attention. But the second she grabbed the bag and ran for the door, Nian mourned the loss of her warmth and raged against the emptiness it left inside him. A moment later he ridiculed himself for his reaction. Females were nothing but trouble, a pleasurable distraction meant to last a few hours, not a lifetime.

And he'd had enough for one night.

Now he must focus and get back in the game. The first order of business? Getting a message to Haider and Gage. He couldn't connect to either warrior through mind-speak (the method of communication required proximity and magical consent by both parties), so…no question. An old-fashioned note would have to do. The Nightfuries needed to know about Rodin's profitable yet oh so illegal business—and where that money was being funneled.

The intel was prime. And Nian planned to leverage the hell out of it. Crank it so hard he ended up getting what he wanted…a face-to-face meeting with the Nightfury commander.

Chapter Twenty-Five

Feeling lighter than she had in ages, J.J. hummed one of her new tunes, trying out different lyrics for the chorus, and pushed the door to the prison library open. As she stepped over the threshold, the smell of old paperbacks and furniture polish floated on the slow roll of air kicked out by the heat vents. Hmm, heaven. Her good mood quadrupled within moments, beating a happy tune inside her heart. She loved it here, in the peace and quiet, surrounded by stacks of books in all shapes, sizes, and colors.

The fact that judgment day loomed less than a month away didn't hurt her state of mind, either. Soon. So very *soon*. Any day now, really, and she'd get another letter... be given the exact day and hour she would meet with the parole board. Couple that news with the fact the prison librarian had asked for her by name and...

Yup. On a scale of one to ten, today qualified as a solid eight. No doubt about it.

Now if only Daisy the Destroyer would leave her alone that eight might turn into a happy-go-lucky ten. But J.J. wasn't that fortunate. The woman was dogging her again, mouthing off at mealtime, slinging insults, bumping her in line, trying to get a rise out of her. With a sigh, J.J. hung a left and headed toward the checkout desk, wondering what the heck Daisy thought she was doing.

The question reeked of redundancy.

Dum-dum Daisy didn't have a clue...couldn't figure out, never mind understand, why J.J. never rose to her bait. But then, thinking required a working brain. Something J.J. was pretty certain her nemesis didn't own. Too many drugs before her prison stint, maybe. Or maybe she'd hit herself on the head one too many times while doing bicep curls out in the yard.

Ding-dong. Lights-out. Brain damage assured.

The mental snapshot made J.J. smile. Swallowing a laugh, she stopped in front of the head librarian's desk and rang the bell. As the ding echoed, movement flashed behind the counter. A second later Mrs. Smithers popped up in front of her, round face red from exertion, plump frame encased in a neon-green T-shirt.

Accustomed to the librarian's odd shirt collection, J.J. squinted, protecting her retinas from color overload, and said, "Good morning, Mrs. Smithers."

"Oh, hello, dear," the librarian said, sweat beading on her upper lip. With a huff, she picked up the *Vanity Fair* magazine sitting on the countertop and fanned herself with it. "Menopause, dear. Avoid it as long as you can."

"Good advice."

"I think so. Now..." Mrs. Smithers trailed off as a fly buzzed into her field of vision. She swatted at it with the magazine, missing by a mile. Distracted by the uninvited guest in her library, she glanced around and muttered "infernal little bugger" a second before turning to refocus on J.J. "Now, what can I help you with, dear?"

J.J. blinked. "Ah, you asked me to come down?"

"Oh, right! Of course I did. Silly me." The housefly flew past again. Mrs. Smithers's eyes narrowed in annoyance. On the hunt, she abandoned the magazine, grabbed a copy of the *Seattle Times*, and rolled the newspaper. "We received a new shipment of books this morning, J.J. I need you to sort and catalog each one, then place them on the shelves."

Excitement bumped J.J.'s internal scale, elevating her mood from an excellent eight to exuberant nine. A whole day spent in the library with books. Oh happy day. Could there be anything better? Well, other than a baby grand piano?

Nope. Not much better.

Unable to hold it in, J.J. grinned. "Thank you for thinking of me, Mrs. Smithers."

"Off to work with you now, dear," she said, a smile in her dark eyes even as she shooed her away. "You know the drill."

Yes, she did. Every once in a while, Mrs. Smithers called her in. Sometimes it was to dust and clean. Sometimes to reorganize shelves or set up new displays. But her favorite all-time activity was sorting through the new orders that arrived at the prison. The librarian always gave her the pick of the litter, allowing her to take a book back to her cell before anyone else read it. Creased the spine. Or dirtied the pages with their fingertips. All right. So it wasn't much, but a privilege was a privilege, no matter how small.

And honestly? On the inside, you took what you could get and thanked your lucky stars.

Retreating toward the back of the library, J.J. walked between two tall stacks. Silence reigned but wouldn't for long. The other inmates would arrive soon, taking turns in the resource center, listening to music or reading in the hallowed corner of the prison. A sharp left and two doors later, J.J. crossed the threshold into Mrs. Smithers's sorting room. Two large stainless steel tables with scuffed tops sat at its center, waiting patiently to be used. J.J. didn't waste a moment. She attacked the first box, flipping the cardboard top open.

New releases emerged along with some solid classics.

Lost in the activity, she read title after title, loving the slide and rasp of the binding against her palms, organizing the books by author and category. As the tables filled up, she surveyed her handiwork.

The sharp click of a door closing dragged her attention away from the books.

With a frown, J.J. glanced over her shoulder and—

Froze.

Daisy stood inside the room, a vein pulsing at her temple, two of her thuggish friends by her side. But worse, with the door closed and the room situated at the back of the library, no one could see them. J.J.'s heart started to pound. Oh God. Oh crap in a dozen different languages. She was in serious trouble. The kind that got inmates killed.

Chapter Twenty-Six

The elevator's smooth descent into Black Diamond's underground lair was torture—plain, simple anguish without end. Too bad Tania didn't know how to stop the pain. Or stem the flow of worry killing her inside. Moment by moment, the pressure got worse, upping the ante, turning her head into a pressure cooker, making her want to scream. Explode. Yell at Mac for pushing her away in the psychological sphere.

She could feel it happening. Sensed his retreat and the growing distance between them, even though she stood right next to him. The elevator swayed. Her arm brushed against his, cranking her tighter, stretching the emotional bond she shared with him until it threatened to snap her in two. Tania closed her eyes and breathed deep, battling to stay calm.

Agony. It was pure agony. And 100 percent her fault.

She'd screwed up in a major way.

She should never have told Mac that she loved him. Her unwitting slip had sent him into a tailspin, one that included a fast exit and even quicker escape as he hustled out of his bedroom and down the main corridor. Which, yup, you guessed it. Put them in the elevator, heading toward the other Nightfury warriors, silence ringing between them, tension rising like a tidal wave, her panic at an all-time high.

Tears threatened, clogging the back of her throat. Tania swallowed, holding them back, and looked straight ahead. A double set of steel doors stared back, mocking her with the beauty of Mac's reflection. God, what a joke. His silence. Her need. The awful feeling of isolation. Less than ten minutes ago, she'd been one half of a whole. Now she stood alone, cracked wide open, torn into tiny pieces with no hope of ever putting herself back together.

It was sad, really, how much she needed a hug right now.

But comfort wasn't in the cards. The moment belonged to survival and developing a solid action plan. What should she do...ignore the problem or face it head-on? A chasm of indecision opened inside her, and as uncertainty wreaked havoc, her heart ached. Tania swallowed past the knot in her throat. Maybe she should say something. Talk. Explain. Take it back and tell him it had been a mistake, a slip of the tongue, a reaction born out of relief, but...

Stow that thought. Put it away forever. She couldn't do it.

Lying wouldn't help. Neither would clinging to him. Begging him to love her back probably wouldn't work, either. And honestly? Acting like a lovesick ninny didn't tick any of her boxes. In fact, the thought unchecked everything, then turned up its nose in disgust. She needed to be reasonable. Think logically and put her brain in gear. Some things, after all, were doomed to fail, weren't meant to be... yada yada yada, whatever. The world was full of people who slept together, had a good time, then moved on. No sense getting bent out of shape about it. Right? Tania indulged in a mental nod. Exactly. No problem. If Mac wanted a fling with no strings attached, well then, she would just...

Kill him.

Poke his eyes out with the business end of a sharp stick or something.

Tania blinked. Oh thank God. She was back, reconnecting to the tough, in-your-face girl she knew and loved. So, yup. Forget about a fast escape for Mac. She would have her fairy tale and the love required to nurture it. If he thought for one moment she would roll over and die, he could go straight to—

The elevator pinged.

A second later the doors slid open to reveal another corridor. A quick snapshot provided Tania with the details. Less fancy than the one upstairs, the one she faced epitomized utilitarian: no art or curved moldings, no gleaming hardwood floors or expensive wall sconces. Nothing but an ocean of white walls, high ceilings, and polished concrete floors.

Rolling his shoulders, Mac put his combat boots to use. Nowhere near ready to let him go, Tania reached out, disrupting his getaway by grabbing the sleeve of his jacket. Leather creaked in protest. She held on tight, feeling him tense before he glanced at her, surprise in his eyes.

Her gaze clashed with his. Tania dug deep and found her courage. It was now or never. And *never* was not acceptable when it came to her and Mac. "Listen...about before. I—"

"Bloody hell. 'Tis about time, lad." The deep growl rumbled from the corridor. Less than a second later, the warrior who owned it stepped into view. Tania glared at him. Forge took one look at her face, blinked, then retreated, bumping into the wall opposite the open doors. "Apologies, lass. But honestly, an elevator isnae the best place for a heartfelt chat."

Frustration surged, unleashing her temper. She glanced at Mac. "Can I kill him?"

Mac's lips twitched. He shook his head.

"Maim him then?" she said. "Just a little?"

"For what...my timely intervention?" Amethyst eyes glinting with good humor, Forge raised a brow. "Overkill, if you ask me, lass."

"I didn't ask *you*."

Mac grinned. "No killing...or maiming of Nightfuries allowed. House rules."

"Figures." Releasing her death grip on his jacket, she threw both warriors a dirty look. It was a conspiracy. Or a club, one called the get-your-butt-out-of-a-sling brother-hood. Flipping guys. With a grumble, Tania stepped into the corridor. The scrape of Mac's footfalls sounded behind her, but unable to let it go, she spun and leveled her finger at him. "But don't think for one minute you escaped. We *will* talk about it."

Forge laughed. "Oh-ho. Watch out, lad."

"Talk about what?" Myst asked, walking into the conversation from an open doorway farther down the corridor.

Tania took a breath, preparing to answer. Mac swatted the curve of her behind, landing a stinger with his palm. As she gasped in outrage, he caressed the abused area with one hand, cupped her nape with the other, and leaned in. His mouth brushed hers. Her heart hitched, pausing midthump as he pulled back to gauge her response.

Stunned was a good word. *Needy*, though, might be a better one.

Her fingers curled into his leather lapels. Tania tipped her chin up and, lips parted, asked for more. A hairbreadth away, his mouth curved, the satisfaction in his eyes easy to see.

"Gotta go, honey," he murmured, then nipped her bottom lip.

The love bite startled her enough to let him go. The instant her grip went lax, he gave her another pat on the derriere, then turned and strode away, following Forge's retreat toward the end of the corridor. Tania blinked. Good lord. What the heck had just happened? One minute he pushed her away. And the next? He stoked her fire, increasing her internal temperature by about five bazillion degrees.

And it wasn't getting any better. Not her lack of brain power. Nor her amped-up libido. The thing started up like a nuclear fallout siren, squawking rah, rah...red alert, red alert!...as Mac walked away.

But boy oh boy, what a beautiful sight.

He looked just as good going as he did coming. Each stride long and even. Impossibly wide shoulders rolling. Gorgeous backside a marvel to behold. And ah, jeez. Too bad for her, 'cause, yup, she was in nympho territory. Sexed up and out of control for a man heading...Tania frowned... where exactly?

The corridor dead-ended. Nothing lay in that direction, except—

Static electricity crackled through the air, raising the fine hair on her forearms. The chiseled blocks undulated, morphing from solid stone into a wavy, indistinct blur. A doorway formed in the wall face, the ripple of movement transforming from murky to clear as Forge walked through into what looked like a cave on the other side. Tania's mouth fell open. Although why the wall-to-magical-portal surprised her, she didn't know. It wasn't as if she hadn't witnessed ten times worse in the last few days.

Red fire-breathing demon dragon included.

Mac glanced over his shoulder. Aquamarine irises shimmering, his gaze roamed over her, making her body tighten as he tipped his chin. "Behave while I'm away, beautiful."

And just like that, he was gone. Leaving nothing but the memory of his touch, the promise in his heated gaze, and a now solid wall in his wake.

"Holy crap. Talk about incendiary. I'm about to burst into flames over here."

Her brows drawn tight, Tania barely heard her best friend. She stared at the dead end, struggling to regain her balance.

Myst nudged her. "What's wrong?"

"I don't know. It's just…he was totally freaked out. So quiet in the elevator, about to jump overboard, and then he goes and does…" Her gaze still glued to the wall, Tania threw up her hands, waving them around in front of her. "*That.*"

"What? Undressing you with his eyes?" Myst huffed, laughter in her voice. "One hundred percent normal. Bastian does it to me all the time."

The news flash should've made her feel better. Worry sank deep instead, making her wonder whether his actions were just another sidestep. A way to deflect her while he made a quick getaway. "I think I screwed up."

"What did you do?"

"I told him I love him…by accident."

"Oh boy," Myst said, a grimace in her voice. "Hence his tumble into *freaked out?*"

"Elementary, my dear Watson."

Her friend snorted. "Okay then. Let's go find Sherlock and pick her brain. Maybe she can shed some light on Mac's behavior."

"Thought I was Sherlock."

"Nope. That's Ange." Linking arms with her, Myst towed her down the hallway. "She's in the gym, buried under a crapload of paperwork."

"Doesn't sound fun."

"Ha! She's in heaven, sniffing out leads." Taking a sharp left turn, Myst led her through a double-wide doorway. As Tania got dragged over the threshold, a couple of things registered: weight room complete with treadmills and elliptical machines to one side, NBA-size basketball court in the center, open area with T-shaped contraptions at the back. And Angela (aka Detective Keen) standing beside an enormous stack of file boxes, elbow-deep in a clear plastic bag full of shredded documents. "Hey, Ange… found anything yet?"

"Just getting started. But wow, I think Wick and the boys hit pay dirt last night." Hazel eyes sparkling with excitement, Angela looked away from the huge pile of little paper strips and smiled. "The raid on the Razorbacks' old lair was so worth the trip. Look at all this stuff."

And Tania did. Wow was right. It looked like an archive with the boxes, file folders, and stained leather-bound ledgers scattered around a raft of blue exercise mats in the sea of center court. The smell of musty paper and damp bookbinding joined the scent of floor wax as she skirted the first stack, trying to read the labels on the boxes. No luck there. Water damage had done its job, smearing the ink.

Flipping the top off one of the cardboard boxes, Myst peered inside. "Still miffed Rikar didn't let you go?"

"Freaking guy," Angela grumbled, a look of consternation on her face. "Can't fault his methods, though. While the other guys walked the crime scene, he put me into a pleasure coma."

"Oh yeah." Tania flipped open a file sitting on one of the tables set up end-to-end, each butted up against the next, providing a large working surface. Large industrial lights shone down from above, illuminating the whole, giving Angela the perfect place to do, well...whatever her detective brain did. "I do love a good pleasure coma."

Myst laughed and, after dragging a box into the middle of the mats, sat cross-legged beside it.

"Show me a woman who doesn't, and I'll call her pathological," Angela said. "I just never expected Rikar to use it as a weapon against me."

Tania raised a brow. "Turnabout is fair play."

"But not nearly as effective."

The three of them shared a grin. Tania rolled her eyes then asked, "So how can we help?"

"Dig in." Plopping the plastic bag on the table, Angela turned to lean against the wood edge. A frown on her face, she scanned the organizational nightmare sitting in the center of the gym. "We'll sort things into categories...like information with like. Sloan's bringing me a light table so I can reassemble the shredded pages, but until then..."

As the detective trailed off, Tania and Myst nodded. No problem. Organization was Tania's specialty. The anal-retentive tendency served her well, helping her keep the many different projects she headed in shipshape order and on schedule. Although she guessed her job was nothing but history now. She couldn't go back. Didn't want to, either, which…

Surprise, surprise, didn't bother her all that much.

All right, so she would miss her job. She loved what she did; got real satisfaction from designing incredible landscapes and making her clients happy. But staying with Mac took center stage. He mattered more than a high-powered position in a highfalutin firm. More than designer handbags and gorgeous shoes. More than her life in the human world and—

Way to go, Tania.

She finally got it. Understood why a woman sacrificed for a man. Some things were better than total independence. Sometimes autonomy made for a lonely life. And somehow loving Mac made all the difference. And as her paradigm shifted, peace came, showing her the way home.

Did it matter that it looked like a bumpy road? Or that Mac's reaction might be insurmountable? No. Absolutely not. She'd made her decision and would see it through. No matter how painful.

But first things first.

Tania glanced up from her stack of papers. "Hey, guys… do you know if Sloan's around tonight?"

Scanning a file, Myst shook her head.

"Com center," Angela muttered, frowning at the document in her hand. "Down the hall to your left."

Leaving the distracted pair behind, Tania made her way across the gym. When she reached the door, she turned left. Two doors put in an appearance. A quick glance through a wall of windows and she found the medical clinic. She veered left, the fast click of fingers on a keyboard drawing her toward Sloan's domain. Her rubber soles squeaked as she stopped between the jambs. The warrior's head came up. A second later he glanced over his shoulder. Dark brown eyes met hers as he swiveled in his...ah, well, yikes. That was the ugliest chair she'd ever seen.

Huge. Beat-up. And purple. The thing needed to be driven to the nearest garbage dump.

Reading her expression right, he rubbed his palms along each armrest. "A thing of beauty, isn't it?"

"In what universe?" she asked, making a face and him laugh. Beautiful in the dim light, his mocha skin glowed as his eyes sparked with good humor. But as his amusement morphed into a smile and his white teeth flashed, Tania's nerves got the better of her. She didn't want to impose, but...she needed to know if Mac was right and the Nightfury computer genius could help. Chewing on the inside of her lip, she shored up her courage and said, "Did Mac happen to mention anything about—"

"Your sister?" Arching a dark brow, Sloan waited. When she nodded, he spun back to face the wall-mounted computer screen and said, "He gave me a heads-up. Wanna stick around while I find out what's up with the parole board?"

"Yes, please." Anticipation picked up her heart and then her feet, propelling Tania across the room. Please, God, let it be real. She needed a miracle for J.J. Wanted to see her sister free and happy, starting a new life instead of locked inside the mistakes of the old one. And as she stopped behind the awful purple chair and stared at the computer screen, Tania dared to hope. Allowed herself to believe for the first time in a long time. "Hey, Sloan?"

"Uh-huh."

"Thanks."

"No sweat," he said, shrugging off her gratitude. With a couple of keystrokes, Sloan cleared the screen and opened a new search window. Fingers flying, he went to work, hacking into the Washington State Department of Corrections database. "Mac's part of the pack. He asks, I do. Family helps family."

Thank God for that. And Mac. His foresight and willingness to help had put her here. With Sloan. Just moments away from finding a solution to J.J.'s problem. And as she watched Sloan jump from screen to screen, her love for Mac grew. For an ex-cop, he was remarkably understanding about having a felon in the family. She hadn't expected that. Then again, not even a psychic could have guessed at what hid in plain sight. A whole gaggle of dragon-guys, one of which possessed wicked IT skills.

God bless him and his fast fingers.

Tania leaned forward as her sister's file popped up on-screen. Sloan scrolled through the information and—

"Ah, fuck."

"Oh my God," she whispered, alarm making her heart thump hard. "Hold on. Go back. What did it say? Is J.J.—"

"Tania, I need you to step out for a minute." Sloan tapped a key. The screen went black.

"Bullshit. I'm not going anywhere." A death grip on the back of his chair, she spun him to one side and reached for the wireless mouse on the desktop. She jiggled it. Nothing happened. She glanced at Sloan. "Put it back on-screen."

He shook his head.

And Tania knew she couldn't win. Not with an IT wizard in the computer department. But she needed to know. Couldn't step out and leave Sloan to his digging with words like "blunt force trauma" and "deep lacerations" buzzing inside her head. She'd seen those two phrases up on-screen. Maybe she'd misread. Maybe she hadn't, but—

"Please, Sloan," she whispered, not above begging. Panic twisted into dread, then took a nosedive into terror as she imagined the worst. "She's my sister. If she's hurt, I need to know. I have a *right* to know."

A muscle flexed in Sloan's jaw. She whispered her plea again. With a muttered curse, he turned back to the computer. "You have to promise me something first."

"What?"

"That you won't run," he said, hand poised above the keyboard. "Whatever the situation, you wait for Mac to get home."

"But—"

"Jesus H. Christ, female. That's the deal. Take it or leave it."

Willing to agree to anything for the truth, she nodded. "Okay."

One click and a prompt screen flashed on-screen. Lightning quick, Sloan typed in a password and scrolled down. Tania skimmed the information, looking for—

"Oh no." Tears blurring her vision, she shook her head, denying the truth even as it stared her in the face. Curling her hand in Sloan's shirtsleeve, she rasped, "Is she alive? Please tell me if...I can't tell from this."

"They evac'ed her from the prison," Sloan said, his tone gentle. A tear rolled over her bottom lashes. Tania wiped it away, struggling to keep it together, forcing herself to think as he read to the end of the report. "So she's alive."

"Which hospital?"

"Looks like…" He paused to open another screen. "Swedish Medical."

The information sank deep, setting her resolve. Action plan time. She needed to get to the hospital ASAP. Being evac'ed in a helicopter meant one thing. Her sister was fighting for her life, and Tania would be damned if she would let J.J. do it alone.

Pushing away from the desk, Tania spun toward the door, her mind whirling. What did she need first? A car. Preferably a really fast one.

"Shit." Sloan left his chair on the fly. Growling something about Mac killing him, he leaped in front of her, blocking her path to the door. Startled, Tania flinched, then hopped backward to avoid colliding with him. Holy jeez, he was fast and…way too intense. His expression spoke volumes before he said, "You promised, Tania. Night fell an hour ago. It isn't safe for you outside the lair."

Maybe. Then again, maybe not.

Her crash course in Dragonkind had taught her well. She understood the energy angle; how Mac fed, drawing the nourishment he required to heal and stay healthy through her; how she connected, drawing the power of the Meridian through him when they touched. Strange? Yes. Normal for her now? Absolutely. But not for the Razorbacks.

None of those assholes could track her energy. Only Mac could do that, which meant…what? She could slip out of the lair, stay under enemy radar, and protect her sister all at the same time.

Good news for her. Not so great for Sloan.

Promise or no promise, she wouldn't be sticking around. But as she met Sloan's gaze, Tania knew her attitude—never mind her game plan—wouldn't fly. Especially since he was doing an excellent impression of a dragon-guy barricade. So new plan. Lie like a pro and hope for the best. 'Cause the second Sloan realized she planned to bolt, he'd lock her in the nearest broom closet and wait for Mac to get home.

No way she would let that happen. Not while J.J. lay bloodied and broken, surrounded by a bunch of people who didn't give a damn about her.

"Look, I know it's hard," Sloan said, his tone full of understanding. "But you need to stay here. Give me some time, Tania. I'll get into the hospital records…get a status report on your sister's condition."

Raking the loose tendrils of hair away from her face, Tania hesitated. God, she hated to do it. Didn't want to deflect Sloan, but what other choice did she have? She couldn't sit on her duff and do nothing. J.J. needed her. And Tania needed to be there, protecting her, making sure her sister got the best care. So screw right. She was diving straight into wrong.

"All right, I'll stick," she whispered, shoving her conscience aside. "But promise me something."

"What?"

"The second…the *millisecond*…you know something, you'll come get me."

"Done," he said, his dark gaze on her face. "Where will you be?"

"In the gym…with Myst and Angela." Oh, the lies. They just kept coming. She had no intention of staying put. Knew exactly where the garage was situated from her flight to Black Diamond and Mac's landing beside it. All she needed to do was sneak past the girls, backtrack to Mac's room, slip through the window, hop over some hedgerows, and…bingo. She'd be steps away from the car she required to make a fast getaway. The perfect plan. Well, except for the lying, cheating, and stealing part. "I can't stay here and watch you. I'll go nuts with nothing to keep me busy and—"

"Go, female. I'll find you when I'm done."

His trust sent regret prickling through her. Her lack of integrity made her want to cry. Tania swallowed the tears and turned toward the door. Her conscience squawked again, trying one last time to dissuade her. She ignored it and, with a whispered "thanks" and a silent *sorry*, crossed into the corridor, one thought on her mind.

Mac.

Please, God, let him understand. Her sister couldn't wait. And neither could she.

———

The stench of decomposing human flesh rose like steam from a gutter grate, making Ivar's stomach roll as he tossed the last body into the fire pit. The corpse rolled, skin sloughing off its flopping limbs as it bumped into its neighbor. Revolting…inferior…stinking race. Even in death, humans were disgusting. Proof positive lay piled like kindling inside the stone-walled circle, each one nothing but a saggy-skinned bag of bones waiting for the moment he set the blaze.

He grimaced. Another reason to miss Lothair.

His late XO had never minded taking out the trash. Or incinerating them in the pit outside the Razorbacks' lair. But now the job fell to Ivar, and he hated it. Despised the fact a second batch of test subjects lay here—proof of another failed experiment—instead of out in the world, infecting others of their kind, wiping the inferior species from the face of the earth.

A waste. And total freaking fuckup.

Project Supervirus was going to kill him...with frustration.

With a sigh, Ivar rolled his shoulders and glanced skyward. Clouds darkened the view, blocking out the moon, hiding stars behind a blanket of thick, gray, and terrible, heralding the coming winter. Not his favorite season. Typical of his fire dragon roots, he didn't like the cold. Spent more time inside from December to March than any male he knew, but...

Not this year.

With Lothair gone, the Nightfuries on the hunt, and the potential Rodin problem, he needed to stay front and center. His soldiers required a strong leader—something he could give them, but honestly didn't want to. Full-time command of his ever-growing pack would keep him away from the lab. Not an idea he relished, never mind wanted to implement. Science required intense concentration, commitment to detail, and careful observation. So cutting his hours in the laboratory? Not the best strategy. Especially when whipping up a lethal viral load to jump-start a global epidemic.

Too bad circumstance didn't give a shit about his plans. Or his preferences, either.

Proof positive of that sat just feet away, stinking up his airspace and the crisp night air. With a muttered curse, he refocused on the dead heap of human waste. He scowled and reached for his magic. His palm tingled as a pink fireball appeared in the center of his hand. With a flick, he tossed the flames into the pit. Fueled by human kindling, the blaze caught hold. Ivar fanned the inferno and, enjoying the glow, watched the pink tendrils lick skyward.

Sensation crept over his shoulders, then prickled down his spine. Ivar closed his eyes and listened, waiting for...

Ah, there it was. The soft crunch of footfalls behind him.

Without turning, he returned his attention to the fire and murmured, "Denzeil. Whatcha got?"

"The female is out of pocket."

"The one the water rat saved?"

"Solares," Denzeil said, stepping up alongside him. Dark eyes met his. Satisfaction radiating off him in waves, his soldier handed him the iPad he carried. "Check out the green dot. She's in a car on I-90, using OnStar to call a hospital."

"And now we've got her real-time location." His heart pounded, beating triple time as he watched the dot travel along the virtual map. Oh lucky night. The H-E female was his for the taking...destined to be number six in his breeding program after all. Anticipation streaked through him. Firelight crackled and ash danced, drifting down to land on the edge of the screen. Ivar brushed it away and handed the tablet back to Denzeil. "Where is everyone?"

"Those that are uninjured? Downtown hunting."

"Call them all back." Turning away from the pit, Ivar leaped onto one of the rusty backhoes littering his backyard. Heavy-duty steel groaned, bending inward as he landed on the roof and shifted into dragon form. Red, black-tipped scales expanded, wrapping over his body, around his spiked spine and the jet-black horns on his head.

Pink eyes aglow, he mind-spoke, *"Give them the longs and lats of her position. We rendezvous over I-90. I want that female, D."*

"And Hamersveld?"

"Leave him to me."

An excellent plan from start to finish. Hamersveld wouldn't respond to anyone else. The male was unpredictable most of the time, but wouldn't be tonight. Ivar would bet his fangs on it. The promise of a high-energy female always brought a predator out to play.

Chapter Twenty-Seven

Mac walked into the Gridiron in a wrecking-ball frame of mind. The cloying scent of perfume and hard alcohol didn't improve his mood. Neither did the thumping bass of heavy metal nor the throbbing strobe lights. Normally not things that bothered him. But tonight, everything rubbed him the wrong way. He was on overload, keen dragon senses bombarded by the violent rush of sensory input.

Laser beams flashed above the dance floor. Technicolor streamed across the nightclub.

He turned his face away, protecting his light-sensitive eyes, but not before he got the lay of the land. Large, round bar to his right, people three deep around it. Goth decor with a death rock vibe. And the ratio? At least two guys to one girl on the dance floor. The public bump and grind should've amused him. It usually did. Right now, though, the sight of sex in dark corners annoyed the shit out of him. For good reason too. All he wanted to do was go home to Black Diamond...and Tania.

Ironic, wasn't it? He'd waited four long weeks for tonight. For the green light from Bastian and the right to join his brothers-in-arms on the hunt for Razorbacks. For his maiden voyage, so to speak. Now here he stood, a full member of the pack—fledgling status revoked…thank fuck—and all he could think about was his female. And the way he'd left things with her.

I love you.

Three little words. Nothing special alone. But together, they packed a wallop, cracking through his defenses, allowing a lifetime of hurt to spill into the open. Now he bled, for the little boy he'd been and the emotionally crippled man he'd become. So much rejection. So much "you'll never be good enough." So much pain.

Mac shook his head and scanned the club again, looking for a target. A Razorback—or five—to provoke. He needed a fight, a ball-busting, claw-ripping brawl to clear his head. Otherwise he would lose his cool. Go ape-shit crazy, freak out again, and—

Jesus. He couldn't wrap his brain around it.

Tania loved him. Wanted to stay with him…be with *him*, a guy so undeserving of her it made his chest ache. She needed so much better than him, a male tainted by his past, unworthy of a future with a female so smart, so funny, so fucking beautiful she took his breath away every time he looked at her.

I love you.

Mac rubbed the sore spot between his brows. God, he was a first-rate jackass. He should've said the words back to her. Should've admitted what he'd known for a while but had been too much of a dickhead to realize. He loved her too. So much his heart wasn't big enough to contain the magnitude of feeling. And as his love for her overflowed and spread, infusing every cell in his body, Mac wanted to turn around, fly home, and tell her. Before he lost his nerve. Before she gave up on him. Before *too late* became the story of them.

The screeching wail of guitar riffs shrieked in his ear. A throb started up between his temples. "Motherfuck."

Stopping beside him, Forge slapped him on the shoulder. "You'll get used to it."

What? Loving Tania? Shit, he hoped so.

"Nay, you wanker," Forge said, picking his thought out of thin air. "The abundance of noise...the sensory overload is normal at first. Dragonkind senses are much sharper than a human's. It'll take some time tae become accustomed tae it. So next lesson. Tae-night you learn tae control what you let in and what you block out, aye?"

As Mac nodded, a tingle slid across the nape of his neck. He glanced over his shoulder. Venom and Wick crossed the threshold and entered the club, looking like a pair of straight-up killers. A group of gothed-out guys scattered, scrambling to get out of the way. As the pathway opened, a curvy redhead hopped off a bar stool and latched onto Venom. The warrior welcomed the female with a smile, wrapped his arm around her, and, without breaking stride, brought her with him.

Tipping his chin, Mac greeted his comrades, then glanced sideways at Forge. "Can I block out Ven?"

Amusement sparked in Wick's golden eyes.

Venom rolled his. "Only if you want your ass kicked."

Mac grinned, liking the new arrangement much better than the old. Sometimes calling a truce was a good thing. Especially when it came to Venom. With the tension between them gone, he could tease the guy and be razzed in return without getting bent out of shape. Or suffering the overwhelming urge to rip the male's head off.

"You need some time?" Forge's gaze drifted over the female tucked against Venom's side. Her aura glowed softly, nothing like the brilliance of Tania's high energy, but enough to take the edge off a male's appetite. "Probably should, Ven. You took a serious hit the other night."

Anticipation sparked in Venom's ruby-red gaze. "Private bathroom in the back. Give us twenty minutes."

Us? Mac blinked. Did he mean—?

Ah, yeah. And Wick made three. The redhead was in for a big surprise. Except...

Venom whispered in her ear. Peeking over her shoulder, she ran her gaze over Wick. Her lips curved up a moment before she nodded. Mac huffed. Well, all right. Crisis averted. No need for intervention. The female was all in, A-okay with the fact she would be getting two for the price of one.

Wick on the other hand? Not so much.

With a mental click, Mac refocused, shutting out the peripheral stimuli, and sent a ping out to surround Wick. Unease came back in a winding curl. His cop instincts woke up, adding observation to the intuitive swirl. Dark head bowed. Wide shoulders hunched. Dread encircled the usually lethal male, hanging like a noose around his neck as he followed Venom to the back of the club. His brows drawn tight, Mac wondered about Wick's reaction for a moment, then shrugged it off. It wasn't any of his business. Besides, butting in where he didn't belong with Wick?

Not a good idea if he wanted to stay in one piece.

Putting his boots in gear, Mac headed for the VIP section. The human sea parted. His mouth curved as he strode through the opening in the crowd and mounted the steps. Not much had changed. Even before his *change,* people had treated him like a predator, scattering the moment he stepped into a room. Ange called the phenomenon the "Mac Effect." He called it awesome. The mad scramble meant smooth sailing instead of rough waters, which…and it never failed…involved cracking a few skulls together.

Setting up shop in an empty booth, Mac slid along the deep bench seat and glanced toward the bar. He tipped his chin. A waitress hopped to, hustling toward him as Forge took the spot on his right-hand side. His mentor's gaze raked the female. Reacting to the search and sweep, she slowed, moving to the beat of thumping bass, giving them time to look her over. Hunger sparked in Forge's eyes. Mac didn't blame him. Dressed in a sequined tube-top and a skirt slit thigh high, she put the bombshell in blonde.

She stopped in front of their table. Her gaze flicked over him. Seeing his noninterest, she turned to Forge, planted her hand on the tabletop, and leaned in, gifting the male with a glimpse of cleavage. "What can I get you, baby?"

"An ale, luv." Forge's nostrils flared as he drew her scent into his lungs. "Whatever you've got on tap."

"You?" she asked Mac, her focus still trained on his mentor.

"Dos Lunas," he murmured, ordering his favorite tequila. "Neat."

She nodded, then said to Forge, "I have a minute, if you do."

"Go," Mac mind-spoke, keeping it on the down-low. Discretion, after all, was the better part of valor. *"We got time. And I'm good here. If you need—"*

"I don't need shite, lad. I'm not leaving you alone," he said, his tone tight. Strobes flashed, bathing the waitress's pale skin in bright light. Lifting his hand, Forge drew his

fingertip along the underside of her chin, caressing her softly. High-gloss lips parted; she purred. His throat worked as he withdrew and leaned back in his seat. "Many thanks for the offer, luv. But just the drinks tae-night."

"Another time?"

"Mayhap."

In a pout, she headed for the bar and their drinks. Mac shook his head. "Fuck off, Forge. Stop being overprotective. I can handle myself."

"Nae doubt, but—"

"Shit," Mac growled as an unfamiliar prickle danced across his skin. His tattoo tightened, reacting to the magical charge in the air. He shot to his feet. His eyes narrowed on the crowd beyond the VIP section, he breathed deep, sifting through human heat and club stench, hunting for the almost imperceptible scent. "You smell that?"

"Nay."

"Salt water and seaweed."

Forge slid out from behind the table. Shitkickers planted beside him, he asked, "Female perfume?"

"A male…Dragonkind."

Mac swept the undulating crush again, seeking the source. He knew it was there. Could feel the electrical snap, the magical shift in the air, and smell the danger. Animal instinct screamed a warning. A second later, he located the threat. Big, blond, exuding a lethal amount of aggression, the male leaned against the curved edge of the main bar one level down. Next to the dance floor and covered with swirling yellow-white stone, the bottom curve of the round structure glowed, illuminating the stranger's face. Black eyes rimmed by a thin band of light blue shimmered as the fucker blew him a kiss and—

Recognition struck him like a sledgehammer. Mac sucked in a quick breath. Motherfuck. A water dragon, another male who possessed his brand of kick-ass.

"Forge."

"I see him."

"Yank Ven and Wick's chain," he said, wanting extra backup. "I'm going over there."

"Bullshite." With a quick hand, Forge grabbed a fistful of his leather jacket, anchoring him in place. "Wait, lad. Let's see what the asshole does and who he's got with him first."

Good plan. Starting a brawl inside the club wasn't the best idea. Not in a place where camera-happy humans outnumbered them hundreds to one. CNN didn't need to know about what went down in the sky above Seattle.

Still, Mac itched with impatience. Territorial instinct ripped through him, acting like a rabid dog frothing at the end of his chain. Magic flared, dusting the air as Forge sent out the call, raising Venom and Wick through mind-speak. One hundred percent focused on his target, Mac barely noticed. He locked gazes with the male instead. A smirk on his face, the bastard raised his glass in salute, taunting him. Mac bared his teeth on a snarl, then breathed deep. Something was off. The newcomer wore another scent, a deadly one not his own.

"He isnae alone."

"I know." Mac swept those seated at the bar on high stools, skimmed over a guy dressed in a black karategi, then snapped back. His gaze narrowed on the male: slight build, of Asian descent, narrow vertical pupils. Definitely not human. Rotating his arm, he broke Forge's hold and growled, "The small male three stools down. What the—"

"A wren. Miniature dragons…small, vicious, highly maneuverable in flight, and hard to hit," Forge said, stepping around the table edge and in front of him. Amethyst eyes aglow, he glanced over his shoulder. "Watch yourself when we get out there. Block out all sound. A wren's shriek is a powerful weapon. The little bastard'll scramble your wits with his scream…try tae bring you tae ground."

Made sense. A downed dragon became a dead one… fast. "Let's go."

His gaze on the corridor at the rear of the club, Forge shook his head. Raising his hand, he held up his index finger and pointed to the red glow of the exit sign. A door halfway down the corridor flew open. Venom roared over the threshold and into the hallway, ruby eyes narrowed, aggression on display along with his bare chest. Conjuring a shirt and his leather jacket, the male buttoned his fly as Wick rolled in behind him.

Looking like a pair of twins called Kick-ass and Hardcore, the warriors strode across the VIP section. Mac didn't wait. He shoved Forge to one side and beat feet for the stairs. He needed to reach the blond bastard before he turned tail and disappeared. Four against two, after all, wasn't good odds…for Mr. Cocky and his wren. The second the enemy got wind of the extra backup, Mac knew… just *knew*…the fucker would run, hide, and not resurface for a while.

Which was…yeah. Not happening tonight.

Tapping into the collective psyche, Mac kept his attention glued to his quarry and cleared a path. The crowd parted, scurrying out of his way like mice before a hungry cat. Just as he reached the railing, Mr. Cocky broke eye contact and tilted his head. The sharp movement put Mac on high alert. The bastard's body language spoke volumes and provoked an immediate conclusion. He was talking to someone, linking in through mind-speak.

Mac leaped the staircase. As he landed at the bottom, the enemy male smiled, the baring of teeth more aggressive than amused, then turned and hauled ass toward the front of the club.

"Motherfuck. Forge, get to the—"

"*Mac!*" The growl came through mind-speak loud and clear.

"*Screw off, Sloan.*" Racing for the exit, Mac answered on the run. "*I'm busy.*"

"*Get unbusy and your ass headed toward I-90.*"

Hot on his heels, Forge asked, "*What happened?*"

"*Tania happened.*" Sloan cursed. Something clanged as though a fist had just hit metal. "*Fucking female. She lied right to my face, then flew the coop.*"

Mac slid to a stop beside the dance floor. Humans scattered like bowling pins. "*What the fuck?*"

"*Her sister was attacked…evac'ed from the prison earlier today.*"

"*Where is Tania now?*"

"*In Gage's new Corvette…on the built-in satellite phone with Seattle Medical.*"

"*Motherfuck.*" Fear grabbed Mac by the throat. "*Please tell me she hasn't used her name.*"

"*Wish I could, but if I picked it up on the wire so have the Razorbacks.*" The scrape of claws came through mind-speak a moment before the flap of wings sounded. "*I'm airborne now, but she's got a half hour lead on me. You're closer from downtown.*"

Holy fuck, he hoped so. 'Cause if the rogues reached her first?

Adrenaline hit Mac like rocket fuel, turning him into a human torpedo. Shoving the bouncers aside, he planted his foot on the top step and leaped skyward. Magic exploded around him. The cloaking spell took hold, making him disappear into thin air as he shifted into dragon form. His wings caught air. Blown off their feet by the wind gust, the people in line screamed. Mac didn't care. Cuts and bruises on a few innocent bystanders were nothing. He needed to reach Tania. Now. Faster than fast. Before the rogues found and captured her.

Oh God, please. Let him reach her first.

If he didn't, Mac knew he would never recover. Tania meant everything, and if she died, he would lose it all—his heart, mind, and soul—and die right along with her.

———

The purr of the high-performance engine rumbled through the quiet. The sound should've calmed Tania. Slipping behind the wheel of a finely tuned automobile had that effect on her. Under normal circumstances, anyway.

Tonight, though, wasn't normal.

She was too tense to enjoy the smooth perfection of the clutch and shift. Or the way the Corvette's racing tires hugged the road. Worry distracted her, winding her so tight she barely noticed how well the car cornered, flying around S curves, roaring down straightaways, its sleek lines and maneuverability man's gift to driving aficionados everywhere. All Tania cared about was that it went fast.

Mind-bending, heart-torquing *fast*.

Taking her eyes off the road, she glanced at the onboard navigation system. The little blue screen glowed, showing her location on the digital map. A little over an hour to go before she reached Seattle. Before she found out whether her sister would live or die. All right, so maybe that was a bit melodramatic. She didn't have any of the details, after all. Not the how, when, or why. Which was a problem. Especially since her imagination never said quit. Right now, it kept kicking out terrible yet oh so plausible *maybes*, tormenting her with enough worst-case scenarios to sink a battleship.

Par for the course for a worrywart. And some things never changed.

Bad luck seemed to be one of them. 'Cause, yeah, the road? Two lanes of twisting blacktop and stomach-clenching turns. Hell for a girl in a hurry.

White-knuckling the steering wheel, Tania sped down another hill. As she swung around the next bend, the Vette's headlights pierced the darkness, throwing illumination out in a wide arc before splashing over the side of the road. Huge pine trees rose beyond the gravel shoulders, moonlight painting their midnight needles with a silver brush as a lake glinted in the distance. Tania shifted into fifth gear. A quick glance at the speedometer confirmed her suspicions. She'd broken the speed limit fifty clicks ago. Now she rode the razor's edge, in control of the powerful car, but not by much.

Instinct made her tug on her seat belt. Yup. Two thumbs up. The five-point racing harness checked out, the shoulder straps secure and…annoying as hell. The thing hadn't been made for her, but for someone much bigger. Which made sense considering the size of the Nightfury crew and the fact she'd stolen one of their cars. Tania grimaced, feeling terrible about that, but…oh, snap. She might as well face it.

She was in a crapload of trouble.

Her heart clenched at the thought. Tania eased off the gas pedal. As her speed went from supersonic to just-kill-me-now fast, she imagined Mac's reaction to her midnight run. Furious would be the least of it. Afraid for her, however? Bingo. That about summed it up. Despite her uncertainty about how he felt about her, she knew… just *knew*…he'd freak out—be worried, terrified, half out of his mind—when he learned what she'd done and where she'd gone.

Guilt collided with regret and then tumbled into remorse. She swallowed past the lump in her throat, wanting to kick herself, hating the distress she would cause him. But there was no other way.

J.J. was in trouble.

Injured and alone. Maybe even dying. So, no. Waiting for Mac to come home hadn't been an option. The need to protect her sister was simply too strong for that.

Blinking away her tears, Tania gave herself a pep talk. She was safe, winding her way toward Seattle, untraceable by Dragonkind standards. That counted for something, didn't it? God, she hoped so and that, in the end, Mac would understand. He was, after all, a reasonable guy.

She frowned. Right?

Downshifting into the next turn, she examined that bit of logic and realized she was a first-class pinhead. Who was she kidding? Mac wouldn't care about the whys and wherefores. He'd be one giant ball of I'm-gonna-tan-your-hide the second he got hold of her.

Which…wow, wasn't going to be any fun. At all.

"She's my baby sister. Please don't be mad," she whispered, practicing her defense only to recognize the futility. No matter how good her excuse, she would still catch hell.

Mac would make sure of it, so…time to come up with a new prayer. "Please make him love me so much he can't help but forgive me."

Well, all right. That was more like it. A heartfelt wish she put all her weight behind while—

The OnStar satellite phone crackled.

"Seattle Medical…"

Oh thank God. It was about time. "Yes, hi. This is Tania Solares. I'm still waiting for information on—"

"Please hold."

"Goddamn it!" She glared at the rearview mirror and its little black button.

Not that it was OnStar's fault. The guy at Chevrolet Central had been superhelpful, downloading directions to the Vette's onboard navigation system, connecting her call to the hospital. The receptionist at Seattle Medial, however? The antithesis of helpful. Nowhere near the ballpark, never mind in the same league in the customer service department.

A death grip on the steering wheel, Tania cursed under her breath. Oh, just wait until she arrived at the ER. She was going to find that receptionist and smack her. Right upside the head. With whatever the woman used to keep tabs on incoming calls. She hoped it was a binder, one of those thick heavy-duty suckers. 'Cause Queen-of-the-Phone-Lines had just put her on hold for the third flipping time.

"Double goddamn it."

Tossing caution out the window, Tania put her foot down again. The engine growled as she crested the top of a rise and swung around another bend. A caution sign flashed past her passenger side window, twin skid marks on display. With a muttered curse, she powered down, slowing the car before whipping into the hard turn. A steep hill led her down, making her stomach dip as it propelled her toward the bottom. One more blind curve, and she was out the other end and into a straightaway that stretched along one side of a lake.

Moonlight winked at her, rippling across dark blue water.

Alive in the ebb and flow, the waves frolicked, then called to her. Tania smiled a little, wishing she could join them for a midnight swim. Foolish, she knew, to allow her love of water to distract her. She didn't have time to waste but honestly needed the respite. And as the chaotic clamor inside her head died down, the pressure banding her rib cage loosened, allowing her to take a full breath.

Tania took advantage, filling her lungs to capacity as her gaze skimmed over the lake. The quiet moment reconnected her, sharpened her awareness, and…warned her. Something was off. Not by much, and yet she sensed the disturbance ripple around her. Her heart picked up a beat. Tania shook her head. It couldn't be. She understood how the Meridian worked and how Dragonkind tracked its prey. None of the Razorbacks had touched her, which made it impossible—

The air went still, and the crickets' song quieted.

Energy snapped, flicking at her already frayed nerve endings. The prickle ghosted down her spine, making the hair on her nape stand at attention. Tania held her breath and listened over the hard thump of her heart. Nothing. Not even a rustle of sound. Eerie. Alarming. So unnatural her internal warning system went off. As the thing clanged, lighting her senses on fire, she glanced out her side window.

Backlit by moonlight, the corvette's silhouette drifted over tree trunks. And above her...

Her breath stalled in her throat.

The large winged shadow hung over her car. A growl rolled over the silence, flooding her with terror, washing in like a tidal wave. Not Mac. It wasn't Mac. She could feel the son of a bitch and the vicious crackle in the air.

Foe...not friend.

With a wild cry, Tania put the hammer down. The Vette lurched, engine roaring, torquing left as rubber snarled against pavement. Another growl rippled. She saw a wing tip dip low a second before the beast flipped fast and set down hard. Pink eyes aglow, red scales flashing, his sharp talons ripped up the roadway, throwing chunks of asphalt into the air. Rock rained down, slamming into her windshield. The glass smashed, fissuring into a spiderweb of destruction. Tania screamed as she lost control. The back end of the car fishtailed, heading toward the lake. The rear tires caught the shoulder of the road. Gravel flew, cracking against the steel undercarriage as she rotated into a 360-degree death spin.

She ripped through the guardrail and careened over the embankment. The car shuddered. The harness clamped down, cementing her to the bucket seat. Bracing for impact, adrenaline punched through, jolting her into action. Slamming both feet onto the pedal, Tania stood on the brakes. The Vette whined, shrieking in protest. Twin headlights swung around, painting thick tree trunks with revolving splashes of white light. One wheel rim caught rock and threw the car sideways. Steel groaned. A huge pine tree clipped her front bumper. As wood splintered, the air bags deployed, blowing her hands off the steering wheel.

Pain exploded up her right arm. But the brutal slide stopped. Thank God. Now all she needed to do was breathe. Easier said than done. Her lungs were empty, fighting the clamp-down of the harness strapped over her chest. Fighting through the agony, Tania wheezed, struggling to unclip the racing seat belt and get away from the wreckage.

She refused to panic. Not now. Later would be soon enough to freak out. She needed to keep her head and get moving. Run. Hide. Lie low until the sun came up and the dragon asshole chasing her went home before he got fried. As far as plans went, it was a good one. The only one, really, because without Mac to protect her, she was a sitting duck. Nothing but dragon bait in the middle of nowhere.

Cursing herself and her fumbling fingers, she yanked on the harness. Once. Twice. The third time, the clasp gave way. Not wasting a second, Tania turned sideways in her seat and kicked at the door. The Corvette cooperated, releasing the locking mechanism. She didn't pause or stop to think...she bolted, stumbling on the uneven ground, rounding the front bumper, her gaze fixed on the glint of water through the trees.

The lake. She must reach the shoreline. Immerse herself, get under the water—a place all dragons hated... with the exception of Mac—before Mr. Asshole-of-the-Red-Scales took flight. It was her only chance. The only way to outwit a hunter with predatory instincts and razor-sharp senses. The second the pink-eyed bastard spotted her, she was done.

As good as caught.

But screw the odds. Tania refused to give up or break down. Not without putting up a fight. Or sending a distress call in Mac's direction.

Far-fetched? Wishful thinking? Probably. But Tania didn't hesitate.

Sprinting beneath ancient pines, she reached deep, dipped into her energy—the one she felt each time Mac touched her—and stoked the flame high. When she couldn't hold it any longer, she threw the electrical charge like dice in a casino. Power whiplashed, then tumbled, swirling out into the night air. An answering ping came back and—

She felt him. Sensed him in flight. Felt the pulsing edge of his bond with her.

Oh God. He was close. So very close.

Clinging to the fragile connection, she gasped, "Mac."

"Hold on, honey." Mac's voice rang inside her head, giving her courage. *"Run harder. Buy me time."*

Raw with hope, fighting her fear, she obeyed and ran, injured arm throbbing, legs pumping, each breath sawing at the back of her throat. Blood trickling from the cut above her eye, she reached the lakeshore and splashed through the shallows. The mucky bottom sucked at her sneakers, weighing her down as water flew from her heels. Knee-deep now, she checked over her shoulder. Nothing. No glowing pink eyes. No fireball coming to eat her alive. Not a glimmer of red scales anywhere.

Daring to believe, Tania waded in farther. Cold water washed over her stomach.

A loud splash snapped her head around. Water rippled out in a horrifying ring in the center of the inlet. A second later, a dragon—scales the color of sharkskin, dorsal fin as jagged as a sawtooth blade—surfaced like a crocodile. Horned head half-submerged in the water, black eyes ringed by pale blue narrowed on her.

Tania froze, disbelief warring with terror. Another water dragon, but...how was that possible? The Nightfuries believed Mac was the only one and—

The beast flicked his thin alligator tail, then slithered through the water, leaving no doubt about his pedigree. Or her peril.

Chapter Twenty-Eight

Coming out of the cloud cover with hurricane force, Mac left the city behind and leveled out over the forest. Night vision pinpoint sharp, nothing escaped his attention. Not the shape and size of individual pine needles, the texture of the bark on redwoods, nor the glint of spider eyes gazing up from their thin webs. Magic married instinct and intellect, honing his senses, narrowing each thread toward one purpose.

Tania.

He must find her first. Nothing else mattered.

Rain splattered over his scales as Interstate 90 rushed up to greet his rapid descent. Linked into Tania's bioenergy, he tracked the electrostatic trace she left in her wake. So close. He was so close now. Minutes away from having her in his arms. From making sure she was all right. From bringing her back home to Black Diamond, where she'd be safe and he'd have peace of mind. Enough to give her hell for leaving in the first place. Mac snorted. Yeah, right. No way would that ever happen. 'Cause guaranteed…the second he got his hands on her? No scolding would get done. For good reason too. All he wanted to do was hold her, love her…curl up with her for days on end and never let go.

"Mac." With a nifty flip, Venom settled on his right wing tip. *"Fill us in."*

"A minute out," he said, mining his connection with her. As his dragon radar picked up more information, Mac banked hard, flying fast toward a cluster of lakes in the distance. *"Close to water."*

"I hate water." Black, amber-tipped scales flashed as Wick rolled in, taking up the wingman position on Mac's left side.

"Bloody hell, aye." Forge feigned a shudder, then somersaulted up and over, taking the shadow position over Mac's spine. *"Doonae know how you do it, lad. All that awful, slimy—"*

"Fuck off or I'll drown you." Whipping up a minicyclone, Mac tossed it into his mentor's path.

With a "fuck me," Forge splashed through it, then sent him a dirty look. *"Wanker."*

He snarled at his friend. Forge grumbled but backed off as Mac mind-spoke, *"Rikar…ETA?"*

"Now." Frost blew in on frigid air. Rikar uncloaked, rocketing behind the pack.

An electrical charge rippled, ghosting around the horns on his head. Mac glanced over his shoulder. *"Bastian?"*

"On your six." Midnight scales rattling, B flew in, his wing tip inches from Rikar's. *"Heads up, boys. We got multiple rogues converging, flying hard, but not yet on-site."*

"Lay it out, B."

"Twelve total," Bastian said as his magic flared. The powerful surge gathered speed, rushing in front of Mac's commander, allowing him to read the enemies' strength and weakness from a distance. *"All fire-breathers but one."*

"*Motherfuck,*" Mac growled, guessing at the one. The fucker from the bar. Pure water rat, the rogue was not only older but more experienced than him. Too bad Mac didn't give a shit. If the blond bastard got anywhere near Tania, he'd rip the male's head off, then play basketball with his skull. "*The water rat is mine.*"

All the guys hoorayed.

Mac didn't make a sound. He fixated, speed supersonic as he went wings vertical, blasting between two huge redwoods. Caught in the wind gust, wood groaned. Tree trunks snapped, then blew sky-high as the road curved into a rolling hill. As he rocketed over the next rise, a tingle slid around the horns on his head. He mined the energy, sifting through information as his sonar pinged, guiding him in flight.

Almost there. Just a few more seconds and—

His magic whiplashed, triangulating Tania's position. Mac's heart clenched, then jumped, slamming into the wall of his chest. Jesus. She was out of the car, on the run, terror fueling her burst of energy. Dread hit him dead center as he felt each pain-filled breath she took. Sensed her struggle as fatigue and injury sapped her strength.

"*Run, honey,*" he mind-spoke to her, pushing the words toward her. "*I'm coming, Tania. Run!*"

She whispered his name, static swirling around her voice.

Mac flew harder, pushing himself to maximum velocity. Wisps of air curled from his wing tips, streaming like jet fuel in his wake. As he banked into another tight turn, a flash of yellow caught his eyes. His head snapped to the left.

Holy fuck. Oh God...no, the Corvette.

Twisted and torn, the wreckage lay at the bottom of a shallow gully. Time slowed, filtering perception like images through a camera. His eyes shuttered, fixing the details in his mind. The stench of gas. Dented metal. The driver's side door…wide open and hanging off the bottom hinges.

A growl ripped through the frigid winter air.

Mac exploded around a copse of trees. A nanosecond, that's all it took for him to size up the situation. Tania, waist-deep in water, frozen with fear as two dragons hemmed her in. Red scales glinting in the moonlight, Ivar hissed at her from the shoreline while the water rat swam, slithering toward her like a sea serpent. Rage ripped through Mac, amping into aggression. With silent ferocity, he breathed deep and unleashed, exhaling hard. Water-acid flew from between his fangs.

Dragons snarled overhead as Nightfury intercepted Razorback. The horrific shriek of claws raking scales exploded, echoing across the surface of the lake.

Caught by surprise, the water rat cursed.

Ivar wheeled and, pink eyes aglow, spun to avoid the deadly stream of Mac's exhale. Too little, too late. The acid splattered across his red scales. The rogue leader roared and took flight. Mac let him go. The boys would chase the bastard down. He had bigger fish to fry.

And a female to protect.

Flying fast, Mac conjured a triton. He hurled it like a thunderbolt from fifty feet away. Magic spun and lengthened, propelling the weapon over the surface of the water. Jet-black eyes rimmed by blue widened, and shark-gray scales clicking, the rogue dove to avoid the deadly three-pronged weapon.

The second the fucker disappeared, he yelled, "Tania, run!"

She spun toward the embankment, obeying him without hesitation. The water rat surfaced and lunged, swiping at her. One razor-sharp claw caught the back of her T-shirt. Tania screamed. Blood welled on white cotton as the force of the blow threw her into the shallows. With an anguished roar, Mac splashed down and attacked. Battling to keep himself between the water rat and his female, he tore at the rogue's smooth scales. Shifting right, the enemy slashed at him, grazing his shoulder with his claws. Mac retaliated, fought dirty, and kung fu'ed the motherfucker, pushing the rogue deeper into the lake. As his horned head connected, hammering the enemy's rib cage, he checked Tania's vital signs.

Energy-fuse flared, connecting him to her life force. Strong heartbeat. Fatigued and hurting but all right.

Time to get her the fuck out of Dodge.

"Forge!"

Dark-purple scales flashed overhead. *"Here."*

"Catch."

Forge swooped in and circled overhead. Mac gave the command. Water washed in around Tania, then surged, shooting her skyward like the cork from a bottle of champagne. The water rat cursed. Mac elbowed him in the face, heard teeth rattle as he spun. Pond scum flew in a wide arc as he treated the enemy to the sharp blade of his tail. Warm dragon blood splattered over his cold scales as, eyes on Tania, Mac watched his mentor pick her out of thin air.

"Got her, but..." Forge paused, as though checking something.

Mac dragged the water rat underwater, taking the fight to the bottom of the lake. Air bubbles swirled. Sandy debris at the bottom kicked up, screwing with his visibility. Grit washed over Mac's scales. His tattoo shimmered, then glowed, illuminating the water around him. An instant later the murky conditions cleared, giving him an uninhibited view of the enemy...and the tribal ink on the bastard's dragon skin. Similar to his own, but not quite the same, the marking glowed along the rogue's back.

The water rat swam left.

Mac circled right, his gaze on the male's tattoo as he assessed his strength. Jesus, the bastard was powerful. A hulking male with huge webbed paws and a jagged, sawtooth dorsal fin. But then, so was Mac. And the blade along his spine? Way more deadly. Proof of it crisscrossed the rogue's forearms and claws, the myriad of slicing cuts telling the tale. The vicious SOB couldn't grab him without suffering the consequences.

Which might include a severed limb if Mac timed it just right.

"Nice ink, asshole," Mac said, taunting the enemy, searching for a weakness.

"It's Hamersveld, whelp," he growled, thick accent warping through water. Baring his fangs, the male hissed at him. Mac dodged as boiling water streamed past his shoulder. "And like sire, like son."

Mac frowned. What the fuck was the male saying?

"Always knew I would produce strong sons. Your marking is proof enough of that, Nightfury. Only warrior males of my line wear it. My sire before me, and now...you." Hamersveld's dark eyes gleamed, piercing through the dark depths. His bladed tail swished, increasing his swimming speed. "Too bad there can only be one."

Shock flared through Mac. His father? Was the bastard really claiming—?

Hamersveld surged, closing the distance between them. The bastard sideswiped him. Sharp claws gouged his shoulder. With a snarl, Mac countered, kicking out with his hind paw. Fury made him strong. Aggression made him ruthless. The kick connected and...crack! One of the male's horns snapped off and sank, heading for the bottom. As Hamersveld howled, the violent crack rippled, sending sound out in concentric waves. Mac turned and, showing no mercy, whacked him with his tail, cutting through scales to slice muscle. Hamersveld retreated. Whipping around, he swam after the bastard. No way would he let him—

"Mac!"

The urgency in Forge's voice turned Mac's attention. *"What?"*

"Drag your arse out of there. Tania's—"

"Motherfuck," he snarled, watching Hamersveld disappear into the shadows.

Frustration lit him up. And yet, even as his dragon half raged, Mac let his prey escape into the murky depths and, muscles straining, rocketed toward the surface. He didn't need Forge to tell him. He already knew what his mentor meant. Could feel Tania's vital signs weakening as her heartbeat took a downturn and she gasped in pain.

His female needed him. So fuck the water rat.

There would be time and more to kill the newest member of the Razorback organization. Another time. Another place. Another battle. But for now, he must reach Tania… faster than fast. She needed an energy infuse to stabilize her life force—medicine, Dragonkind-style—and he was the only one who could give it to her.

Chapter Twenty-Nine

Pain faded on a slow, peace-filled swirl. Tania sighed and settled deep, content to drift into relaxation as a soft current coaxed, pulling her along. Prickles of pleasure ghosted over her shoulders. A moment later the sensation curled inward, streamed down her spine, then circled beneath warm weight pressed to her lower back. It urged her to take. Drink deep and draw more, soothing sore muscles, the knot in her chest unraveling with every breath she took.

Hmm, so good. Strange, sure. Yet somehow lovely too.

Bliss rushed in her veins, keeping time with her heart. Someone murmured. The deep voice held her high, tethering her to the nourishing tide that washed through her. Tania purred. Oh yes...just what she needed. All that she wanted, a sweet burn that went on and on, easing the bruises, banishing the ache in her wrist, infusing her with awareness. And as she surfaced, buoyant with gentle need, her mind slipped from neutral into drive. Mental gears turned. With a hum, she nestled into the curve of a warm body. Strong arms tightened around her. A muscled thigh pressed between her own.

Her mouth curved.

Mac.

It had to be. No other man had ever made her feel so good. So completely comfortable in her own skin. So beautiful, loved, or accepted…just the way she was. No need to worry. Except…

That wasn't quite right. She seemed to remember…

Struggling to clear the mental fog, Tania told her eyes to open. A no go. Her body refused to cooperate, sending all the wrong signals. With a grumble, she gave herself a mental kick. Her brain cranked over. She tried again. Her lids resisted, then rose. A fuzzy collection of, ah…trees, maybe?…met the attempt. She rubbed her eyes, trying to wipe away the visual haze. Her focus sharpened, becoming clearer by the second. The sticklike smudges morphed into trees. Leafless limbs waved at her as a huge, smooth-topped boulder floated by.

Tania frowned at it. No, that wasn't right. The rock wasn't *floating*, she was the one adrift. Warm water washed in, flowing in an unnatural circle around her. A whiskered cheek rubbed against hers. Clarity rushed to the forefront, flooding her with memory.

Dragons. The red one and others. Shrieking in battle. Fireballs flashing against the night sky. The horrific sound of claws ripping through scales. The hot splash of dragon blood on her skin. Mac deep in the lake with the shark dragon that wanted to kill her.

The recollection pounded through her. Tania flinched. Pain dinged her, shooting up her right arm.

"Shh, *mo chroí*. It's all right." One hand spread wide on the small of her back, Mac stroked over her hair with the other. The gentle caress grounded her in reality. Exhaling a shaky breath, she clung to him, wrapping her good arm around his bare shoulder. He nuzzled the side of her throat, then lifted his head. Shimmering aquamarine eyes met hers. "You're safe."

She swallowed, working moisture back into her mouth. "Where…?"

"The river outside Black Diamond," he said, holding her close, supporting her weight in the water. "The waterfall's around the next bend."

Oh, well, that made sense. Trees. Rocks. The beaver dam walling up the small inlet she spotted over Mac's shoulder as they drifted by. All of it pointed to the great outdoors. Add that to the fact she was chest-deep in water, buoyant in Mac's arms while pinpoint stars played peekaboo with wispy, faraway clouds? Yup. Definitely. Outside said it all. One thing, though…

Another wave of warmth washed in, swirling over her skin. She met Mac's gaze and raised a brow. "Any reason I'm naked?"

"Other than the fact I prefer you that way?"

She rolled her eyes.

He grinned. A moment later his expression smoothed into serious lines. "I'm sorry, honey, I should've taken you inside, but I couldn't wait. I needed to check you…to make sure you were okay. I couldn't do that with your clothes on."

"I'm not complaining." An understatement if there ever was one. 'Cause, yup, the whole skin-on-skin thing with Mac? Umm, boy…it so worked for her. Along with almost everything about him. Awed by his strength and courage, Tania traced his mouth with her fingertips. God, he was beautiful, all that she wanted, more than she deserved. "Guess I'm okay then, huh?"

"A little banged up, but you'll live."

Her throat went tight. "Thanks to you."

Big hands roamed over her back as he whispered her name. Tania tipped her chin up, craving his kiss. He gave it to her, burying his hand in her hair, holding her still, demanding entrance. With a hum, she opened, parting her lips, inviting him in, asking for more. Dipping into her mouth, he kept it light, delivering his taste one gentle stroke at a time. Pleasure and need collided in a heated swirl, and Tania purred, loving the feel of him. Minutes later—or maybe hours...Tania didn't know—he retreated, relinquishing her mouth.

Muttering "no," she protested his retreat.

He came back to nip her, then pulled away again. The river rush increased, twirling them in a circle as she pouted. His lips twitched a second before he turned his attention to her sore wrist. Tania tensed, expecting the throb of agony to return. But he was gentle, and the pain was so much less, as though her body had kicked into high gear, healing at an accelerated rate.

Cradling her hand in his, he asked her to move her fingers. As she obeyed, he glanced at her. "Does it still hurt?"

"A little, but not much anymore."

"Good. The bone is knitting." With a gentle touch, he examined her bruised thumb. "Fuck, I love energy-fuse. Another day and you'll be good as new."

Her breath caught. *Energy-fuse.* She knew about it from Myst. Her best friend had explained the bond she shared with Bastian. Rare. Powerful. A magical connection that enabled a Dragonkind male to feed his female healing energy—a fusion so strong it mated hearts and entwined souls. Hope whispered through her.

Oh God, please. Make it so. Let it be true.

Holding back tears, she whispered, "You fed me?"

"I'm still feeding you." Raising his hand, he traced the ridge of her cheekbone with his fingertip. "Feel that current...the nourishing wash of sensation?"

Tania let her eyes drift closed. The rush intensified, thrumming through her veins. Her love for him surfaced, finding a permanent home inside her heart. "Yes."

"All me."

"It's nice." Opening her eyes, she met his gaze. "Is it like that when I feed you?"

"More intense. Not as gentle."

"I like giving you what you need."

His throat worked as he swallowed. "I love the way you taste...like honey and ocean breezes. Beautiful."

Any other time, she would've enjoyed the compliment. Right now, though, his praise shamed her. *Beautiful.* Yeah, right. She hadn't been so hot an hour ago when she'd lied, cheated, and stolen a crazy-expensive car. One that now lay in a twisted heap beside the lake where she'd nearly gotten everyone killed.

God, how messed up was that? All she'd wanted was to reach her sister. But in doing so, she'd risked them all. Herself. The Nightfury warriors. The man she loved.

Tears filled her eyes. With a sob, she covered her mouth with her hand. "Oh my God. I'm so sorry."

"Tania, honey, it's all right."

"No, it isn't. I'm an idiot." She shook her head, her chest so tight she could hardly breathe. "I didn't realize. I thought I would be okay...that they couldn't track me, you know? Because of the energy thing and..." Her bottom lip trembled. The first tears fell, tipping over her bottom lashes. Mac brushed each one away as she rasped, "Is everyone all right? The guys and—"

"It's all good, *mo chroí*," he said. "B and the boys are having fun."

Tania blinked. "Fun?"

"Hammering rogues. Chasing the assholes back into the city."

Oh, well, all right then. As long as they were having *fun*. But even as she accepted the Nightfuries' absurd notion of a good time, another worry rose to replace it. Fear prickled through her, tightening muscles over bone, spinning toward a full-blown panic attack. Her heart picked up a beat and then another, thumping hard as she stared at Mac.

His focus sharpened on her face. "Don't, Tania."

She frowned at him. "Don't what?"

"Even think about it." His arms flexed around her as he gave her a warning look. "I know about J.J., honey. Sloan filled me in."

"Then you know why I have to go."

A muscle twitched along his jaw. "I get that you're afraid for her...that it seems unnatural not to be with her right now. But Sloan's hooked into the hospital mainframe now. The second he knows something, so will we."

She opened her mouth to argue.

He shook his head. "Forget it. You can't help J.J. by putting a bull's-eye on your back. You pop up on the grid again and the Razorbacks will find you. Just like they did tonight."

"I'll be careful. Tell me what to do...what to avoid and—"

"No." His snarl rippled, the sound full of over-my-dead-body. The river followed his lead, surging into a whirlpool around them. As warm water splashed over her bare shoulders, he growled, "It's too dangerous, Tania. I love you too much to risk you. I won't do it."

Struck stupid, Tania blinked. Had Mac really just said, well...*that?* Yearning pushed hope to the surface, making her heart ache as she stared at him. "You love me?"

"Yes," he said, looking shocked by the admission. But as he held her gaze, the uncertainty she saw in his eyes cleared. Stone-cold resolve took its place, obliterating doubt. "I love you, Tania. So much it wrecks me. So much I want it all. You with me always. The mating ceremony... happily-ever-after...every single thing you're willing to give me."

Everything. She wanted to give him *everything*. Every last piece of herself.

"I love you too." More tears fell. "With all my heart."

"Then trust me." A kiss accompanied the plea, and as his mouth brushed hers a second time, he murmured, "Trust me, *mo chroí*...to make it safe for you, and J.J. too."

"How?" Burying her uninjured hand in his hair, she held him close, matching him caress for caress. "I can't leave her there. She's all alone. If they take her back to prison—"

"Fuck the prison. The parole board too." Sea-blue eyes full of mischief, he nipped the tip of her nose and leaned away to look at her. "I play by Dragonkind's rules now, my love. The second she's able to travel, I'll bring your sister home to you."

"Dragonkind rules." Gratitude mixed with love, tying her up inside. Beautiful man. His generosity—the love and commitment—made her go teary-eyed all over again. "I think I like that."

"You'd better." Wrapping a lock of her hair around his fingertip, he grinned and gave it a playful tug. "You're stuck with me now."

"Excellent," she whispered, awe circling as she kissed him softly. "So…forever, then."

"And every day after."

Sounded about right. Felt right too with Mac in her arms wearing nothing but skin. And as she slow danced with him, twirling in the water, Tania knew it couldn't get any better. A man to love and be loved by in return. A sister with the hope of a new future. The end of a journey, but the beginning of another…one she'd always been meant to take.

Perfection didn't begin to describe it.

Keep reading for a peek at how the saga continues in *Fury of Desire.*

Chapter One

"Goddamn it, Sloan! Get the hell out of there before—"

The explosion cut Venom off. The concussive *boom!* ripped through the frigid air, blowing him back past a row of parked dump trucks. Ravenous flames followed, lighting up the night sky, blistering yellow industrial-grade paint and melting steel like ice cream in the noonday sun.

Perfect. Just what he didn't need. Wick on the rampage.

Flipping guy. Trust the male to come in hot, hammering the enemy while threading the needle between his comrades with a nasty exhale. His best friend needed his head examined. Or a serious boot to the ass. Venom couldn't decide, but either option would do. Maybe then Wick would exercise some caution and use the gray matter between his ears. Of which he possessed a considerable amount...

Under normal circumstances.

Tonight, though, didn't qualify as *normal.*

The Razorbacks had tried to take one of their own—a female who belonged to a member of their pack. Why Wick cared was anyone's guess. The male hardly ever talked, even to Venom, so yeah, it was a crapshoot. One big "what the hell's he thinking now?" Not that anyone gave a damn at the moment. The Nightfury warriors were too busy, 100 percent dialed in and on the warpath, chasing the rogues back into the city, away from Mac and his injured mate.

The target had been a natural one. High-energy females always were for the bastards. And no wonder. Rarer than four-leaf clovers, women who drew pure power from the Meridian—the source that fed Dragonkind and kept them alive—were valuable. Which meant the war raging between Nightfury and Razorback had reached new heights.

Escalation to the nth degree.

And Ivar, leader of the Razorbacks, was to blame.

The bastard kept crossing the line. He shamed Dragonkind at every turn, targeting H-E females, imprisoning them inside his lair, conducting scientific experiments designed to…

Hell, Venom didn't know exactly. But whatever the nutbar's endgame, it couldn't be good. Especially considering the fact he called his pet project a "breeding program." Jesus, the asshole was hurting females…innocents in a world that preached honor, discipline, and the protection of those weaker than themselves.

The thought of what Ivar planned made Venom cringe. Then again, so did Wick.

Equal parts vicious and crazy, his best friend was uncontrollable. A casualty of his upbringing, Wick's rage ran hot, neck and neck with the death wish he carried around like luggage. Venom understood his friend's propensity for violence. Encouraged it even, at least in battle. But sometimes his intensity got to Venom. Made him sad on a soul-deep level he found difficult to ignore. Especially since the compulsion had nothing to do with right and wrong, never mind honor or duty. What drove Wick went deeper than that, and, like it or not, Venom couldn't do anything to help him.

He'd been there, tried everything he could think of... all to no avail.

With a curse, Venom extended his wings, slowing his free fall toward cracked concrete and twisted steel. Air caught in the webbing, and his muscles squawked, stretching under the strain. Good thing he was armored up and buttoned down. His dragon scales were doing their job, making him fire-retardant. Convenient really, 'cause, yup...the flames were gathering speed, heading toward the shoulder of the road.

Oh so not advisable.

A forest fire would bring the humans running. They'd call in air support along with cops, forest rangers, and firefighters. And a crowd wasn't something Venom wanted, never mind could afford. Not with the rogues in full retreat, desperate to find a way out, one Venom refused to hand them by sending up a giant smoke signal to human authorities.

One eye on the sky, the other on the inferno, Venom banked hard, his wing tip inches from the ground, and breathed out. A luminous green wave shot from between his fangs, frothing over broken asphalt, stealing the air to douse the flames. Smoke billowed, throwing the smell of burned rubber and sweet grass up to meet moonlight.

Mission accomplished. No firefighters required.

Now for the Razorback jack-offs dogging his tail. Or rather, on his radar. His sonar pinged, picking up movement over the forest. Ah hell. Not again. The buggers were playing hide-and-seek, hopscotching across rough terrain, hightailing it back to the city in the hopes of losing the Nightfury warriors somewhere along the way.

Losing the enemies' signal in the smoke, Venom fired up mind-speak. *"Wick."*

A yellow Razorback streaked over the ripped-to-shreds asphalt.

Right on the rogue's tail, Wick's black amber-tipped scales flashed in the gloom. *"What?"*

"Holster the fireworks, will ya? I'm in the target zone."

"Well, get the fuck out of there," Wick said, his tone all "Elementary, my dear Watson." *"I'll smoke the rest out."*

"Give me a minute."

"You got thirty seconds before I unleash."

Terrific. His buddy was a flipping peach. *"Remind me to kick your ass when we get home."*

"Right," Wick said, eagerness in his tone.

Flipping into a somersault, Venom flew over a downed crane to scan the gully on the opposite side of the highway. Piled up like broken Tonka toys, the steel carcasses, tires still alight and smoking, littered the bottom of the ravine. Hmm...good cover down there. A nice place to hide if a rogue felt so inclined.

Venom rounded the end of a downed dump truck and...bingo. He spotted the Razorback within seconds. Bright blue scales smeared with motor oil, eyes trained on the sky, the male crouched like a cat, no doubt waiting to blow him to kingdom come when he flew over. Venom snorted, a load of "you gotta be kidding me" making the rounds inside his head.

He sighed and, angling his wings, changed course. Slithering in on a slow glide, he snarled at the male, startling the idiot. The enemy dragon jumped like a jack-rabbit, then dodged to avoid his razor-sharp claws. Too late. Venom struck, grabbing the bastard by the tail. Sharp spikes sliced the palm of his talon. He ignored the pain and yanked. A quick flip. A sickening twist and...*crack!* He snapped the rogue's neck, leaving his ashes to float above blackened field grass.

Using the roof of a backhoe as a launchpad, Venom leaped skyward. He had five seconds before Wick exhaled and—

A flash exploded through the darkness.

"Jesus H. Christ," Sloan growled, catching Venom's updraft as he cleared the tops of the ancient redwoods hugging the stretch of blacktop.

Venom growled as round two rolled in. Blue-orange flame streaked over the treetops, a horrific missile-like sound whistling in its wake. Heat went cataclysmic, sucking the oxygen from Venom's lungs. Choking on the smell of sulfur, he tucked his wings and rocketed into a tight spiral. The fireball roared past, singeing his scales, missing him by inches. He counted off the seconds, eager to see what Wick's arsenal unearthed. Three. Two. One...

The ravenous ball of poisonous gas struck.

Sound boomed, warping perception as shock waves expanded into a brutal surge. Newly poured concrete buckled then heaved, erupting skyward as enemy dragons screamed, abandoning their hidey-holes behind hapless graders and industrial-size bulldozers.

Venom almost snarled in satisfaction, then thought better of it. No need to get cocky. He wasn't out of the woods yet. Especially with Wick unleashed and on the loose.

Acknowledgments

A tremendous thank-you to the readers of the Dragonfury novels for falling in love with the dragon warriors and sharing your enthusiasm with me. I so enjoy hearing from you and fielding all your questions, even when I can't answer them for fear of giving too much away!

A thousand thanks, many times over, to Christine Witthohn, Eleni Caminis, Melody Guy, Nancy Berland, and Kim Miller for all your hard work, incredible insight, and support. Working with each of you is a joy.

And also to the entire Amazon Publishing team, whose talents, energy, and dedication know no bounds.

With love to my family (those related and the ones I've adopted) and all my writer friends.

As always, hugs and kisses to my husband. None of this would be possible without you.

Last but not least, to Kallie Lane—thank you for showing me the way.

I raise a glass to all of you!

About the Author

Image © Julie Daniluk

As the only girl on all-guys hockey teams from age six through her college years, Coreene Callahan knows a thing or two about tough guys and loves to write about them. Call it kismet. Call it payback after years of locker-room talk and ice-rink antics. But whatever you call it, the action better be heart stopping, the magic electric, and the story wicked good fun.

After graduating with honors in psychology and working as an interior designer, Callahan finally succumbed to her overactive imagination and returned to her first love: writing. And when she's not writing, she is dreaming of magical worlds full of dragon-shifters, elite assassins, and romance that's too hot to handle. Callahan currently lives in Canada with her family and her writing buddy, a fun-loving golden retriever.